FACE
HER
FEAR

BOOKS BY LISA REGAN

FACE
HER
FEAR

LISA REGAN

bookouture

Published by Bookouture in 2024

An imprint of Storyfire Ltd.
Carmelite House
50 Victoria Embankment
London EC4Y 0DZ

www.bookouture.com

ISBN: 978-1-83790-948-3
eBook ISBN: 978-1-83790-947-6

In loving memory of Elaine M. Boris

ONE

The edge of a cliff was a terrible place for an argument. She hadn't intended the fight to happen here. She hadn't intended to have a fight at all. Her husband had suggested that the three of them go for a hike. Get outdoors. The weather was warm and inviting. Low humidity. Up here, this high on the mountain, cool breezes caressed the backs of their calves and ruffled their hair. Overhead, birds trilled happy little ballads. Ben had wanted to give the news to her child out here, where it was serene, the beauty of nature all around them. Why not on the summit? he'd said. They'd be alone, uninterrupted by the trappings of daily life. Surely, it would be welcome news. But she had been wrong. They'd both been wrong. Now she stood with her back to a sheer drop. Hundreds of feet. Sweat dotted her upper lip. Her shoulders heaved with indignation as the child she had borne so many years ago sneered at her with disgust and called her a sick, deluded, selfish bitch.

Ben tried to step between them. Both his hands were raised. "Please," he said. "Stop. Let's take it down a notch."

But it was too late. The damage was done. Her anger gained strength like a forest fire. Every glare from her child's ungrateful eyes were blasts of oxygen feeding it. "How dare you?" she said. "I did everything for you. I gave you everything!"

"You gave yourself everything," came the response. "You just used me to get it. How can you even sleep at night? Does he know what you did?"

For a moment, the fire raging inside her went silent. The flames still licked at her insides, heating her skin, making her fingers twitch with the desire to hurt someone, but now there was no sound. Ben's brows knit together in that look he gave her when he didn't understand something or when he knew she was holding something back from him. He made no attempt to defend her. He only looked at her, confused and expectant, but there were some things he could never know because he would never understand them. A hawk screeched in the distance.

"Tell him," said her child. "Or I will."

A primal noise came from deep in her lungs. She sprang forward, pushing as hard as she could, her outstretched hands making contact with her child's shoulders. But her progeny wasn't a small thing anymore.

"Don't you dare touch me!"

Strong hands shoved back, sending her sprawling on her ass.

Ben said, "Stop, please."

As much as she loved him, he had never been good when it came to physical confrontation.

Small stones bit into the palms of her hands. She staggered upright, fists closed, and swung at her child only to be rewarded with a kick to her stomach. The breath left her lungs. Her feet stumbled backward, slipping on loose gravel among the rocks that made up the edge of the cliff.

Ben cried, "No!"

She fell. Flailing for purchase, one of her hands found a vine. The other searched the dirt and stones for something to grab. Pain streaked through her fingertips as her nails broke off. Her legs dangled, their weight pulling her down into the chasm.

She felt muscles in her shoulders pull. Something made a popping noise and her grip on the vine loosened. Adrenaline blunted the pain. Somewhere, the hawk shrieked again.

Ben's face appeared. His eyes were wide with terror. He must be on his stomach, she thought. He shimmied forward and held both hands out to her. She fumbled to catch one of them with her free hand. Relief ran through her like an electric current when she felt his palm against hers.

She could always count on him. After all this time, she'd finally found someone true, someone pure and kind. Someone who would always come to her rescue.

"Hold on!" His voice was strained.

She let go of the vine and clutched his other hand. He smiled. Then a shadow appeared behind him. In what felt like slow motion, it resolved into a face. Her own child. Gone was the anger and hurt. Now there were only pursed lips and a chin set in steely determination.

"No. No, no, no." She shook her head vigorously but all it did was loosen Ben's grip on her.

"Stop moving," he said. "I'm going to pull you up."

But it was too late. She saw the sickening realization on his face as he slid inexorably toward her.

He clutched her hand the whole way down.

TWO

SACRED NEW BEGINNINGS RETREAT,
SULLIVAN COUNTY

Day 1

"Tell me why you're here."

Josie stared at the woman seated across from her. Waning sunlight streamed through the windows, backlighting her as if she were some kind of supernatural figure instead of a psychologist. Then again, the room didn't exactly scream therapist's office with its taxidermied deer heads affixed to the walls and a group of pheasants lurking in one corner. It looked like the exact opposite of a place you would expect to find the Sacred New Beginnings Retreat. The name still grated on Josie. "It sounds like a cult," she had told her husband, Noah, when she signed up for it. He had laughed. She knew he would laugh now if he could see this room.

Dr. Sandrine Morrow, or simply Sandrine, as she preferred to be called, followed Josie's gaze from the eight-point buck over the door to an atypical thirteen-pointer on the wall across from it. She laughed softly. "I didn't choose the location well, I'm afraid. This property is typically rented out to hunters. I asked Cooper to remove some of these more..." she looked around at the animals, searching for the right word before settling on, "majestic creatures."

Cooper Riggs was the caretaker of the property. "I'd say Cooper had his hands full getting this place ready for the six of us for the entire week," Josie said. "Hauling supplies, filling the generators, chopping wood."

The property seemed like a lot for one person to manage. Josie had expected a single chalet at the summit of the mountain. Instead, there were several buildings arrayed like steps in a clearing high along the side of the mountain. At the base of the glade was a small outbuilding, no bigger than a shed, then a larger building, painted red like a barn. After that was the main house, which was where Josie and Sandrine currently sat. It was a behemoth, fashioned out of logs. Built as an A-frame, it had large windows that overlooked a sizable porch and a wall of trees beyond. It was the most impressive structure on the mountain and certainly the largest, dwarfing the six tiny cabins that lay on the other side of it.

Sandrine's beatific smile stayed in place. "Yes, I suppose you're right. The hunters do all that themselves when they're here. I'll talk to Cooper about all of us taking on some chores this week to make it easier on him. We haven't been much help so far though it's only the first day."

Josie smiled tightly. "Great."

That's what she needed on a retreat for processing trauma: housework. Or, given the rustic nature of the place, camping. It was mid-December, and freezing. Josie was worried that the well supplying the water that ran to each building would freeze. The main house and cabins were powered by gas-guzzling generators and heated using wood-burning stoves.

Sandrine chuckled. "I promise I won't make you chop your own wood, Josie."

"I'd like to go on record that it's probably safer for everyone if I chop wood rather than cook."

This elicited a full-throated laugh from Sandrine. She tossed her head back, her long salt-and-pepper curls undulating. Beneath an oversized black sweater, her thin shoulders shook. Josie felt some of the tension that had been knotting her shoulders all day loosen. Things had been tense between her and Noah in the few days before she left, and the retreat had suddenly seemed like a welcome distraction. Driving the three hours to Sullivan County had given her a feeling of relief. Until she arrived in one of the most remote areas of the county at a small gravel parking lot, miles from anything resembling civilization.

"You're not the outdoorsy type?" asked Sandrine.

Josie shook her head. "No. I like modern technology. Like putting on the heat by pressing some buttons on my thermostat. Also, my car and phone."

And Netflix, she added silently. What was she supposed to do with all her downtime this week?

That morning, Sandrine and Cooper had met Josie and five others in the parking lot. They had been told not to bring their phones or any electronic devices—including tablets. They'd left their vehicles there, each one of them taking their turn riding in a John Deere Gator, driven by Cooper. He'd escorted them up an uneven path that zigzagged across the face of the mountain. The path was just wide enough for a small car to pass but falling rocks had blocked part of it, thus necessitating the use of the Gator to get them up the mountain and deposit them into a clearing at the base of the camp. From there, they'd had to lug their bags the rest of the way up to their assigned cabins.

"Owner says he'll get those cleared next spring so people can drive up again," Cooper had told her.

Sandrine smoothed the fabric of her dress over her knees. Black yoga pants peeked from underneath. On her feet were a pair of white sneakers. "To be perfectly honest, I enjoy creature comforts, too. I've got subscriptions to just about every streaming service in existence. Even the British ones! But there's no Wi-Fi up here, even if we had all brought laptops and tablets."

Josie wasn't entirely unfamiliar with the location. Sullivan County was north of her home in the small, central Pennsylvania city of Denton. Josie had been here on several occasions for cases in her capacity as a detective for the Denton Police Department. Her ex-fiancé's family had a farm in the county.

When Josie didn't say anything, Sandrine said, "I know it's difficult to go without those things, but I really do find that the more we disconnect from the outside world during these retreats, the more beneficial it is to everyone. It gives us all more time and energy to focus on the things inside of us that need attention, to do the necessary work of accessing and processing some of the trauma we're all carrying. Tell me, Josie, why are you here?"

"To sleep," Josie blurted out, not thinking.

She expected Sandrine to admonish her for what must have seemed like a flippant answer but instead, she simply nodded. "Insomnia is one of the ways that stress and anxiety, particularly surrounding trauma, manifest physically. It can be crippling."

Josie nodded, though her inability to sleep for the last ten months hadn't been crippling so much as it sometimes made her feel like she was drunk, delirious, or losing her mind.

Sandrine said, "I understand you're a police officer."

Josie swallowed over the lump in her throat. "Yes."

Josie had grown up in Denton and after college, joined their police department, working her way up from patrol to detective.

"Is it a busy department?" asked Sandrine.

Denton was a small city tucked away in a valley surrounded by mountains. While its central district was concentrated along the banks of a branch of the Susquehanna River, much of Denton included the more distant areas that spider-legged out into the mountains. In spite of its many rural and remote expanses, it had its fair share of crime.

"Yes," Josie answered. Her eyes drifted toward the mounted head of a twelve-point deer above the windows. It stared down at her with derision. *You asked to be here*, it seemed to say. *Stop being coy.*

She really was delirious from lack of sleep. Imagining a deer speaking.

"We're a very busy department," Josie added, shifting forward in her chair. "My insomnia started in February. My colleague, Finn Mettner, died in the line of duty. I was holding his hand."

More of the tension in her shoulders fell away.

Sandrine also shimmied her way to the edge of her chair, matching Josie's posture, closing some of the distance between them. "I'm so sorry, Josie. Obviously, I knew you had experienced some great losses. It was on your application. Thank you for telling me about Finn. It gives us a great starting point. What was he like?"

Josie had expected Sandrine to delve directly into Josie's feelings surrounding Finn's murder. No one ever asked Josie to talk about him. In fact, even her colleagues, who had also been close to Mett, refused to mention him at all. For them, it was too painful but for Josie, the painful part was acting like he had never existed at all. It felt wrong to her. She wanted to keep his memory alive.

Almost daily she thought about him and reminded herself: he was here; he was real; I loved him.

Talking about Mett lightened the weight of her grief. Normally she couldn't bear to burden others with it. But here was Sandrine, offering a space for Mettner and Josie's memories of him. Josie waved her hands, indicating the rest of the room. "Mett would love this place. I mean, he would have loved it. He was an avid hunter and fisher. He had three brothers. They grew up doing outdoorsy stuff. He would probably laugh if he knew I was here, in a place like this, to talk about him. He was in love. Deeply in love. Her name is Amber. God, if he could see her now, the way she suffers, it would break his heart." She wiped a tear from her cheek and clasped her palms together, feeling the ghost of his hand in hers from the night he'd died. "He, uh, loved the job and he was good at it. He was hard-working. Very serious. He, uh, challenged me all the time. It always annoyed Noah—that's my husband, he's part of our investigative team, too—but I liked it."

Sandrine's gentle smile deepened with each fact that Josie shared. "Why? Why did you like it?"

Josie rested her elbows on her knees. Now the twelve-pointer seemed to look down on her with approval. "Because he made me better. Better at my job. Better at... being a human."

Josie waited for Sandrine to ask if she thought she needed to be a better human. Her regular therapist, Dr. Rosetti, would have pounced on that. Instead, she said, "Why do you think your body has responded to his death by keeping you from restful sleep?"

Josie looked again at the twelve-pointer. It had no answer. "I don't know."

Softly, Sandrine said, "You've lost people before, by violence."

"Yes." Josie squeezed her hands together until the skin blanched. "My first husband, Ray, and my grandmother. Both were shot. Like Mett. I couldn't save them."

"But you were there," Sandrine said. It wasn't a question.

"Yes."

"Josie, I am so sorry. That is so much for one person to carry."

"Wait till you hear about my childhood."

THREE

The joke fell flat. Sandrine continued to stare at her. Josie searched her face for pity but found only compassion. The last of the tension in her shoulders melted away.

Sandrine said, "Hypervigilance is extremely common in complex PTSD cases. Your brain and your body are constantly on high alert, trying to be ready in case something else traumatic occurs, so that it can protect you."

"But it can't protect me," Josie blurted. "Nothing can protect any of us from traumatic things happening. We can be careful. Avoid certain situations, try to prepare for any eventuality, and still get blindsided by something absolutely horrifying."

She thought about the news she had received only a few days before leaving for the retreat. The terrible truth that had caused the rift between her and Noah. Did it count as trauma? She had certainly felt blindsided. It was definitely terrible. She'd been getting less sleep than ever.

"You're right," said Sandrine. "It's a very difficult truth to live with, isn't it?"

Josie touched a hand to her chest where her heart now pounded. "You can't fix me in a week."

Sandrine smiled again. "I know. I'm not trying to 'fix' you, Josie. What I would like to do is offer you—all of you—some tools that might be helpful to you in dealing with your PTSD. Things you can take with you when you leave here, or techniques you can work on at home with your own therapist. Hopefully, you'll find something valuable. Sometimes just getting out of our usual environment can be helpful as well, even if we're roughing it."

Josie's heartbeat slowed marginally. She respected Sandrine's honesty. Her hand moved from her chest to the thin scar that ran from just beneath her ear, down the side of her face, terminating at the center of her chin. A relic from her childhood. One of the first acts in the shitshow of her life. She had always prided herself on being so much stronger than the traumatized little girl who had endured so much, but here she was, an adult who routinely took down criminals, and she couldn't sleep through the night to save her life.

"Often our bodies react far more quickly than our minds when it comes to processing trauma," Sandrine added. "For you, especially in a job where you have to compartmentalize on a regular basis just in order to get through a shift, I'd like to start by trying to get you more in touch with your body. Has your therapist ever recommended a body scan?"

Josie could not stop her eye-roll.

Sandrine laughed again. "Not a fan?"

Josie felt her face flush. "Sorry. My therapist has tried this with me. Many times. It doesn't work. She thinks I have a 'negative attitude' about it—which is probably true—but I just don't understand how knowing where my body feels the most crappy is supposed to help me get past all this trauma."

"That's fair," Sandrine said.

Josie looked to the twelve-pointer. Silently, she asked him, *Can you believe this lady?*

Dr. Rosetti had proselytized endlessly about the benefits of body scans. She could not and would not force Josie to avail herself of the practice but the way she made it sound, a body scan was like some miraculous cure for every emotional wound. All it did for Josie was make her feel more uncomfortable.

Sandrine went on, "Josie, when you are fairly relaxed, let's say at home having dinner with your husband, and when you are in a high-stress situation, maybe working on a difficult case at the department, do you feel any differently? Or are those two things more or less the same to you, emotionally?"

Josie took a moment to think this over. With dawning horror, she realized that aside from the physical exhaustion that came with a high-stakes case, her emotional state was pretty much always the same. She was calm. Steady. Steely. Rarely did she break down. She was all those things no matter what was happening. This had always seemed like a good thing. "Are you saying that I can't tell the difference between what feels stressful and what feels relaxing?"

The twelve-pointer's glassy eyes looked sad.

Sandrine said, "I asked you. Is that what you think?"

"Shit," Josie said.

Sandrine pushed her rear end to the very edge of her chair. "Josie, you'll know this, I'm sure, from your work. When we are under threat, our sympathetic nervous system goes into a fight-or-flight response. One of the other responses, governed by our parasympathetic nervous system, is a freeze response."

"Yes," Josie said. "You don't know which of those your body will do until you're tested." Luckily, her own body responded by fighting.

"Because these responses to danger are governed by our autonomic nervous system. They're involuntary, physical responses to threats. Rapid heartbeat, labored breathing, flushing or paling of skin, a rise in blood pressure, muscle tension, dry mouth. Those are just a few things that can happen when our body's sympathetic nervous system is activated."

"Okay," said Josie. "But I don't need to mentally scan my body to tell you that I feel the stress in my chest and stomach."

Sandrine's serene smile was back. "It's good that you can identify these areas. Let's keep talking about our physical responses to trauma."

"Why?" Josie asked bluntly. The twelve-pointer gave her a decidedly judgy look.

Sandrine was unfazed. "Josie, in the same way that our bodies have immediate, automatic responses to danger, they also have a process for calming us down. That's the parasympathetic nervous system response. It reverses the rapid heartbeat, loosens the tense muscles, brings your blood pressure down, that sort of thing. It is a state of rest and healing. Your body should be able to switch between these two states—fight or flight and rest and healing—with ease and regularity. Do you see where I'm going with this?"

"I can't switch," Josie said. As if to put the exclamation point on this realization, her heart did a double tap. "I'm stuck."

"Your body should be spending more time in the rest and healing stage but if you cannot get there, it is a problem. The body scan, when done consistently, will help your mind to align more with your body and help to slowly remind your body to go back to its relaxed state when it doesn't need to be on high alert. But if that doesn't work for you, we can try something else."

Sandrine stood up and circled behind her chair. The room was furnished like a sitting room with their two chairs, a long couch, and a couple of end tables. In the corner was a credenza with a record-player on top of it. Inside were hundreds of vinyl records. Sandrine thumbed through them.

"Does that thing work?" asked Josie.

Sandrine beckoned her over. "We'll find out." She chose a record and placed it on the turntable. Then she turned to Josie. She rolled her neck and began to shake her arms. "First, we shake."

Josie raised a brow. "Shake?"

Sandrine started shaking her legs out one by one. Soon, her entire body was juddering. "It's called neurogenic tremoring. It helps release muscle tension, burn off your adrenaline. Get your body back to a more neutral place. Try it."

Josie imagined the twelve-pointer laughing at her. She looked around at all the other fake animal eyes. They seemed disinterested. Sandrine twitched, unabashed. "Come on! Try it!"

She was on top of a mountain, alone in a room with Sandrine and a dozen taxidermied animals. She'd come to this retreat because nothing else was working. "Sure," she said.

She started moving her head side to side, then shaking out her arms and her legs. She followed Sandrine's lead, imitating her. After a few minutes, Sandrine stopped long enough to drop the needle on the spinning record. First, there was only a whirring sound, followed by a crackling. Then came the first notes of a song Josie recognized from the oldies station in Denton. The Four Tops began singing "I Can't Help Myself". Sandrine started swaying along with the rhythm. "Now we dance!" she announced, grinning. "Catchy, right?"

It was one of Josie's favorite songs.

Sandrine turned up the volume and they danced.

That night, for the first time in ten months, Josie slept soundlessly until morning.

FOUR

SACRED NEW BEGINNINGS RETREAT, SULLIVAN COUNTY

Day 5

Screams cut through the stillness of the winter day. Josie froze on the dirt path and scanned the area. They were coming from somewhere near the lower part of camp. Josie turned away from the path that led to the mountain's summit and raced down toward the cabins. The weather had only gotten colder as the week progressed. The ground was hard and unyielding beneath her boots. Her breath came out in clouds as she sprinted. No smoke puffed from the cabins' small chimneys. Still, she checked each one as she went, pounding on the doors and trying the knobs. They were unlocked and no one was inside. With each building she came to, her hand went to where her gun holster normally sat on her waist. Of course, it wasn't there. She wasn't a detective here, she was just a woman on a retreat, trying to process years of trauma. Somewhere in the back of her mind, Sandrine's voice narrated the science of what was happening to her body in this moment.

The screams continued, unabated.

As she neared the last cabin before the main house, the one

in which Sandrine was staying, she heard a thwacking sound nearby. Josie took a quick look inside to confirm it was empty and went around to the back. Brian Davies leaned against the back of the structure, smacking a long, flat vape pen against his open palm. His shoulders tensed slightly as he registered her presence.

"Busted," he said, offering her a pained smile.

She pulled up short, turning her head in the direction of the screams, but they'd stopped.

"You okay?" asked Brian, shaking the pen.

"I, uh—" She stopped when she thought she heard another scream.

Brian held out the vape pen. "I know we're not supposed to have stuff like this, but I needed it. Unfortunately, I haven't been able to get the damn thing to work all week."

When Josie didn't respond, Brian added, "It's juvenile, I know."

"No," Josie said, still listening for more screams. "It's not. I get it." There had been many times that week that she'd wished for a shot of Wild Turkey, even though she had given up drinking years ago. Sandrine had offered them a wide range of methods for destressing, and for processing trauma, some of which were relaxing, like guided meditation and yoga, but they were still there to do difficult emotional work.

Brian nodded, seeming relieved, and used a palm to hit the end of the vape pen. He squinted at it as he then tried to slip his nail under the cover to the slot where the vape cartridge went. "I can't even get the damn thing open," he mumbled. "Although I couldn't get it to charge either so maybe it's totally shot."

Josie noticed he wasn't wearing his coat, hat, or gloves. He hadn't worn them all week, in spite of the freezing weather. He was dressed as he always was—in a T-shirt, basketball shorts, and a pair of beat-up sneakers. His brown hair curled at the ends, no two strands moving in the same direction. He looked chronically unkempt.

He reminded her of a high school boy, but he was in his early forties. He was the only man at the retreat, not counting Cooper, and he'd come with his wife, Nicola. There were only six of them in total on the retreat. They had daily group sessions in which they'd gotten to know one another somewhat. Sandrine's only caveat during those sessions was that they weren't required to give much biographical information other than their names and why they were there.

All Josie knew about Brian was that he had had a rough upbringing in a group foster home that had eventually burned to the ground. That wasn't the only reason he was there, though. He and Nicola were there because they'd lost a child in one of the worst ways imaginable. Their five-year-old daughter had been abducted while playing in front of their house. A week later, her battered and broken body was found in a drainage ditch a mile from their home. The perpetrator turned out to be a man who drove an ice cream truck through their neighborhood each day in the summer. The abduction hadn't happened in Josie's jurisdiction. The Davies couple were from New York.

During every single one of their group sharing sessions, Josie had had to hold herself back from peppering them both with questions about their daughter's abduction and murder. A man in an ice cream truck abducting a little girl. Josie immediately began to wonder if there were more victims out there. During one chat, she'd overstepped, and Sandrine had pulled her aside to remind her that she was not a police officer right now. She was just a woman at a retreat, and she was there to process her various traumas.

"Seriously," Brian said, giving up on the pen and sliding it into his pocket. "Josie. Are you okay?"

"I heard screaming," she said. "But it seems to have stopped."

Brian laughed. "You forgot, didn't you?"

Josie jammed her gloved hands into her pockets. "Forgot what?"

"Sandrine was holding a rage-room session today."

Josie fought the urge to face-palm herself. She had forgotten. One of the things Sandrine had offered them that week were sessions inside the "rage room" she and Cooper had created in the red building. It was a large space filled with furniture, small appliances, glassware—anything breakable. They donned thick protective suits and goggles and then used baseball bats to smash everything in sight. Sandrine had cautioned them that not all therapists believed in its benefits, but in her experience, it was a way for people with a lifetime of repressed feelings to finally get in touch with their unexpressed anger. For others who were already in touch with their rage, it offered a safe environment in which to vent it. For both types, Sandrine had explained, it could be a good outlet. Josie had participated in the rage-room session on Tuesday, along with everyone else, and had declined to do it again. Although Josie had enjoyed the freedom and abandon of the rage room, smashing things had not been as cathartic as she had hoped. She'd watched the faces of a few of the other members of the retreat, seen the relief and invigoration in their expressions, and realized she hadn't quite gotten what she'd expected from it. Sandrine said it was because she had pushed her anger down so far that she'd lost touch with it altogether. Just like all of her negative feelings. She was a work in progress.

"You didn't want to go again?" Josie asked.

He shook his head. "No. I didn't really want to do it the first time. I've seen rage. I don't want to be close to it again."

Josie nodded. "Understandable."

Brian lifted his chin in the direction of the rage room. "You didn't want to go again either?"

Her right hand closed around the contraband cell phone in her coat pocket. "I just didn't feel up to it," she lied. She took a few steps back, ready to be on her way now that she knew there was no emergency.

"Josie," Brian called.

She turned back to him.

"Can I ask you something?"

She tried to calculate how much time she had before they would all have to meet for lunch and their afternoon sessions, but time was meaningless here. They had no clocks, no phones, no electronics. They relied on Sandrine and Cooper to tell them when to be where. A new scream cut through the air. If they were still carrying on in the rage room, she'd have at least another half hour, maybe more. "Sure," she said.

"Do you think this retreat has helped you?"

Josie took a moment to consider this. She'd been in therapy for over three years, ever since her beloved grandmother was murdered. Dr. Rosetti had spent less time on her grandmother's murder and more time unpacking her considerable childhood trauma. Noah insisted that it had helped, even though Josie couldn't always tell whether or not it was making a difference. After Mettner's death and the resultant insomnia, Dr. Rosetti had thought that this retreat—seven days of intensive trauma therapy in a secluded setting with a group of people who were also processing extreme trauma—would benefit her.

Had it, though?

She had slept well the first night there but then her insomnia returned. It wasn't as bad as before, but it was still there.

"I don't know," Josie said honestly. "But I usually can't tell with these things."

Brian laughed. "You can't tell?"

She shrugged. "This kind of stuff? Therapy? There's never a moment where I suddenly feel better. It's more of a gradual effect. I get a little more sleep at night. I stop wanting to down a bottle of Wild Turkey every time something goes wrong. I ask for help when I wouldn't have in the past. I talk with my husband instead of hiding my feelings behind work."

Brian nodded along with her words. "You're saying you won't know if this has helped until later?"

"I mean, I guess." Uncomfortable with the line of questioning, Josie asked, "Is it helping you?"

He looked toward the trees that lined the area at the back of the cabins. He slid the vape pen out of his pocket and used its edge to scratch at a burn scar on his wrist. Snowflakes began falling, small and light. They landed in his hair, twinkling. He didn't seem to notice. His eyes had a faraway, unfocused look, as if he was no longer present but stuck in some pocket of time from his past. Josie had seen it happen in their group sessions whenever he talked about the fire at the foster home. Sandrine often told him not to disassociate and to stay present.

"Brian?" Josie said.

He blinked, awareness coming back into his eyes, and gave her a weak smile. "Sorry. I was—"

"I know," Josie said. "You don't have to explain."

He rolled his vape pen in his palm. "I want to feel better," he said. "But I just wonder if there are some scars that aren't meant to heal."

FIVE

The snow fell harder as Josie left Brian behind the cabin and trudged back up the hill. It wasn't yet heavy enough to cover any surfaces, but ominous gray clouds hung low in the sky, portending a storm. At this altitude, Josie felt as if she could reach up and touch them. It was only a matter of time before they unleashed the rest of their contents. This was what she'd been worried about—a bad snowstorm. While she had been enjoying the retreat, she was concerned about them getting stuck on the mountain. Sandrine had chosen the property for its isolation but leaving the camp would not be easy—or even possible—if a big enough storm came through.

Before Josie had left home, she'd checked the forecast for Sullivan County. A week ago, there had been a chance of snow during the late part of the week, but the weather models predicted everything from a dusting to several feet. Basically, meteorologists didn't know what would happen. Without any word from civilization since then, Josie had no idea what the forecast called for now. Although she'd charged her cell phone, there was no Wi-Fi or service in her cabin so she couldn't check.

The day before, as she passed back and forth between her cabin and the main house, she'd noticed a change in the air around her. There was a heaviness, a thickness to the atmosphere that usually preceded a significant amount of snow. It wasn't something she could explain but from growing up in the mountains of Central Pennsylvania, Josie knew what it felt like.

She was afraid they were about to get hit with a blizzard.

She had said as much to Sandrine after breakfast the day before, but this notion had been dismissed immediately. "If I thought that there was any chance of a storm this week, I would have postponed the retreat."

Josie pulled her knit hat down more firmly over her black hair and then felt for her cell phone inside her coat pocket once more. The trek was taking longer than she expected. She hadn't been this far from the cabins since her arrival when she had taken her free time to get an idea of what lay beyond the camp. If she hoped to get even one bar on her cell phone, she had to get to the highest point possible. Even as her breath puffed out before her, sweat dampened her back. Her calves burned but her nose felt frozen. The wind whipped through the barren tree trunks, spinning the snowflakes into tiny funnels that twirled furiously around her before breaking apart. The snap of a branch stopped her. She scanned the naked tree trunks and large boulders around her but saw no one. Hearing nothing more, she continued on, climbing until she came to a small clearing near the summit of the mountain.

She took off her gloves and jammed them into her right pocket. From her left pocket, she pulled out her phone. Along with it, a crumpled tissue and a folded piece of notebook paper tumbled out, fluttering to the frozen ground. The tissue bounced away like a tumbleweed. Josie used the toe of her boot to capture the paper.

"Shit," she muttered.

She flashed back to sitting at her desk at work, phone trapped between her ear and her shoulder as she scribbled notes onto the small pad she kept next to her computer. She had listened to the voice on the other end of the line while she jotted down words she didn't yet understand. Words she knew in her heart she never wanted to understand. Some whimsical and childlike part of her wondered now if she let the slip fly out from under her boot and into the sky, would her problem fly away as well? Like a magic trick?

Afterward, she'd torn the page from her notepad and stuffed it into her coat pocket before anyone could see it. Later, at home, Noah had caught her reading it. He'd pressed her on the contents, and she had told him. She could still remember the look on his face. It had hollowed her out, hurting her in ways she hadn't been hurt in years.

Feeling as if she'd been punched in the stomach, she'd accused him, "My God. You're disappointed."

He had looked up from the paper, confusion creasing his forehead. His hazel eyes told her everything she needed to know, even before he spoke. "I'm..." he'd faltered. "I—I mean, aren't you disappointed?"

That was a few days before she left for the retreat, and yet it seemed like an eternity.

Another noise startled her from her thoughts. Steps crunching over dead leaves and hard-packed dirt. As she bent to retrieve the page, a scuffed pair of brown work boots appeared before her. In her chest, her heart did a strange little flutter. Her mind was trying to make sense of this other presence so far from the camp when a large, wrinkled hand with hairy knuckles plucked the notebook paper from under her foot. The next thing that Josie saw was the back of a man's head. Thick gray hair curled at the nape of a ruddy neck. The collar of a flannel shirt peeked out of a thick blue coat. Josie exhaled, relieved.

"Cooper," she said. "You scared the shit out of me."

He stood and smiled at her, yellowed teeth showing through his white beard. He was about a foot taller than Josie and although he was likely in his seventies, he was one of the sturdiest-looking people Josie had ever met—broad shoulders, thick forearms, and feet that could put a Sasquatch to shame. He handed her the slip of paper. "Looks like you dropped this."

Even though he had likely not seen anything written on the page—and even if he had, the words would mean nothing to him—Josie felt her face flame as she took it from him. She stuffed it back into her pocket, along with her phone. "Thanks," she said. "What are you doing up here?"

Cooper took a slow look around them. He held out a hand to catch some of the snowflakes which were growing fatter and heavier. "The better question is what are *you* doing up here?"

It wasn't lost on Josie that he'd answered her question with another question. "I was taking a walk," she said.

Blue eyes sparkled from beneath his bushy white brows. "Nobody comes up here just to take a walk."

Josie couldn't tell if he was teasing her or trying to get her to admit to doing something that Sandrine would definitely frown on. Regardless, she didn't owe him an explanation so she repeated her question. "What are you doing up here?"

He opened his mouth to answer but clamped it shut when a loud huffing sound came from behind him. He turned and Josie stepped up beside him as they both tried to find its source. Was yet another person up here on the top of the mountain with them? The noise came again, low and deep, followed by the sound of clacking.

"Oh shit," Josie said, dread sending her heartbeat into overdrive.

There was another long exhale of air and then the sound again: *clackclackclack*.

Cooper pointed to a boulder about thirty feet away from them. "There," he said softly.

The enormous head of a black bear rose up above the boulder. It pointed its light brown snout upward, scenting the air. It huffed again and snapped its jaws several more times in succession, its inch-long canines sharp and gleaming wet with saliva. Josie felt a shudder run the length of her body. "Shouldn't that bear be in hibernation by now?" she whispered.

"Some bears den from October to now. Others don't den at all if they can't find sufficient food," Cooper answered quietly.

One of its feet appeared on the top of the boulder. Two-inch claws scratched against the stone. The bear drew itself up onto the top of the rock, its massive black fur-covered frame seeming to take forever to come fully into view. It paused, bobbing its head and letting out an exhale that sounded like a large piece of machinery lurching to life. Then it hopped down, drawing closer. *Clackclackclack.*

Josie reached for her pistol and was again reminded that it wasn't there. Not that a 9-millimeter would take down a bear of this size. Its massive body lumbered around, searching for the source of the alien scent. With dawning horror, she estimated it to be between five and seven hundred pounds. She'd never been up close and personal with a black bear before. Its legs were almost as thick as her body. Its powerful shoulders moved with a sort of savage grace as it walked, taking a step or two directly toward them and then sidestepping right and left, as if it was still trying to decide whether to attack or not.

Again, it lifted its nose. Huff. *Clackclackclack.*

The air in Josie's lungs stopped moving as the bear spotted them. Panic dried up every ounce of sweat on her body. Suddenly she felt cold, like an ice statue, rooted to the spot. Some part of her brain tried to remember everything she'd been taught about what to do when encountering a black bear, but came up with nothing. All she could think about was how she couldn't breathe, and she was probably going to die in the next few minutes. She'd fought a lot of killers in her time, and won, but she was no match for a black bear, especially without her gun.

Cooper's callused palm closed over her hand. It was surprisingly warm. In a voice low enough for only her to hear, he said, "Keep still. Stand your ground."

Josie was sure she'd heard that advice before. Her police department was filled with hunters, most of whom had encountered a black bear at some point in their outdoor endeavors, but now, at the mercy of a creature so massive and with the power to potentially kill her with a single swipe, this sounded like the worst advice Josie had ever heard.

"You have to be out of your mind," she whispered from the side of her mouth.

Cooper gave her hand a gentle squeeze. "It's the only way we survive this if he decides to mess with us. You're looking at an apex predator. You run, he runs after you, and I can assure you that he is much faster than he looks."

Clackclackclack. The next huff that emanated from the bear's throat seemed like part growl. The sound vibrated in the air all around them.

Cooper said, "He's going to bluff-charge us."

"What?" Instinctively, Josie began to pull her hand away, but Cooper held her in place.

Now his voice was much firmer. "Stay still. Do not run. Follow my lead now."

He let go of her hand, raised his arms, and started waving them in the air. Loudly, firmly, and with no trace of fear, he yelled, "Go on! Get out of here now! You get on out of here! Get lost!"

The bear paused, regarding them steadily, but the clacking and huffing had stopped momentarily.

Josie's arms felt like lead weights, but she thrust them up

and over her head, waving them like Cooper was doing. Her voice came out shaky at first but grew stronger with each exhortation. "Get out of here! Leave us alone! Go! Leave!"

Cooper continued, "Get on out of here, you stupid old bear! Go!"

The bear continued to stare at them, perplexed.

Cooper stopped yelling. Over her own shouts, Josie heard him say, "Be ready and remember, don't move."

The bear had no tells. It gave no indication that it was going to attack. One moment it was staring at them, dark eyes inscrutable. The next it was charging at them, a solid mass of muscle and destruction bearing down on them faster than Josie imagined an animal so large could move. Her bowels loosened. Cooper's arm was a bar across the middle of her back, holding her in place. She had time for one thought.

Noah.

Then, abruptly, the bear stopped within a foot of them and darted off to the side, loping away from them.

Cooper had the wherewithal to start yelling at it again. "That's right, you son of a bitch! Get out of here!"

It disappeared, heading in the direction it had come, down the mountain, but luckily, away from the camp.

With one large hand, Cooper patted Josie's back. It was hard, as if he were trying to dislodge something stuck in her throat. Her breath, maybe. "You did a good job there, Miss Quinn."

Josie's body sagged. She leaned forward and put her hands on her knees. Cooper patted her again, gently this time, then squeezed the back of her neck in an overly familiar way that, in the moment, felt oddly comforting.

"You're okay," Cooper said with a little chuckle. "First time staring down a black bear then, is it?"

"Yeah," she muttered.

"Well, don't worry. Don't think he'll come back real soon

but we still shouldn't stay here. Go ahead and do what you came to do. I'll wait over there, where the path back to the cabins starts."

His footsteps faded before Josie could think to ask how he knew she'd come to this place to do something.

SIX

Standing, Josie sucked in several deep breaths, using the box-breathing technique she had learned along with everyone else during their first group session. She emptied her lungs of air. Then, she breathed in through her nose for four seconds; held it for four seconds; exhaled for a four-count; held that for four more seconds and began again. After a few cycles, she felt more settled in her body again, more solid and less like a pile of jelly limbs. Still, anxiety pricked at her like a porcupine rolling inside her chest. A quick scan of the area reassured her that Cooper was right. The bear hadn't come back—yet—and Cooper was not in sight.

Her hands shook as she reached into her pocket once more and pulled out her cell phone, careful not to dislodge the notepaper again. The tip of her index finger felt numb as she pressed the power button. The power-up process seemed to take forever. Josie stamped her feet to keep some warmth flowing through them as she waited. Another glance around her revealed that there were still no intruders—animal or human.

Finally, the lock screen appeared. She punched in a pass-code and waited for the home screen to follow with its photo of her, Noah, and their Boston terrier, Trout. Her heart gave a funny little skip at the sight, and she wished desperately to be snuggled into bed with the two of them at that very moment. She wished that she hadn't fought with Noah before she left. She wished she'd given him a chance to explain, like he'd asked. She wished she'd given in to his pleas to talk it out.

Would it have made any difference?

Josie didn't know but she missed both husband and dog with a yearning that took her by surprise with its intensity. She had little time to let her notifications populate or to do much of anything except attempt to check for messages from Noah—there were none—and the weather forecast. She had left the phone powered up with its volume off when she arrived at the retreat on Saturday. When she checked it on Tuesday, even though she had not used it, its battery was almost completely drained. It had gone into roam as soon as they arrived near the bottom of the mountain and remained in that battery-sucking mode ever since. The charger was barely keeping up. Even now it was only at fifty-six percent. She held it up and circled around the outside of a large pine tree, waiting to see if it would pick up any network connection.

"Yes!" She found a spot that gave her one bar. Raising her other hand, she brought up the weather app. The phone dropped to fifty-five percent, and a tiny tornado icon spun on her screen, indicating that the app was loading. Whatever connection she'd achieved was not enough to access the app.

"Shit."

The snow had picked up. Fat, wet flakes landed on her face and her phone screen. She scrubbed it with the sleeve of her coat, trying to keep it dry. Putting the phone to her ear, she tried to call Noah but after dialing, there was nothing but dead air. Next, she began to type in a text to him, hesitating over every word. She knew she should start out with an apology, but it galled her to write the word "sorry." She was still wounded from his response to the news. She couldn't exactly act like nothing had transpired and ask about the weather. She made a few attempts at a cohesive text but couldn't bring herself to send it. Finally, she pulled up the contact information for her friend and fellow detective on the Denton PD, Gretchen Palmer. This time, her fingers moved swiftly, with no hesitation.

All is well. Couple more days to go on this retreat. Worried about weather. Can't get internet here. Can barely get cell. Storm coming?

She pressed send and waited as a tiny icon in the shape of a stopwatch whirled below her message. It wasn't going through.

"Dammit."

She stamped her feet again, noticing now that the snow was plentiful enough to crunch beneath her feet. Her eyes wandered over to the boulder the bear had climbed over. Its surface was now covered.

If she left her phone on, it was possible, though unlikely, that the message might go through while she was working her way back to camp but if Gretchen responded, she wouldn't get it unless she came back here—which she most definitely did not want to do.

Josie was so engrossed in her dilemma, eyes locked on the screen, mouth murmuring "come on, come on" over and over again to the unsent message, that she didn't look up when she heard footsteps approaching.

She assumed it was Cooper, there to hurry her along, but Sandrine's voice rang out, loud and appalled.

"Josie! What are you doing? Is that—is that a phone?"

Sandrine said the word "phone" as if she'd caught Josie holding a severed head. Her light brown eyes were wide with shock and disappointment. Snowflakes caught in her long lashes, and she blinked them away. The long brown and gray hair that cascaded from beneath her knit hat sparkled with more flakes. Of all of them, Sandrine seemed to be the most ill-dressed for winter that week. The rest of them had brought heavy coats, gloves, scarves, hats lined with fleece, and winter boots. Sandrine wore an overly large utility jacket, its olive color faded with too many washes. The bottom of yet another thin maxi dress swirled from under the jacket. Beneath that were her standard black yoga pants. Running sneakers completed the mismatched ensemble. Not for the first time that week, it appeared that all of Sandrine's planning had gone toward the activities of the retreat, with none left over to pack a wardrobe suitable for Central Pennsylvania in December. Yet, she didn't seem cold as she eyed Josie with a frown.

"Where's Cooper?" Josie said, craning to look behind her.

Sandrine ignored her question, shaking her head sadly. "You brought a phone?"

Sandrine would have had to pass Cooper to come this far. Surely he'd warned her about the bear? Josie used the phone to gesture all around them. "Sandrine, I'm sorry, but this weather—"

With another shake of her head, Sandrine interrupted. "You've been very focused on the weather today. I'm not sure it's that much of a concern."

"It is," Josie insisted. "If we get a lot of snow, we could be stuck here for days with little food and dwindling wood to keep the cabins warm." And bears.

Sandrine took a step toward her. Josie wondered if she was going to ask for the phone but instead, she put a hand on Josie's forearm and pressed it downward. "Put that away. Josie, this isn't about the weather at all, don't you realize that?"

One last glance at her phone screen told Josie that her message hadn't gone through yet. She put the phone into her pocket. Slipping her gloves back on, she met Sandrine's intense stare. "You saw Cooper on the way up here, right?"

"Yes," Sandrine said. "He's on the path waiting for us. Don't deflect, Josie. I think we need to discuss what your fixation on the weather is really about."

Josie took a deep breath. "Not here."

Sandrine pursed her lips momentarily, now looking like a disappointed school teacher. "You're right. It doesn't have to be here. It's cold and Cooper said you've just seen a bear! But Josie, we will unpack this."

"Sandrine, it really is very simple," Josie said. She started to walk back toward the path to camp. "This retreat has been wonderful. Really. I'm even sleeping better! But if we get stuck up here for a long time, it could be very bad for all of us."

Sandrine trudged alongside her. With a sigh, she brushed snow from her shoulders. "Josie, you've worked so hard this week. I've been very impressed by your commitment to processing the traumatic events of your childhood as well as the painful losses you've experienced as an adult, but in our private sessions, I've felt as though you were holding something back."

Josie didn't say anything. As usual, Sandrine was right. She used the sleeve of her coat to wipe snow from her nose.

More softly now, Sandrine said, "Will you tell me what's bothering you?"

Josie kept moving down the path, annoyed at how long it was taking. Her boots slipped several times in the wet snow.

Sandrine went on. "Maybe the real issue here is trust. We don't know one another that well. It's been less than a week. Given your life experience, I can certainly understand why you have issues trusting people—and processes—but you will never get past your trauma if you don't try to trust people."

"Trust is earned," Josie pointed out. She took one last look over her shoulder. The boulder was still in sight. The bear hadn't returned.

"Has anyone in your life ever truly earned your trust?"

The answer came to Josie instantly. The first person had

been Lisette, her grandmother, but she was gone now. That left her husband, Noah. Did she still trust him? She had never thought him capable of hurting her until last week. He'd skewered her with that single look. It still took her breath away when she thought of it.

Aren't you disappointed?

For the very first time since she had received the news, a voice in the back of her mind needled, *Well? Aren't you disappointed?*

"Shit," she said.

"Josie, it is very difficult to have meaningful relationships without trust."

"No," Josie said quickly. "It's not that. I do trust people."

She felt some modicum of relief at the realization. She did trust her colleagues: Chief Bob Chitwood and Detective Gretchen Palmer as well as her found family, Misty DeRossi and her son, Harris. There was also her biological family that she'd only been reunited with six years ago.

And Mettner. A memory sprang loose in her brain, popping up like the automated villain in some twisted carnival game: his pale face, the way he had stared up at her while he bled out, eyes moving from the sickening realization that he'd been badly shot to resignation that his life was about to end. With a small shake of her head, Josie mentally squashed the memory. She knew she was supposed to sit with these memories, with the feelings that came with them, but she'd always hated that advice with every fiber of her being and neither the time nor the place was right for such a thing.

Sandrine's feet slipped as they stepped over a cluster of stones. Josie's hand shot out, clutching her arm to keep her upright. In the distance, Josie saw Cooper waiting beneath a barren oak tree. "I trust your methods as a therapist, Sandrine," Josie clarified. "But I don't trust your assessment of the weather."

Sandrine laughed, using both hands to grip Josie's arm for support. "I do enjoy your frankness."

"I've lived here my entire life," Josie added. "I can tell when a storm is coming."

Sandrine kept her eyes on the ground before them, treading more carefully now. "If you're that concerned, I'll send Cooper down and into the nearest town tonight to find out what's going on. Happy?"

"Yes," said Josie. "Thank you."

Sandrine stopped just before they came within earshot of Cooper. She brushed Josie's hand away. Her eyes darkened with concern. "Would you like to go home? I'm not keeping you here against your will, Josie. You're free to go anytime. We've only got tomorrow and Saturday morning left. Whether it snows or not, it doesn't change our program here or the work we're trying to do. It's all indoors anyway. Cooper can dig a path from each cabin to the main house if necessary."

Josie didn't argue with her. She could leave, it was true. She could go directly back to her cabin, pack up all of her things, and hop on the back of the Gator for Cooper to take her down to her vehicle. She could be home in a few hours.

As much as she missed Noah, did she really want to have the difficult conversation that awaited her at home? Today?

Sandrine stamped her feet to warm up. "So you're not that worried about the weather?"

Josie took off her glove and jammed her hand into her coat pocket, fishing for the notebook page. When her fingers closed over it, she drew it out and handed it to Sandrine, who took it, staring at the words. "Oh Josie," she said. "Is this... do these apply to you?"

The tip of her nose felt numb. "Yes."

Maybe Sandrine was right. Maybe her fixation on the weather was just a way to distract herself from what awaited her at home. The week was nearing its end and the fact that she was going to have to face some difficult truths and discussions loomed large. Rather than think about that, it was easier to focus on a disaster of a different kind.

Sandrine read off the diagnoses. "Diminished ovarian reserve. Uterine septum. You've been trying to get pregnant?"

Josie closed her eyes. Snow pelted her cheeks. A wet flake landed on her eyelid. After taking two deep breaths, she wiped at it and opened her eyes to face Sandrine. "Yes. My husband and I decided earlier this year that we would try to have children. When I couldn't conceive, I went to my OB/GYN and had some tests done. I don't have a lot of eggs left. There's still a slim chance I could get pregnant but even if I did, I would likely miscarry because the inside of my uterus is shaped weird. There's a wall of tissue that shouldn't be there. That septum thing." Tears spilled from her eyes, in spite of her trying to hold them back. She gestured toward the page. "The septum doesn't have a good enough blood supply for an embryo to implant. That's what would lead to the miscarriages. I could have surgery to correct it but with how few eggs I've got left, I still might not ever get pregnant, even with fertility treatments—which are expensive. It's possible to spend our life's savings on this and still be left with nothing."

Snow fell onto the page, blurring Josie's scribbled words. Carefully, Sandrine folded it up and put it into her own pocket. Josie felt a strange sort of relief, as if some part of the burden that came with this horrible knowledge had been lifted.

"Have you and your husband discussed other options?" Sandrine asked.

"No. We didn't get that far. He saw the notes I took from my conversation with the doctor. I told him what they meant. Then he—he had this look on his face." In spite of the cold that cut through her entire body, a hot stab of pain punched into Josie's abdomen as she remembered the crestfallen look on Noah's face.

Sandrine said, "You didn't expect him to be disappointed? He wanted children as well, didn't he?"

"Yes, but he always told me that I was enough for him. Even if we never had children, he said, I was enough." Josie pounded a gloved fist against her chest. Now the tears came fast and furious. "And I believed him. I believed him all this time. Then when I told him the news, I saw in his face that that was a lie."

Sandrine pulled a clump of tissues from somewhere in her jacket pocket. Her hand shook with cold as she handed them to Josie. "I'm not sure that you can infer so much from just a look, Josie. What did he say?"

The words scraped raw across her throat. "That he was disappointed."

Sandrine looked past her to where Cooper stood, glancing all around, likely checking for the bear. Returning her attention to Josie, she said, "People are very complex, Josie. I'm not sure you should take his initial reaction so much to heart. What else did he say?"

Josie dabbed at her face with the tissues. Her tears felt frozen to her skin. "Nothing."

"Because there was nothing else he wanted to say or because you didn't give him a chance to say anything else?" From anyone else's mouth, the words might have sounded pointed, but Sandrine had an uncanny way of softening even the bluntest questions. When Josie didn't answer, Sandrine smiled gently. "Don't go home yet, Josie. Think about why your instinct was to flee rather than to talk it over with him. I know the answer but I'm not sure you do. I can tell it to you, but it won't have the same impact as it will if you get there yourself. Stay here with us. I think it would be beneficial if you took the next day and a half to explore this issue before you go home and face reality. What do you say?"

Josie sniffed. "Sure."

"Now let's get out of this cold."

SEVEN

DENTON, PA

In spite of the fact that he'd showered before he left his house, sweat dampened the back of Noah Fraley's neck. His legs felt heavy from the run he'd taken earlier that day. He'd pushed himself, covering nearly double the miles he normally did. He'd run until his mind could no longer focus on anything but keeping oxygen in his lungs and his body upright. Until thoughts of his wife, Josie, and the way she'd stared at him in the days before she left for her retreat disappeared from his mind. Shattered. That's how she'd looked. It hadn't come to him until she was already gone. The right word for it. Or any of the right words, for that matter.

"Dammit," he muttered to himself, heaving up one more short flight of steps. It was only two floors. Why did it feel like an eternity today? And why the hell was it so hot? Was it always this hot in the stairwell?

He paused on the first landing to peel off his coat. A uniformed officer came flying out of the first-floor door, hitting Noah like a wall. He fell backward, almost toppling down the steps. His hands caught the railing just in time. His coat tumbled down the stairs. The officer muttered a sorry and disappeared below, hopping over the coat without a glance. Seconds later, the ground-floor door to the municipal parking lot banged open and a gust of cold air rushed upward, lifting the lock of thick dark hair that had fallen across Noah's forehead.

With a sigh, Noah went back to the lower landing and picked up his coat. This time, as he passed the first floor, he kept his distance from the door. He'd never given much thought to the fact that the building had no elevators, but now he wondered why none had ever been installed. Probably because the Denton Historic Society wouldn't allow it. Housed in a massive three-story stone building that boasted a bell tower, it had once been the town hall. Nearly seventy years ago, it was converted into police headquarters. The second-floor great room was where Noah and the other investigators spent most of their time. It was a huge open-concept area just outside the office of the Chief of Police, filled with desks for officers to make calls and complete paperwork. Only five of those desks had been permanently assigned to specific people on the force. One belonged to their press liaison, Amber Watts. The other four, pushed together to make a large rectangle in the center of the room, belonged to the investigative team: Josie, Gretchen, Noah, and their fallen colleague, Finn Mettner. Although Mett had died ten months earlier, the Chief had not replaced him right away, and no one had touched his desk other than to access official files needed for police business. The Chief had left it up to Amber, Finn's girlfriend, to remove his personal effects. It had taken about six months before they noticed that she'd begun, little by little, to remove a few things. Framed photos of his extended family. The fishing mug he used as a pen holder which said *The Rodfather* on it. A badly painted ceramic bass his nephew had made for him.

But it still held many of Mett's things. In Noah's mind, it was still Mett's desk.

Which was probably why he completely lost his shit when

he walked into the great room and saw Chief Chitwood putting the remaining contents of the desk into a box. Before Noah's rational mind could impress upon him that it was a terrible idea, his body sprinted around the desks, hip-checking Chief Chitwood out of the way, and snatching up the box. The files inside jostled around, a few pages slipping out of the one on top.

The Chief stumbled backward, gripping the back of Mettner's chair to stay upright. From behind him, seated at her own desk, Gretchen stared at him, stunned.

Red suffused the Chief's acne-pitted cheeks and crept all the way up to his scalp, where strands of thin white hair floated. One bushy eyebrow shot upward. He crossed his arms over his thin chest. As he drew in a long breath, Noah knew he was in deep shit. "Fraley!" the Chief boomed. "Just what in the hell do you think you're doing?"

Noah looked down at the box, then back at Amber's desk. Empty. The sweat at the back of his neck increased, pouring down the column of his spine and wicking his Denton PD polo shirt to his skin. "This is Mett's desk," he blurted.

Some of the Chief's bluster seemed to dissipate. "No," he said. "This *was* Mett's desk. You three have been up my ass for months to hire a fourth investigator, and so I did. He starts tomorrow."

Gretchen's chair creaked as she stood up. In her late forties, with more experience than any of them, having worked fifteen years on Philadelphia's homicide squad, she was often a calming force. Moving around the Chief, she gently reached out for the box. Noah's knuckles ached as he tightened his grip on it. He was being childish. He knew it. He was glad Josie wasn't here to see this. If she had been here, maybe he wouldn't be acting this way.

"Fraley," said Gretchen. "This day was always going to come."

He swallowed hard and then let her take the box from his

hands. She placed it back on the desk, pushed both hands through her short, spiked salt-and-pepper hair, sighed, and then picked up where the Chief had left off.

"Don't think you're off the hook," the Chief said, pointing a finger at Noah.

Gretchen, still between them, pushed the Chief's arm down but the Chief was undeterred. Anger flashed in his flinty eyes. "Son," he said. "I don't know what crawled up your ass this week, but you better shit it out real quick because I am not putting up with it any longer."

Noah eyed him. "What are you talking about?"

"You've been acting like a child all week. Now I know Quinn is away but that's no excuse."

"I haven't—" Noah said.

"You have," Gretchen cut him off. She turned to the Chief. "It's not that she's away. They had a fight."

Noah felt as though she had slapped him. "What? How the hell do you know?"

Gretchen sighed again and stopped packing the box so she could take out her cell phone. She waved it in the air. "Because your wife texted me about the weather today. That's how I know. No internet. Limited cell service. She's worried about the storm that's coming and instead of contacting you, she texted me. Doesn't take a genius to figure out she's not speaking to you. So, you had a fight."

The Chief shook his head slowly, as if in disapproval.

Noah said, "You don't understand. What happened—"

Chief Chitwood raised a hand, stopping him mid-sentence. "Fraley, I don't need to know your personal business."

"True story," said Gretchen.

Noah felt the last of his energy bleed through his feet into the tile beneath him. He closed his eyes, tipped his head up toward the ceiling and sucked in a few deep breaths. Again, he pictured the look on Josie's face after she'd told him that she couldn't have a baby. He had thought she was devastated by the news, but she had had hours to digest it before they spoke. It was only after she left that he realized it wasn't the news that had shattered her, but his reaction to it. It was true that he hadn't even known how much he wanted to have children with her until that moment, when it was no longer an option, but that didn't mean he didn't want her. He would never not want her.

He had spent the three days before she left begging her to talk to him, but he should have known what was really bothering her. He knew her better than anyone else. As closed off as she could be, this was a point of pride for him. Not only had he married the most extraordinary woman on the planet, but he was good at being her husband. Now he replayed the conversation, the look, the three days afterward, the deafening silence in their normally loud and happy household.

A simple reassurance from him could have prevented all of this strife.

He opened his eyes and looked back at the Chief and Gretchen. "I screwed up."

Gretchen laughed. "You think?"

The Chief said, "Well, you better figure out a way to unscrew things fast, Fraley."

EIGHT

Dinner at the main house was either a very lively event with lots of chatter or a very morose event that felt like a funeral. It all depended on the type of day that the retreat members had had. Tonight, Josie was relieved to see that everyone was in a good mood, in spite of the snow accumulating outside. When they had all participated in the rage room on Tuesday, everyone had been in good spirits then, as well. They sat at a long rectangular table, presided over by Sandrine. It was positioned near the back of the large central room. Normally, they were treated to a view of the trees out front but now, the darkness outside showed them only their own reflections in the wall of windows. Josie was still pondering Sandrine's earlier question about why her first instinct had been to shut Noah out. She pushed the evening's dinner around on her plate. It was some sort of rice and vegetable concoction. Sandrine insisted on feeding them healthy, organic dishes, most of which Josie had never heard of before.

An elbow landed softly in Josie's ribs. She looked up to see Alice Vargus grinning surreptitiously at her. "I would give up a non-essential organ for a slice of pizza right about now. You?"

Josie laughed softly. "You read my mind."

"Here," said Alice, plucking a soft roll from her plate and depositing it onto Josie's. "It's just about the only thing that's edible."

Alice was right. Sandrine had made two dozen gluten-free dinner rolls to go with the meal and placed them in the center of the table. Josie had taken one, not expecting it to be very palatable, but it was delicious. When she reached for a second, they were all gone.

"You don't have to—" Josie began, but Alice huffed at her in a way that made it clear she was accepting no arguments. "Thanks."

Although Alice was about twenty years older than Josie, in her mid- to late fifties, the two of them had made fast friends. Back home in New York City, Alice was an emergency room nurse. She had confessed that there were things she saw on the job that traumatized her. Josie had related instantly to that. But none of them were there for just one issue. To get on the retreat, you had to reach a certain bar for trauma. All of them there had complex PTSD. In addition to Alice's traumatic work experience, she had been raped at the tender age of nineteen and gone on to bear a son. Raising him with few resources and parents who wanted little to do with a grandson fathered by a rapist, Alice had turned to drugs and alcohol, spiraling out of control until she lost custody of her son. After hitting rock bottom, going to rehab, and slowly piecing her life together, including taking several years to complete nursing school, she had tried to reconnect with her son. He had wanted nothing to do with her. Although Alice tried, year after year, to make amends, he did not welcome her overtures.

Alice dropped her voice again so that only Josie could hear it. "I saw Cooper riding the Gator down the path before dinner. He was really struggling in the snow."

Josie nodded and told her about the conversation with

Sandrine. With a sigh, Alice sat back in her chair and put her fork down. She regarded the others around them, each one locked in conversation with someone else. "I suppose there are worse places to be stuck although the company could be better. Bunch of sad sacks, we are."

"I'm not worried about the company," Josie said. "I'm worried about supplies."

Alice frowned. "How long could we be stuck here?"

"Depending on the amount of snow, a week, maybe? I'd hope. People know we're here so I'd expect someone to try to get us off the mountain as fast as possible but we're miles from the nearest town, on a road that would need to be cleared, and since there aren't many residences out here, it would be low on the plowing priority list. Plus with those fallen rocks along the path between the parking lot and here, no car or truck would make it all the way."

Alice picked her fork up again, pushing the rice and vegetables around on her plate. "The wood supplies for heat would be an issue. Not sure how long those would last, but I'd think that Brian could use the axe from the rage room and cut us up some wood if necessary. To stay warm, we'd all have to stay here though, in one central location, then try to stretch the food as much as possible. That big generator out back will run out of gas which would make cooking difficult but I'm sure we could just start a little campfire outside. All of our nighttime lanterns are solar-powered so if we just charge them during the day like we do now, they'll be fine at night."

Josie pushed the last piece of dinner roll into her mouth and chewed.

Alice added, "But Cooper will be back soon with news. If he thinks we all need to get off this mountain, then we will."

Josie didn't mention that at least two inches of snow had fallen since Cooper left. She wasn't sure he'd even make it back to the camp with his news at this rate. Looking at the faces gathered round the table, she tried to imagine being stranded here in this building with these people. They'd achieved a tentative closeness during the week of oversharing about their personal traumas. With Sandrine's gentle guidance, they had formed some bonds, but Josie wasn't sure it was enough to sustain them under extreme stress.

Some of them were barely hanging on, like Brian's wife, Nicola, who sat across the table. A waif of a woman, Josie estimated her to be in her early thirties. Pale skin, strawberry-blonde hair, long, willowy limbs that hung listlessly from her mostly inert frame. As she pushed her vegetables around her plate, her left elbow kept clashing with the right arm of the woman next to her, Meg Cleary. After accidentally knocking Meg's fork out of her hand, Nicola suggested they switch seats. "Sorry," she told Meg in a flat voice. "I'm left-handed. I always end up bumping right-handed people."

Meg picked up her plate and stood. Nicola moved into her empty chair but that left the seat between Brian and Nicola open. Brian smiled and motioned for Meg to take it but Nicola said, "You move down, too. Let her have the seat on the other side of you."

Brian's cheeks glowed red but he did as Nicola told him. The three of them lapsed into silence.

Alice bumped Josie's shoulder gently with her own. In a conspiratorial whisper, she said, "You're wondering which one of them would break first, aren't you?"

Josie lowered her head to hide her smile and used her fork to spear a piece of broccoli.

"My guess is Meg," said Alice.

A polite smile was plastered across Meg's face as Brian started talking to her. On his other side, Nicola watched him with annoyance. Josie couldn't tell if it was because of what he was saying or because he was so focused on Meg. Unlike Nicola, everything about Meg was robust—from her curvy figure to her long, lustrous brown hair. Well, everything except her personality. Nicola was prone to lashing out, which Josie found completely understandable, given what had happened to her daughter. Meg, on the other hand, carried herself like an abused animal. Her brown eyes were usually wide and wary, as if she were waiting for something bad to happen.

"I can see why you would choose Meg," Josie told Alice.

"Can you though?" Alice asked, leaning more closely toward Josie so that her words could not be overheard.

Matching Alice's tone, Josie whispered, "After what she went through, of course I can."

Josie was close enough to feel the shudder work its way through Alice's body. Meg had been the victim of a stalker. Austin Cawley, a male coworker at a restaurant where she'd worked, had seemed sweet and harmless when he first took an interest in her. Meg didn't view him in a romantic light and thought nothing of it when she turned him down for a date. Until he kept asking. After rejection number six, he'd subjected her to two years of terror that no restraining order could stop. She had changed jobs, apartments, and phone numbers multiple times but he still found her. Cawley always found a way to make her life hell, whether it was inundating her with calls and texts, breaking into her home and masturbating on her bed, or hiding cameras in her bathroom so that he could distribute the resulting photos to her neighbors and coworkers.

The criminal justice system didn't take his offenses seriously enough, nor did it move quickly enough. Josie had always thought the anti-stalking laws in most places were too weak and her opinion was borne out in Meg's case. Although the stalker was charged with a slew of criminal acts after the bathroom photos started showing up everywhere, he was let out of jail on bond. In a final desperate attempt to possess Meg, he had kidnapped her and her sister at gunpoint and held them in his apartment for three days. Meg's sister never made it out. She died of a heart attack while being held captive, caused by a combination of a pre-existing heart condition and the stress of their ordeal.

This time, Cawley was charged with more serious offenses but again, he was let out on bond, pending trial. He immediately fled. It had been almost six months but no one had found him, according to Meg. She had moved several states away in an attempt to stay off his radar and evade him.

"Whenever I think I had it bad," Alice said softly, "I think about Meg. I don't mean to sound cold. I just don't think that Meg would handle being stuck very well. It's too soon after what she went through. The guy isn't even in prison."

Josie quickly shoved another piece of broccoli into her mouth. "I get it, but my money is on Nicola."

Alice's fork froze halfway between her mouth and the plate. "Really? Over Taryn?"

Josie followed Meg's unwavering gaze which was fixed on Taryn Pederson. Taryn sat where she always did, right next to Sandrine. Like Josie, Brian, and Nicola, Taryn was in her mid- to late thirties. She acted more like Meg, who was ten years younger, but dressed similarly to Sandrine, in long, flowing maxi dresses over yoga pants, even in winter, using a worn UPenn hoody to keep warm. She even wore her long, dark hair parted in the middle like Sandrine's though it lacked the curls and the threads of gray of Sandrine's locks. Even though Taryn showed little interest in the rest of them, Josie had found her to be generally warm and pleasant. That didn't keep Meg from watching her as if she were some kind of domesticated animal that might turn feral at any moment. Taryn had garnered more and more of Meg's quiet stares as the week went on. Josie thought back through the various group sessions and other activities they'd done together but she couldn't remember anything transpiring between the two women.

Josie said, "I feel like Taryn would see getting stuck here as an adventure rather than a catastrophe."

"Hmmm, maybe you're right," Alice conceded. She lifted a piece of asparagus to her mouth, wrinkled her nose, and dumped it back onto her plate. "She lost her parents in a camping accident. Then her husband. What a weird way to go, too. How many people a year are killed from whales crashing into their fishing boats?"

"Not many, I'm sure," Josie said.

"This is all in, what? A two-year period? She'd probably rather be trapped here with us than home alone."

As usual, during mealtimes, Taryn was bending Sandrine's ear about various sorts of therapy available to trauma survivors. Currently, they were discussing primal scream therapy, which Taryn thought might be of use, but which Sandrine advised had been debunked as having no actual benefit to patients.

Alice said, "What does it say about us that neither one of us has even considered Brian as the weakest link?"

"I'm not sure," Josie said. "But I don't think it would take much to get Brian to lose his composure."

"Agree," Alice said. "To be honest? I don't think either him or Nicola are really processing what happened to their little girl."

Josie felt sadness nipping at her insides. "It will take a lot more than a retreat to get them to that point."

"If it was me? I would have offed myself. I don't think I could live with something like that."

Josie turned her head and looked at Alice. In the dim light of the room, the flecks of green in her hazel eyes sparkled as she blinked back tears. Her eyes always reminded Josie of Noah's and the way they subtly shifted color depending on his mood.

"I'm sorry," Alice said. "I shouldn't have said that. It was awful. We shouldn't be making fun either, I suppose. I just thought I would lighten the mood. You seem so sad tonight."

Josie leaned her head against Alice's shoulder. "Thanks."

The sound of dishes clattering and ceramics breaking startled her upright. Across the table, Nicola stood, fists clenched at her sides. Her chair had fallen over. What was left of her dinner now lay in Brian's lap. Her plate and water glass were shattered on the wooden floor.

"You son of a bitch," she snarled, eyes aglow with rage. Brian stared at her, a strange expression on his face. It almost looked like boredom. All week, he had not been as vocal as his wife or as engaged in any of the sessions. He barely spoke and when he did, he talked about the fire that had burned down his first foster home and left him with a lifetime of nightmares. Sandrine had spent the entire week urging him to stop avoiding the topic of his daughter's death by focusing on an earlier trauma. He often looked uncomfortable and usually stared at Nicola with sympathy writ large across his face but now, he looked indifferent to her display of emotion.

Sandrine was out of her seat, moving toward Nicola, but before she could reach her, Nicola stepped back, away from the table.

Brian said, "Nicola, please just sit down."

"Don't tell me what to do, you bastard," she shot back. "You don't care about me or my feelings. You never have!"

Taryn stood up. "Nicola," she said sweetly, "I'm sure that's not true. Why don't you come back to the table, and we'll talk it out."

Anger twisted Nicola's delicate features. "Oh shut up, bitch. No one wants to"—here she lifted her thin arms to use air quotes—"'talk it out' with you."

Alice gasped.

Taryn opened her mouth to speak but nothing came out. Her lower lip trembled. Meg put her fork down and rested both palms on the table, as if ready to spring from her seat. For once, her big brown eyes narrowed and locked on Taryn.

Every muscle in her body seemed tensed, as if bracing for something.

Sandrine put her body between Nicola and Taryn, shaking her head, her tone gentle but firm. It always amazed Josie how Sandrine kept her poise around all of them, especially when one of them was having a meltdown. "Nicola, I understand you're upset right now, but Taryn's right. Whatever is bothering you, why don't we talk about it? I could take you and Brian into a private session if you—"

"Oh, you shut up, too!" Nicola snapped.

Taryn said, "Hey!"

Softly, Alice said, "Nicola."

Her voice—gentle and almost motherly—seemed to get through to her. The angry lines of her face loosened as she looked over Sandrine's shoulder and met Alice's eyes. "I know you're frustrated right now, but we promised we would have compassion for one another this week and be respectful, remember?"

"Yes," Sandrine agreed. "Those were the rules. I can see that you're angry right now. I understand what that's like—better than anyone..."

At this, Nicola's features twisted again. She opened her mouth to speak once more but changed her mind abruptly when Alice gave her another maternal look.

Taryn wiped tears from her cheeks. "We're all angry here, Nicola, but barking at each other is not a good way to go about expressing or processing that anger."

Nicola groaned. She rolled her eyes and spun on her heel, striding toward the front door. As she passed through it, a gust of icy wind burst into the room, bringing with it a snow squall. After it slammed shut, the eyes of everyone in the room turned to Brian. He hung his head and heaved himself out of his chair. The remains of his dinner tumbled to the floor. As he bent to clean them up, Meg stood to help. Brian made a half-hearted attempt to get all the food up from the floor but seeing how efficiently Meg worked, he left her to it, drawing to his full height. He looked at the rest of them, then at the door. "I'll go talk to Nic," he said in a tone that implied that someone was making him do it.

"No," Sandrine said sharply. "You stay. Help with dinner clean-up. I'd like to speak to her."

Once Sandrine was gone, Josie and Alice helped Meg finish cleaning up while Taryn started clearing plates. Brian stood awkwardly, watching, until Taryn snapped at him to do something. Instead of helping, he left. After that, no one talked. The only sounds were the dishes clinking and Taryn's sniffles.

In the kitchen, Josie started washing the dishes. Moments later, Alice joined her, carefully drying each dish once Josie finished with it. She glanced at the door to the kitchen and, satisfied that neither Taryn nor Meg would hear her, whispered in Josie's ear, "Now, which one of our retreat mates do you think would get mauled by the bear first?"

NINE

By three a.m. Friday, Noah felt like he'd downed two pots of coffee. He hadn't been able to sleep after his Thursday evening shift. Now he sat in bed checking and rechecking the radar on his weather app. Although Denton wouldn't be badly impacted by snow, a major storm was bearing down on Sullivan County at an alarming rate. Before he'd left the stationhouse, Gretchen had texted Josie back to tell her a blizzard was on the way, but had gotten no response. Nor had Josie come home early, which meant that she was going to get stuck on that mountainside— possibly for days—with no electronics and limited supplies, surrounded by people she barely knew.

No matter where things stood between them, he wasn't letting that happen to his wife.

As if sensing his anxiety, their Boston terrier, Trout, whined and pawed at Noah's arm. The dog had been inconsolable since Josie left. The first two days she'd been away he had refused to eat his meals and wouldn't go to the bathroom unless Noah carried him outside and sweet-talked him into doing his business. Trout had done nothing but lie in the foyer, watching the front door. Even at nighttime, he would not come to bed with

Noah. By day three, he'd come to some sort of grudging accep-
tance that Josie would not be walking through the front door
any time soon, eating meals and sleeping in the bed with Noah
again. Still, every chance he got, he made his displeasure with
the situation known, just like he was now, in the middle of the
night.

Scratching behind his ears, Noah said, "I know, boy. I
should go get your mom, huh?"

Trout huffed in agreement and then stared into Noah's soul
until he got up and started getting dressed. Noah packed a small
overnight bag, in case he, too, got stuck in Sullivan County, and
then he dropped Trout off with their friend, Misty DeRossi.
She was one of their best friends and often came to their rescue
in emergencies, just like Noah and Josie did for her. She wasn't
upset in the least at being disturbed in the middle of the night.
She often watched Trout, as well, so taking their dog was not an
imposition. After planting several kisses on Trout's squishy face,
Noah hit the road. It was slow going on narrow, winding roads
through mountains and valleys with few residences, snow
already on the ground and more of it falling relentlessly. There
was no major highway or thoroughfare to get to Sullivan
County. Route 220 was probably the most well-traveled, well-
maintained road but even that sliced through some extremely
high mountains. Near dawn, he found himself on a steep
incline in nearly a foot of snow that had not yet been plowed.
The tires of his SUV strained to find purchase as he neared
Laporte, the county seat, and the small town in which the sheriff's office was located. It seemed as good a place to start as any,
especially since he needed help locating the retreat and might
also need help rescuing the members of the retreat from the top
of a mountain.

His hands ached from gripping the steering wheel so hard.
His GPS had lost its connection miles ago. At this point, any
town would be welcome. Although he'd passed a few lone resi-

dences, and a recycling plant, the rest of Sullivan County so far was wilderness. Relief loosened the knot forming in his stomach when, through the onslaught of snow, he made out a green sign ahead. *Laporte, 2 miles.* He punched the gas pedal harder. He was making progress up the long hill when the SUV started to fishtail. He tried to regain control of it but he jerked the wheel too hard, sending it sideways. It started to drift slowly back down the hill. He tried again to exert some control over the vehicle's direction or speed, but it was caught in an inexorable sideways slide, gaining momentum back down the hill. From the driver's side window, he watched the bottom of the hill rush toward him.

A pair of headlights appeared, bright pinpricks in the white fury.

He was headed directly toward them.

There was only time for one thought. Her name came out as a whisper, even though there was no one there to hear it. "Josie."

TEN

Day 6

Josie woke to the sound of someone pounding on her cabin door. She sat up in bed, blinking rapidly. Her eyes felt like they were full of grit. Across the room, the last of the small logs she had fed into the wood-burning stove glowed orange, nothing left but embers and charred husks. Muted daylight streamed through the gauzy curtains, a dull gray.

"Josie? Josie? Are you in there?" Sandrine's voice was high-pitched, her knocking urgent. This wasn't how she normally woke them for breakfast.

"I'm here," Josie called, but her throat was so dry, it came out as a croak.

She threw off her comforter and padded across the tiny room. Even through her thick socks, the cold bled up from the floor and into the soles of her feet. She unlocked the door and turned the knob. The door flew inward and Sandrine burst through in a squall of snow, knocking Josie onto her ass. Blistering cold air whooshed over her, driving out the heat from the stove. Sandrine held onto the knob to stay upright. She was dressed much as she had been the day before, a utility jacket over a thin maxi dress, black yoga pants, and a knit hat. This time, at least, she had on a solid pair of winter boots.

Josie threw up a forearm to cover her eyes from the brightness exploding through the doorway. Snow, snow, and more snow. It was still coming down hard and fast outside, just as it had been when she'd returned to her cabin after dinner the evening before. A miniature drift about a foot high had gathered at the cabin's threshold and now it stood, flattened along the side where it had rested against her cabin door.

Sandrine said, "You're okay? You're all right?"

Josie stood up, rubbing her bottom, and looking around for where she'd thrown her jeans the night before. "Yes. Why wouldn't I be okay? Is something wrong?"

Sandrine used the inside edge of her right boot to try to sweep the snow back outside onto the stoop. It was a losing battle. Her cheeks were bright red. Snowflakes snagged in the long, twisted locks of her hair. "I was waking everyone for breakfast and Meg is not in her cabin. It was unlocked, but she isn't there. She's not in the main house. Taryn ran down to the outbuilding where we hold the rage room and said she's not there either."

"Taryn?"

Looking at her feet, Sandrine said, "Cooper never came back last night. There must have been too much snow for him to get here. Please don't launch into a 'told you so' lecture, Josie. Right now, I just want to find Meg."

"That's not my style, Sandrine." Josie looked around the tiny cabin. All of them had the same layout. A single room with a small bed, a short wooden dresser, and a wood-burning stove. In the back of the cabin was a bathroom. Josie found her jeans in a pile of clothes on top of the dresser and pulled them up over her thin pajama pants. Then she shoved her feet into her boots and snatched her coat from a hook along the wall, pulling it on. "When you went inside Meg's cabin, how did it look?"

Sandrine's brows drew together in confusion. "What do you mean?"

Josie had to remind herself she wasn't conducting an official investigation with her team. Instead of asking if it looked like there had been a struggle, she said, "Was everything neat and in its place, or did it look messy?"

"Oh, it was fine. Neat."

"Was all of her stuff still inside?"

"All of her things look like they're still there," said Sandrine.

"Did it appear as though she'd slept in her bed?"

Sandrine twisted her gloved hands. "You think she left in the middle of the night? Or early this morning? There's so much snow!"

Josie found her hat inside one pocket of her coat and pulled it over her head. "I don't know. That's why I'm asking."

Another gust of wind blasted through the doorway, scattering snow across the floor. Sandrine quickly closed the door and pressed her back against it. "I don't know. I guess. The covers were rumpled at the bottom of her bed."

Josie fished in her other pocket for her gloves. "Do you know if Meg is the type to make her bed?"

Sandrine blinked. "Why are you asking me all these questions?"

Josie slid her hands into the gloves. "I'm trying to help you locate Meg."

"You sound like... like you're investigating a crime."

In truth, a bud of anxiety had bloomed in the pit of Josie's stomach the moment she saw Sandrine's face. It was far more likely that Meg had tried to leave or taken a walk and gotten lost or stuck in the snow than that a crime had been committed. In fact, the greater concern was the bear that Josie and Cooper had encountered. Josie couldn't stop thinking about its beady brown eyes and the loud clacking of its massive teeth. Hopefully, Meg hadn't run afoul of the beast. Josie forced a smile onto her face. "Sorry. Habit. I'm sure Meg is fine but if we want to locate her quickly, we have to eliminate certain things."

Sandrine swiped at the snow in her hair. "Things like what?"

"Like if she's not in her cabin, how long has she been gone? If we can ascertain whether or not she slept in her bed, that could help. On the other hand, if Meg is the kind of person who never makes her bed, then it will be impossible to tell."

"Oh, well, I don't know if she made it or not."

"What about her wood-burning stove?" asked Josie, gesturing for Sandrine to move away from the door.

Sandrine shuffled to the side. "The fire was out."

"Stove still warm?"

"Oh, I don't know. I didn't feel it."

Depending on how many logs Meg typically loaded into the stove at bedtime, this could mean nothing. Or it could mean she'd left her cabin many hours ago. Perhaps she'd never loaded it at all the night before.

Josie opened the door and stepped onto the porch, which was little more than a three foot by three foot wooden slab atop four rickety steps. All of it was covered in snow. Josie estimated about twelve to fourteen inches. Deep footsteps, already being filled with new snow, were visible from below the main house to where Josie now stood. On the deck of the main house, Taryn stood hugging herself and stamping her feet. Nicola stood in the open doorway of her cabin. Brian wasn't visible.

Josie counted off the cabins in her head. From the bottom of the slope, after the rage room and the main house, first was Sandrine's, then Nicola and Brian's; Taryn's, Meg's, Josie's and Alice's at the top of the hill.

There were no footsteps to or from Alice's cabin. Josie headed there first with Sandrine in tow. The wind whipped more snow into their faces as they battled the short distance to Alice's door. She opened it after the first few knocks. "What are you doing he—" The question died on her lips as she looked beyond Josie and Sandrine to the snow coming down. "Shit. This retreat just got a lot longer."

ELEVEN

They stood in a loose circle in the great room of the main house. Everyone wore their winter coats, hats, gloves and boots except for Brian who had trudged in with nothing on but a T-shirt, basketball shorts, and a pair of sneakers. No socks. Snow melted against his ankles but if it bothered him, he didn't show it. All eyes were on Sandrine. For the first time that week, the preternatural calm she exuded in every moment was gone. Wringing her hands, she looked toward Josie.

Taryn was on Sandrine's other side, eyes wide, her teeth working at her bottom lip. When no one spoke, Josie said, "Did anyone see Meg after dinner last night?"

Alice said, "She stayed here for a bit after dinner. Taryn and I did the sound bath in the meditation room, and she joined us."

"Yes," Taryn said.

Josie looked to Sandrine who nodded.

Josie had retreated to her cabin after the scene at dinner, her mind still on Noah.

Nicola pushed a hand through her short strawberry-blonde locks and sighed. "What does it matter when anyone saw her?"

"Nic," Brian whispered.

Nicola glanced at him and then her gaze swept downward. Quietly, she twisted her wedding band around her finger. She fiddled with it so much that the gold's sheen had dulled.

Josie said, "I'm trying to figure out how long she's been missing."

Brian put a hand on Nicola's shoulder, but she shrugged it off. "Is that important?"

It was an odd question from a mother whose daughter had been abducted and murdered. Then again, Nicola had spent almost no time at all discussing the police response or logistics of what had happened, only how the loss had affected her.

Josie glanced at the wall of windows. It was a white-out as far as the eye could see. Even the naked tree branches were no longer visible in the onslaught of snow. "If she walked off somewhere, it will give us an idea of how far we need to search. If she left at eleven last night, she might have gotten to the bottom of the mountain, but if she walked off early this morning, she might still be nearby."

Alice looked around the group. "Why would she have 'walked off'? Why leave her cabin without telling anyone? If she left sometime after the sound bath last night, it was already snowing pretty heavily."

The room fell silent. Josie could hear the wind whistling through the trees outside, but the generator was silent. For the first time, she noticed how cold it was inside the building. Without Cooper, no one had started the generator or lit the wood-burner.

Nicola said, "Everyone here is fucked up. Who knows why she left?"

"Nicola, please," Sandrine admonished.

"Come on, Sandrine," Nicola shot back. "It's true."

"Well," Taryn huffed. "I take issue with that. You might be... messed up but I'm not."

Nicola laughed. "You're at a retreat for trauma, Taryn."

Taryn folded her arms across her chest. "We're all here for the same reason. To try to get better. I went through some things, just like all of you, but I'm dealing with it. I'm fine."

Nicola smirked at her. "Sure you are."

Sandrine put both palms up. "Please. That's enough. Let's keep the focus on Meg. She's not in her cabin. There is a great deal of snow outside and it doesn't seem to be stopping. We need to find her."

Josie said, "Did anyone see Meg after the..." she couldn't believe the words were coming out of her mouth as the practice had seemed so odd to her when she first heard of it but was actually very soothing, "sound bath?"

Heads shaking all around.

Alice waved a gloved hand at the windows. "Shouldn't we just follow her tracks in the snow?"

Brian said, "How could we even tell what tracks are hers? We've all just trampled anything that might be out there."

Josie said, "Sandrine, did you notice any tracks coming from Meg's cabin when you came out of the main house?"

Sandrine shook her head. "No. None. I was looking because I hoped Cooper had come back and maybe he was rattling around somewhere, but there was nothing."

"Cooper didn't come back from checking on the weather?" said Nicola. "That's suspicious."

Taryn rubbed two fingers against the hollow of her throat. "Why is that suspicious?"

"'Cause how long does it take to check on the weather? He could have gotten back up here before the snow got bad, which means he chose not to come back." She stabbed Brian's ribs with her elbow. "It's weird, right?"

"I, uh, don't know."

Taryn adjusted the hat on her head, pulling it down more firmly over her ears. "Maybe something happened to him! He could have been hurt or something. We should be looking for him, too."

Josie had had the same thought but there had not been much time to examine it. Cooper seemed to handle himself quite well in the woods and, as caretaker of the remote property, he knew the area better than anyone. Josie thought it was more likely that he either hadn't been physically able to get back to the cabins in the dark or he had seen an opportunity to get away from them for a night and taken it. Either way, she hoped he was in a nearby town, in a position to get them some help.

"Sandrine," Josie said. "Do you have a phone? Is there a landline here in the main house?"

Sandrine slowly shook her head.

"What about a SAT phone? Surely, Cooper had one on the property for emergencies."

Sandrine grimaced. Her voice was almost a whisper. "He took it with him."

"What?" Brian blurted. "Are you kidding me? Why?"

Sandrine held her hands out, palms up. "In case something happened to him in the snow and he needed help."

"And you let him take it?" Alice said.

"We're fine here," Sandrine said. "We've got heat and food and shelter. Cooper was navigating in the snow. If he had an accident, he would need it more than us."

Trying to tamp down her annoyance, Josie asked, "What was your plan if something went wrong? If there was an emergency of some sort?"

"I, uh, Cooper was supposed to come back! Or one of us could walk to the bottom of the mountain and find the closest area with cell service."

There were grumbles all around them. Alice said, "What if someone was injured?"

"I—I have a first aid kit," said Sandrine.

Nicola glanced at the windows. "I don't think we can get to the bottom in this."

Brian, finally feeling the cold, walked over to the wood-burning stove and knelt in front of it. He took logs from a bucket beside it and started loading them into the stove. "There is no cell service anywhere on this mountain. Not even in the parking lot."

Taryn gave him a sharp look. "You brought your phone?"

"Of course I did."

Josie sighed. "I did, too, but Brian's right. The service is practically non-existent. I got something yesterday when I was at the top of the mountain, but it wasn't enough to get through to anyone."

"How can that be?" asked Nicola. "There's like no place in this country where you *can't* get cell service."

Alice huffed. "There are plenty of places you can't get service, especially in remote areas like this."

Sandrine said, "Sullivan County is definitely remote. That's why I chose it for this retreat. Did you know there's only one traffic light in the entire county?"

"Great," said Nicola with an eye-roll.

"Even if we can find service somewhere, my phone can't keep a charge." Brian rifled through a second, smaller bucket for kindling. "Stupid roam sucks the battery dry so fast that my charger can't keep up."

Alice said, "Brian, you and Josie should charge your phones as much as you can before the generators run out of fuel. Can you make emergency calls?"

Brian shrugged and then turned his attention back to the stove, using a lighter with an extension on it to light the kindling he had placed atop the logs.

"Possibly," said Josie.

She'd been in situations before where she was out in the mountains, on the outskirts of Denton, with limited cell service.

Situations in which she had tried to make an emergency call. It hadn't worked. But she didn't want to scare the others. It was possible they could get back to the summit and try to make a call from there. There might also be pockets of service elsewhere on the mountain.

Alice looked at Josie. "Why were you trying to use your phone yesterday?"

"To check the weather," Josie said. "But listen, none of this is important right now. Our priority is finding Meg. Once we do that, we'll reassess things and figure out our next steps."

"Next steps," said Taryn, voice wobbly. "We're stuck here. There is over a foot of snow out there and it's not even slowing down. It's a long way to the bottom of the mountain. Without Cooper's Gator, we can't get down there. Even with it, at this point, there's too much snow for the Gator to operate."

Brian watched as the flames caught the kindling. Quickly, he closed the door to the stove and jumped back from it as if he might get burned. "We might be able to walk to the bottom."

"That's too dangerous," Josie said. "It's at least two miles, if not more. None of us have the proper winter gear for a trek like that in this weather. Don't forget, there is also a bear out there."

Alice moved closer to the stove. "Even if we could walk to the bottom, our cars would be snowed in. Then we'd just be stuck down there."

Brian watched as the window of the stove began to glow orange. He took another step back. "But we could wait for someone to drive by the parking lot and flag them down."

"That's a big risk. What if that's what Cooper was doing and something happened to him—" Nicola began.

Sandrine put her hands up again. "Okay, everyone, let's take some deep breaths. I'm sure Cooper is fine. He's got the SAT phone in case any issues arise. He may have simply stayed in the nearest town so he could find resources to get us off this mountain tomorrow as scheduled. I have every confidence that he is just fine."

"Really?" Alice took off her gloves and held her palms over the stove where heat from the fire within now shimmered. "Not to be disrespectful, but he's got to be in his seventies, at least."

Sandrine gave a strained smile. "Like I said, I have every confidence he is fine and lining up some help for us as we speak. Josie is right though, we need to find Meg. Immediately."

TWELVE

They split up to search for Meg. Nicola and Brian were assigned the area north of the camp, in the direction of the summit. Taryn was tasked with searching behind the line of cabins while Alice took the wooded area across from them. Josie and Sandrine headed down the path leading from the camp to the bottom of the mountain. Josie was heartened to find that, at the very least, Cooper kept walkie-talkies in the kitchen of the main house. There were four. Exactly enough. Josie toggled the volume button as she and Sandrine made their way down the path past the rage room and shed.

Brian's voice came through as a series of squawks. "Can you hear me?"

Before Josie could respond, there was a screech of static and then Taryn said, "Yes. Can you hear me?"

Once everyone had checked in, Josie pressed the talk button and said, "We don't know how much of a charge these things have or how long the batteries will last. Let's try to conserve for now."

In return, she received three bursts of static followed by three agreements. Then the device went silent. Sandrine huffed along beside Josie, holding up the edge of her maxi dress as they walked into the trees. "How far do those reach?"

"No idea," Josie said. "I'm guessing we'll find out."

The snow overtook the tops of Josie's boots, making a band of ice around her calves. Ahead, it was undisturbed except for what looked like the slightest of depressions where drifts hadn't formed. Were they from footsteps made in the initial snowfall that had then been filled in by the overnight storm? Cooper's or Meg's? Or both? It was impossible to tell. It could be nothing at all. It could be from the bear.

The wind lashed at them, stinging Josie's face. The snowflakes were coming down more quickly than before.

It was only going to get worse.

Josie said, "You led the sound bath last night. When Meg left, did she seem upset about anything?"

"No," Sandrine said.

"Had she complained to you about anything this week other than what was discussed in sessions?"

"What do you mean?"

A gust of wind tore through the trees to their left and slapped at them, so strong that Sandrine stumbled. She grabbed onto Josie's arm for balance. As Josie helped her regain her footing, she noticed her teeth were chattering. She took a moment to gather the bottom of her maxi dress and tie it into a knot that fell alongside her left thigh, keeping it from hampering her steps.

"I mean was she having any issues at this retreat? Were any other members bothering her? Was there anything that was not to her liking?"

"Oh," said Sandrine, holding onto Josie's arm as they pushed ahead. "No. Not really."

"It's just you and me here, Sandrine. Can you think of any reason why she would run off in the middle of the night during a snowstorm?"

"No, I can't. Meg was very engaged in all the activities this week. She even said that she wished the retreat was longer."

That was the impression that Josie had gotten as well, which made the blossoming dread in her stomach expand with every moment they were out looking for Meg. If she hadn't had a reason to leave, why had she? Maybe it was the police officer in her, but Josie immediately wondered about the possibility, however slim, that she had been taken. While it was hard to imagine someone stalking the woods here in Sullivan County, given the size of the area they covered, Josie knew from experience that sometimes monsters lurked in remote places. Denton had been known to harbor monsters in its forests. The kind who masqueraded as men and targeted young women and girls. Of everyone there, Meg was the youngest. She was also very attractive, and small enough to be easily overcome in a physical altercation. It had already happened to her once with her stalker. But the more likely possibility—the one Josie had been trying to fend off, even in her own mind—was that someone at the retreat was responsible for Meg not being in her cabin.

Sandrine's hand was hooked inside Josie's elbow. Josie's shoulder burned with the weight of half dragging her along.

As if reading her mind, Sandrine said, "I know what you're thinking. I was not prepared for a Pennsylvania winter. Well, I'm sad to say that you're right. I wasn't. This is my first winter retreat. I wasn't even going to do it, but I thought, I've never done one in winter. People are stuck inside during this time of year. Depression is more prevalent. Maybe the winter is the best time to do this. With all of these, there's a learning curve."

Josie could barely feel her feet any longer. The cold sliced through her jeans, chilling her skin painfully. Her eyes scanned every part of the trail and its surroundings as they struggled along. She could feel Sandrine shivering against her. To keep both their minds off the cold, Josie tried to keep the conversation going. "You're not used to this weather, are you?"

"N-no. I'm originally from California. Well, I guess I'm not from anywhere. I bounced around my entire life—Oregon, Texas, New York—but spent a lot of time in California—and later, Florida. I always preferred w-warmer p-places."

Josie tried to remember what she had read on Sandrine's website back when she was deciding whether or not to go to the retreat. Sandrine had received her doctorate in psychology from UC Berkeley. Although in private practice she was Dr. Morrow, on the retreat she was simply Sandrine, warm, calm, soft-spoken, and aglow with some inner knowledge and peace that none of them possessed. Had Josie met her in a different context, she would have pegged her for a yoga instructor or the owner of an organic food market. Josie couldn't remember where she had done her undergraduate work but other than her considerable professional accomplishments, the biography had not contained much personal information. She had shared little more with them during the week, joking that they weren't there to unpack her baggage before neatly segueing into their first group session.

"Were your parents in the military?" Josie asked. "Is that why you bounced around?"

"Oh, no." Sandrine gave a dry chuckle. "That would have been lovely, wouldn't it? But no. It was because of my mother's job."

Another sharp blast of wind batted at them from behind, hurrying their descent along the path and causing them to stumble once more. Sandrine fell to her knees, pulling Josie along with her. The snow soaked the knees of her jeans in seconds. They struggled back to their feet. Josie looked behind them. It felt as though they'd been walking for hours and yet, Josie could still see the red of the rage-room building behind them as well as the small shed beside it.

"Shit," she mumbled.

"What is it?" Sandrine said, teeth chattering now.

"You should go back," Josie told her. "Back to the main house and wait."

"No. I can't. I can't stay back while the rest of you search. I —I'll be f-fine. Keep talking. It's helping."

Josie managed a frozen smile as they dragged on. "Why did you come to Pennsylvania to do these retreats?"

"I was asked to do a series of guest l-lectures for the University of Pennsylvania. I knew I'd be here on the East Coast for a year, s-so I thought I'd do a few of these here. I'd done m-many before in other states, though never during a blizzard. The ones I did h-here earlier this year were very successful. N-not here in Sullivan County. This is my f-first time here. I guess I should have stayed closer to the E-east Coast."

Before Josie could think of another question, her vision snagged on something to her left, just off the path. A flash of hot pink in an unending sea of white. "There!"

Sandrine hobbled as Josie dragged her off the trail. At the base of a large maple tree, the cuff of a coat sleeve poked up from a small snowdrift. Josie disentangled herself from Sandrine and dropped to her knees, brushing the snow away. Her heart was in full stampede mode.

Sandrine said, "That's Meg's coat."

But Meg wasn't inside it.

Josie looked past the maple tree. Behind it, barren tree trunks went on as far as the eye could see, some of the smaller ones bending in the wind. Josie focused on the swath of ground before her, walking carefully into the woods. Snow lifted from the ground and whirled around, redistributing itself along the terrain. As it shifted, she began to see slight lumps.

"There!" Sandrine shouted. She let go of Josie's arm and surged forward, falling to her knees. She dusted off the first lump she came to, uncovering a black hat.

Josie said, "Wait."

Sandrine crawled to the next lump, hands brushing rapidly. A glove. A few feet away, atop the snow, was another glove.

"Sandrine, wait!" Josie said.

Catching up to Sandrine, she touched her shoulder before she could reach the next half-covered item. A boot on its side, its laces undone.

"What—what is this?" Sandrine said, staggering to her feet. "Oh God. Is that—is that...?"

Josie looked beyond the boot to where a foot clad in a thick pink sock stuck out from behind the trunk of another maple tree. Blood roared in her ears as they circled the tree. On her back, partially covered by snow, lay Meg. Sandrine sobbed into Josie's shoulder. The wind lashed at them again, lifting the last of the snow that clung to Meg's face, exposing her lovely features, frozen in forever sleep.

THIRTEEN

Josie didn't need to take Meg's pulse. She'd seen enough dead bodies to know that Meg Cleary had been deceased for some time. Sandrine slid down into a heap in the snow, weeping. Josie took a moment to try to calm her thundering heart and focus on the scene, looking at it in its entirety. Meg's arms lay at her sides. One of her legs was bent, the knee falling outward, while the other was straight. Her blouse was unbuttoned, exposing her bra and abdomen. Her jeans were still zippered and buttoned but her boots and one of her socks had been cast off just like her coat, hat, and gloves. Had someone been trying to take her clothes off, or had she taken them off? But why would she?

Mettner's voice came from somewhere deep in her brain, floating up from memories of various conversations they'd had over the years. "Hypothermia," he had told her once. "As your body gets colder, it sends your blood away from the extremities, toward the core of your body, where it is needed the most. It's called vasoconstriction. But the longer you're exposed to freezing temperatures, that process starts to fail. At some point, your body releases all that blood back to your extremities. The vessels near your skin are wide open and the blood comes rushing back. That part is called vasodilation. Makes people feel suddenly very warm. They're already disoriented and confused. They start taking off their clothes."

"Paradoxical undressing," she mumbled. That's what it was called. She remembered Mett saying that it usually happened just before a person lapsed into unconsciousness. Had Meg left her cabin to walk to the bottom of the trail and frozen to death? It seemed unlikely. Yes, it was below freezing, and the snow had come down in force overnight, but they weren't that far from the camp. She couldn't have frozen to death at this distance. Josie and Sandrine had not.

Josie was jarred back to the present by Sandrine's high-pitched cries. "Oh Meg! My poor Meg!"

Sandrine reached out to touch Meg's face.

"Stop!" Josie said, rushing forward and grabbing Sandrine's wrist before her hand made contact with Meg.

Sandrine's eyes went wide with surprise. "What?"

"Don't touch her. Please."

Slowly, Sandrine withdrew her arm from Josie's grip. Hurt darkened her eyes.

"I'm sorry," Josie said. "We shouldn't disturb her—" She stopped herself before she said "body", instead concluding with, "I just want to have a look at some things, if you don't mind."

Sandrine stared at her, uncomprehending. "What do you mean?"

"We don't know what happened here. I'd like to make some assessments." Josie leaned down and gently tried to move one of Meg's arms from the side of her body but couldn't. "She's in rigor."

"What?" said Sandrine.

"Never mind."

Meg Cleary wasn't just frozen from having lain out in the snow for several hours. Her body was in full rigor mortis. Now that she was closer, Josie could see a small cut on Meg's right cheek. Dried blood smudged beneath it. It was thin, only half an inch long, with a slight curve at the end. Had it come from a fingernail? Josie couldn't tell. Moving on, she used a gloved finger to lift each of Meg's eyelids. The whites of her eyes were dotted with petechiae, pinpricks of pink where blood vessels had burst from lack of oxygen.

Josie's heart sank.

It might not mean anything. She heard Mettner's voice in her head as if he were right there with her.

Her eyes were drawn to the scarf around Meg's neck. *True,* she told him silently. Petechiae could be caused by something as simple as coughing or vomiting rather than strangulation. But to Josie's knowledge, Meg hadn't been doing either of those things this week.

You need to see what's under her scarf, Mettner's voice advised.

But she couldn't just look. If she was right about what had happened to Meg then she needed to treat this as a crime scene. Even though she wasn't in her own jurisdiction, her oath as a sworn officer of the law would not allow her to contaminate the scene. If someone had killed Meg, they might have left trace evidence behind—fibers or DNA. Josie had to make an attempt to preserve anything that might be there. That meant she couldn't allow anyone to touch the body any more than the minimal amount required to move it. She couldn't even brush or blow the snow away. The best option would be to get her onto a clean sheet exactly as she was and then take her back to one of the unoccupied buildings. Once her body was transferred to an environment above freezing, the snow would melt and leave any trace evidence in place.

Josie took out her walkie-talkie and pressed the talk button. It took effort not to speak into it as if she were communicating with her own team. "This is Josie," she said. "Sandrine and I found Meg along the path. I need help down here right away to move her."

Brian's voice came back. "Roger that. On our way to you now."

"Stop in the main house and see if you can find a clean sheet."

There were a few beats of silence and then Taryn responded, "Roger."

Josie took a deep breath. "Alice? You copy?"

There was a burst of static and then Alice's voice. "I'm here."

"I need you, too. Can you stop at my cabin and bring my journal and a pen? Bring my phone as well."

"Sure. See you soon."

Sandrine stood on shaky legs. Her yoga pants were soaked through. Her entire body shivered from cold and shock and grief. "What are you doing, Josie?"

Josie debated whether or not to tell Sandrine her suspicions and decided it was best not to say anything until she had a clearer picture of what had caused Meg's death. Instead, she said, "I need you to stand over there, closer to the path, and make sure the others see us when they get down here."

Sandrine covered her mouth before another sob escaped. She looked down at Meg again, the sadness in her face piercing Josie's heart. "Poor Meg."

"Please, Sandrine. I know this is hard, but I need you to stand over there so that the others find us. Then we need to get you back to the main house as soon as possible. Try not to touch anything."

Sandrine walked past the trail of Meg's discarded clothes and stood near the treeline. Josie estimated that Meg was twenty feet off the path, based on the distance between the body and Sandrine. There were no discernible footprints near Meg's body other than the ones Josie and Sandrine had just made. Josie saw some faint depressions now filled with snow like the ones they'd followed along the path, but it was impossible to tell anything from them. They didn't even form a continuous trail since the snow had been blowing and drifting for hours.

As they waited, Josie kept scanning the woods, worried the bear might find them. Relief pulsed through her when she heard the others call out to Sandrine. Soon, Brian, Nicola, Alice, and Taryn came into view. One by one, they looked beyond Sandrine to where Josie stood sentry over Meg's body. Their eyes took in the scene. Their expressions changed from curiosity to concern. All they would be able to see from where they stood were Meg's discarded items and her foot.

"Is she hurt?" Alice said, surging forward.

Josie held up a hand. "Stay there. Please."

Alice froze. Josie walked over to them, careful to avoid the items of Meg's clothing that she and Sandrine had unearthed. "I can help," Alice said, trying to muscle past Josie. "I'm an ER nurse. Remember?"

Taking hold of Alice's shoulders, Josie kept her in place. "She's gone, Alice. I checked."

"Wh-what?" Taryn said, voice high-pitched. "Gone? What do you mean, gone?"

Sandrine touched Taryn's arm. "Meg is dead."

"No," Taryn breathed. She pulled at the knit scarf around her neck, loosening it. "No. She can't be dead. Did you—did you try to render aid? Alice—Alice has medical training. She can—"

Josie said, "I'm sorry, Taryn. Sandrine is right. It's too late for that. Meg is dead."

"You're kidding, right?" Brian said.

"I'm sorry," Josie repeated, keeping her voice calm. "I wish I was joking. I truly do."

"But what happened?" Brian asked.

"I don't know," Josie said. "Right now, I need my phone, journal and pen."

A new voice came from behind Sandrine, Alice, Taryn and Brian. "Why do you need all that?" asked Nicola. The others parted to reveal her standing along the path. "Did you say that Meg's dead? How can she be dead? What the hell happened?"

Alice handed over Josie's phone, journal and pen and Josie held them up. "I don't know what happened and because I don't know what happened, I have to treat this as a suspicious death."

"Someone killed her?" said Nicola.

"I didn't say that," Josie said. "I don't have enough information to conclude that but what I'd like to do is to make a sketch and take some photos before we move the— her."

Josie felt Alice's eyes boring into her. Nicola said, "You wouldn't do any of that if it was an accident. You think someone killed her."

"That is not true, Nicola," Josie said.

Taryn's lower lip trembled. "Who would want to kill Meg?"

"You sure the bear didn't get her?" asked Brian.

Alice pointed to the ground where the snow still swirled and eddied in the fierce wind. "Are those her clothes? Maybe she got hypothermia." She turned toward the rest of them and explained how hypothermia caused paradoxical undressing. Then she added, "I've seen it before with people brought into the ER in various states of undress. Believe me, it's probably best if Josie documents everything so that when help gets here, no one gets blamed for anything that didn't really happen."

Mollified, everyone fell silent. Alice turned back to Josie and gave her a barely perceptible nod. Her eyes spoke volumes. She wasn't buying hypothermia either, but this would give Josie her best shot at preserving what evidence she could if it turned out that Meg had been murdered.

Josie looked at her phone. The battery was charged to

seventy-eight percent. In the upper left-hand corner of the screen it said: *Searching*. The tiny icon that told her how good her connection was, was blank with an X in the center of it. Briefly, it blinked to a single bar of connectivity. A text notification flashed across the top of the screen. Gretchen's name filled her with relief but then when she pulled up the message, the relief changed to horror.

> *Bona fide blizzard coming your way. Leave now if you can. Get everyone out of there. Hope this gets to you in time. PS Noah is a damn mess.*

Tears stung the backs of Josie's eyes briefly. She breathed as deeply as she could, pushing all thoughts of Noah out of her brain.

"Are you okay?" Nicola asked. "You look like you're going to throw up."

Brian turned to look at his wife. "She just found a dead body, Nic."

Nicola sighed. "She's a detective, isn't she? That's, like, her job."

Josie pushed everything that did not have to do with the task at hand inside a box inside her brain and then she shoved the box deep into the back of a mental closet. "I'm fine." She held up the phone, Gretchen's message now safely hidden by the lock screen. "Before I do anything, I'm going to try to make an emergency call, just in case Cooper wasn't able to use the SAT phone or get to the nearest town. Ideally, someone can get to us and get all of us out of here."

She dialed 911 and waited.

It didn't ring. She hung up and tried again. And again. On the third attempt, it rang once and then the call died with a series of rapid-succession beeps.

"What's going on?" Nicola called.

Josie sighed. "I can't get through."

Alice took a step forward, careful to avoid any of Meg's discarded clothes. "Even if you can, it could be hours before anyone can get up here. The snow is still coming down hard, Josie. It's freezing. We can't leave her out here, and we can't station someone out here to stay with her until help arrives."

Josie nodded. "Then we'll go with my original plan."

She left the group on the trail and went to work, making a quick sketch of the entire area inside her journal and then taking as many photos as possible with her phone. After documenting everything as they'd found it, she knelt and used a gloved finger to pull back the edge of Meg's scarf. Her heart did a double tap, paused, and then roared into overdrive. The blood rushing through her ears drowned out the wind whipping and shrieking all around her.

"Oh Meg," she whispered.

Without removing the scarf completely, she shifted it around enough to get the rest of the photos. She'd seen enough to confirm her greatest fear. She'd leave the rest for the county medical examiner. She considered Meg's cast-off clothing. Under normal circumstances it'd be collected in order to be processed for evidence. However, Josie was in no position to do any sort of evidence collection. If she attempted it, she could damage or lose any evidence that might be there. On the other hand, if she left it, it could be blown away or buried by snow or even disturbed by animals. It was a no-win situation. Ultimately, she decided that the least damaging option was to leave everything in its place. She took photos and marked each item in her sketches.

Once she was finished, she made her way back to the others. They stood along the trail, everyone but Brian crying softly. His eyes shone with unshed tears, though, as he held Nicola to his chest while she sobbed. Josie, too, felt like sinking into the snow and crying, but there was no time. They would all freeze.

"We're sorry," Taryn sniffed, wiping her nose with the back of her glove. "It's just so awful."

"Poor Meg," Brian said huskily, squeezing Nicola more tightly against him.

Alice pulled a crumpled tissue from her coat pocket and dabbed at her red-rimmed eyes. "After everything she went through..."

She didn't finish the sentence. Sandrine patted her shoulder. "It's very sad. This is a terrible day for us all, not just Meg."

"I know this is hard," Josie said. "I'm devastated as well, but right now, the best thing we can do for Meg is get her back to camp."

She handed her phone to Sandrine, instructing her to try to reach emergency services. Then she led Taryn, Brian, and Alice back to Meg's body. Nicola stayed with Sandrine, arms crossed over her chest, wiping tears from her pale face.

"Who has the sheet?" Josie asked as the four of them surrounded Meg's body. She took up position at Meg's head.

"Holy shit." Brian stood next to Meg's left hip. "She is really dead. Like, dead dead."

From Meg's right side, Taryn handed Josie a white sheet. "I'm sorry, Josie. I don't think I can do this."

Brian tore his eyes from the body to look at Taryn. "Are you kidding? She's not going to bite you."

Taryn stared back down at Meg, lower lip trembling again. She adjusted the scarf around her neck, tugging at it as if it was too tight.

Alice, closest to Meg's feet, glared at Brian. "Her husband died in front of her, remember?" She turned to Taryn. "It's okay, Taryn. Go back to the trail. See if Nicola or Sandrine will help us. We need four people."

Mumbling another apology, Taryn stomped back toward the trail, lifting her knees high to maneuver through the thickening snow.

Josie snapped the sheet open and laid it out beside Meg. "Alice," she said. "You get her feet."

Brian watched, seemingly fascinated, while they quickly and efficiently moved Meg's stiffened body onto the sheet. Josie winced as some of the snow covering her torso shifted. There was nothing to be done about it. Alice was right. They could not leave her. A moment later, Nicola appeared, eyebrows disappearing under the brim of her knit hat as she craned to get a look at Meg.

"Oh wow," she breathed. "That's creepy as hell."

FOURTEEN

By the time they reached the shed beside the big red rage-room building, Josie was soaked through with sweat, in spite of the freezing temperatures and heavy snow. Her arms felt weak and rubbery as they laid Meg down on the floor inside. Sandrine had gone ahead with Taryn to make sure they could get the doors open and clear an area for Meg. In the center of the small building was a riding mower. Neither Sandrine nor Taryn could get it started so it stayed where it was while they cleared out a space next to it. Just outside the shed, Taryn and Sandrine had piled a weed whacker, a toolbox, two small gas cans, a bottle of motor oil, two shovels, and a log-splitter.

Once they got Meg settled onto the concrete slab, Josie took off her hat and gloves and swiped a hand through her hair. It was wet with perspiration. She fought the urge to take off her winter coat. Her goal was to get everyone out of the shed and away from the body as soon as possible. Brian and Nicola shuffled back to the door. They, too, pulled off their hats. Alice's short dark hair was wet and plastered flat against her skull. She stood nearest to Josie, her back to the riding mower, and stared down at Meg.

Now that the initial shock of Meg's death had worn off, Nicola watched them with naked curiosity. "So, what?" she said. "We just leave her in here? Why here?"

"Do you want to help carry her up the hill to her cabin?" Alice asked pointedly.

Nicola didn't answer. Josie was happy to let her think that the real reason they had brought Meg's body to the shed was because it was closest to where she'd been found. In reality, since Meg's cabin was the last place she'd been seen, Josie wanted to treat it as a crime scene. Bringing Meg's body back there would only taint it. With everything but the riding mower removed from the shed, there was no reason for anyone to return to it. Later, she'd have to find a way to seal off both the shed and Meg's cabin, or at least lock them up.

Brian used his hat to wipe the sweat from his flushed face. "Won't she smell?"

Before Josie could answer, Sandrine pushed her way between the two of them and shooed them away from the door. "Go," she said. "I want everyone at the main house immediately. We need to regroup and talk about what's happened here."

Before he disappeared, Brian said, "We need to figure out how to get the hell out of here."

Sandrine shook her head but stood in the doorway for several moments. Turning back to Josie and Alice, she said, "They're gone. What do you need?"

Josie looked around. There was only one entrance, and no windows, which was good. "We need to seal this building off somehow so that no one can enter it. It's best if no one disturbs the body. I'd also like to seal off Meg's cabin, if possible. I'll have to get some photos of it first, but then it's best if no one goes inside."

Alice said, "You didn't find her key with her?"

"No," said Josie. She hoped Alice wouldn't press the issue and ask about whether or not Josie had searched Meg's pockets.

She hadn't because that would mean further disturbing any evidence that might be on Meg's body or at the scene of her death, but that was not a conversation she wanted to have right now.

Sandrine put her hands on her hips. "I'll go to the main house. I know there are keys to lock up this building. I don't know where Meg's cabin key is but I'll see if there's an extra one."

"Thanks," Josie said. "Alice and I will wait here for you."

Once Sandrine was gone, Alice strode over and closed the doors, plunging them into darkness. "That's not going to work," she mumbled to herself, opening the door a crack to let the light back in. She stuck her head outside and peered around. When she turned back to Josie, she said, "They're all gone. Tell me the truth. What is going on here, Josie?"

Josie looked down at Meg's body. A shiver of fear worked its way through her frame. She tried to suppress it, but the cold and her anxiety made that impossible.

"Josie?" Alice said, voice softer now. The wind whipped against the outside of the shed. The door quivered in Alice's grip.

Josie's chest felt tight, as if she couldn't get enough breath. Her heartbeat felt like it was out of rhythm. She was alone. Utterly alone. Stuck on the top of a mountain in one of the most rural counties in the entire state during a blizzard. Even if they could reach 911, it might still be days before anyone got to them and there was a murderer among them. Josie was walking a tightrope with no safety net. Sandrine's words came back to her: *the real issue here is trust.*

Could she trust Alice?

"Josie, I know something is up."

Josie swallowed. The inside of her mouth felt like sandpaper. "We're in the middle of a blizzard."

Alice laughed, battling the wind to keep her grip on the

door. "No shit. It's been coming down at least an inch per hour out there all night long and it's still going strong. I think everyone here knows that this is a blizzard. Obviously, Sandrine dropped the ball, and Cooper? Well, for all we know, he got sick and tired of hearing all this new age, self-help, I've-got-issues crap and decided he'd spend the rest of the week drunk in some local bar while the rest of us toughed it out up here. You know that's not what I'm talking about. What is going on?"

It didn't really matter whether Josie trusted Alice or not. She already knew something was very wrong. It wouldn't be long before she figured out what—whether Josie told her or not.

"Someone strangled Meg."

Alice didn't gasp or show any outward signs of surprise or shock, but she went very still. The door hinges whined as she nearly let go. For a second, Josie couldn't tell if she was still breathing. Lips barely moving, she said, "How can you tell?"

"Ligature marks under her scarf," Josie said. "Petechiae in her eyes."

Alice swallowed, the only movement visible on her entire body. "Her clothes—do you think she—do you think that someone—"

"I don't think she was sexually assaulted," said Josie. "But I can't be sure. I think that the clothes and other items were staged to make it look like she had hypothermia."

Alice's body relaxed slightly. Her chest rose and fell rapidly. "What you're saying is that someone here, someone at this retreat, strangled Meg to death but tried to make it look like she walked into the woods and froze to death."

Josie nodded.

Alice swallowed again. "Are you sure?"

"I wish I wasn't."

The door shuddered again in Alice's hand. Snowflakes burst through the opening, twirling in the shaft of light. "But who? It had to be Brian, don't you think? I bet it was him. He was always talking to her even though he's married. She didn't give him the time of day, but he kept talking at her. Face it, he's just a giant douche. I don't know what Nicola sees in him. Or what if it's her stalker? That Cawley guy? No one has seen him for months. He's crazy. What if he followed her here? Wait, wait! What if it was Cooper? He seems so mild and fatherly but maybe he's really not. Maybe that's why he didn't come back. He killed Meg and rather than face us all, he just left. But then why make it look like she died of hypothermia? I mean, that's what this killer did, right? Made it look like natural causes? Who would know to do that?"

Josie edged around Meg's body, navigating the small space until they were face to face. "Alice, stop."

"You haven't thought about this yet? You're a police officer."

Josie had learned a long time ago that in homicide cases, the only thing that mattered was the evidence, and she didn't have enough evidence to form any theories as to who had killed Meg. "There is no point in speculating."

Alice pursed her lips. The fine lines at the corners of her eyes crinkled. The green flecks in her irises shimmered.

"What is it?" Josie said.

With the sleeve of her coat, she wiped a wet strand of hair from her forehead. "I saw something this week. I didn't think it was important or that it meant anything, but now..."

"Tell me."

Alice took a quick glance out the door again then turned back to Josie. "Cooper and Meg. I saw them talking. Privately. Behind her cabin. Three times. The last time was yesterday right before he left."

Josie felt the muscles in her shoulder blades tense. "Did you hear what they were talking about?"

"No. I was too far away."

"Did they see you?"

Alice shook her head.

"How did they look?"

The door shimmied in Alice's grip, and she clutched it harder. "What do you mean?"

"Did Meg look scared? Were they standing close together? Far apart? What was Meg's posture? Guarded? Was Cooper in her personal space?"

"Oh. They were a little closer than you might normally stand if you didn't know each other well. Like maybe they didn't want to be overheard. Meg had her arms crossed but she always stands—stood—like that. But she kept uncrossing them and gesturing, like she was talking with her hands. Fast, jerky movements. Yesterday, when she was finished, he kind of nodded and then he put his hand on her neck."

Josie felt a flutter in her chest. "How?"

With her free hand, Alice reached around the back of Josie's head and squeezed her neck. The glove was wet and heavy, but the motion was similar to the way Cooper had gripped her neck when they were on the summit together. But he'd done it after the two of them successfully ran off the bear. At the time, it had seemed the equivalent of a pat on the back, even if it was overly familiar.

"How did Meg react?"

Alice dropped her hand from Josie's neck. "She pulled away. You know how she hates—hated—to be touched. She told us in the group session on our first day, remember?"

Josie nodded. They'd all had to set their physical boundaries on the first day.

"So it was Cooper then, right? He was fixated on her or something and she rejected him so he killed her."

Josie held up her hands to stop Alice from continuing. "I know it's odd that Cooper and Meg were having private conversations, but we can't make the leap from a couple of chats behind her cabin to him killing her. Alice, we could go round and round all day coming up with theories that we have no evidence to support. It won't help us."

"Okay. I'm sorry. I'm just... really freaked out."

"I know," Josie said. "You might not like my next suggestion then. I don't think that we should tell any of the others that Meg was murdered."

Alice sagged against the door, causing it to swing open abruptly. Josie caught her before she fell. With her feet back under her, Alice peeked outside again toward the main house. Satisfied that no one was coming, she said, "You want to keep this a secret?" The word "secret" was tinged with incredulity and horror.

"The alternative is causing a panic and putting the killer in a position where he or she feels like their back is against the wall. It's not a good idea."

"You really think this could have been one of the women? Who? Taryn is strong enough but she's so sweet. Nicola. I could totally see her doing something like this. She is so angry all the time but who wouldn't be after what happened to her daughter? Wait. Sandrine! What about her? She was the one who woke us all up to tell us Meg was gone."

"Alice," Josie said, keeping her voice calm and even. "You're missing the point. Please. I need you on board with this if we're going to get out of here safely and quickly."

Josie held Alice's gaze, making sure her own breathing was slow and steady. After a long moment, the rapid movements of Alice's chest mirrored Josie's own. She licked her lips and nodded. "You're right. Yes. Our priority should be getting off this mountain." Glancing over Josie's shoulder at Meg, she added, "Hypothermia it is. You want to leave Meg here, right? It's cold. Freezing. She'll be preserved that way. Like being in the morgue."

Alice was right. This building had no source of heat at all. In fact, snow still covered parts of Meg's body. "Yes," Josie said.

"It's the best chance we have to preserve any fibers or trace evidence. Keeping it secure will be an issue but locking this place up will have to do. Once Sandrine gets back with the key, I need to go up to Meg's cabin and take some photos. Sandrine was already inside the cabin when she went to wake Meg, but I can't help that."

Normally, Josie would not enter the cabin at all. Legally, she couldn't—at least not to search it. The criteria for a warrantless search could not be met. It was up to the law enforcement department whose jurisdiction the cabin was in to go inside and process it for evidence. However, she could photograph the inside of the cabin to ensure nothing changed before that happened. Toward that end, the current circumstances would fall under exigency.

More snow burst through the door. Alice pulled it closed so that only three inches of light shone through. "What do you mean?"

"Since this is a homicide and the last place Meg was known to have been was her cabin, that needs to be processed as a crime scene. It has to be kept sealed off until the local police can tend to it. If that procedure isn't followed, then anything found inside the cabin—any evidence that might implicate the killer—becomes fruit of the poisonous tree."

"Poisonous tree?"

Josie sighed. "It won't be admitted in court."

"Even if it was a murder weapon with the killer's prints on it?"

The sweat from her earlier exertions had dried up. She started to feel the cold again. Searching inside her pocket, she found her hat and pulled it back on. "That doesn't really apply in this case, but yeah, basically. It's already problematic that Sandrine was in there but like I said, there's nothing I can do about that."

They both heard footsteps crunching over the snow outside.

Alice poked her head out again and then quickly retreated. "That's Sandrine with the keys."

"Okay," said Josie. "Once Sandrine gets here, we lock this place up. I'll take photos of Meg's cabin while you go back to the main house and cover for me. I'll meet you there as soon as I'm done."

Alice grimaced. "I really don't want to see any of those people. Josie, one of them is a stone-cold killer!"

"I know," Josie said. "But right now, our survival depends on not raising any alarm. Please, Alice. I need your help. Are you with me on this?"

Reluctantly, Alice nodded.

FIFTEEN

Noah clutched the steering wheel and turned it, trying to spin his SUV back in the direction he'd come and out of the path of the oncoming lights. The vehicle slid from side to side and then jerked to a stop, tires stuck in the unplowed snow. He pumped the gas, trying to free them but all he accomplished was to send the SUV into a backwards slide. The rear bumper kissed the metal guardrail with a gentle thud. With relief, he saw that he was no longer in the path of the approaching car. He tried the gas again, but he wasn't going anywhere. He got out of the car. There was a bucket of salt and a shovel in the back. Maybe he could get himself out of this predicament.

As Noah reached the guardrail, the air in his lungs froze. The other side was practically a sheer drop-off into a valley. There was nothing but trees and what looked like a lake. He was lucky he hadn't hit the guardrail more forcefully.

He turned back to the road when he heard the rumble of an engine. The lights he'd almost crashed into resolved into a large silver pickup truck. Chains were wrapped around all its tires. Along the side of it were emblazoned the words *Sullivan*

County Sheriff. It came to a stop along the road as it reached Noah's SUV.

A man in a thick blue coat hopped out. Noah estimated him to be in his fifties, tall and solid. He smiled as he approached. "Looks like you're in need of some help."

Noah nodded. "I was actually headed to your office." He introduced himself and fished his credentials out of his coat, even though he wasn't there on official business.

The man extended a gloved hand. "Deputy Ehrbar. Patrick Ehrbar. What are you doing all the way up here, Lieutenant?"

"There's a camp up here somewhere. My wife is at a retreat there. Her and a few other people. I haven't heard from her and I'm afraid she's stuck—that they're all stuck."

Ehrbar frowned. He scratched beneath his blue knit hat. "You have any information on the property? That sounds like a lot of places up here."

Noah told him what little information he had.

Ehrbar nodded. "Okay, yeah. I think I know the place. It's out by World's End."

"I'm sorry," Noah said. "What did you say?"

Ehrbar laughed. "World's End State Park. I'm pretty sure my boss, Sheriff Hunter Shaw, owns that camp. Rents it out all year round but usually to hunters. Has a caretaker who manages it. Let's get you out of here and we'll see what we can find out."

"Thank you," said Noah. "I really appreciate it. I'm worried about my wife."

Ehrbar's frown returned. He looked overhead. Snow continued to fall fast and heavy. "You should be," he said. "It's not going to be easy getting to them."

SIXTEEN

The mood at the main house was somber. The initial upset after Meg's death had turned to dull shock. They sat around the dining table while Sandrine dished out food that no one touched. It was already well into the afternoon. None of them had eaten breakfast. Although the last thing Josie wanted to do was eat, she knew that she needed food to keep up her energy for whatever was to come. She chose a sandwich from one of the two plates that Sandrine had put in the center of the table and forced herself to take a bite. Other than the tomato, lettuce and alfalfa sprouts, she recognized nothing Sandrine had crushed between the two pieces of gluten-free whole-grain bread. It wasn't bad. Soon, she was devouring the entire thing. Next to her, Alice watched and then hesitantly chose her own sandwich from the other plate. It looked like peanut butter and jam.

Nicola said, "How can you two eat at a time like this?"

"You just saw a dead body," Brian added. "You touched a dead body."

Alice shrugged. Around a mouthful of food, she said, "Josie's a police officer. I work in the emergency department of a very busy trauma center. We've both seen a lot worse than that."

Taryn picked a sandwich from one of the platters. "Josie and Alice have the right idea. We should all eat. We don't want whatever fresh food we've got to go to waste."

Nicola and Brian took the last two sandwiches from the plates. A few seconds later, Josie heard Brian speaking to Nicola under his breath. "Switch with me."

"What? Why?" She picked up her own sandwich and prepared to take a bite, but he quickly reached over and touched her arm to stop her. "What is your problem?" she demanded.

"I'm allergic to peanuts," he said through gritted teeth. "Remember?"

"Oh shit." Nicola quickly switched with him. Glancing around the table, she realized that everyone was watching them. "Sorry," she said. "My brain hasn't been right since we lost our little girl. I forget important things."

"I think we're all in a bit of a fog right now," Sandrine said. "After the morning we've had. I'm so sorry, Brian. I put the peanut butter sandwiches on a separate plate but forgot to mention it. I'm just so... stunned by what's happened. I wasn't thinking. I didn't bring it, by the way. As we discussed before the retreat, everything I brought was peanut-free. I found the peanut butter in one of the cabinets. Probably from the last group that was here. We're running low on supplies so I didn't think the others would mind. I'm terribly sorry. Forgive me."

"It's fine," he mumbled.

No one spoke again. Josie surreptitiously glanced at each one of them. Even though she'd told Alice not to theorize as to who might have strangled Meg, she couldn't stop her own mind from going there. Meg had been wearing all her winter gear when she either left her cabin or was lured from it. Her cabin gave nothing away. Sandrine was right—all of her things were still there and there was no evidence of a struggle, which likely meant that Meg had left the cabin of her own free will and had intended to return to it. Why would she have gone out for a walk in the snow? Even on the sunny days before the storm came, walking was unpleasant in the cold. The scenario that made the most sense given what little Josie knew was that Meg had either been going to meet someone or had been following someone.

But who?

Silently, Sandrine and Taryn began clearing the dishes. They'd been doing it after each meal almost the entire week so that now their movements were practically synchronized. They picked up dishes with their left hands and then tucked them into the crook of their right elbows before heading to the kitchen. Nicola and Brian retreated to the armchairs circled around the wood-burning stove, sitting across from one another. Nicola stared into the glass door of the stove, while Brian fiddled with his phone.

The way Josie saw it, there were three possibilities. The first, and most likely, was that Meg had followed, gone to meet, or been lured by someone on the retreat. Someone in this room. The staging of the body to make the death look like it was from hypothermia made sense if someone here had killed her. They might want it to look like a tragic accident so as not to arouse suspicion. Who here knew enough about hypothermia to stage the body correctly? There was Alice, obviously, although Josie's gut told her Alice was not a killer. Taryn's parents had been very outdoorsy, according to all the stories she'd told about them that week. Josie didn't know enough about the others to make a guess as to their knowledge of death by hypothermia.

Josie heard Mett's voice float from somewhere deep in her mind. *You're focusing too hard on the hypothermia thing. What if the killer didn't stage her body at all? What if he sexually assaulted her and simply didn't bother to put all her clothes back on?*

"Shit," Josie muttered.

"What?" Alice said.

"Nothing."

Mett's ghost voice was right though. Josie was getting tunnel vision—only seeing one thing. She didn't really know that the killer had staged the body. In fact, the sexual assault theory was far more likely. She'd seen it before on the job. But there was no way that Josie would know whether Meg had been sexually assaulted until her body was autopsied by a medical examiner. She just had to live with the uncertainty for now.

The next question was which of the people in this room would Meg follow or go to meet late at night in the woods during a snowstorm? Josie understood why Alice immediately zeroed in on Brian. In these situations, a male always seemed like the obvious suspect but in her last several cases, she had learned never to make assumptions when it came to finding a perpetrator. Also, it was hard to imagine Meg sneaking out under such conditions to meet a man after what her stalker had put her and her sister through. While Josie hated to think it, she could not eliminate the others.

The second possibility was that Meg had run into Cooper somehow. Paradoxical undressing seemed like something he might be familiar with. Something had obviously been going on between him and Meg. The nature of it was anyone's guess. Josie would like to think that if Cooper had been harassing Meg, or making her uncomfortable, she would have told someone at the camp, but she knew that women, in particular, were so hard-wired not to cause a stir, lest they be accused of overreacting, that they often put up with almost anything. Plus, Meg had already been so beaten down by her ordeal, she might not have had the mental energy to report any inappropriate behavior.

It was also possible that Meg had simply been complaining to Cooper about some issue with her cabin—the generator, perhaps. There was one behind each of their cabins. It was Cooper's job to maintain the property. They'd all gone to him for help with something at various points in the week. Maybe the chats meant nothing at all.

Regardless, there was the logistical issue of how Meg ended up part of the way down the trail. Cooper had already been gone for a couple of hours when they'd had dinner, long after the last time he and Meg spoke behind her cabin. No one mentioned hearing the Gator buzz up the hill during the night. If Meg had walked all the way down to where her body was found and ran into him there, at which time he killed her, it was possible no one would have heard the Gator at that distance. He could have gone back down the mountain, and no one would have been the wiser.

The third and most remote possibility was the one that Alice had suggested in the shed: Meg's stalker had somehow found and followed her to the retreat and attacked her. Josie couldn't discount this theory, but it had been months since Meg had had any contact from him. Josie had no doubt that Austin Cawley was every bit as desperate as he had been when he kidnapped Meg and her sister. She was sure he'd illegally procure any means necessary to cross multiple state lines to get to Meg. If Cawley was the killer, maybe he hadn't been trying to stage her body but instead attempting to assault her. The real question was that if he was still stalking her, how would he find her here? Josie had been to Sullivan County before. She was used to rural Pennsylvania, but even she had had difficulty finding the parking lot at the bottom of the mountain. Every single one of them had—even with directions from Sandrine's office. Nicola and Brian had gotten lost. Then there was the issue of how he'd navigated the snow successfully.

Alone at the table, Josie leaned toward Alice and whispered, "Meg was from Texas, right?"

Alice's eyes widened. She looked around to make sure no one was watching them. "She lives in Maryland, now. I mean, she did. She moved after her stalker disappeared. But before that, yes, it was Texas. Why? You think her stalker did this? You think he's here?"

Josie smiled reassuringly. "No. I don't think it's likely."

"Oh God, then it's someone here. Or Cooper. Is it wrong to say I wish it was Cooper? At least he's not here right now."

Before Josie could answer, Sandrine and Taryn returned to the room. Sandrine carefully pushed the other chairs up to the table while Taryn took a seat near the stove with Nicola and Brian. Under the table, Alice reached over and squeezed Josie's arm. The reassuring feel of her hand sent a wave of warmth through Josie. Immediately, her mind turned to Noah and the way his touch always seemed to calm her and settle her anxiety. What had Gretchen meant when she said he was a damn mess? Was it because he was upset about the news they'd received, or the way she had left things? As hurt as she was, she found herself wishing for him. She missed his soothing hands, his easy smile, the way his dark hair stuck up in the morning, the way nothing unnerved him.

Well, almost nothing.

Before her mind could go down that road again, Josie pushed thoughts of Noah deep into the back of her mind. She had to focus on the situation at hand. Sandrine was standing in the center of the room, addressing them. "I think we need to talk about what happened today."

Josie and Alice stood and followed her over to the chairs, sitting beside one another while Sandrine took the centermost seat where she had a good view of each one of them. Josie was grateful for an excuse to sit near the wood-burning stove, although it wasn't giving off as much heat as it had been after Brian first lit it this morning. After taking photos of Meg's cabin, she'd stopped at her cabin and changed into dry clothes, but she still felt cold. Now she pulled her hands inside the sleeves of her Denton PD hoodie, trying to warm her fingers.

Nicola got up and went over to the stove, feeding more logs

into it. "You mean talk about the fact that we came to this place to process our trauma and found a dead body? I'll start. It's really fucked up."

Taryn's fingers traveled to the hollow of her throat, scratching. "Nicola, please. Language."

Nicola rolled her eyes. "It is." She closed the door to the stove but stayed on her knees in front of it, looking around at the rest of them. Josie noticed that in spite of her usual bravado, tears glistened in her eyes. "Don't you think so? Isn't anyone else thinking that?"

Brian tucked his phone into his pocket and leaned all the way back in his chair, limbs sprawled. "I've been thinking that."

"And Meg. Poor Meg," Nicola added. "She was here to try to get her life back, to feel some control over things again, and she dies? It's fucked up."

Sandrine clasped her hands together. "While I would not have chosen those words, Nicola, you're right. This was supposed to be a week where I hoped to provide a safe space for all of you and offer you multiple ways in which you might process some of the life trauma you've all endured and instead, what's happened is that you've all been retraumatized and Meg lost her life. I think at this time, we should all take a few minutes to gather our thoughts and then share how we're feeling about Meg's death. Then I'd like you each to think about what would be the most effective way for you to begin to process Meg's death."

Alice crossed her arms, hugging herself. "Sandrine, that's all well and good but I think we should be figuring out how to get off this mountain as soon as possible."

Brian lifted a hand in the air. "I agree."

Sandrine sighed. She looked toward the windows; Josie followed her gaze. Since they'd brought Meg back to camp, at least three more inches of snow had fallen.

Turning back to the group, Josie said, "We need a plan. Not

just for getting off this mountain—which is going to be next to impossible in this weather—but for how to spend the next day or potentially two or three days."

"Two or three days?" Taryn blurted out. "You want us to spend two or three more days up here with a dead body?"

Alice shuddered silently.

Josie said, "There is a very good chance that no rescue efforts will begin until the snow has stopped. It may be too dangerous. Also, we don't know what kind of equipment will be needed to reach us and how long it will take county officials to amass it and bring it here. So yes, we need to prepare ourselves for the reality that we could be here until Sunday or Monday—or even later. That means we need to conserve whatever supplies are on hand. Food, wood, and fuel for the generator."

"You mean generators," said Brian.

"No," Josie said. "One generator. What makes the most sense is for us to pool all of our supplies and stay here together in the main house."

"What? Like sleep here together?" Nicola said.

Alice slid her feet out of her boots and tucked them up under her. "Josie's right. We should gather all the wood from our individual cabins and bring it here. We can try to find something to siphon out the fuel from the other generators so we can use it here. That way we all benefit from it."

Taryn scratched again at her throat and glanced at Sandrine, who offered no objections. "Someone should catalog the food supply so we can start to ration it out. We should eat the fresh food first, then go to the nonperishables."

"What about sleeping arrangements?" Brian asked. "We all just sleep in here?"

Alice said, "We'll just have to grab our blankets and pillows from our cabins. Maybe when the snow lets up, if we're able, we can work together to move mattresses from the cabins to here."

"We can split up and sleep in the breakout rooms if you prefer that," said Sandrine.

The breakout rooms were on either side of the great room. One of them was where Josie had had her first private session with Sandrine—the one with all the taxidermied animals. The other room had been fashioned like a game room with an air hockey table in the middle of it, dartboards on the walls and some cornhole kits stacked in one corner. Cornhole was a game that had gained a lot of popularity in Pennsylvania the last several years. Each kit contained a wooden goal board which was raised and angled and had one small hole along its surface. The object was to throw small bean bags into the holes for points. Cooper and Sandrine had moved the kits and the air hockey table aside so they could use the room for yoga, guided meditation, and sound baths.

In spite of the extra warmth coming from the wood-burning stove now that it was restocked, Alice shivered. "I think we should all sleep here, in this big room together."

"Why?" Nicola said, brows scrunched.

Alice shrugged. "So we can look out for each other. If any one of us had noticed Meg leave her cabin last night, we wouldn't be in this position. If we're all together—"

Brian narrowed his eyes. "You want to keep an eye on all of us."

"That's not what I said."

"But it's what you meant," Brian insisted. "Why else would you want us all to sleep in the same room?"

Before the conversation could devolve further, Josie cleared her throat and said, "We can worry about sleeping arrangements later. Our first priority should be trying to get in touch with someone to make sure help is on the way."

"I agree," said Sandrine, the smile on her face now strained.

Taryn glanced toward the windows as a strong gust of wind shook the house. "Help must be on the way. Cooper is probably trying to find help as we speak. He has the SAT phone! Why else didn't he return to camp last night?"

Nicola held her palms out toward the stove to warm them. "For all we know, Cooper could be dead, too. We don't have any proof that he made it all the way down the mountain."

Brian said, "Cooper didn't come back because he was sick of listening to a bunch of whiny losers. He manages this property year-round. I'm sure he's used to bad weather. No way is he dead."

Josie tried to get them back on track. "Regardless, it won't hurt if one of us got in touch with emergency services and let them know that we're stuck up here and that one member of our party is deceased. Even if Cooper did have some sort of accident and used the SAT phone, he wouldn't have known about Meg, so that's not something that he would have reported to authorities. They might prioritize the call differently if they know someone on the retreat died. We should do it before the weather gets any worse—while we can still move out there."

Taryn returned her hand to her lap. Two pink slashes were visible at the hollow of her throat where she'd been scratching. "How will we get in touch with anyone?"

Josie pushed her hands out of her sleeves and gestured toward Brian. "We've got two phones. We split up. One group goes toward the summit and the other group goes down the path. That gives us a better chance of reaching someone. Then we meet back here."

Sandrine interjected, "Why don't we all get our blankets, pillows, and any personal items and bring them here first. That should only take a few minutes."

"Yes," Josie agreed. "We should do that first. Then try to make some calls."

As everyone pulled on their winter wear and trudged toward the door, she considered the possibility that someone in the room might be the killer and whether it was wise to split up.

Ultimately, she decided that as long as they stayed in groups, they would be fine. Once everyone had brought their things to the main house, three could go up the slope and three down the slope as far as they could manage. The snow was coming down so furiously, they only had a small window of time during which they could attempt to make contact with the outside world. Josie's gut told her that if Meg's killer was among them, he or she would not be likely to try to overpower two other retreat members in order to kill them as well. They had to take their chances.

SEVENTEEN

Noah's ass hurt from sitting on the bench inside the sheriff's office while he waited for Deputy Ehrbar's boss to show up. After helping get Noah back on the road, Ehrbar had followed Noah up to the top of the long hill, sometimes having to push him along with his front bumper, until they reached the road into Laporte, which was not much easier to navigate. Once in the center of town, the road flattened out and became easier to manage since it had just been plowed. At the sheriff's office, a deputy named Carrie Roeder had been assigned to the front desk and was taking a steady stream of calls from county residents in distress because of the storm. Ehrbar had been called right back out, promising Noah that Sheriff Shaw would be in any moment.

That had been over an hour ago and so far, no one had come in or out. Noah took out his phone for the fifteenth time since his arrival. No messages. No calls. He wondered if Josie had tried to contact Gretchen again. But Gretchen would have told him. He'd called her and the Chief before he left for Sullivan County to let them know what was going on. He'd had to take sick time. He felt badly for leaving just as the new guy was about to start. The Chief hadn't told them much about him except that he had a lot of experience. Noah would have preferred to be there to meet their new investigator, but Josie needed him. Noah was sure of that.

Most of all, he needed to talk to her. He couldn't let another day go by with her thinking that she wasn't enough for him. It wasn't something he wanted to tell her by text or over the phone. He needed to see her face.

The lobby door swung open and Ehrbar entered, followed by a blast of snow. He shook it off his head and looked over at Noah. "Still here?"

"Yeah. Listen, the storm is getting worse. Is there any way you could just get me the name of the caretaker or maybe the location of the property so I can check it out on my own?"

Ehrbar frowned. "And get stuck out there again?"

Noah stood up. "I need to get to my wife. If there is even a chance of reaching her before this storm gets any worse, I need to try."

With a sigh, Ehrbar said, "Just how do you think you're going to get to her? I know the property. You can't drive up to it, especially in this weather."

"What about the caretaker?" Noah asked. "Wouldn't he have a way to get up there in bad weather?"

Deputy Roeder took another call. As soon as she picked up, somewhere else in the room two more phones rang.

"I suppose he would," said Ehrbar. "Won't hurt to find out. Let me see what I can do."

EIGHTEEN

The snow was nearly to their knees this time and coming down steadily. Josie fought through it, pulling her scarf up so that it covered everything but her eyes. Behind her, Sandrine and Alice trudged along, fitting their boots into the path she had already trod. They were headed down the mountain, toward where Meg had been found. The other group—Nicola, Brian, and Taryn—had gone in the opposite direction, toward the summit. Taryn had not been happy about being separated from Sandrine, but Sandrine had convinced her that she would be the most help accompanying Nicola and Brian. Like everyone else, Josie had gone back to her cabin to get her blankets and pillow to bring to the main house. She'd also put on some extra layers but now, they'd only just passed the shed that contained Meg's body and already she was soaked through. Plus, the extra bulk made it harder to move through the thick snow. The muscles of her legs burned mercilessly.

She paused to catch her breath, estimating that they were about halfway to where Meg had been found. Turning, she saw Sandrine hunched over, hands on her knees. Josie had tried to get her to stay back at the main house, but she refused. Alice watched her with concern, placing a hand on her back and saying something into her ear that Josie couldn't make out. Seconds later, Sandrine pushed herself upright. Her face was red and wet with snow, but she did her best to smile. "I'm fine," she insisted. "Please, let's go."

What felt like a frozen eternity later, they reached the place where she and Sandrine had found Meg's body. Josie could tell from where the snow had been tamped down by all of them walking. New snow now covered it, but their old tracks were still visible. For now.

"Come on," she said. "Let's keep going. I don't want to disturb that scene if we can help it."

"But you had a signal there," Alice said.

Sandrine said, "Scene? Josie, really, is there something you want to share with me?"

Josie paused, turning back. Over Sandrine's shoulder, Josie caught Alice's wide-eyed look. Alice shrugged. It was Josie's call how much to tell Sandrine. She did the calculations in her head. On one hand, it was Sandrine's retreat. Perhaps she deserved to know. On the other hand, what difference would it make? Whether Sandrine knew Meg had been murdered or not, it changed nothing. They were still stuck here for the foreseeable future, a killer among them.

Josie said, "Sandrine, do you know what an unattended death is?"

Gloved hands came up and pushed her hat down more firmly over her skull. "Yes," she said. "I do. It's when someone who was otherwise healthy dies with no witnesses, and it is not immediately clear why or what happened."

Again, Alice shot Josie a look. This time, one of her brows arched severely as if to say, *How the hell did Sandrine know that?*

"That's right," Josie said.

Sandrine glanced toward the trees that had hidden Meg's

body. "Meg was young and healthy. There was no reason for her to die." She looked back at Alice. "You said she died of hypothermia."

Alice nodded. "That's what it looked like."

"It would still be investigated as an unattended death," Josie said. "Usually by police, although more commonly the coroner or medical examiner, but the scene where the deceased was found is treated like a crime scene just in case the investigation reveals that foul play was involved. The reason is that you only get one chance to preserve and process a scene."

"You've jumped right into police mode, Josie," Sandrine said with a weak smile.

Josie swiped at snowflakes landing in her eyelashes. "Yes. I'm trying to follow procedure as best I can out here. This is not my jurisdiction, but I'm still trying to do everything I can to make the job of law enforcement and the coroner or medical examiner easier once help arrives. Now come on, let's keep going. We'll find a spot lower on the trail but parallel to where I got the signal last time."

They trudged onward until Josie found a natural opening among the trees. "Here," she said.

Sandrine and Alice started to follow her into the woods. As they walked, Josie took off her gloves and got her phone out again. Holding it up in the air, she walked from tree to tree, waiting for it to show any connection to the cellular network. Finally, two bars appeared. Josie waited a moment to see if any notifications would pop up. None did. She punched in 911 and hit call. At first, it didn't ring. On her third try, the sound of the line ringing on the other end made them all whoop with joy.

Finally came a click and then a tinny voice, "Nine-one-one. Where's your emergency?"

"We're at the Sacred New Beginnings Retreat," Josie began.

"What's the address, ma'am?"

Sandrine stumbled over and put her face near the receiver,

shouting the address. The 911 dispatcher repeated it back and then Sandrine confirmed it.

"What's your emergency?" asked the operator.

Before Josie could answer, the line went dead.

"What happened?" Alice cried.

"It disconnected," Josie flexed her fingers, trying to fight the numbing cold. "I'll try again."

The call went through once more on her fifth try. Again, they gave their location, this time advising that they were stuck, and a member of their party was deceased but once the word "deceased" was out of Josie's mouth, the line died again.

They tried again and again until the phone had dropped to forty-nine percent and the three of them were shivering badly. Josie's legs below the knees felt like they were encased in a block of ice. The wind stung every inch of her exposed skin.

Alice brushed snow from her shoulders and hair. "It's not going to h-hold. They'll n-never get to us."

"They'll have to send someone," Josie said. "Even if the call wasn't completed. They've got a location."

For the second time that day, Sandrine's teeth chattered. "H-how can you be s-sure?"

"Because that's how this works," said Josie.

Alice moved closer to Sandrine and put an arm across her shoulders. "But what if they don't send someone?"

"They will," Josie said, but already doubt ate at her insides. She was sure that the county's emergency services would investigate the multiple partial calls, but would they prioritize them? Cooper had left with a SAT phone and yet, no one had come for them when the snow was still navigable. Josie questioned how quickly authorities would be able to get up the mountain now.

Alice hugged Sandrine close to her side. "You're sure?"

"Yes," Josie replied. She looked at her phone again, this time pulling up text messages. Nothing new. She tapped in a message to Gretchen. It had worked before.

Blizzard hit us full force. Trapped with few supplies. One member of retreat is deceased. Looks like a homicide. Tried to call 911. Call keeps dropping.

Sandrine clung to Alice. "We need to t-try again. To be s-sure."

They did, making asymmetrical patterns in the snow as they moved around the clearing to try to get and maintain a connection. Alice and Sandrine stayed huddled together, trying to warm one another, as they followed Josie around. She tried 911 several more times. But the calls wouldn't go through, or they would drop so quickly that Josie didn't have enough time to explain their situation. With the phone down to thirty-two percent, Josie stopped. The screen kept getting wet with snow and her fingers were numb. She checked her text messages again but there was no response from Gretchen. Yet.

Alice dragged Sandrine over to a large sycamore tree and leaned against its trunk. "You are a police officer. Can't you bypass 911 and just call someone you know?"

Josie was about to point out again that Sullivan County was not her jurisdiction but then she realized it didn't matter. If she could get hold of any member of her team, they could intervene on her behalf. Fingers trembling, she pulled up her contacts. Noah was on top of it, favorited. She hesitated. Would he pick up if she called?

Of course he will, the voice in the back of her head told her. *He was the one who wanted you to talk things over. Gretchen said he was a mess.*

"Can you d-do that, Josie?" Sandrine slumped against the tree, sinking into the snow beneath her. Wind shrieked through the branches over their heads. "Call one of your colleagues? Can they help?"

She could just as easily try calling Gretchen, or the Chief. They would help her. She left Alice and Sandrine at the tree and started walking again, circling back to the places where they'd found service. Suddenly, three bars appeared. Before she could think about it, one of her shaking fingers pressed down on Noah's name. Then came the sound of ringing.

Relief flooded through her.

Then a voice that was not Noah's answered. "Hello?"

Josie hesitated. She took the phone from her cheek and stared at it. She had dialed Noah's desk phone at work, not his cell phone. "Wh-who is this?" she said, realizing that her own teeth had started to chatter.

"Who am I?" said the man. "Honey, you called me. Why don't you start with telling me who you are."

"I'm looking for Lieutenant Fraley," she said. "My—my husband."

"You're going in and out, sweetheart," said the man and Josie wondered why she was "going in and out" when she could hear everything he said perfectly. "Did you say you're looking for your husband? Looks like you have the wrong number."

"Noah Fraley," she said. "I need to speak with him. This is Josie. Detective Josie Quinn. I'm in Sullivan County. I'm at a retreat. We're stuck in the snow..." She rattled off the address. "Someone is dead. We need help."

"This is Denton you called," he said. "Alcott County. You've got the wrong department. Listen, I've got to keep this line open. Best of luck to you."

"Wait," Josie cried. "I work for the Denton Police Department! It's Detective Josie Quinn!"

But the line was already dead.

Josie stared at the phone screen, something between shock and fury bubbling up inside her.

Alice and Sandrine appeared, hobbling together, following the path Josie's feet had made. "What happened?" asked Alice. "What did he say?"

Josie wiped the snow from the screen again and checked the number to make sure it was correct in her phone. It was the right number. Who in the hell was answering Noah's desk phone?

"Josie?" Sandrine said.

The Chief had talked about hiring a new detective to replace Mettner, but he'd been tight-lipped about it. Had he brought someone new on while Josie was away? Had he not even briefed the guy about the rest of the team?

Alice shook Josie's shoulder. "What happened?"

"The call dropped," Josie said. "The snow is getting worse. We better go back. Maybe the other group had better luck."

NINETEEN

The other group hadn't had any luck at all making an emergency call. They arrived at the main house moments after Josie, Alice and Sandrine. It was almost dark and everyone was shivering and soaked. While Sandrine loaded logs into the wood-burner that heated the building, the rest of them took turns using the bathroom to change into dry clothes. Everyone seemed as exhausted and frozen to the bone as Josie felt. They placed their blankets and pillows around the perimeter of the central room, since that was the location of their main source of heat, and then they gathered around the dining table while Sandrine and Taryn threw something together for dinner.

Brian took one of the solar-powered lanterns and the only flashlight they'd been able to find out back to check on the generator. It was still running but no one had checked the fuel all day. Cooper usually took care of that. Josie wondered just how much fuel was left. They hadn't had a chance to search for materials that might help them siphon the gas from the other generators. They could survive without the electricity the generator provided but she and Brian would not be able to charge their phones. They hadn't been much use yet, but Josie didn't want the one tenuous link to the outside world severed. She found her phone in her coat pocket and plugged the charging cord into it. The screen came to life, showing a text message. Josie's breath caught in her throat as she opened it.

Gretchen had replied. Sometime between Josie, Alice, and Sandrine leaving the forest after their last attempt to reach 911 and now, the message had come through.

Homicide??? Are you safe? Chief and I are making some calls to Sullivan County. The Chief knows their Sheriff, Hunter Shaw. Says he's a good man. But the storm there is bad. Not sure how long it will take for them to get to you. Noah's already up there. He left when the snow started. I tried calling his cell but can't get through. Hang tight. Help is on the way.

Josie tipped her head back and let out a long sigh of relief. Noah. Here in Sullivan County. She hadn't contacted him. Had refused to call him or text him. She'd shut him out even before she left for the retreat, and he'd come after her anyway.

He left when the snow started.

Tears pricked at Josie's eyes. Blinking them back, she set the phone down and joined the others for dinner. Brian reported that there was enough fuel to get them through one more day. The next day he would search around to see if he could find anything he could use to get the remaining gas from the other generators. The news was met with silent nods. No one seemed to have the energy for conversation. After they ate, Nicola and Brian cleaned up. The rest of them moved to the chairs around the wood-burning stove. Josie wrapped herself in her blanket and plopped down. In spite of the heat radiating from the stove, she couldn't get warm. It was like the cold of the day had seeped so deeply into her bones, she might never be rid of it. As her body started to relax for the first time that day, she felt aches in her feet, legs, back and shoulders, the unwelcome results of trudging through almost knee-high snow the better part of the day, and transporting Meg's body. She knew she should dig through her bag for her ibuprofen, but she didn't have the strength to move from her chair.

Josie looked over her shoulder to the windows, now black, showing only the reflections of the rest of them inside. It was eerie, as if the rest of the world no longer existed. But outside those windows, two doors down, the frozen body of poor Meg Cleary waited for the proper authorities to claim it. Once everyone else was gathered around the stove, Josie gave them the good news that her colleagues in Denton were getting in touch with local authorities to let them know what was going on.

Alice clapped her hands together, eyes alight with relief. "Help is on the way!"

"That's great," said Brian. "But how will they get up here? How long will it take?"

"I don't know," Josie answered honestly. She didn't tell them her fear that whatever resources Sullivan County had would already be stretched thin in conditions this bad. On the other hand, a homicide here would likely fall under the purview of the state police, which might mean a second agency trying to reach them.

Sandrine dragged her fingers through her long hair. "Let's not worry about that right now. All we need to know is that help is coming. We'll just try to stretch our resources as far as they'll go. I really think we should all take this opportunity to talk about how we're feeling. About Meg's death."

No one spoke.

The only sounds were the crackling of the fire and the shrill whine of the wind outside.

Sandrine added, "I know you're all very tired. Exhausted. In addition to the shock of Meg's death, we've all been pushed to our physical limits today. But I do think it's really important that we don't lose sight of the emotional impact all of this is having on us. Pushing your feelings aside now will only lead to more problems later."

Taryn, seated beside Sandrine, raised her hand. "I feel sad—obviously. I guess that's stupid to say."

Sandrine smiled. "No, Taryn, it's not stupid at all."

"Yes it is," Nicola interjected. Only her head was visible from the cocoon of her brown blanket. The short locks of her hair stuck out like the points of a star. "Of course you're sad. We're all sad. We're here because we're sad."

"Nicola, please," Sandrine said. "We talked about this last night after your outburst at dinner. You're very welcome to express your feelings but please do it in a respectful, civil manner."

Taryn scratched her throat again, glaring at Nicola. "You're very disrespectful—especially to Sandrine."

"Please, Taryn," Nicola spat back. Her head rose up from the blanket like a snake, exposing her slender neck. "Stop acting like this woman is the greatest therapist in the world. How do we even know she's qualified to help any of us"—here her hands emerged from under the blanket to form air quotes—"'process our trauma'? How do we know she's qualified at all?"

Sandrine's mouth hung open.

"Where is this even coming from?" Alice laughed. "You didn't research her before you signed up for this retreat? Must be nice to spend money like that. I had to work three extra shifts just to cover the cost of this!"

Josie said, "My therapist recommended Sandrine. You didn't hear about her through yours?"

Nicola faltered. Her pinched features slackened. Josie wasn't sure what it was that flashed across her face. Confusion, maybe. She looked at Brian. He shifted in his chair, looking around at each one of them sheepishly. "We, uh, don't have a therapist."

Nicola added, "There was no requirement that we be referred by a therapist."

Alice straightened her spine and smoothed her blanket over her knees. "You two lost a child, in one of the most horrific ways possible, and you don't have a therapist? At all?"

"Alice," Sandrine said softly. "It's okay. Mental health treatment is often difficult to obtain."

Josie could tell by Alice's posture that she wasn't going to let the issue go. "But you thought that a week in a group environment was going to solve all your problems?" Alice said to Brian incredulously.

"You are missing the point," Nicola said. "It doesn't matter how we got here. What matters is that the person who brought us here is not qualified to help us at all. We've all got trauma. How do we know Sandrine does? Because she says she does?"

Again, Alice laughed but there was an edge to it now. "Yeah, that's kind of how it works. It wouldn't be appropriate for her to ask us to carry her baggage as well as ours."

Sandrine held up a hand to silence them all. "Nicola, I'm very sorry that you feel this way, that you've lost confidence in my ability to help you—"

Brian interrupted. "Sandrine, I think what my wife is getting at is maybe it would help if you shared just a bit of your own journey with us."

Sandrine smiled stiffly. "I'm afraid not, Brian. I will not be put in the position of having to 'prove' that I am qualified to treat patients based on things that happened to me. I'm qualified due to my education, research, and experience in the field. I've worked with hundreds of patients."

Nicola pressed on. "But how do we know you're not a fraud? Not everything can be learned by reading books or taking college classes. It's completely different when you experience something first-hand. Everyone in this room has seen trauma up close and personal. Except you!"

Alice slid to the edge of her chair. Color had returned to her cheeks. "I think finding Meg's dead body counts as trauma, Nicola. Can you just drop this—whatever this is? We're all tired. Sandrine has done her best to keep everything moving along in spite of some pretty extraordinary circumstances."

Ignoring Alice, Nicola threw off her cover and stood up, stepping toward Sandrine. "I've seen a dead body before." She looked over toward Brian, for encouragement or permission, Josie wasn't sure. His face was inscrutable. Turning back to Sandrine, Nicola continued, voice shaking. "Our daughter's dead body. The police took me to the drainage ditch and showed her to me. They made me go down into the muck to make sure they had the right child. I had to climb through sewage to get to her. To see my baby desecrated."

"What?" Josie blurted out.

If Nicola heard her, she didn't show it, keeping her gaze on Sandrine. Her voice gained strength, getting louder. "Has anything like that ever happened to you? Have you ever lost a child?"

She said the word "child" with extra emphasis, her throat quivering. Sandrine blinked, eyes filling with tears. She looked around the room at each one of them. Josie saw her lower lip tremble ever so slightly. The day—Meg's death, all the hours out in the cold, the grief, confusion, and fear—it was all getting to her. Sandrine had been unflappable all week. Josie had the sense that she was used to being in charge and that angry, combative people did not intimidate her but this situation, with the loss of Meg during a blizzard, was uncharted territory for her. She was their de facto leader. If she cracked, what would happen?

And what in the hell was Nicola talking about?

Josie put her blanket aside and stood up. "Nicola, are you saying that the police took you to the site where your daughter was found for an ID?"

Nicola spun on her. A momentary blip of confusion crossed her face but was quickly replaced with a scowl. "What? Yes. It was—it was horrible."

Josie put her hands on her hips. Just the small movements reminded her how sore her body felt, but she could not let this go. How she wanted to sit back down and just go to sleep. The detective in her would not allow it. "How soon after she was found?"

She was aware of everyone staring at her now. She knew it sounded insensitive. It *was* insensitive to ask a grieving parent these types of questions about the murder of her daughter when there was no investigation at stake.

Except that Nicola was lying.

Josie glanced at Brian briefly, but his expression gave away nothing. She stepped closer to Nicola, encroaching on her personal space. "How long?"

Nicola looked to Brian again, but all he offered was a half-hearted, one-shoulder shrug. Without meeting Josie's eyes, she answered, "I don't know. A few minutes after they found her. They came and got me and took me to her."

Sandrine stood and walked over, inserting herself between them. "That's enough. Please, let's everyone just sit down and take a breath."

"Nicola," Josie said, keeping her tone matter-of-fact. "No law enforcement officer would ever do that."

Taryn said, "What are you talking about, Josie?"

Josie kept her eyes on Nicola. She could see her resolve wavering slightly in the way her eyes widened, fear filling them. Josie said, "No police officer would ever bring a parent to a crime scene like that. Not only is it cruel but it would taint the scene, making it very difficult to bring a case against the murderer. They would have sealed that scene off, Nicola. No one in or out except for evidence techs and investigators. You or your husband would have been asked to make an ID at the morgue, after your daughter had been cleaned up. So tell me, what really happened?"

Sandrine stepped aside. From where Josie stood, she saw hatred flare in Nicola's eyes.

No one spoke, the tension in the room growing thicker each second. The silence went on so long that Josie began counting in her head. When she reached nineteen, Brian jumped out of his chair. "We made it up," he said. "It's not true."

Josie was aware of a few gasps. Taryn said, "What do you mean, you 'made it up'?"

Nicola turned to her husband and pushed him, her palms meeting his shoulders. He fell back into his chair. "Why?" she growled at him. "Why would you say that?"

Sandrine's voice had a slight tremor. "Is that true, Nicola?"

Alice said, "That's despicable. How could you? Both of you!"

Brian climbed out of his chair again. "Wait, wait," he said. "Let me explain."

"Don't," Nicola said, tone low and menacing.

Ignoring her, Brian said, "It didn't happen to us as parents, okay? We don't have any kids. When Nicola was a little girl, her sister was abducted and murdered."

Alice said, "Why would you pretend it was your child? Do you know how sick that is?"

"We have experienced bad things," Brian said quickly. "Okay? Just not as a couple."

"Yes," Nicola said. "Brian lost people in that fire when he was a kid, and I lost my sister."

"Why would you lie about all of this?" Alice said. "There is absolutely no reason for it."

"I'm sorry," Brian said. "I can explain—"

"And how dare you accuse Sandrine of being a fraud when the two of you have lied to all of us the entire week?" added Alice.

"She is a fraud!" Nicola shouted, advancing on Alice. "We actually did experience trauma, Brian and I! So we fudged the details a little. It's still real!"

Still seated, Alice recoiled. Josie walked over and stood between the two of them, getting so close to Nicola that she was forced to back away. "Calm down," Josie told her.

Nicola turned away but Sandrine was right there, blocking her way. "I think we should talk about why the two of you felt the need to 'fudge details.'"

"We don't owe you an explanation," Nicola said. "Any of you. I'm done with this."

With a huff, she pushed her way past Sandrine and stalked off. She snatched her coat from a hook along the far wall and punched her arms into it. Then she threw open the front door, seemingly intent on stomping out of the building, but a blast of snow and cold air rushed at her, knocking her back into the room. She gave a frustrated grumble and pushed the door closed, using all of her weight to do so. With a glance back at them, she instead tromped off to one of the breakout rooms, slamming that door behind her.

"I, uh, I'm really sorry," Brian said. "I'll go talk to her."

Sandrine watched him go, nonplussed.

Taryn stood up and walked over to her, putting a hand on her shoulder. "Maybe we should all just get some sleep. Everyone is exhausted. This would have been the last day of the retreat. We were scheduled to go in the morning."

"I'm so sorry," Sandrine whispered. "I didn't want it to end like this."

Taryn pulled her into a side hug. "It's not your fault."

Alice got up, pulling her blanket tight around her. "Can you believe this shit?" she said.

Nicola and Brian argued in the breakout room for another half hour—their voices muffled and indistinct—before getting into their makeshift beds, each under their own blanket. Alice had placed her cover and pillow next to Josie's. Once everyone was wrapped in their own bedding on the floor, she leaned toward Josie and whispered, "Can you really sleep? We don't know who any of these people are at all! One of them could be a killer!"

In spite of the overwhelming fatigue weighing down every inch of her body, Josie knew her insomnia would be in full force under the current circumstances. "Want to take shifts?" she asked Alice.

"Yes, thank you. I'll go first. I'm used to working night shifts."

Josie wanted to tell her that they didn't need to take shifts, but realized she had to try to sleep. Even if all she did was rest her achy body, it would be something. So she thanked Alice and closed her eyes. She was too exhausted to care about how hard and uncomfortable the floor felt beneath her. Moments later, she found herself skimming the edges of sleep. Her mind worked through the events of the day, and she realized Alice was right. She knew nothing about the people on the retreat. One of them was dead and two of them had been lying all week.

What were the others hiding?

TWENTY

Deputy Ehrbar had given Noah directions to a parking lot and the home of the retreat property's caretaker. The residence would not come up in GPS, Ehrbar warned—not that Noah's GPS would work in the mountains—and the lot had no address. It was just a spot, around a bend, a quarter mile past a sharp curve in the road along Route 154. Luckily, the home of Cooper Riggs was only "a coupla three" miles past the lot.

In the middle of nowhere, Noah thought.

It was almost dark by the time Noah found the parking lot. Maneuvering the rural route in over a foot of snow, with more coming down rapidly, took every bit of concentration he had, especially when he realized a creek ran alongside the road. If he lost control of his vehicle, he wasn't just risking getting stuck in the snow miles from anyone who might help, he was likely to meet his death in a freezing watery grave.

Noah was relieved when the parking lot came into view. It wasn't big. Half of it was filled with vehicles, their roofs carrying over a foot of snow each. He pulled into it, slotting his tires into tracks that had been made by another vehicle. Snow had nearly filled them back in, but they were still lightly visible.

Leaving his vehicle in park, Noah hopped out and looked around. He counted seven vehicles, all parked side by side, snow up to their undercarriages. Josie's was in the middle. He walked slowly along the row, the wind batting at him.

At the end of the row, there was a spot that looked as if it had been vacated either before or shortly after the snow had started. Noah could just make out the rectangle of ground that had fewer inches of snow in it than the rest of the lot. Beyond that was an opening in the trees, just wide enough for a car. What looked like footprints came from there, barely visible now that they were filled with new snowfall. Someone had made it off the mountain and driven away. Several hours ago, given the rate of snowfall and the fact that both the footprints and tire tracks were almost covered now.

But who? The caretaker? If he'd gotten off the mountain, why hadn't he called to get help for the others? Where was he?

Noah pulled his phone from his coat pocket to call Ehrbar, but the call wouldn't go through. Nothing was coming or going. He had no network connection. Sighing, he put it away and walked up the path, following the partially covered prints until he came to a John Deere Gator. It was covered in snow. Even if he had keys to it, there was no way it was traversing over a foot of snow.

Night was closing in. Soon he wouldn't even be able to see, and he didn't trust the battery on his phone to power his flashlight app long enough to get back to his vehicle. He wondered how long the path was and whether he could walk it or not if he got his actual flashlight out of his car. Based on what Ehrbar had told him, he didn't think so. Maybe on a warm day with no snow. But not now. He needed help to be able to get to Josie and bring her back. Freezing to death halfway up the mountain wasn't going to do either of them any good.

He trudged back to his vehicle, snow stinging his face. Turning the heat to full blast, he considered his options. Ehrbar hadn't known if the caretaker was home or not. He had tried calling his landline but got no answer. Noah wondered if the missing car had belonged to Cooper Riggs. But if Riggs had made it off the mountain and gone home, why didn't he answer his phone? Or had he not made it home at all? Had someone else from the retreat found their way to the bottom and left everyone else stuck there in a blizzard?

There was only one way to find out.

TWENTY-ONE

True to her word, Alice woke Josie from a fitful sleep four hours later for them to change shifts. Josie sat up, rubbing the sleep from her eyes and looking around the room. It was lit only by the orange glow of the fire from within the wood-burning stove. Someone had kept it going during the night. While Alice turned onto her side and quickly began to snore, Josie leaned against the wall, drawing her knees to her chest and watching the others, just lumps beneath their blankets. Awake and alone with her thoughts, her brain instantly went to Noah. She had hoped he would somehow make it up the mountain to them before they went to sleep even though, given the snowfall outside, it was clearly not feasible. She wondered if Gretchen or the Chief had gotten in touch with him and told him they'd had a homicide. She thought about poor Meg, her frozen body alone in the dark on the side of a mountain.

Guilt felt like a vise around her chest. Mett's voice floated up from somewhere in her brain. *You did the best you could under the circumstances.*

What do I do now? she asked him.

She swore she could hear his laughter. *You already know what to do,* he said. *You don't need me.*

The band around her chest tightened. Tears threatened. *But I miss you so much.*

A rustling drew her attention. Across the room, Brian rolled over and threw his cover aside. Although they'd laid on the floor next to one another, Nicola was now several feet away from Brian. He didn't look at her and she didn't stir. He heaved himself to his feet and walked over to the stove. When he opened the door, Josie felt a light wave of heat wash over her. Inside, the last log was almost gone. She watched as Brian took another from the bottom of the bucket beside the stove and placed it inside. Flames flared as the wood caught fire. Brian felt around the bottom of the bucket and came up empty. He got onto his hands and knees and searched around the stove.

Josie whispered, "The rest of the wood is in the kitchen."

Startled, Brian jumped back and landed on his rear end. His eyes searched the semi-darkness until he found Josie. She stood up and padded over. "Sorry, didn't mean to scare you. I couldn't sleep."

She extended a hand and helped him to his feet. She pointed to the bucket and he picked it up, following her into the kitchen. She tried the light switch and a bulb flickered on overhead.

"Guess the generator is still working," Brian said.

"For now." Josie showed him where Sandrine and Taryn had stacked extra logs earlier in the day. They were lined up along the wall next to the back door. Mumbling a "thanks," he knelt and began loading some into the bucket.

Josie leaned a hip against the counter. "It doesn't bother you? Getting that close to fire?"

Brian stopped and looked up at her. He rubbed a palm over a burn mark on the back of his wrist. It was something she'd seen him do many times that week whenever he talked about the fire that burned down his foster home. "You think I lied about that, too, don't you?"

"I didn't say that."

He stared into the bucket. "But my big trauma is that fire, and here I am loading up the wood-burning stove all day with no issues at all. I guess everything I say or Nicola says now will be subject to doubt."

"You can't really blame us," Josie said. While she had him here, out of earshot of everyone else, during the quiet of the night, was the perfect time to ask him some questions. "Why *did* you lie?"

He shook his head. "I—I don't know. I don't have a good explanation. We both wanted to be on the retreat together, but Nicola was afraid she wouldn't meet the criteria of complex PTSD because what happened didn't happen to her. She didn't think losing a sister as a child would qualify her. Listen, I know we shouldn't have lied. Believe me, I'm sorry. But I couldn't talk her out of it. I didn't lie about the fire. It was real. I was there."

Josie watched him as he arranged the logs in the bucket to make more room. Then he paused to pick a splinter out from under his wedding band. Unlike Nicola's his was a soft black silicone. "But you had already found a way to be comfortable around fire before you came here."

"No. I didn't. I still get, like, triggered. Just not in this kind of situation. These fires are pretty well-contained. I will admit, I was upset when we got here, and I found out the cabins were heated with wood-burning stoves."

Josie laughed softly. "So was I but for different reasons. I don't like roughing it."

He loaded a few more logs into the bucket and then stopped again. "The smell still bothers me sometimes. It's like I can't ever really get it out of my nose or something. Sometimes I feel like I can still taste it in the back of my throat. If it's too strong, I get flashbacks."

Josie tapped her nose. "That makes sense. Remember what Sandrine said? Our olfactory bulbs are right in front of our brains. Odors go directly to our limbic systems, specifically our amygdala and hippocampus."

Brian stood up, nodding. His hand kneaded at the scar again. "Yeah, I remember. Emotion and memory. We talked about it in one of my private sessions."

"Did it help?"

His palm went still. His eyebrows rose a bit, as if his own answer was surprising to him. "Yeah. Actually, it did. We used the flashback halting thing. Remember that? From Monday?"

"Yes, I do." Josie clasped her hands together, still feeling the ghostly sensation of Mettner's palm against her skin. "She used it with me but for when my colleague died."

Brian recited the exercise. "Right now, I'm feeling scared and panicked. In my body, I feel dizzy, sweaty, and a little sick because I'm remembering the fire and at the same time, it's actually December, twenty-nine years later. I'm here at the Sacred New Beginnings Retreat in Pennsylvania. I can see Josie, a bucket of logs, a sink, that countertop, and that shelf full of coffee mugs, and so I know that the fire isn't happening now."

"Wow," Josie said. "You remember the whole thing."

He gave a half-hearted smile. "It's better with a breathing exercise, but yeah. It helped."

Josie decided to ask the question she'd been wondering all along. "Do you think Sandrine is a fraud?"

Some of the color drained from his face. "Like I said, I'm really sorry about Nic. That we lied—"

Josie held up a hand to silence him. "No judgment from me, Brian. I get why you did it." In reality, his reasoning for why they had lied made little sense to her, but he didn't need to know that. "I'm just wondering whether or not you agree with Nicola. Do you think Sandrine is a fraud?"

He reached down and picked up the bucket of logs. "It's not

that I think she's a fraud. I know she went to school for this stuff. I know she's got years of experience. It's just that... I'm not sure she is who she says she is."

In the quiet, Josie could hear the wind lashing the outside of the house and the steady hum of the generator. She let a few beats of silence settle between them. When Brian offered no explanation, Josie asked, "What does that mean?"

Before Brian could answer, footsteps sounded from behind Josie. "Nic," he said.

Josie turned around to see Nicola in the doorway, strawberry-blonde hair spiked on one side from her sleeping position. She squinted at them. Immediately, annoyance sent the corners of her small mouth downward. "What are you doing? It's the middle of the night."

"Getting some more wood to load up the stove. I didn't know where it was so Josie showed me." Brian's tone sounded almost frightened. He held out the bucket of logs as if in offering.

Nicola's eyes raked over Josie, steeped in suspicion. Of what, Josie couldn't fathom. Did she think Josie was coming on to Brian?

Josie pointed to the sink. "I was just getting a glass of water before I go back to sleep."

Brian brushed past her, leaving her with a look that seemed to say, "Don't tell Nicola what we were talking about."

Josie gave him a barely perceptible nod that she understood. His shoulders sagged momentarily in relief and then he hurried off. Nicola scowled once more at Josie for good measure and disappeared after him.

Early on in the week, Nicola had barely shown any signs of life. By the middle of the week, she had become petulant and angry. Now, she was downright caustic. Given that she had lied to all of them, Sandrine included, about her reason for being at the retreat, Josie did not understand her sudden vitriol toward

Sandrine. What had Sandrine done or said to make Nicola—and Brian—believe she was hiding something? What could Sandrine possibly be hiding that would have any effect on the retreat? Her personal life and her past were no business of theirs and had no bearing on her ability to help them. She had explained the day they'd arrived that not all the techniques and skills she would present to them during the week would be useful. Processing trauma and treating complex PTSD was not a perfect science. What worked for some of them did not work for others. That didn't make Sandrine a fraud. But as Brian pointed out, it wasn't her methods he was calling into question.

I'm not sure she is who she says she is.

What did it mean? What had made them think that? Why were they bringing it up now, at the end of the week when they were stuck here?

Josie's thoughts were interrupted by a whisper fight going on in the main room. Nicola and Brian. Sighing, she decided to wait until they had settled before returning to her own sleep space.

She reached onto the shelf that held the mugs and took one down, filling it at the sink, and sipping it. The window above the sink was rimed with frost on the outside. Inside there was too much condensation for Josie to even see her own reflection. A succulent in a planter no bigger than the palm of Josie's hand sat in the center of the windowsill. Josie wondered how it survived in the winter when the main house wasn't heated. Maybe it was fake. She reached out to touch one of its plump spikes. Fake, indeed. As she took her hand away, something caught her eye. The glint of the half-light on something shiny nestled inside the fake spikes. Josie put her mug down and picked up the planter, pinching the tiny object between her thumb and forefinger.

Staring at it, she muttered, "Son of a bitch."

TWENTY-TWO

Josie looked toward the doorway to be certain no one was there. Beyond it, Nicola and Brian still spoke to one another in barely audible tones. She heard the sound of the wood-stove door opening and then closing a few seconds later. Then some rustling. Nicola and Brian turning in, finally, although their hushed voices still carried. Josie couldn't make out anything they were saying, only that they were still engaged in what sounded like a very tense argument. Focusing on the small object in the palm of her hand, Josie's mind raced.

A hidden camera.

She bounced it in her palm so that it turned over. She saw the casing for a micro SD card. That made sense. There was no way anyone was streaming via Wi-Fi on this mountain. Whoever had put the camera here was recording to the SD card. If it had been going on all week, the person would have had to change it several times and probably charge it. Who had the most access to the kitchen at times when they might not be seen swapping out the card? At the opposite end of the room, the door to Cooper's closet-turned-bedroom stood ajar. The light from the kitchen cut across the small space, revealing a cot with a pillow and blanket piled on it. Josie stopped halfway to the room.

She could not legally enter it. The room was Cooper's and even though he was not there, he had a reasonable expectation of privacy. As a law enforcement officer, she had no probable cause to request a warrant to search it—even if this was her jurisdiction. The circumstances did not meet the criteria for a warrantless search either and Cooper was not there to give her permission to search.

But why would Cooper be taping them? Was he doing it on behalf of the property owner? The camera was in the kitchen, where there was no reasonable expectation of privacy, which meant that even if some or all of them on the retreat had an issue with it being there, they would not have much legal recourse at all. Unless the camera also recorded audio. Although there was no law in Pennsylvania against installing a hidden camera on private property, it was a felony to record oral communications without the consent of all parties. There was no way to tell whether or not the camera recorded audio. Her phone didn't have a micro SD port and she had not brought her laptop.

Brian and Nicola's voices rose sharply. Nicola said, "Shut up and stay out of it."

In a sleep-tinged voice, Taryn said, "Both of you shut up! We're trying to sleep."

Josie considered the tiny camera again. It could have had a very innocent explanation. The property owner rented out the premises all year round. Perhaps the camera did not record audio and it was merely there to account for any property damage that might occur during rentals. It was, after all, in the kitchen. What scandalous things happened in the kitchen?

Beyond the darkened doorway, Josie heard footsteps. She closed her hand around the camera and picked up her mug, sipping water from it again. Elsewhere in the building, she heard a door close. A moment later came the sound of the toilet flushing and then the door opening again. The floor in the main hall creaked. More rustling and then a long sigh. Someone getting back under their covers.

Her heart ticked back down to a more normal rate. She opened her palm. Everything in her told her that there was no innocent explanation behind this camera. Though any recording it might make of activity in the kitchen would be innocuous, what if there were other cameras elsewhere in the house? The main hall wasn't of much concern. It would merely show them eating, lounging about, sometimes meditating, and now sleeping. Even the breakout rooms would not show much, assuming there was no audio component to any hidden cams on the property. In the main house, that only left one room, save Cooper's sleeping area.

Discomfort bubbled inside Josie's stomach. The bathroom. She thought of how many cases her department had caught in the last several years where someone had put a hidden camera inside a store dressing room or some public bathroom. Was it possible that someone at the retreat had installed a camera inside the bathroom? Were they dealing with a pervert? A digital Peeping Tom? Josie would not have pegged anyone there as the type, but a week wasn't long enough to make that kind of judgment. With the things she saw on the job on a daily basis, nothing would surprise her. Acid burned her gut as she remembered that Meg's stalker had planted a camera in her bathroom.

No, Josie thought. It wasn't possible. Austin Cawley could not have come onto the mountain and planted hidden cameras without being noticed by someone.

Josie tried to quell the nausea she felt at this idea as she pushed her mug toward the back of the counter and placed the tiny camera behind it where no one would see it before walking softly to the bathroom. She closed the door. Leaning against it, she did her box breathing again until her heartbeat calmed a bit. Since it was a common bathroom, there was no legal issue in her searching it. She lifted the toilet seat and the back of the tank. The only other thing in the room was a freestanding sink. No hidden camera. Relief quieted the sick feeling building inside her—for the moment. So they weren't looking at a pervert, most likely.

Josie tiptoed out of the bathroom and went down the hall, standing at the threshold of the main hall, wondering if she could access the two breakout rooms without waking anyone. She had to try. When would she have another opportunity to go into them without raising questions? The glow of the wood-burning stove gave off enough light for her to maneuver around her slumbering retreat mates. First, she went to her bedding and got her phone so she could snap photos if necessary. The door to the game room creaked as she opened it. It sounded like a scream in the night, but if anyone heard it, they gave no indication. Josie watched each person's sleeping form, snug in their blankets, for several minutes before she disappeared into the first breakout room. She just had to hope no one would notice the light from under the door.

She moved as quickly and as quietly as she could. The camera would be hidden but it would have to be in a place where it could capture what was happening inside the room. She found its miniature lens twinkling from the puck return of the air hockey table. Leaving it there, she snapped several pictures, doing her best to make it look like she was simply using her phone in case the person who had placed it there accessed its SD card and saw her poking around. Then she stood in front of it and panned the room. Given its position, whoever put it there had done so after Sandrine and Cooper moved the air hockey table. It would have captured their group sessions, more meditation, yoga, and sound baths.

Moments later, she was in the taxidermy room, conducting

another search. She found the third camera tucked beneath the wing of one of the stuffed pheasants.

"Son of a bitch."

Leaving it there, she took more photos, this time attempting to make it look like she was simply taking photos of all the stuffed animals in the room. She tried not to think about all of the private things she had shared with Sandrine in this room during the week. Things about her childhood that she had not shared in the group sessions. If the cameras had an audio component, it was even more of a violation than taking secret videos. When she finished, she went back to the kitchen. Legally, she could collect the other two cameras as evidence. However, if the killer saw that all three cameras were missing rather than just one, she couldn't predict how he or she might react. She didn't want to risk additional conflict if she could avoid it. She had to figure out what to do with the camera she had found there, especially since she had already moved it. Her mug was where she'd left it with the camera tucked safely out of sight behind it. She took a sip of the water, her mind on overdrive. Who would have placed the cameras in the main house? Were there cameras in their cabins, as well? Josie had not seen any in her own but she hadn't been looking. It would be easy enough to return to her cabin after daylight to look. She could not search the other cabins, however, not without permission from their occupants.

"Are you okay?"

Josie jumped, the water in her mug sloshing up and splashing across her chest. Luckily, her other palm had closed over the camera, holding it out of view. Alice stood in the doorway, rubbing sleep from her eyes. She picked up a towel as she crossed the room and held it out to Josie. "I'm sorry I scared you. When I woke up, you weren't there."

Josie set the mug down and took the towel, dabbing her chest with it. She managed a smile. "I came in to show Brian where the rest of the wood was stored and then I thought I'd have some water. It's easier to stay awake in here than lying in my bed."

Josie watched Alice carefully to see if her eyes darted toward the succulent on the windowsill, but they didn't. She ran through her interaction with Brian. He hadn't looked at it either. If Cooper hadn't planted the camera, Josie might discover who had by whether or not they glanced at the plant to see if the camera was still there. Then again, that would require her getting each person into the kitchen, close enough to the plant to check it. What would happen if they noticed that it wasn't there? They'd have no way of knowing that Josie took it.

"Seriously, Josie. Are you okay? You're a million miles away."

She decided not to tell Alice about the camera. At least not yet. She still had no idea what it meant or if it was even important. Why make Alice even more freaked out than she already was if the cameras had been placed in the main house at the direction of the property owner?

"I'm fine," Josie replied. "Just exhausted. Worried about all of us getting out of here safely."

Alice hugged herself. "Yeah, me too,"

"But I'm okay for now," Josie added quickly. "Thanks for checking on me. Get some sleep."

Alice nodded and padded back into the big hall.

Josie couldn't put the camera back now. What if Meg's killer had placed it there? She had no evidence that Meg's murder and the hidden cameras were connected but her gut told her they were. If it was the killer who had placed the cameras, she didn't want them to access the SD card somehow and see her finding the one in the kitchen. Plus, if the killer put it there, it was evidence. Even though she'd already touched it— not realizing what it was—she still had to treat it like evidence, just in case it was connected to Meg's murder. It took several

minutes of careful rifling through the kitchen drawers and cabinets as silently as possible to find a small sandwich bag to
deposit the camera into. It wasn't ideal but nothing about her
present circumstances was ideal. Once the bag was sealed, she
found a pen and wrote down where and when she had found it.
She tucked it into the pocket of her pajama pants and took
photos of the fake succulent. Turning off the kitchen light, she
padded back to her sleep area in the main room. As quietly as
she could, she unzipped her suitcase and pushed the bag deep
inside one of the inner pockets.

She spent the hours until dawn watching everyone else
sleep and wondering if it had been one of them who'd planted
the camera and if so, why?

TWENTY-THREE

After taking nearly an hour to get out of the parking lot, Noah took several more to travel the three treacherous miles to the small house that Deputy Ehrbar had described as belonging to Cooper Riggs. The snow was so thick and coming down so fast and hard that he got stuck several times. He had to use his shovel and salt after all. He kept his phone plugged into the car charger but got no service. By the time Riggs's small, one-story house came into view, it was the middle of the night. Noah's headlights swept over its blue siding as he pulled into the driveway. There were faint tire tracks, already full of new snow, leading from the road to a Dodge truck. The house had a small square of a front yard and two sheds next to it. He was relieved to see light glowing from the windows at the front of the house.

He parked his SUV behind the truck and pushed through the snow to get to the front stoop. He rapped against the door several times, getting no answer. If Cooper Riggs was inside, he was probably asleep. Noah was considering his options when the door finally swung open. A man with a shiny shaved head and a thick, dark beard stared at him, one bushy eyebrow raised.

"Help you?"

"Cooper Riggs?" asked Noah.

The man looked behind Noah. "Who're you?"

"Noah Fraley. I'm looking for my wife," said Noah. "She's up at Hunter Shaw's property. The Sacred New Beginnings Retreat. Josie Quinn."

Recognition flickered in the man's eyes. "Oh yeah, of course. The retreat. Sorry. I just got up. Fell asleep on the couch."

Noah felt the wind at his back like a slap. Snow swirled around his face. "Why aren't you with them?"

"With them?"

"On the mountain," said Noah. "At the retreat."

Riggs opened the door wide enough to fit his hand through, gesturing behind Noah. "Can't get up there in this, not the way it's coming down so hard and fast. Gotta wait it out. Once the snow stops, I was going to try to get up there. I've got a snowmobile out in one of the sheds. I was gonna try to get back up there on that."

"You were already down here when this started?" Noah asked.

"Yeah." The man stroked his beard. Noah noticed he was wearing faded blue jeans, a flannel shirt, and a pair of boots. Fully dressed in the middle of the night. Riggs continued, "They sent me down to get some supplies but by the time I was ready to go back up, the snow was bad. I couldn't go back up even if I wanted to."

Noah felt a flush creep up his neck to his scalp. "So you just left them all up there?"

Cooper frowned. "I didn't want to. Believe me. But look outside, my friend. This is a bona fide blizzard. Did you, uh, did you try to get up there?"

Snow blew against Noah's back again, some of it sliding down the nape of his neck and into his coat. "I went to the parking lot but I couldn't get up there. Not on foot."

"You went to the parking lot?"

"Well, yeah. It was on the way. I'm sorry to have knocked on your door so late but I got stuck a half dozen times."

Stroking his beard again, Cooper looked past Noah toward the road. "I told you, the snow is bad. We just have to wait for it to stop. Then we can head over there together. Say, where are you headed from here?"

Noah sighed and brushed snow from his hair. "I don't know. My only option is to go back to Laporte for the night, but I'd just as soon sleep in my car right in your driveway knowing how long it will take to get there. If you don't mind. I just need to get to my wife as soon as possible. I'm not leaving Sullivan County without her."

Cooper opened the door wider, revealing a small living room with one sagging couch, dated orange carpeting and a television tuned to WYEP coverage of the storm. "Don't be ridiculous. There's no need for you to sleep in your car. I've got a perfectly good couch right here. Grab a few hours of shut-eye and as soon as it stops coming down, we'll head over to the parking lot together and get everyone down from the mountain."

Warmth enveloped him as he crossed the threshold. He hadn't realized just how tired he was until this moment when Cooper's couch was in sight. He hadn't slept the night before and he'd been fighting snow all day to get to Josie.

"Thanks," he said. "You think the snowmobile will work? There's going to be over two feet of snow by the time this is finished," Noah said.

"Only one way to find out," Cooper said. "We gotta try, right? I could sure use your help with it. Getting it up on the truck and such. Then I can follow you over to the parking lot and we'll head up to the retreat."

"Yeah, sure," said Noah.

The chyron on the bottom of the television screen read:

Several Counties Crippled by Blizzard. The sound was on low, but Noah could hear WYEP reporter Dallas Jones's voice reading off information about power outages, road closures, and the locations of accidents as he stood in front of the Sonestown Country Inn, snow whirling all around him. Noah had passed through Sonestown what felt like an eternity ago.

Cooper pointed to the couch. "Sit, sit. I'll see if I can find you a pillow and blanket."

"Wait," said Noah. "Do you have a landline I can use?"

Stroking his beard again, Cooper shook his head. "No. Sorry, my friend. It's out. Can't get cell service?"

Noah shook his head. He took a step toward the couch but turned back to study Cooper.

Something tickled at the back of his mind, something down deep under the layers of exhaustion and soreness. But what was it? There was no threat here. None that he could see.

"You worried about your lady?" Cooper asked.

When Noah didn't answer, he said, "Don't be. She'll be fine till we get up there. Wait here. Make yourself comfortable. I'll get you that blanket and pillow we talked about."

With that, he disappeared deeper into the tiny house. Noah listened to his footsteps as they carried down a hallway. A doorway near the back of the house revealed kitchen tiles. Quietly, Noah walked into the room. The only light came from over the sink, but it was enough for him to make out the shadow of a table and chairs and the shape of a phone hanging on the wall nearby. He could still hear Cooper rustling around in one of the rooms down the hall. He picked up the receiver and pressed it to his ear.

Dead air.

Why did he think Cooper had lied about the landline being out?

This was crazy. He needed sleep. There was nothing he

could do for Josie at this moment except get some rest so he was ready to go as soon as the roads were passable again.

Cooper's shadow filled the doorway. Noah felt a prickle along the back of his neck. His hand went to where his service pistol normally rested on his waist, but it wasn't there. His off-duty pistol was in his boot, but suddenly seemed miles away. For a split second, his breath stopped. Then the overhead light snapped on and Cooper smiled. "You found the kitchen. Bathroom's down the hall, by the way. I put your stuff on the couch. You hungry? Help yourself to anything here. There's microwave meals in the freezer. I can heat you up one right now."

Air whooshed back into his lungs. He was starving but he was more exhausted than anything. He walked past Cooper into the living room where, as promised, a blanket and pillow waited. "No thanks. Not right now. I think I'll just get some sleep."

"Sure thing."

TWENTY-FOUR

SACRED NEW BEGINNINGS RETREAT,
SULLIVAN COUNTY

Day 7

Breakfast began in silence. Even Sandrine did not bother trying to get them to talk about their feelings. Josie was grateful there was still coffee left and enough power from the generator to brew it. Near the end of the meal, Taryn suggested that they have necessary discussions about what they should do next. The task of assessing their supplies had fallen to Brian, who hadn't found anything in the main house that might help him siphon fuel from the other generators. He estimated that the fuel in the generator serving the main house would only last them another twelve hours. By nightfall, they would be without power. At the rate they were consuming wood to heat the main house, that would likely last until the next morning. The same went for the food. There was enough to feed all of them through breakfast the next morning. But then they would be without food, heat, or power.

"What do we do?" asked Alice when Brian finished his litany of bad news.

"We have to try to stretch the food longer," Josie said.

Taryn raised a hand. "I have some food in my cabin. I brought some snacks in case I didn't like the food." Blushing, she looked at Sandrine. "I didn't know you'd be such a good cook."

Sandrine smiled at her. "I'm not offended, Taryn. There was certainly no restriction on food. It's lovely of you to offer it to the rest of us."

With a sigh, Alice said, "I've got a few protein bars in my cabin. I can add those to the store."

Nicola cleared her throat, drawing everyone's attention. No one but Brian had spoken to her since their big lie had been revealed the evening before. She kept her eyes on the remnants of scrambled eggs on her plate. "It's very nice of you both to offer to share your food. Brian and I have some chips and pretzels we could add."

Brian nodded his agreement.

Josie finished her coffee. "I've got candy bars."

Sandrine clapped her hands together. Her hopeful smile was back. "This is wonderful. I'm so happy to see all of you coming together to help the group."

Taryn pushed her empty plate away. "Josie is right, though. We all need to eat less so we can stretch out the food longer."

Alice leaned over and looked into Josie's empty mug. Then she pushed her own half-filled cup toward Josie. "That's food settled. There's nothing we can do about the generator fuel, but what about wood? There's an axe in the rage room. We could use it to chop more wood."

"You're talking about taking trees down," Taryn said. "That's more work than you think."

"We brought up the log-splitter from the shed," Alice pointed out.

Josie thought about turning down the rest of Alice's coffee but already knew Alice would never take it back. She drank it.

"Yeah, but have you ever tried to chop down a tree?" Taryn

asked. "It's not as simple as you think. My parents loved outdoor stuff. Not just hiking and camping. They used to take me off the grid. We did stuff like that. I'm telling you, chopping down trees in these conditions is probably a last resort. What we should do is scavenge the other cabins for stuff to burn."

"That's a good idea," said Brian. "Each one has a wooden dresser. They'd be easy enough for two people to carry."

Taryn smiled, enjoying the rapid problem-solving. "Then we use the axe from the rage room to chop up the dressers."

"What about here? In the main house?" Josie asked. "Shouldn't we use whatever we can do without here first? There are coffee and end tables in the breakout rooms we could easily chop up and burn. The cornhole games are made of wood."

"Yes," Alice said, bumping her shoulder against Josie's. "Great idea."

Josie didn't want to get into an argument about why she wanted to keep Meg's cabin sealed off so she said, "Once we've used up everything we can find in here, then we start with the dressers. We don't need them all at once. We should start with one—the dresser in the cabin closest, and then as they're needed, we can work our way up. It will be less effort that way."

She was relieved that everyone agreed with her. They'd have to go through three cabins before they reached Meg's. Josie hoped they would be rescued by then.

Sandrine offered, "When we go to get the axe, we could also gather what we can from the rage room that can be burned. All of that stuff is already in pieces."

Josie saw an opportunity to check the shed to make sure Meg's body was undisturbed. She knew no one had snuck out overnight but there was still a bear wandering around outside. "I can do that."

"I'll help you," Alice offered.

Sandrine stood up and began taking their empty plates,

holding them in a pile in the crook of her elbow like a waitress. "We just have to get by until rescue comes. Someone somewhere is already working on it. The snow has stopped, so hopefully they'll be able to get to us soon."

Nicola waved toward the windows. Thick clouds hung low in the sky but the snow wasn't coming down any longer. "Have any of you even looked outside? We're not going to be able to do any of that stuff unless we move some of this snow. Are there any shovels?"

Brian stood up and stretched his arms over his head. "We have two that Sandrine brought up from the shed. We can take shifts."

Taryn leapt to her feet. "I want to be in Sandrine's group."

Nicola scoffed. "This isn't elementary school, Taryn. We're not picking teams for gym class. I know you're in love with Queen Sandrine and everything, but she is really not all she's cracked up to be."

Alice sprang to her feet and pointed an accusing finger at Nicola. "What is your problem?"

Pink circles appeared high on Nicola's delicate cheeks. "A woman died yesterday, Alice! On her watch. Or were you too busy playing survivor with everyone else to remember?"

Alice put a hand to her chest, fingers splayed. "Playing? You think we're playing? You're the one who lied to get here so you could 'play' trauma mom."

Josie heard Taryn gasp. Brian, staring down at the top of his wife's head, flinched. Sandrine opened her mouth to intervene but Alice was on a roll. "The only person here who has forgotten about Meg is you! You're so concerned with Sandrine being a fraud all of a sudden that you don't even care about anything else. Where is this even coming from? It's not Sandrine's fault that Meg died!"

Nicola's eyes narrowed. Her voice was low and taut, a

razor's edge. "How do you know that Sandrine had nothing to do with Meg's death? How can you be so damn sure?"

Taryn said, "What are you talking about? Meg died of hypothermia."

Nicola was firmly focused on Alice. "How can we know that?"

Josie watched a flush creep from Sandrine's neck to her hairline. Whether it was anger or embarrassment, she couldn't tell. Maybe both. What she knew for sure was that she could not let this go on any longer. Matching Nicola's tone, Josie said, "That's enough, Nicola."

All heads turned toward her.

Taryn opened her mouth to speak again but Nicola leaned forward, elbows on the table, and glared at Josie. "What did you just say to me?"

Calmly, Josie said, "You heard me. We don't have time for this. There are two feet of snow outside and it's going to take us the better part of the day to shovel the paths. Whatever beef you've got with Sandrine, it has to wait. Also, stop abusing Taryn. She hasn't done anything."

There was a moment of silence. Only the wind could be heard outside, still whistling through the trees. From her periphery, Josie noted Brian's mouth hanging open, Taryn's saucer-wide eyes, and Alice's smirk.

"How dare you talk to me like that?" Nicola demanded, slamming her palm on the table. Coffee sloshed out of her untouched mug.

"Hey!" Josie shouted. Everyone reared back. Sandrine bobbled the dishes tucked into her arm before regaining control of them. Even Alice took a tiny step away from Josie. Of every person on the retreat, Josie was the calmest, the most even-tempered, the least likely to cry. All because her body thought that her high-alert state and her rest and healing state were the same thing. Everyone seemed shocked to hear her raise her voice. She stood up and reached over, taking Nicola's mug. "Don't waste perfectly good coffee!"

She felt their eyes on her as she slugged down the contents of Nicola's mug in several long gulps. Before she finished, she heard Alice laugh. A few seconds later, Taryn joined in.

A muscle in Nicola's jaw twitched. "This isn't funny!"

Alice stood up as well and started clearing silverware and cups. "Oh, shut up."

Josie finished the coffee and eyed Nicola, issuing a silent challenge. The color in Nicola's cheeks went from rosy to cardinal red. Her lips pressed into a thin line. Josie noticed her fingers trembling on the tabletop. Before she could say or do anything, Brian leaned over and put a hand on her forearm. "Come on, Nic. Let's just go."

"Don't touch me." Nicola ripped her arm from his grip and pushed her chair back abruptly. Glowering at Josie a final time, she walked away from the table. Brian followed her into one of the breakout rooms again. From behind the door came more muffled arguing.

Josie turned to Taryn. "Same groups as yesterday."

The smile on her face died. "I don't want to be in their group. I'm not pouting, I promise. I just don't like her. There, I've said it. She lied to all of us! And she thinks Sandrine is a fraud! She's mean!"

"Oh, Taryn." Using her free hand, Sandrine squeezed her shoulder. "I know this is difficult. You can go with Josie and Alice. I can handle those two."

"No!" Taryn cried. "I don't want you to go with them." She pointed at Josie and Alice. "One of these two—"

Alice cut her off. "I'm with Josie. Period. I don't want to be around them either. Josie and I will shovel from here to the shed while Brian and Nicola take the upper part of the slope. Then we'll get what we can from the rage room to burn. I don't care what either of you does."

Sandrine made a hushing sound. "This is silly. We've only got two shovels. We don't even need to be in teams or groups. Taryn and I can just rotate. Doesn't matter whether it's going up the slope or down. Now, Taryn, help me with these dishes."

Placated, Taryn followed Sandrine into the kitchen. Alice nudged Josie again, whispering, "I hope we get rescued today because I don't know if I can take one more hour with Liar McLiarPants. Well done, by the way."

"Thanks," Josie muttered. It wasn't lost on her that Nicola had all but accused Sandrine of murdering Meg. But why? Did Nicola somehow know that Meg had been murdered, or was she just theorizing? If she truly thought Meg was the victim of a homicide, what made her think Sandrine had anything to do with it?

As Josie helped clean up the breakfast mess, her mind kept returning to what Brian had said to her about Sandrine.

I'm not sure she is who she says she is.

TWENTY-FIVE

The snow was easily two feet deep. They had to shovel their way down the steps of the main house and make their own trail. They split up and began shoveling. Brian and Nicola worked their way up the mountain, creating a path to each of the cabins. Josie and Alice worked their way down toward the trail, making their way to the red outbuilding so they could get what they needed from the rage room. As promised, Sandrine and Taryn rotated, taking their turns on both sides so that everyone had a rest.

Even with the shorter area to cover, it took hours for Josie, Alice, and a third person—usually Sandrine—to dig all the way down to the rage room building. Whenever she wasn't shoveling, Josie took out her phone to check and see if she had any service.

"What are you doing?" asked Alice when they were almost to the bottom and Sandrine was shoveling.

"Somewhere between the main house and where we made the calls yesterday, there was another spot where I was able to get service. I'm trying to find it again."

"To do what?" asked Alice.

"To check on how much longer it's going to take to get off this mountain," Josie said.

It was mid-afternoon by the time they reached the rage room. From its doors, Josie could see that the shed where they'd left Meg was undisturbed. Inside the rage room they searched for anything that could be burned for heat. They worked as fast as they could, picking up any wooden objects or fragments and making piles outside. They were all sweaty from shoveling but their perspiration would dry soon, and they'd be even colder than when they started. Once they had two piles, Sandrine and Alice carried them up to the main house. Josie knew she had been left behind to gather more but she took the opportunity to check her phone again.

Near the rear of the building, she got a bar. Notifications began to pop up. Texts from Gretchen. They hadn't gotten in touch with Noah, but they had gotten in touch with the county sheriff's office. Resources in the county were stretched thin and they hadn't yet figured out how they were going to get up the mountain with over two feet of snow along the partially blocked trail, but everyone was working as quickly as they could to rescue them. However, since Josie had reported a homicide, the state police would be called in to investigate. Gretchen was already in touch with State Police Detective Heather Loughlin to take point, and she would get in touch with Sullivan County authorities to coordinate. But, Gretchen warned, it could still take time. Relief spread through Josie's body as she read the texts.

The last one read:

You hanging in there?

She tried to call Gretchen, but it dropped after only a couple of rings. Two more attempts also failed.

She glanced out the door to see Sandrine and Alice making

their way back to the building. Bringing up the text messages again, she wrote:

> *Still here. Need to get off this mountain ASAP. Supplies will run out in 24 hours.*

She hit send. A moment later, a reply came back, causing her to whoop out loud.

> *Anything I can do?*

Without thinking, Josie tapped back:

> *Can you or Heather run these names for me? I need a better idea of what I'm dealing with in case we don't get out of here soon. Also the deceased had a stalker/kidnapper. He was out on bail in Texas and fled. Can you check him out, too. See if there is any word?*

She gave Gretchen the name of Meg's stalker and then listed the names of everyone on the retreat, including Cooper, Alice, and even Meg. She gave their approximate ages and where they'd said they were from.

> *On it*

Josie typed back:

> *Also, is there any way you can get in touch with the caretaker or property owner to find out if he intentionally hid cameras on the property?*

> *Will try*

The caretaker had a SAT phone with him when he left on Thursday. Has anyone heard from him or tried to call the phone?

Will look into this, too.

"Taking an unauthorized break, I see," Alice joked as she came through the door.

Josie held up the phone. "I got in touch with my colleague. They're doing everything they can to get to us."

Sandrine came in behind Alice, smiling broadly for the first time in hours. "That's wonderful news."

The three of them gathered what little was left in the rage-room area. It wasn't much. Still, Josie tried to delay their trek back to the main house as long as possible, hoping that Gretchen would get back to her with something. It would take a while for her to run the names Josie had given her but the phone call to the property owner or Cooper should not take very long at all.

Alice picked up a large, splintered board that had once been part of a credenza. She held it in one hand and used her other hand to knead at her lower back. "I hate to sound old, but my back is killing me. All that shoveling was worse than working a twelve in the ER!"

Josie said, "You should take a break. If you want to walk back up to the main house, I can finish up here."

Alice gave her a meaningful look. "I'm not leaving you alone, Josie."

"I'll stay," Sandrine said. "I don't think there's much more here to gather. I can help Josie finish while you rest your back for a bit."

Alice waited until Josie gave her a subtle nod before picking up the small pile of wooden fragments they'd gathered and heading back to the main house. While Sandrine picked through the room, Josie turned away from her and checked her phone again. No service. She returned to the place she'd been standing earlier and within seconds two bars appeared, but no text notifications popped up. She thought about trying to call Noah but knew the call probably wouldn't go through and if it did, she didn't want to talk to him for the first time since their rift in front of Sandrine—or anyone. She pulled up his cell phone number in her contacts to send him a text but stopped. She still didn't know how to start or what to say. Every time her fingertips neared the tiny keyboard, her mind fixed on the look of disappointment on his face when she told him she couldn't give him a child.

"Is there an update?" asked Sandrine.

Josie quickly sent the screen back to lock mode and slid her phone into her pocket. "No. Not yet." She walked over to the door and looked outside. High above them, Nicola and Brian were still shoveling paths to the last of the cabins. Josie was alone with Sandrine, and this was a good opportunity to stall for more time until Gretchen could get back to her with something. Once they returned to the main house, there would be few reasons that Josie could reasonably give to keep coming down here so she could check her messages. She could say she was checking on the progress of rescue efforts, but how many times could she do that before arousing the suspicion of the others? "Sandrine, I had an odd conversation with Brian last night. About you."

Sandrine sighed. "I'm not even sure I want to know. He will go along with whatever Nicola tells him to do. I don't know why but she clearly believes I'm a fraud."

"I'm not sure that's it," Josie said. "I don't think it's your methods or your education they're calling into question."

"What then?"

Josie licked her lips. "They seem to think that you're not who you say you are."

Sandrine laughed. "Who else would I be? All my credentials are listed on my website. What do they want? Letters from my colleagues? I don't know what they're grasping at or why, but it's absurd."

"I understand," Josie said.

"Things with them were fine all week. A bit strained, maybe. They were difficult in their sessions. Didn't want to open up. Both of them brimming with anger and grief. But they weren't accusing me of being someone I'm not. Maybe Meg's death just sent them spiraling. More trauma on top of trauma for everyone. I was trying to stay calm, to try to guide you all through this as best I could while we're all still here, but maybe I seemed too composed to them." Sandrine kicked aside a few pieces of shattered ceramics. "Maybe they think that I truly didn't have any trauma." A frustrated groan came from deep in her diaphragm. She looked like she wanted to pick up one of the rage-room bats and start smashing things. Josie watched her take a few cleansing breaths before continuing, "You know how trauma changes you. How different would you have been if you'd grown up with your true family, Josie?"

Josie had shared her life story with Sandrine in their second individual session. Every last, ugly, horrifying detail. They'd spoken at length that week about her childhood, but Sandrine hadn't asked this question before. It was the kind of maddening what-if that Josie turned over in her mind regularly. Every time she spoke to or saw her biological family: twin sister, little brother, mother, and father.

When she was three weeks old, one of the women from her parents' cleaning service had set their family home on fire. That woman, Lila Jensen, had taken Josie and fled to Denton. Authorities investigating the fire believed tiny Josie had perished. Her family had a funeral for her and mourned her from that day forward. They had no idea that Lila had used infant Josie to get back together with her former boyfriend, Eli

Matson. Back then there were no mail-in paternity tests. When Lila showed up on his doorstep almost a year after they broke up and told him that Josie was his, he hadn't asked questions. Instead, he'd loved Josie fiercely and unconditionally—and later, Lila murdered him for it.

Josie touched the scar that ran from her right ear down along the side of her face to under her chin.

"You wouldn't have that," Sandrine pointed out. "Although that scar is nothing compared to what that woman put you through as a child."

"Yes," Josie choked. "You're right."

Lila had been physically and emotionally abusive. In fact, she seemed to revel in finding new and creative ways to make young Josie suffer. It wasn't until Eli's mother—the only grandmother Josie had ever known—Lisette Matson, had wrested custody of Josie away from Lila when Josie was fourteen that Josie knew any peace or normality. Lisette had been a force to be reckoned with, and God help anyone who got in the way of her protecting Josie. She hadn't been able to use brute force to keep Josie away from Lila, so she'd used her wits. For as kind, generous, and tender as she was, Lisette was just as tough and cunning. Capable of a ruthlessness born of the purest love, Lisette had shown Josie the very meaning of grit and grace.

"I wouldn't have known my grandmother, though," Josie said with a smile.

"She made you who you are today," Sandrine agreed. "Every bit as much as Lila did with her abuse. You know, my mother was a lot like yours—like Lila, I mean, not your biological mother. She didn't leave me with physical scars. Well, not directly, but she left me with many, many emotional scars and yes, it shaped me."

"What are you saying?" asked Josie.

"Brian and Nicola are right in one sense. I'm not the person I was as a child, or even as a young woman. The things that happened to me changed me, irrevocably. In some ways, for the worse. But I have devoted my life to making up for it; to helping others heal from similar things. It took a long time and a lot of work to become who I am right now, standing before you. But I am just me." Something flickered in her eyes and her gaze briefly turned upward, to her left side. Without meeting Josie's eyes, she added, "I'm Dr. Sandrine Morrow."

Josie's phone buzzed in her pocket. She took it out and saw that she had notifications. Sucking in a deep breath, she opened her text messages. Gretchen again.

No one can get in touch with the caretaker. Not answering his phone. No luck with the SAT phone either. But I made contact with Sheriff Shaw. He says he's never used cameras of any kind up there or on any of his properties. Josie, just what the hell is going on?

Quickly, Josie sent Gretchen a photo of the camera she had found in the kitchen.

I found three in the common areas. There could be others. If Shaw didn't okay these, that means someone here planted them.

Shit. Still working on those names. Watch your back until we can get to you.

TWENTY-SIX

Outside, Josie could see Taryn and Nicola now shoveling a path to the last cabin. She and Sandrine picked their way along the path the two of them and Alice had shoveled earlier. Their feet slipped and slid on the thin layer of snow remaining. Sandrine hooked her hand inside the crook of Josie's elbow again and let Josie pull her along. Between transporting Meg's body yesterday and all the shoveling so far today, Josie's upper back and shoulders screamed in protest but she didn't object, instead trying to use the short walk from the rage room to the main house to gather any information she could, now that she was pretty positive that whoever had killed Meg had planted the cameras.

"Sandrine, how well do you know Cooper?"

"Oh, not at all, really. When I rented the place, I was told that he manages this property all year round. He lives in the area. I only met him a few hours before you all did. When I booked these cabins, the property owner told me when and where to meet him and said he'd take care of anything I needed, and he did."

Except that he'd left them all stranded on the mountain as soon as the weather got bad.

"Did you and he talk much this week?" Josie asked.

"A little. He was always around, on the periphery, helping to keep everything running smoothly. He asked me about some of the stuff we were doing. Meditation. Yoga. He wanted to know what that had to do with 'head stuff.' I tried to explain the mind–body connection but I'm not sure he got it."

"Did he ever make you feel uncomfortable?" Josie continued. "Or say or do anything you found inappropriate, no matter how small?"

Sandrine stopped in her tracks, forcing Josie to pause as well. "Why are you asking me these things, Josie?"

Josie was not prepared to tell Sandrine about the cameras, but the more she considered it, the more it made sense that Cooper might be the one who had planted all the cameras in the main house. That was where he spent most of his time. It would have been easy for him to place them around and then discreetly change the SD cards. No one would have noticed. But again, she wondered, if he was behind the cameras, what was he trying to capture? A bunch of people doing a sun salutation? Two people sitting on chairs talking for an hour? Sandrine cooking healthy meals while Taryn picked her brain about trauma-based treatments? Even if the cameras had an audio component and he had illegally taped conversations without anyone's permission, what was he hoping to hear? A half dozen horror stories about the depth of human depravity? Tales of how bad luck spared no one? Did he have a perverse fixation with other people's pain?

"Cooper didn't come back," Josie answered. "I can't help but wonder if there's more to it than just the weather."

Sandrine looked toward the main house, only about ten yards away now. "I'm sure there's not, Josie. Cooper never made me uncomfortable or said or did anything inappropriate. I felt very comfortable with him. If I didn't, I would not have allowed him to stay. He could very well have left our supplies here for the week and let us handle everything."

The wind whipped around them, stinging Josie's face. When she licked her lips, her mouth felt dry. "Did Meg ever complain to you about Cooper?"

Extricating her arm from Josie's, Sandrine put her hands on her hips. "What are you talking about?"

Josie saw no harm in relating what Alice had seen during the week so she told Sandrine how Cooper and Meg had been spotted behind her cabin on at least three occasions, deep in conversation. How Cooper had squeezed the back of her neck and Meg had pulled away. Frowning, Sandrine said, "How strange. You have no idea what they were discussing?"

Josie shook her head. The cold was creeping into her toes and the tips of her fingers now. She was relieved to see a column of smoke rising from the chimney of the main house. She couldn't wait to warm herself by the wood burning stove. "It could have been innocent, but I was wondering if Meg ever came to you with concerns about Cooper."

Sandrine turned and glanced to the top of the slope where Nicola sat on the steps of the last cabin watching Taryn shovel. "It wasn't Cooper that Meg was concerned about."

"What do you mean?"

Sighing, Sandrine faced Josie again. "I shouldn't say."

"Is it something Meg confided to you in a private session?"

"Oh no. I just..." Sandrine paused. Her gaze was drawn to the last cabin again. Taryn was still shoveling with enthusiasm. She'd removed her hat, and her long dark hair whipped all around her.

"Taryn," Josie said. "Meg had concerns about Taryn?"

"Please don't repeat this, Josie. I shouldn't even tell you as I don't think it has any merit, but Meg thought that Taryn was unnaturally fixated on me. She thought that—that Taryn was exhibiting the same types of behaviors as a stalker."

The admission took something out of Sandrine. Her shoulders slumped. Josie reached out and linked arms with her once more. She thought about the way Meg had been increasingly on high alert around Taryn as the week went on. Taryn, who insisted on always sitting beside Sandrine; who asked Sandrine endless questions like a star pupil. Taryn even dressed similarly to Sandrine.

"What do you think?" asked Josie.

"I don't know what to think," Sandrine admitted. "It's true that Taryn is very attached to me. I didn't tell this to Meg, but she has come to at least three talks I've given in the last year in different locations."

"And you let her come on this retreat?" Josie said.

"She has never crossed any lines, Josie. I think she sees me more as a maternal figure. You remember what she said in group sessions, don't you? How her mother was cruel to her? So she sees me as a mentor. I don't believe there's more to it than that. She just needs help, the same as everyone else."

"So you don't consider her a stalker."

"No."

Josie watched as Taryn walked over to where Nicola sat and started gesticulating wildly toward the path. Reluctantly, Nicola heaved herself to her feet and took over the shoveling. "But Meg thought she did."

"Yes," Sandrine said. "But Meg was still so shell-shocked from her ordeal. With this guy still out there, she had not even begun to process all that had happened to her. She was on guard at all times. You remember the group sessions, don't you?"

Josie felt a stab of pain in her heart recalling the way Meg had felt so stupid for not seeing the escalation in Cawley's behaviors; how guilty she felt for not being more diligent about reporting him when his behaviors were more benign. "I should have gone to the police when he wouldn't stop texting me multiple times a day," she had said, "and showing up where I was working or eating dinner or going to yoga class, but I didn't want to make a big deal out of things. He really wasn't doing anything wrong at that point. He just made me super uncomfortable."

"Sandrine, I asked you yesterday if Meg had had any problems with anyone on this retreat and you said no."

"I said 'no, not really,'" Sandrine clarified. "Besides, Meg didn't have trouble with Taryn. She only thought that I did. There wasn't any conflict between them directly. I'm sure that Meg would have told me."

Before Josie could press Sandrine further, Alice appeared on the porch of the main house. "Come in and get warm," she called.

Josie looked back up the trail the others had dug from the main house to each cabin. Nicola and Brian had disappeared. Taryn had moved back down the path and now stood in the doorway of her own cabin. "I'll be right there," Josie said. "I want to check something in my cabin."

"I'll come with you," Alice offered.

Josie smiled. "No, you stay here with Sandrine."

"Josie," Alice said, a warning note in her voice.

"It's okay," Josie told her. "You'll be able to watch for me from here."

TWENTY-SEVEN

Noah woke to a stiff back and the smell of bacon and eggs. The starchy white pillowcase scratched at his cheek. He opened his eyes to see that the television was still tuned to WYEP. They were still running coverage of the storm only now Dallas Jones stood in front of the state police barracks between Laporte and Dushore in full daylight. The bottom right-hand side of the screen showed the time. It was well into the afternoon.

Swearing, he sat up and fished around the floor for his boots. He slid his feet into them and secured his pistol. From the kitchen he heard the clink of pots and pans. Ignoring his bladder, he strode in there to find Cooper at the stove. He still wore the same clothes he'd had on the night before. "Hey," Noah said. "The day is halfway over. We're going to lose daylight soon. What's going on? Why didn't you wake me?"

Using a spatula to push scrambled eggs around in a pan, Cooper turned to him, smiling. "Sorry, friend. I overslept myself. I'm just making us something to eat and then we'll get right out there. I'm anxious to get back there, too, you know. Those people are counting on me."

He moved the spatula to a second pan in which bacon sizzled. Noah's stomach grumbled loudly.

Cooper said, "Go on and clean up. This'll be ready in a few minutes."

Noah tried to tamp down his anger. What could he say? Cooper had been kind enough to let him crash and was now feeding him. He still had time to rescue Josie. A peek out the window showed several inches of snow piled on top of his SUV but at least it had stopped coming down. He took his overnight bag with his phone to the bathroom. He tried to get a signal but couldn't. In spite of his having let the phone charge through the night, it was only at twelve percent.

"What the hell?" he muttered.

Had the outlet he'd plugged it into not worked?

There wasn't time to worry about it now. He brushed his teeth and changed his clothes. Back in the kitchen, Cooper had two plates in hand, ready to serve very late breakfast. Noah sat down and accepted his meal with a muttered thanks. Cooper sat across from him. In the light of day, Noah had a better look at the room. The table was Formica and chrome, probably worth a small fortune these days, with matching vinyl chairs for four. A small tabletop organizer held napkins and salt and pepper. The kitchen tile and cabinets were easily twenty years old if not more. The fridge was more modern. Several papers and a few photos adorned it, pinned by magnets. Most of the photos were of a little girl with brown pigtails. She aged over the course of the pictures, starting out as a grinning, chubby-faced toddler, hands held up, covered in what looked like paint. In what appeared to be the most recent photo, she looked to be about Harris's age, maybe a bit older, eight or nine years old. She stood next to an older man in his late sixties, early seventies. He had thick gray hair and bright blue eyes. She leaned into his side, thin arms wrapped around his waist. His hand rested on her back. The two of them grinned at the camera.

"My sister," Cooper said, following Noah's gaze. "When she was little. That's my dad with her. Years ago. He passed on right after that was taken."

"I'm sorry to hear that," said Noah. He shoveled some eggs into his mouth. He just wanted to eat and get on the road. Get to Josie.

Cooper sighed. "Thanks. I just realized I have no photos of myself with Dad. I guess I should update them or maybe take them down. I mean, my sister's in college now. You probably think I'm a weirdo, right? Want something to drink?" He opened the fridge and listed the beverages inside.

"Water's great. Thanks," said Noah. He picked up a piece of bacon, trying to think of what he should say. He'd been rude earlier when he woke up. He didn't want to alienate Cooper. "When's the last time you saw your sister?"

"Not since last year. Now that she's a hotshot at college, she doesn't visit much."

Noah chewed his bacon and looked at the photo of the girl and her father again. There was something off, something wrong, but he couldn't put his finger on it.

"You have kids?" asked Cooper.

He tore his eyes from the photo. "No. We, uh, no. We don't."

A sound came from somewhere deep in the house. A cross between a moan and a creak. The house standing its ground against the wind outside, which was still gusting pretty hard. Cooper seemed not to hear it, or if he did, it was of no concern. He asked, "You don't want kids?"

Noah really didn't want to discuss the issue of children with a complete stranger. "I, uh, I don't know. What about you? You have kids?"

"Nah. I wanted to. Met the right lady but then it didn't work out."

Cooper pushed his chair back, the legs screeching against

the floor. He walked over to the counter, dumping more eggs onto his untouched plate. "Women. Hard to please, am I right?"

Noah glanced at the photo of Cooper's father and sister, and it was then he realized what bothered him. Though he couldn't see the girl's entire shirt because she was turned toward the man, he could see a part of the graphic on the front of it. He recognized the outfit of a character from one of Harris's favorite movies. Harris had made Noah and Josie watch it at least a hundred times.

It had come out the year before.

Which meant that the girl in the photo couldn't possibly have been wearing it when she was Harris's age, 'years ago.' Which also meant that Cooper Riggs was lying about something.

The house groaned against the onslaught of wind again. A draft of cold air slid down the back of Noah's neck.

Cooper turned and leaned against the counter. He scratched at his forehead. "Sure seems like this place is going to fall down, doesn't it? Wind's pretty bad. You think I should be worried?"

Noah stood up to search for the source of the cold air. From beneath his flannel shirt, Cooper pulled a pistol and pointed it directly at Noah's face. His tone changed, going cold and flat. "Do exactly what I say or I will shoot you in the face."

Noah put his hands up. His mind raced. From where he stood, he could tell that the safety on Cooper's gun was off. His finger rested on the trigger. Just four or five pounds of pressure would put a bullet into Noah's brain. "I don't want any trouble," he said. "I just want to find my wife. That's all."

"I don't give a shit about your wife." With his free hand, Cooper gestured toward Noah's feet. "I know you're armed. Take out your gun, set it on the floor and kick it over to me."

Noah knelt slowly, calculating. There was no way he could

draw on Cooper without getting killed before he got his pistol halfway out of the holster.

"Hurry up," Cooper said.

"What do you want?" Noah asked.

"Your gun! Your gun! Come on, hand it over or I will blow your damn brains out."

Noah did what he said. He gave up his off-duty weapon. Then his phone. At gunpoint, he walked to the locked door at the other end of the kitchen. As instructed, he unlocked and opened it. There was a set of wooden steps that vanished into darkness below. Cooper pushed him from behind and he tumbled down them. The wind was knocked out of him when he hit the floor. Then came the most terrifying seconds of his life as he registered Cooper moving down the steps after him. Noah wanted to close his eyes. He didn't want to see the barrel of the gun before Cooper pulled the trigger, but he couldn't get his body to do anything he told it. For what felt like an eternity, he watched Cooper approaching, willing the oxygen to come back into his lungs. It wouldn't.

In his mind, he was already saying the words he couldn't force his body to speak. *I'm sorry, Josie. I'm so sorry.*

TWENTY-EIGHT

Josie trudged up the snowy path, calves burning. She passed Sandrine's cabin, then Brian and Nicola's. Their door was open. Josie caught a glimpse of Brian moving the dresser across the floor as she went past. Taryn's cabin was next. Her door was slightly ajar but Josie saw her moving around inside. Next came Meg's cabin. Josie looked down the slope to make sure no one was watching and then she jogged up the steps and tested the door to make sure it was still locked. When the door didn't budge, a wave of relief washed over her body, warming her momentarily against the freezing temperatures and the cutting wind. She moved on to her own cabin.

She hadn't actually left any of her things inside but now that she knew the property owner wasn't behind the hidden cameras in the main house, she wondered if whoever had put them there had also put them inside the cabins. A sick feeling sloshed in her stomach as she closed the door behind her. It was just as she had left it. Now looking at it, stripped of her personal possessions, there weren't many places one could hide a camera. Still, Josie checked every corner and crevice. She was happy to find nothing. She exited, passing Meg's locked cabin and heading back down the slope. A new thought struck her. Just because there was no hidden camera in her cabin didn't mean that whoever was responsible for them hadn't put them in other cabins. What if Cooper was behind the cameras? He had access to all the cabins. None of them would have found it odd to see him hanging around their cabins.

The problem was that Josie could not legally search any of the cabins occupied by others, not without their permission.

But she could do a plain view search if she was invited inside.

Taryn's door was still cracked. Josie climbed the steps and knocked softly on the door. "Come in!" called Taryn.

She didn't have any of the apprehension or hypervigilance the rest of them had. Josie envied that, but she was also happy for Taryn that she still felt a sense of safety and security in the world.

"Oh hey." Taryn smiled. Her face was flushed. She was likely still sweaty from hours of shoveling snow. She'd taken off her hat, scarf, and gloves and left them on top of the dresser. She was bent over a collection of tote bags centered in the room, rifling through one of them.

Josie scanned the tiny room while Taryn was not looking, again searching for any cameras. Save Taryn's bags, the cabin was identical to Josie's. No cameras in the main room.

"You okay?" asked Taryn.

While she was still occupied with her bag, Josie edged around her, trying to get a glimpse into the bathroom. "Yeah," Josie said. "You?"

From what she could see, there were no cameras in Taryn's cabin.

"Under the circumstances, I guess."

Josie turned away from the bathroom and saw that Taryn was fishing granola bars and packs of trail mix from each bag and consolidating them into a single tote bag. The other bags were filled with clothes, toiletries and what looked like a three-ring binder.

Taryn paused, a small pack of dehydrated cranberries in her hand. "It's a lot for one person, isn't it?"

Josie didn't answer.

"I didn't even eat any of it this week. It just made me feel better to have it. When I was a little girl, my parents would take me mountain-biking or hiking. My mom would bring food but never enough for me."

Josie tried not to visibly flinch. She'd heard some of the stories about Taryn's mother in their group sessions. They mostly revolved around neglect and intentional deprivation. Josie's own fake mother, Lila Jensen, had also routinely starved her by locking her in a closet for days at a time. Josie thought about sharing her own experience, but it was still something she didn't like to talk about. She'd had a difficult time talking to Sandrine about it earlier in the week. Instead, she asked the question she'd been itching to ask all week. "What did your father have to say about her starving you?"

Taryn rubbed the hollow of her throat with her index finger. "He always said I should listen to my mother."

"I'm sorry," said Josie.

She gave a half-shrug and bent again to search the bags for more food. "The truth? I wasn't his."

"What do you mean?"

"My mom adopted me when I was a baby, when she was married to someone else. Then that guy died, and my mom remarried a couple of years later—to the guy I considered my dad. But he wasn't there for me, only her. He didn't care what she did to me. I still don't understand why she wanted me in the first place. To have someone to be shitty to, I guess."

Josie thought of all the horrifying things she'd seen as a law enforcement officer. "Some people are just sick, Taryn. The important thing to remember is that it wasn't your fault. Nothing that she did to you was your fault."

Taryn looked up from the bags and smiled. Her eyes were glassy with unshed tears. "Thanks for saying that. Also, thank you for defending me to Nicola today. That meant a lot."

Josie moved closer as Taryn dug into the bag with the three-ring binder in it. A closer look revealed the words *Dr. Sandrine Morrow* written in Sharpie along its spine. "Sure," said Josie. As Taryn reached into the bottom of the bag, upending the binder even more, Josie noticed colored tabs sticking out from its pages. She couldn't read the handwriting.

Coming up empty-handed, Taryn noticed Josie staring at it. "It looks weird, but it's really not."

Josie lifted her hands in the air, as if in surrender. "I didn't say anything."

Taryn lifted the binder out of the bag as if it was an infant and held it against her chest. "I made this with all my notes from seminars I took and things I learned here because I like Sandrine's teachings, okay?"

It was an odd turn of phrase to use but Josie let it go. "Whatever helps, Taryn. I'm not here to judge."

One of her hands crept from the edge of the binder to her throat and scratched. "Really? Because it seems like everyone else is here to judge me. Except Sandrine."

"You're talking about Nicola," said Josie.

Taryn looked down at the binder. "Not just her. Meg, too. I made the mistake of, uh, leaving this out where she could see it and she freaked out."

That was what had set Meg off, leading her to believe that Taryn was stalking Sandrine. Josie was sure that the way Taryn then hung on Sandrine's every word did not help matters.

"When did you show it to Meg?" asked Josie.

"We hung out at night, after everyone turned in. She got scared at nighttime, even though we've got locks on the cabins. I told her she could come hang out with me here. The first few nights everything was fine. Then on Tuesday we were here and she wanted a snack so I told her to just look in the bags."

The cold was seeping into Josie's bones now that she wasn't moving. She shifted her feet from side to side in an effort to get her blood moving. "She saw your binder?"

Taryn's eyes darkened. "She said I was sick. That I had a 'sick fixation' with Sandrine. She said a lot of ugly things, so I did, too. We had a fight. It wasn't the same after that."

Meg had gone missing Thursday night, two days after that. "She didn't come back here again?"

Taryn looked toward the door, still hanging half open. "After she did the sound bath on Thursday, I tried to make up with her. I asked her to come over after dark and let me explain."

A chill swept across the nape of Josie's neck. "Did she?"

Taryn shook her head. "No. She said she might but then she didn't." Her nostrils flared. "She never even gave me a chance to explain, to be friends again."

"You didn't see her that night at all after you left the main house?" Josie asked.

But Taryn's face twisted into an angry mass of lines. She wasn't listening to Josie anymore. She scratched again at her throat, angrily this time, drawing blood. "Meg *judged* me. She acted like a friend and then she saw one thing and she judged me. I know everyone thinks I'm pathetic, but I'm not."

"I don't think that," Josie told her. At the beginning of the week, Taryn had told the group that she was okay with physical contact. Josie reached over and squeezed her shoulder. "Taryn, I don't think you're pathetic."

Something inside her seemed to shift. She blinked and the anger diminished. "You didn't want to be my friend this week. You're always with Alice."

Josie again felt the cold brush of apprehension along the

back of her neck. "Alice works in an emergency room. I'm a police officer. We have a lot in common, that's all."

Before Taryn could respond, the sound of shouting came from outside. Josie ran out onto the small porch but there was no one in view. A moment later, she heard more shouting. She couldn't make out the words, but she could tell they were coming from next door—Brian and Nicola's cabin.

TWENTY-NINE

As Josie approached their cabin, jogging up the steps to the open door, she could hear their voices, loud and angry. They stood in the center of the main room, facing off. Brian said, "Just give it up. We're not going to get what we want. She's a closed book."

Nicola shot back, "Of course we're not. I'm the only one trying here!"

"This was a total waste of time," Brian complained. "I'm sick of this shit. I just want off this mountain."

Josie was standing in the doorway when Brian turned from the middle of the room to storm out. He pulled up short when he saw her, face turning ashen.

Josie looked back and forth between the two of them. "Everything okay in here?"

He opened his mouth to speak but nothing came out. Nicola walked up behind him, her arms crossed over her chest, eyes like deadly lasers. "What do you want?"

Josie looked up and down the path. Taryn was coming out of her cabin, now wearing her hat, scarf, and gloves, a tote bag over her shoulder. Josie said, "I heard you two shouting. I just wanted to make sure you were both safe. Can I come in?"

Brian stepped out of Josie's way to admit her while Nicola said, "It's none of your business what we were shouting about."

With the three of them inside, the space felt claustrophobic but while she was here, she might as well look for any evidence of a hidden camera. She quickly scanned the area behind Nicola for any evidence of one but saw nothing.

Nicola said, "Are you even listening to me?"

Josie gave her best conciliatory smile. She had Nicola as alone as she would ever get her here in this freezing cabin. Josie was still curious about what had made Nicola and Brian believe that Sandrine was a fraud, but she wasn't going to get any information out of them while Nicola was trying to cut her down with a deadly look. "I just wanted to apologize for before, for forcing the issue about your... sister, and then for being insensitive to you earlier at breakfast. It wasn't my intention to publicly embarrass you or Brian. Everyone is on edge, myself included. I just wanted to say that whether it happened to your daughter or your sister, it's a horrific tragedy and I'm very sorry for your loss."

Josie could sense Brian staring at his wife. Quietly, he said, "Nic."

Nicola's expression softened. "Thank you."

"Yeah," Brian muttered. "We appreciate that."

Josie turned toward him, taking the opportunity to do a visual search of that side of the cabin. Nothing that looked like a camera. While they had a few bags tucked away beside the dresser, the place was otherwise empty. "Can I ask you something, Nicola?"

With a sigh, Nicola said, "I guess."

What Josie really wanted to know was what they had been talking about when she walked up to the cabin. Who was a closed book? What did they want? Nicola had already made it clear that it was none of her business, so she asked, "Why do you think that Sandrine is... what is it that you said at breakfast? 'Not all she's cracked up to be'? Did something happen between the two of you or did she do something that made you feel this way?"

In the silence that followed her question, Josie heard the crunch of snow under boots outside. Was Taryn eavesdropping? Or waiting for them to come up? Or had Alice or Sandrine come looking for them?

Nicola folded her arms across her thin chest. "Why do you care?"

Josie tried to think of an answer that might persuade Nicola to confide in her. "Because we all spent a lot of money to be here this week and someone died here. If there's something you know that the rest of us don't, I think you should share it."

From her periphery, she saw Brian's gloved hand close over his wrist. His coat covered the burn scar but he still rubbed it. Nicola's teeth worked her bottom lip. She glanced at Brian for a beat and then said, "I don't know anything that the rest of you don't. I just think... I think maybe Sandrine is hiding something."

She was lying. Making it up as she went along. But Josie couldn't force her to tell the truth. "Hiding something like what?"

Nicola's gaze drifted toward Brian again, but he had no answer for her. While a silent conversation went on between them, Josie heard more footsteps from outside. She was certain there was more than one person now.

When it became apparent that Nicola wasn't going to respond, Josie said, "How about this? Did you feel this way about her when you signed up for the retreat?"

"No," Nicola said instantly.

Brian added, "We wouldn't have come if we thought she was a fraud."

Josie shifted her feet again, trying to stimulate the circulation in her frozen legs. "Then something happened to make you feel that way while you were here. What was it?"

More silence. More footsteps from outside. Brian and Nicola were so focused on one another and coming up with an answer for Josie, they didn't notice. After a moment, Nicola blurted, "Meg."

Brian said, "What?"

Nicola forged ahead. "Meg. She let Meg come on this retreat when her trauma isn't even really over."

Josie kept her tone even and non-accusatory. "Nicola, you lied about your own trauma to get onto this retreat."

"That's not the same thing. What happened to me—to my sister—that was ages ago. Meg's trauma is ongoing. I mean, she was on the run from her stalker! How do you process everything he did when you know you're not even safe from him?"

Josie said, "I don't think that's how it works, Nicola. From everything I've been told by psychologists, it's never too soon to start getting help after you've experienced something traumatic."

"But she put the rest of us in danger!" Nicola said, her voice higher-pitched now. "Meg's stalker is still out there! He could have followed her here. Sandrine never even took that into account. We're talking about a guy who was so sick, he took secret photos of Meg and then he kidnapped her and her sister! Her sister died because of him, and Sandrine knew he was still out there somewhere and thought it was a good idea to allow Meg to come anyway. I mean, I know that's not what happened to her, but there's no saying it couldn't have happened."

Josie flexed her fingers, trying to urge feeling into them again. Her gloves felt like they were made of ice. Whatever warmth they'd provided initially disappeared hours ago. "You're saying that you think Sandrine is hiding something, or that she is a fraud because she allowed Meg to come here while her stalker is still on the loose?"

"It's pretty messed up," Brian agreed. "I mean, you take money from all these people with complex PTSD to come on a retreat where you promised to help them, and the entire time, you know they're not really safe. Isn't that the worst thing you could do to people like us? Most of us have experienced violence."

"But this didn't bother you all week until Meg died?" Josie asked.

Brian rubbed at his wrist again. "It didn't occur to us until Meg died, no."

Nicola waved one of her arms in the air for emphasis. "Because we felt like we were in this safe bubble until Meg died, and then it made us look at our situation. Sure, Meg froze to death, but she was never really safe. None of us were. Any one of us could freeze to death up here. There's a bear out there wandering around! Any one of us could get mauled. Now we're stuck here and could starve to death! Sandrine knew there were all these dangers, and she just didn't care. She doesn't know what she's doing! No sane person would bring us all here knowing how much could go wrong!"

Brian nodded. "This was a money-grab, pure and simple. She's not interested in our trauma or helping us. She doesn't know anything about trauma. She's playing trauma guru like it's some kind of reality show."

Before Josie could say anything more, the door to the cabin banged open and Sandrine flew in. Alice and Taryn crowded in behind her, watching with wide eyes as Sandrine pushed past Josie, eyes ablaze, and pointed her finger at Brian, only inches from his face. "That's it. I'm sick of this. How dare you call into question my qualifications? The two of you lied to me and everyone else here the entire week! How dare you treat me like this? I've done nothing but try to help you. I've been transparent! I—"

Nicola stepped forward. "No, you haven't."

The wooden floor beneath them quivered as Sandrine stomped her foot in time with her words. "Yes. I. Have! What more do you want from me?"

Silence filled the tiny room. The wind blew a fresh squall of snow through the partially opened door. Taryn closed it and put her back against it.

Brian said, "I just don't think a person who really understood trauma would put us all at risk the way you have this week. That's the difference between someone who has only learned about it in textbooks and someone who learned about it first-hand."

A muscle quivered in Sandrine's jaw as she glared at him. "I do know about trauma first-hand."

Nicola's fingers reached for her wedding band but her gloves stopped her from twisting it. "You haven't told us anything about yourself."

Sandrine threw her arms in the air. Her cheeks flamed red. "Good God, we're back to that again. I haven't told you anything about myself because I am not the focus of this retreat. This isn't about me, and as your guide on this retreat, it should never be about me, but fine! You want to know something about me? Here we go. You want trauma? You want my trauma? When I was a child, I was repeatedly assaulted. Different occasions, different men. It went on for years. It was devastating, physically and emotionally. It was nothing short of torture."

"Oh my God," Taryn gasped. She shifted the tote bag on her shoulder and lifted a hand to touch Sandrine but then decided better of it.

Josie was starting to feel warm with all of them crowded into the small space. Sensation returned to her toes and fingers.

She watched as Brian's gaze dropped to the floor. He tried to back away from Sandrine but there was no room.

"Oh, Sandrine," Alice choked. "I'm so sorry."

Josie said, "Me too. I'm sorry you went through that, and I'm sorry that you felt like you had to tell us when you shouldn't have had to do so."

"Oh shut up," Nicola snapped. "Both of you. What are you even talking about, Sandrine? You lived a golden life. I mean, look at you! The picture of success."

Josie thought about the conversation she and Sandrine had had in the rage room. How traumatic experiences changed you, irrevocably. What had it cost Sandrine to become so successful in spite of her trauma?

Sandrine shook her head. Tears gleamed in her eyes. Her posture sagged. "Lots of successful people have endured horrific things. I had to fight to be here."

"Puh," Nicola scoffed. "I don't believe that."

Alice pushed her way past Sandrine to get closer to Nicola. "Seriously, what is your problem? Sandrine doesn't have to prove anything to anyone. Especially not to a liar. You know what? You're seriously unhinged."

Nicola pointed at Sandrine. "I'm unhinged because I want to hear her story? She's heard all of our stories. Every sordid detail. Why is it so unreasonable that I want to know hers?"

Alice shot Nicola a disbelieving look. "You are out of your mind."

Sandrine remained calm. With one arm, she barred Alice from getting any closer to Nicola. With the other, she raised her palm. "It's okay. Fine. You want my personal horror story? Here it is. My mother was drunk and neglectful and when she wasn't those two things, she found a way to use me for her benefit."

"Your mother?" Brian said. "No way."

Everyone looked at him. "What?" he said. "I'm just saying what kind of mother would do that?"

"Lots of mothers do," Josie mumbled. "You'd be horrified if you knew how many truly terrible mothers there are out there."

"Yes," Taryn said softly from the door. "Look at mine."

Nicola glared at her. "Don't make this about you."

"Leave Taryn alone," Sandrine warned. "It's true that there are a lot of horrible mothers out there, whether you choose to believe it or not. My mother was one of the worst. Now, I'm going to tell you something and I'm only going to say it once and then we're finished talking about this forever."

No one spoke or moved.

"My mother was an actress in the sixties, seventies, and for a bit in the eighties. She was only eighteen when she got pregnant with me. She never told me who my real father was, but she seduced a fairly successful producer and got him to marry her. When I came along, he thought he was my father. For several years, everything was fine. But then my mother started having an affair. The producer found out and he left her. He didn't believe that I was his anymore. He discarded us like we were trash. My mother had to get back out there and get work. Times were different back then. The whole 'casting couch' idea was a very real thing. Not all the time, but sometimes. When she worked, I was left alone on set to wander around. Some things happened during those times, and other times, bad things happened because she made them happen."

"No," Brian said. "She wouldn't."

"She did. There were executives who were willing to give her parts if she let them do what they wanted to me. I was rather young when it started and one of them was so... vigorous... that I was left with permanent injuries that prevented me from ever having children."

"Oh God," Alice gasped.

"No!" Taryn cried. "Sandrine, that's just horrific."

"She was a monster," Sandrine continued. "Life with her was absolute chaos. When she wasn't plotting how I could best help her get ahead, she left me with 'friends' for months at a time. I was never sure if she'd come back or not but she always did. I never knew where she went or why. I just knew that having her back was always the worst thing that could happen to me."

Brian rubbed vigorously at his wrist. "I don't believe this."

"Me either," Nicola said.

Sandrine gave a harsh laugh. "Of course you don't! If I told you there's snow outside, you wouldn't believe me because I said it. But guess what? I don't care what you believe anymore."

"I'm so sorry that happened to you," Taryn said. "If you don't mind me asking, who was your mother?"

"It doesn't matter," said Sandrine. "She died a long time ago. Now, if you'll excuse me, I'm finished with this conversation. I'm going back to the main house. I can sleep in one of the breakout rooms. We needn't speak to one another again for the rest of the time we're together unless absolutely necessary."

Sandrine turned and shuffled out the door. Taryn followed. Alice linked arms with Josie and looked at Brian and Nicola, her lips curled in disgust. "We're going with them."

THIRTY

The sound of duct tape tearing sent Noah's body weak with relief. The air still hadn't fully returned to his lungs, but he was lucid enough to know that if Cooper was tearing duct tape, it meant he wasn't holding a pistol. It was dark in the basement. The other man was just an inky shadow looming over him. Hands fumbled across Noah's body and flipped him onto his stomach. He was still as useless as a landed fish. As much as he willed his limbs to move, his brain and every automatic process in his body was focused on one singular task: getting oxygen. His arms and legs didn't work.

Cooper wrenched his hands behind his back and started looping his wrists with duct tape. Then he began taping his ankles. As Noah's senses returned, he smelled mildew. The concrete floor was cold under his cheek. He tried to set aside his panic long enough to slow his breathing.

"Heh—hey," he tried, but his voice came out barely audible.

Cooper kept wrapping duct tape round and round Noah's ankles.

"Hey," Noah said, voice stronger now. "Let's talk about this."

Cooper grunted and dropped Noah's bound ankles onto the floor. Noah didn't even want to think about how difficult it would be to free himself. He started immediately testing the give in his wrists. Then he felt a hard edge against the back of his skull. It had to be the barrel of the pistol. "Don't even try it," Cooper told him.

Noah went still. He couldn't see the man. Even if he'd been face up, it was too dark for him to see Cooper's face, to gauge his mood or intention. "I'm not going to try to get away," Noah lied. "Or to hurt you. Just tell me what you want. I can help you."

"You're only saying that to save your own hide."

"Well, yeah," Noah conceded. "I'm telling you that you don't have to kill me. I will help you." When Cooper didn't respond, he said, "You helped me last night. Gave me a place to crash. Hell, you even cooked for me. I owe you."

The pressure of the barrel against the back of his skull disappeared. He closed his eyes, sending up a prayer of thanks to anyone who would listen. "Don't twist things," Cooper said. "I'm only going to let you live for as long as you're useful to me."

Noah heard the stairs creak. Cooper walking back upstairs. "Wait!" he called. "Wait!"

The door slammed, plunging him into a darkness so complete, it confused his senses. A feeling of disorientation washed over him. For a moment, it felt like he was floating through endless space. Then he tried to wiggle his wrists and ankles and it brought him right back into his body. Inventorying his aches and pains, he was relieved to find that he hadn't sustained any serious injuries in his fall down the steps.

With nothing else to do, he wondered how long was he going to be useful to Cooper, and how?

THIRTY-ONE

With the group fractured, Josie hoped they'd all be too distracted to give much thought to her stealing away to the rage room again in order to check her phone. Everyone seemed shell-shocked by Sandrine's revelations. Nicola and Brian had wanted so badly to know about Sandrine's traumatic past, but now that they did, their suspicion and anger toward her had given way to shame. A rift opened up in the group. Without conscious thought, Josie chose Sandrine and Alice over the others. Taryn was in their group simply because she clung to Sandrine. Josie helped Sandrine, Alice, and Taryn carry each one of their mattresses from their cabins to the main house. They dragged them all into the taxidermied-animal breakout room while Brian and Nicola retrieved their mattress as well, lugging it into the game room.

When Josie went back to the main room, she could hear Nicola and Brian whisper-arguing behind the door to what was now their room. It was growing dark. Josie didn't want to be out at night if she could help it. With everyone otherwise occupied, she put her coat, hat, and gloves back on and made her way down to the rage-room building. Inside, there was even less light than before. Using her phone's flashlight app to maneuver around the items left scattered across the floor, she found the spot where she'd been able to get service earlier and held her phone out in front of her.

Nothing happened.

She waved the phone around, holding it high over her head, hoping for a signal. As the cold in the drafty room set into her bones, the phone finally buzzed. Josie almost wept with relief. Text messages from Gretchen began to populate rapidly, one after the other. Josie held the phone over her head and scrolled through them.

Loughlin ran those names. Sandrine Morrow, Alice Vargas, and Meg Cleary checked out just fine. No priors. Vargas had a couple of arrests for possession and soliciting from twenty years ago, but charges were always dropped.

Gretchen listed their addresses and ages which lined up with things that Sandrine, Alice and Meg had said during the week.

The Sullivan County Sheriff vouched for Cooper Riggs, even though no one has been able to reach him at his home or via the SAT phone.

Loughlin should still check him out.

She's already on it. She also checked out Cleary's stalker. He hasn't been seen since he was released on bond. Loughlin talked to the local PD in Maryland where Meg was living. They did some investigating. A few days ago, Meg's apartment was broken into—this according to someone else in the building who was walking by and saw her doorknob was busted. Landlord can't tell what, if anything, is missing but it looks ransacked. We asked them if they'd pulled fingerprints or DNA but they said not for a break-in where the resident was not present and it was unclear whether anything was taken.

Josie was certain that the break-in meant that Meg's stalker had been on her trail. Had he made it up here? Had he been able to track Meg to this retreat, in spite of its remote location? Before Josie could run through all the possibilities, the phone buzzed again and again with additional texts.

Sullivan County Sheriff has been given all the information about this guy. So far, they haven't had any sightings but they're not really looking as they're still dealing with the fallout from the snow. Lots of accidents and people stuck. Back to the names. Here's where it gets weird. Brian Davies, Nicola Davies, and Taryn Pederson do not exist. At least not at the ages and locations you gave me. Loughlin contacted Sandrine's home office. Talked to her assistant. Got the intake information for everyone on the retreat. The info those three gave on intake doesn't check out.

Josie's heart fluttered.

What do you mean?

While she waited for a reply, she walked to the door to see if anyone had followed her. Up the trail, she saw Nicola emerge from the main house. At the bottom of the steps, she turned up the slope, eventually going inside the cabin assigned to her and Brian.

Relieved, Josie went back to the spot where she was getting service again and waited a few more minutes. Gretchen replied:

Their addresses were not real addresses. Also, we found no one with those names that match the ages you gave us. We found 147 Brian Davieses in the country. Only 4 in their forties. All of them were contacted. They are accounted for. Not on retreat. Same process and result for Nicola and Taryn. All Nicola Davies in their thirties have been accounted for as well as all Taryn Pedersons in the same age range. None are on your retreat.

Brian, Nicola, Taryn.

All of them lied on their intake paperwork. It could not be a coincidence that three people going to the same retreat lied about their identities, which meant that they were connected. It also meant they had known one another before they came to the retreat. They came together. But for what purpose?

Josie thought back to whether or not there had been any familiarity among them. Brian and Nicola were married so their connection was no surprise. They didn't seem particularly close but not all married couples had the same level of intimacy as others. They did possess the kind of low-level annoyance with one another that Josie often witnessed between long-married couples whose dynamic was less caring and more critical. Not every marriage was the same. Also, you couldn't live with someone and spend almost all of your time with them without getting annoyed by something. As much as Josie loved Noah, there were always small things that drove her crazy about him, like the way he flipped television channels without ever choosing something to watch, or how he always left only a few drops of half-and-half in the carton instead of just throwing it away and purchasing a new one. As devoted and caring as he was toward Josie, he couldn't stand the way she always forgot that she had a load of wash in the dryer. "The dryer is never empty!" he always complained to her.

What about Taryn? There hadn't appeared to be any famil-

iarity at all between her and the couple. In fact, there had been
tension between Taryn and Nicola. Then again, in the last day,
there had been tension between Nicola and everyone. But
Taryn had seemed just as surprised as everyone else that Nicola
and Brian had lied about their reason for being there. Unless it
was all an act.

Why had they come at all? What was their purpose?

Josie thought about what she had overheard between
Nicola and Brian earlier.

Brian said, "Just give it up. We're not going to get what we
want. She's a closed book."

Nicola shot back, "Of course we're not. I'm the only one
trying, here!"

"This was a total waste of time," Brian complained. "I'm
sick of this shit. I just want off this mountain."

They wanted information. Given the way that Nicola had
been going after Sandrine since Meg's death, they had to be
seeking it from her. This theory put Taryn's binder about
Sandrine into a new light. Maybe she hadn't been stalking her
as Meg had thought but instead compiling information. Yet,
Taryn had never seemed interested in Sandrine's personal life,
only in her methods. What did it mean? What kind of information would warrant the three of them lying about their
identities?

Who were they really?

"Wait," Josie muttered to herself.

They hadn't given their real names or their correct
addresses, but Josie was certain that their stories were real. She
recalled the way Brian's eyes went glassy and unfocused sometimes when he remembered the fire at his group home as well as
the way he rubbed at his burn scar whenever he was under
stress. Taryn hoarded food. Nicola had admitted to lying about
her own reasons for being there, but Josie was sure that she told
the truth about her sister being abducted and killed. The detail

about the perpetrator being the driver of an ice cream truck did not seem made up.

Why were they lying about some things but telling the truth about others?

Outside, something crunched over snow. Josie crept to the door and looked out but saw nothing. Then a familiar huff sent a lightning bolt of fear through her body.

THIRTY-TWO

Josie froze in place when the bear loped around the side of the building, maneuvering through two feet of snow with far more grace and finesse than any human she had ever known. It paused when it reached the path they'd carved so they could move among the camp buildings. Its snout lifted, scenting the air. Above, Sandrine stepped out of the main house. Without looking around, she made her way down the steps. Before Josie could call out to her and warn her about the bear, she disappeared into her cabin. If the bear noticed her, it gave no indication.

Josie watched as it scented the air once more and then lumbered off toward the trees, a massive dark splotch against the snow. She wasn't going anywhere just yet. She wanted to give the bear time to get far from the camp. Closing the door firmly, she hurried back to the spot where she best got service and tapped in a response to Gretchen.

> *Not sure what's going on. These people might not be who they claim to be but I think their stories are real. Can you or*

Heather try to track them down? Check news articles? Reports from local PDs?

She was typing in the rest when Gretchen came back with:

Tell me what you know.

Josie's freezing fingers flew across the screen. She racked her brain for every detail of what each one of them had said during the week. Brian and the group home fire. Nicola's sister and her abduction by the ice cream truck driver. Josie had no idea what type of accident had killed Taryn's parents, but she did know that Taryn's husband had died in a tragic boating accident involving a rogue whale. Again, it was the sort of specific detail that Josie doubted had been made up. She gave her best guesses at the time frames and locations of each of their stories.

A few minutes later, Gretchen responded.

We'll see what we can dig up. Again, watch your back.

Josie wanted to get back to the main house but she couldn't resist asking.

Have you heard from Noah?

Still working on getting in touch with him. Chief is going to drive up there in the morning. He'll find Noah. Then all he'll have to do is be himself and emergency services will have you off that mountain in no time at all.

In spite of the grim circumstances, Josie smiled at the joke. She did feel reassured that Chief Chitwood was personally inserting himself, but her gut burned with fear. Cell service was limited in the more remote places of Sullivan County, but it wasn't impossible to find. Why wasn't Noah in touch with the rest of the team? Or trying to get in touch with her? Had something happened to him? Her hands trembled at the thought. Suddenly, the argument they'd had seemed inconsequential.

Aren't you disappointed?

Yes. Of course she was. Why had she expected him to feel any differently? They were in this together. They faced and endured everything together. He'd been by her side for years now, even before they became romantically involved. He had never wavered in his feelings for her. Why had she thought that this one thing would change that? After he'd gone to such great lengths to reassure her that it wouldn't? Why hadn't she believed him? He was the one who'd wanted to talk things out after they got the news. She had shut him down. That's what she did. When things got too difficult emotionally, when they hit too close to the torn and tender parts of her that had been wounded in childhood, she shut down. Better to close off every avenue that might lead to pain than to face her fear, which had been imprinted upon her by Lila Jensen, that she wasn't good enough. That she wasn't lovable. Not really. Because what kind of person didn't inspire love in her own mother?

But Lila wasn't her mother. That had been a massive lie.

And yet, the wounds Lila had inflicted were permanent and irrevocable. It didn't matter that Josie now knew, decades after the fact, that Lila wasn't her mother—that her real mother had been out there somewhere pining for her all along. Josie had believed that Lila was her mother and Lila had tortured her. It was a cut so deep that it had never healed. Not even with the love and devotion of her grandmother or her first husband. She'd lost them both and still blamed herself. She blamed herself for Mettner's death, too. If she was a better person, stronger, faster, smarter, more worthy—the kind of person whose own mother could love her—they'd all still be alive.

She was old enough and wise enough now to understand

that, factually, that wasn't how things worked. She'd been an innocent child stolen away from the people who loved her. Lila's behavior toward her was not a reflection on Josie, but on Lila herself. Josie's worth was not the determining factor in anything, really. People hurt people. She couldn't stop that. No one could. She couldn't stop a cold-blooded killer from taking Mettner away from them. She couldn't stop Ray or Lisette from coming after her in her time of need and then being killed. They'd loved her. Like Noah. Obviously, he still loved her enough to come after her in blizzard conditions. No disappointment, no matter how big, was going to stop him from coming for her, from wanting her unconditionally.

"I'm so dumb," she mumbled to herself.

Tears stung her eyes. Quickly, she brought up his name in her contacts, making sure she got his cell number. She tried to call him. The first time, the call didn't go through. The second time, it rang twice before dropping. The third time it rang until the voicemail picked up. The sound of his voice almost brought her to her knees. She swallowed over the lump in her throat just as the beep sounded. "Noah," she said, voice coming out higher than she intended. She tried again. "Noah, it's me. I'm sorry. I'm sorry I didn't talk it out with you. I should have given you a chance. I love you. I hope you're okay. Please come as soon as you can. I—"

The call died before she could go on.

She considered trying again but she needed to get back to the main house. Outside, darkness was closing in. She hadn't brought a lantern with her. Her thoughts turned from Noah to her current situation. She was stuck on this mountain with three people who had intentionally concealed their identities to get some sort of information out of Sandrine. If it was personal information they were after, did that mean they were the ones who had planted the cameras? Obviously, they didn't know about Pennsylvania's two-party consent law when it came to audio recordings. Then again, even residents of Pennsylvania weren't always aware of it.

What had they hoped to get out of Sandrine? What was so important that they would go to so much trouble? It clearly wasn't the horrific story of Sandrine's childhood. They'd all seemed ill-prepared for that. What, then? Whatever it was, had one of them been willing to kill to conceal their intent? Or were they all in on Meg's death? Had she seen or heard something that either one or all of them hadn't wanted her to know?

Another thought occurred to Josie. Where did Cooper fit in? Was he somehow involved? Why hadn't anyone heard from him since he left them on the mountain? Why hadn't he returned? Had Meg confided in him about whatever it was she'd seen or heard? Was that what they'd been discussing during the week? Had it gotten him killed as well? Would his body be found somewhere farther down the path to the road? Had the three liars conspired to kill him and Meg both, to hide what they were planning?

If that was the case, it meant that Josie, Sandrine, and Alice were all in danger.

"Shit."

Josie pocketed her phone and stepped outside. It was completely dark now. She followed the lights of the main house up the path. Bursting through the front door, she saw that Brian was wrapped in a blanket, ensconced in one of the chairs by the wood stove. Josie sprinted toward the breakout room that she, Sandrine, Alice, and Taryn had claimed for their own. She threw the door open, relieved to see Sandrine asleep, curled up on her mattress and, across the room, Alice sitting cross-legged on hers, scribbling in her journal.

Alice looked up at her and smiled. Her pen stilled, hovering over the page. As she studied Josie's face, her smile disappeared. "Josie, is everything okay?"

Josie looked behind her. Brian's head was visible over the

back of the chair he sat in but he was too far to hear her words. "I just wanted to check on you."

Or maybe he wasn't. He lurched upward, the legs of his chair moaning against the wooden floor. Josie's heart was in her throat. There was no way for him to know, she reminded herself. There was no way for any of them to know that she'd discovered they were lying. She watched as he crossed the room. He stopped just before he reached Josie, turning his head toward the kitchen. "Nic?" he called.

Nicola walked in from the kitchen and joined him.

Josie positioned herself across the doorway. "What's going on?"

Nicola folded her arms across her chest and glanced at Brian. He said, "We wanted to apologize to Sandrine. We were out of line. The stress of everything—Meg's death, being stuck up here, not knowing when we're getting rescued—it got to us."

Josie looked over her shoulder to see Alice standing nearby. On her mattress, Sandrine sat cross-legged, rubbing sleep from her eyes. "What's going on?" she asked.

Josie looked behind Nicola and Brian. "Where's Taryn?"

Brian said, "She was with you guys."

Alice drew up beside Josie, crowding into the doorway. "She said she was going up to her cabin."

"How long ago was that?" asked Josie.

Alice laughed. "Time doesn't exist here, remember?"

Josie looked from Nicola to Sandrine. "Was it before or after Nicola and Sandrine went up to their cabins?"

Alice glanced back at Sandrine, who was now on her feet, trudging toward them. "It was before Sandrine left."

"Wait," said Nicola. "Were you spying on us?"

"No," said Josie. "I was in the rage room, trying to get service on my phone to see if there were any updates on when we might be rescued. I saw you walk up to your cabin and then later on you, Sandrine. I didn't see Taryn. I did see the bear, though so I'm a little concerned that if Taryn walked up to her cabin, she's not back yet. She doesn't even have a lantern with her—all of them are over by the door—which means she's in the dark."

"Wait. You saw the bear?" asked Nicola. "Where?"

"Along the path," said Josie.

Nicola elbowed Brian in the ribs. "We should go check on her. Do you still have the flashlight?"

"I have it but the batteries are dead."

"We'll just have to use the lanterns." Josie walked over to the door. "I'll go with you."

"Me too," said Alice.

Brian threw his arms up in the air. "Why don't we all go, then?"

Sandrine walked out of the breakout room, pulling her sweater tight around her. "I'll stay behind. I can throw something together for dinner while you all get Taryn. I'm just glad to see you working together."

Josie considered this. Leaving Sandrine alone while the rest of them were out searching for Taryn was probably the safest bet. She would not be at the mercy of Taryn, Nicola, or Brian and neither would Josie or Alice if they stuck together. "Okay," she said. "Let's go."

THIRTY-THREE

Josie held her solar-powered lantern out in front of her, lighting the way up the path to the cabins. The moon was just a dull orb behind the clouds, barely giving off any illumination. Her boots slid against the snow. Now that it was evening, the temperature had dropped even lower, making the path icier and more treacherous. A hand clutched her upper arm, holding her upright so she didn't fall. Alice said, "I've got you."

Josie turned back and did another head count. Alice, Nicola, and Brian. Each one of them had brought their own lanterns. They didn't give off much light, but it was something. Enough to see a bear approaching, she hoped. "Stay together," she said.

"This is stupid," Brian said. He cupped his hands around his mouth and yelled, "Taryn!"

They passed Sandrine's cabin, then Nicola and Brian's before stopping at the bottom of the steps to Taryn's cabin.

From her periphery, Josie saw the lights behind her pitching back and forth. Alice said, "I'll go in with you."

"We'll watch for the bear," Brian said.

But the cabin was empty. Only Taryn's tote bags

remained. The edge of the binder about Sandrine peeked from the top of one of them. Alice didn't notice. "Where is she?"

Josie's heartbeat ticked upward, beating like the wings of a butterfly inside her chest. "I don't know." She checked the bathroom a second time. The building was empty.

Outside, Josie gave the rest of the group the news that Taryn was not inside. Nicola's lantern lurched violently. "What do we do now?"

Brian spun slowly, his long arm swinging his lantern in an arc, casting light more widely around them. Josie noticed there were no footprints in the snow around the cabin or leading from the shoveled path to the woods. Clearly, Taryn had left her cabin, but she must have stayed on the path.

"We have to keep looking," Brian said. "If she's out in the snow, she could freeze to death, like Meg."

Nicola shivered, her light shaking along with her body. "Don't say that."

Alice huddled close to Josie. "Where do we start? Where could she be?"

Josie's mind raced with possibilities. Her heartbeat approached the speed of a hummingbird's wings. She took a couple of deep breaths and pushed the thoughts invading her brain aside. Right now, she had to find Taryn. That was the main priority. There would be time for theories and fear later. She pointed up the path. "I think the most logical thing would be to check inside all of the structures first. We can start with Alice's cabin and work our way down the hill."

"Why would she be in Alice's cabin?" asked Nicola.

"I have no idea," Josie answered. "But it makes sense to check all the buildings. I will need your permission though."

"Done," said Alice.

A gust of wind smacked into them. Nicola stumbled backward into Brian's chest. Getting her balance again, she said,

"Permission? Why do you need our permission to look for Taryn?"

Josie didn't want to explain that as a law enforcement officer —even though she was off-duty and in someone else's jurisdiction—she still needed to follow procedure as much as possible. After all, she was investigating what was right now the disappearance of one of her retreat mates. If Taryn hadn't gone off of her own accord, Josie could potentially be looking at a crime. If Meg hadn't already been murdered, then she would likely not be thinking in these terms, but there had already been one homicide on the mountain. It was not a stretch to think that whoever killed Meg had also killed Taryn and hidden her body somewhere. That meant Josie had to treat the camp the same way she would as a sworn officer of the law. Legally, she could not enter any of the cabins without the permission of the people staying in them. If she did, and found Taryn's body, any evidence on it or at the scene could be called into question in a court of law, should Taryn's killer be brought to justice.

"Josie?" Brian coaxed. "We're freezing out here. Can we go?"

"No," Nicola said. "I want to know why she needs our permission."

"Courtesy," Josie said finally. "But also, keys. We need keys to everyone's cabins—in case they're locked."

Nicola put one hand on her hip. "How would Taryn get into our cabins if they're locked?"

"I don't know," Josie answered honestly. "But I still think we should check."

Brian said, "You can have our keys. I can't feel my face. Let's go."

"We don't need to search mine and Brian's cabin," Nicola said, thrusting her lantern in Josie's face. "I was just in there. She's not there."

"We should still look," Josie told her. "You were in the main house with us so there's a chance she could have gone into your cabin."

Before Nicola could argue more, Brian raised his voice to a shout. "There's a bear out here somewhere! It's not safe for us out here! Let's just go! Please!"

Alice turned toward the upper part of the path, her lantern leading the way. "Come on. Nicola, you can be difficult while we look for Taryn."

Josie expected Nicola to continue arguing, but instead, she fell into line behind Josie. It felt like an eternity before they reached Alice's cabin. The wind got worse the higher along the slope they got, as if it were purposely trying to push them back down the hill. The four of them crowded into Alice's cabin to get out of it for a few minutes. Taryn was not inside. She wasn't in Josie's cabin either. Moving back down the hill, Josie unlocked Meg's cabin and looked around, doing her best not to track snow inside. No Taryn.

As they made their way back past Taryn's cabin, Nicola said, "Why do you have Meg's key?"

"It's the extra," Josie said. "Sandrine gave it to me."

"But why you?"

Brian said, "Nic, who cares? Let's just check the other cabins."

Alice said, "After your cabin, there's only Sandrine's. We'll need her key."

They stopped at the bottom of the steps to Brian and Nicola's cabin. Brian kept walking. "I'll go ask her for it."

Josie felt some apprehension letting him be alone with Sandrine, even if it was only for a few moments. "Alice," she said. "Why don't you go with him. The two of you can warm up. Nicola can let me inside here."

Brian was already halfway to the main house. Alice held up her lantern so that Josie could see the look of hesitation on her face. Josie managed a smile for her. "It's fine," she said. "Go ahead."

Josie watched until both Brian and Alice were inside the main house. Then she turned toward Nicola. "Let's go."

She expected Nicola to protest again but instead, she tromped up the steps and unlocked the door. Pushing it open, she stood aside, ushering Josie in. Josie held the lantern up, moving it back and forth so she could see each corner of the room. There were a couple of small bags but no Taryn. Nicola stood by the door as Josie made her way into the bathroom. No sign of Taryn there either.

"She's not here," Josie said, returning to the main room.

Still in the doorway, lantern at her side now, Nicola was just a shadow. "I told you."

Josie slowly swung the lantern back and forth again as she walked toward the door. Some object on top of the dresser glimmered in the passing light. Josie stopped and walked over, holding her light closer to the scuffed wooden surface. A gold ring. Nicola's wedding band.

"Hey," Josie said, picking it up between her gloved thumb and forefinger. "You left this here."

Up close, she saw that the ring was pitted and scratched. It looked older than Josie had initially thought. She turned it in the light, noticing that there was an inscription on the inside of the band. *Till Death. Love, B.*

The words were faint, the "v" and "e" in "Love" faded. Josie saw the curve of the top of the "B" had also dulled. Nicola rushed into the room and snatched the ring out of her hand. "Give me that!"

Josie stepped back from her, almost tripping over the empty bed frame. Her lantern swung wildly as she tried to get her footing. Nicola offered no help, merely clutching the ring in her fist and watching Josie struggle.

Finally, Josie's free hand found the wall and she righted

herself. Nicola held her own lantern near her face so that Josie could see her glare. "Don't touch my ring."

A few choice expletives rested on the tip of Josie's tongue, but she held them back. "I'm not interested in your ring. I'm surprised you left it in here."

Nicola put her lantern on the dresser, yanked off her left glove and shoved the ring onto her finger. "I didn't mean to leave it."

Josie moved into the doorway, keeping her body at an angle as she stepped outside. She no longer trusted Nicola enough to turn her back. The wind whipped around her, cold stinging her exposed face. "Let's go. I want to search the other buildings."

THIRTY-FOUR

They met Alice and Brian at the steps to Sandrine's cabin. Josie and Alice searched inside while Brian and Nicola waited on the path. After that, they searched the rage room, even though Josie had been inside it when Taryn disappeared. Then Josie unlocked the shed where Meg's body lay and took a look in there.

No Taryn.

Finally, they returned to the main house. While the others warmed up, Josie searched there as well. This time, she entered Cooper's small sleep area. There was nothing inside but his cot and a small end table with a lamp on top. Josie got down on her hands and knees to look beneath the cot but found nothing.

Taryn wasn't in any of the buildings.

There were also no footprints leading away from camp.

Once everyone was sufficiently warm, Josie insisted that they go back out and look again, this time circling each structure to see if Taryn was behind or beside one of them. She was not. Finally, with the waning power left on their lanterns, they formed a line and trudged down the path they'd tamped down the day before when they found Meg and brought her back to camp.

Taryn was nowhere to be found and there were no footprints except the ones they'd made themselves.

With each moment that ticked past, the dread in the pit of Josie's stomach became more and more unsettling.

At the main house, they broke the news to Sandrine and then everyone gathered around the stove again, still in their coats, gloves, and hats. They crowded together, hands extended toward the orange glow behind the glass, stamping their feet to bring the feeling back. While they were gone, Sandrine had loaded the stove with pieces of wood they had scavenged from the rage room. Behind them, she set out plates and silverware on the table. Glasses of water stood by each place setting. A large bowl of pasta sat in the center beside a wilted salad. It seemed so strange to see something so normal in circumstances so bizarre and frightening.

They were stuck on this mountain in almost three feet of snow. One of them had been murdered and now one of them was missing. At least three people on the retreat were imposters of some sort. Josie still couldn't figure out why.

Why lie? Why go to so much trouble? What did they want? Why was one of them now missing? Had the other two done something to her? Or did they truly know nothing about her disappearance? They'd both willingly searched for Taryn, seeming concerned. How much of it was an act? They'd been putting on an act all week pretending not to know her.

"Come," called Sandrine. "Sit down and eat."

Reluctantly, they all peeled off their coats, gloves, hats and scarves and made their way to the table. As usual, Alice sat next to Josie. She stared at Josie with wide, mystified eyes. They silently asked the same question Josie's brain was trying to work out.

Where the hell was Taryn?

Sandrine sat across from Josie and Alice, beside Nicola and Brian. In the dim light, Josie could see that her eyes were red-rimmed from crying. She motioned toward the bowls. "We only had gluten-free pasta and a cream sauce and that is what's left of our fresh vegetables. There's a half-bottle of balsamic vinaigrette as well."

No one moved.

Once again, Josie knew she needed to eat but it was the last thing she felt like doing. The only sound in the building was the crackling and popping of the wood inside the stove and the wind shrieking outside. Josie would give anything to go back to the beginning of the week when they were all alive and unharmed, unaffected by this new tragedy, when the dinner conversation was lively and laughter came easily.

Sandrine folded her napkin in half. "There was no sign of her at all?"

"None," said Josie.

Alice picked up a glass of water and took a sip. It trembled in her hand, water sloshing over the rim and onto her chest. Ignoring it, she said, "Where the hell could she be?"

Nicola twisted her ring around her finger. "Maybe she left the camp. You heard how her parents were all outdoorsy. For all we know, she could survive in the wilderness for days."

"In this weather with no resources?" Josie reached over to the bowl of pasta and spooned some onto her plate even though the smell of the cream sauce turned her stomach. "I don't think so. She didn't take anything with her."

"How do you know?" asked Nicola.

Next, Josie deposited some salad onto her plate. "Because there were three tote bags in her cabin earlier when I was there. One of them is in the kitchen—she brought her food to share with us—and the other two are still in her cabin."

"But her coat and all that are gone," Nicola offered. "How

do we know she didn't take some of her food with her? Did you inventory that while you were with her?"

"No," said Josie. "I don't know if any of it is missing. What I do know is that unless Taryn has a lot of Arctic expeditions under her belt, she has no chance of surviving in this cold. She didn't leave camp."

Brian went for the pasta next. "There's no reason for her to leave camp. It's not like anything happened to make her want to leave. Maybe the bear got her."

Nicola turned to him, mouth hanging open momentarily. When he didn't acknowledge her, she slapped his shoulder. "How can you say that? How horrible!"

He rubbed at his shoulder, shooting her a dirty look. "I'm being realistic, Nic. She's not here. Josie spotted that bear twice this week and she saw it in the camp today. I know you don't want to think about it, but it's not impossible."

"There were no tracks," Alice said. "Anywhere in the camp. At all. Only the ones we made looking for her. There was also no blood. Wouldn't we have found blood if she got mauled by a bear?"

Nicola slumped with relief. "You're right. So she wasn't killed or dragged off by the bear."

Brian started to spoon pasta onto Nicola's plate, but she shoved him away, knocking the large pasta spoon out of his hand. It clattered onto the table, splattering sauce all over the wood. "What the hell?" he said.

"I'm lactose intolerant, remember?" Nicola snapped. "I'll just have salad."

Brian picked up the pasta spoon and tossed it back into the bowl. He didn't attempt to serve Nicola salad. "Whatever," he said. "If there are no footprints and no blood, then where the hell is she?"

Josie said, "She's still here."

Nicola used the salad tongs to fill her own plate. "Still here? What are you saying? She's... hiding?"

Josie doubted very much that Taryn was hiding, although she could not rule it out completely. The most likely scenario was that someone in this room had killed her and hidden her body well enough that their exhaustive search hadn't found it.

"Why the hell would she hide?" Alice said testily.

Josie could feel the fear and agitation rolling off her in waves. Under the table, she reached over and patted Alice's knee. Instead of answering either question, Josie said, "Where were all of you when Taryn walked up to her cabin?"

Brian said, "I was here. I went out back to check how much fuel was left in the generator and then I came in and sat by the stove."

Everyone looked toward Nicola. "You know where I was," she said. "I walked up to our cabin to change my clothes. Then I came back. I was in the kitchen getting a drink of water when Brian called me."

One of Alice's hands found Josie's and squeezed it tightly. "I was here, in the breakout room."

Nicola looked over at Sandrine. "What about you?"

Sandrine spooned food onto her plate. "I went to my cabin for a bit. I needed some space. Some time alone."

"In the cold?" asked Nicola.

Sandrine kept her eyes on her plate. "Yes. In the cold. I wasn't in there long because it was freezing. I came back and went to my bed to rest."

Josie said, "Did anyone actually see Taryn leave this building?"

A few beats of silence ticked by. No one answered.

"I saw her leave the breakout room," Alice said. "That was it."

More silence. They looked around at one another. Josie was

struck by how different everyone looked now than they had just two days earlier. Every one of them was pale with dark circles under their eyes. They looked tired and haggard, afraid and uncertain.

Nicola speared a cherry tomato with her fork. Its juice squirted across her plate. "Does it matter if we saw her leave? She's not here. The real issue is finding her!"

Brian added, "What are we missing here? I mean, people don't vanish into thin air."

Alice's voice shook. "No, they don't. I think we all know what really happened to Taryn but no one here wants to say it."

Under the table, Josie tightened her grip on Alice's hand. "Alice."

Brian looked up from his plate. "You think she's dead."

"No," Sandrine whispered. "No, don't say that."

Alice wrenched her hand out of Josie's and stood up, slamming both palms onto the table. Their plates jumped. Sandrine put a hand to her chest. "Alice, calm down."

"I will not! How can you all sit here like this, so calm? There is only one explanation for what happened to Taryn. She's dead!"

Josie tried to think of a way to keep the conversation from escalating, but she was exhausted, and her brain felt slow and foggy. Not only had she not gotten much rest since Sandrine woke her to say Meg was missing, but she'd been traipsing all over the camp in nearly three feet of snow, shoveling, and searching for Taryn all while the disturbing information Gretchen had given her spun round and round in her head.

Nicola's eyes were glassy with tears. Her fingers worked at her wedding band. "Shut up! Don't say that! You don't know that! Why would she be dead? How could she have possibly died?"

Alice's next words exploded out of her. "Someone here killed her! Just like Meg!"

THIRTY-FIVE

The darkness in the cellar was so complete that Noah couldn't make anything out, even once his eyes had time to adjust. For a time, a small sliver of light outlined the door at the top of the steps but eventually it disappeared. Had it grown dark? Was it evening again? Or had Cooper just turned off the kitchen light? Noah lay on his stomach for what felt like hours, turning his head back and forth to keep his neck from aching. The floor felt like hard-packed dirt. He could barely feel his extremities. There was no heat, in spite of the fact that somewhere nearby, a furnace roared to life every so often. He'd spent a great deal of time trying to loosen the tape around his wrists, pulling at them until his shoulders screamed in pain. When sweat started to pour from his scalp and burn his eyes, he took a break.

For a long time, he listened, trying to make sense of the noises he heard above him. There was barely anything. Occasional footsteps which he couldn't hear if the furnace was running. He didn't even realize he had dozed off until he woke from a dream thrashing against his restraints. In it, he'd been going door to door in Denton, entering homes and tearing open closet doors, looking for Josie. This was the kind of darkness she had described to him when she told him what Lila Jensen had done to her in childhood. He had always thought he understood it but now he knew that it wasn't something you could ever understand unless you experienced it. Not just the fact of having no light source but of being trapped, completely help-less, and vulnerable, like he was now.

Overhead, the house groaned. The wind again. The furnace kicked off and Noah listened for footsteps. There were none. A few minutes later, he heard what sounded like a vehicle's engine purring. Was Cooper leaving? Was he leaving in Noah's SUV? Noah hadn't taken much time to consider what was actually going on. One thing he was fairly certain of was that the man upstairs was not the real Cooper Riggs. If he was the real Cooper, he wouldn't have lied about the photo on the fridge. Noah would put money on it that the older man in the photo was the actual Cooper Riggs.

But where was he?

Noah tested his legs, bringing his heels toward his rear end, trying to get his circulation going. He strained against the tape around his legs. There was very little give. He would have better luck freeing his hands. He squirmed, contorting his body until he was in a sitting position, his hands touching the floor behind his back and his feet out in front of him. He rolled his shoulders forward, trying to use them to put added pressure on the tape around his wrists.

The sound of tires spinning out in snow was faint but audi-ble. Cooper was having trouble getting out of the driveway. For some reason, this filled Noah with relief. He didn't want that psychopath anywhere near Josie.

Assuming he hadn't already been up the mountain.

Had this stranger been to the retreat? Had he wreaked havoc there? Killed the real Cooper and then taken up in his house until the storm was over? Was that the reason Josie hadn't come home? Was she dead?

Adrenaline surged through Noah's body, sharpening every one of his senses. His wrists were on fire, but he kept tugging and twisting, hoping to free his hands. It felt as though one of his hands was close to coming loose. He worked harder.

He refused to believe that Josie was gone. If Cooper had killed everyone on the retreat and was here to ride out the storm, why would he keep Noah alive? He still needed Noah for something. Had he been telling the truth about needing Noah's help to load the snowmobile onto his truck? Was there a snowmobile, or had he made that up as well? Did he intend to go up the mountain or had that been for Noah's benefit? There was no way to say for sure. The only thing Noah knew for certain was that the only chance he had of getting out of this alive and rescuing Josie was to get out of his bindings so he would be ready when Cooper finally came for him.

THIRTY-SIX

In the silence that followed Alice's outburst, Josie could hear the hum of the generator out back joining the whistle of the wind and the popping of wood from the stove. No one spoke or moved for several beats. Josie looked around at their faces. Brian's mouth hung open. Nicola's eyes were wide with shock. Tears spilled down Sandrine's cheeks. She was the first to speak. Her voice came out scratchy. "What are you talking about, Alice?"

Alice looked down at Josie. The green flecks in her eyes had gone dark. "I'm so sorry, Josie."

Before Josie could respond, Nicola said, "Why are you apologizing to her? What is going on here?"

Josie sighed. "I believe that Meg was murdered."

Sandrine used the sleeve of her sweater to wipe away her tears. "And you kept that from us? From all of us?"

"I didn't want to cause unnecessary panic," Josie explained.

Brian closed his mouth and swallowed twice, his Adam's apple bobbing up and down. "Are you sure?"

"As sure as I can be."

"Someone strangled her," Alice blurted out.

"Alice—" Josie began but Nicola cut her off again.

"You knew all this time that someone strangled Meg and you didn't tell any of us? You knew that we were in danger, and you didn't say anything? I thought you were a police officer. What if Taryn is really dead? Her blood is on your hands."

The accusation hit Josie right in the chest. An ache bloomed over her heart. Was that true? If Taryn was, in fact, dead, could Josie have prevented her death by telling everyone that Meg had been murdered? Would they all have been more careful? She'd been so worried that the killer was among them and that telling everyone would only escalate the killer's behavior, putting them all at risk. But if she had told them, would the killer have de-escalated instead? Would Taryn be sitting with them right now, safe and sound? If the killer was somehow not in this room, would he or she have been prevented from picking Taryn off if Josie had told the truth about Meg's death? Had she made a fatal miscalculation?

Brian rubbed at his scar. "Nic," he said softly. "Come on."

Nicola shot out of her seat. "Shut up! It's true! If she had told us that Meg was murdered, we could have been on guard. We could have stuck together more. Taryn would not have been in her cabin alone."

"No!" Alice exclaimed. "That's not true. Josie was trying to protect us. I agreed with her decision. She wanted us to stay calm and focused so we could get off this damn mountain. Why would she have shared that information? For all we know, one of you is the killer!"

"What?" Brian said.

Josie's head started to pound. Was Nicola right? Was Taryn's disappearance and potential murder her fault?

Alice kept going, throwing gasoline on the flames. "When we found Meg, I thought maybe her stalker somehow tracked her here and killed her. Then I thought maybe it was Cooper since he never came back, but now with Taryn missing, there's only one possibility. One of you killed Meg and Taryn! Were we supposed to announce that we knew one of you was a murderer? What if you came after us? That's probably what happened to Taryn! She figured out one of you was a murderer and you had to kill her to keep her quiet."

Brian's nails dug into his scar, drawing blood. "This is crazy. This can't be happening."

Could Josie have prevented what happened to Taryn? The ache in her chest felt crushing. She could barely breathe.

Sandrine tugged her fingers through her long hair. "Stop! Stop this instant! We don't know that Taryn is dead. We simply don't. While I don't know why she would choose to hide out from us in this cold, we simply cannot and should not assume that she's dead."

Mettner's ghost voice floated up from the back of Josie's mind, reminding her of what she had told him many times when they'd worked together, what she told victims' families. *Boss*, he said, *only killers are responsible for killing.* There were only six of them on the mountain, trapped in a relatively small area together. They had rarely been apart since the snow started. Killing Taryn was a huge risk which made Josie think that the killer didn't much care about the circumstances—he or she would kill no matter what. Still, she couldn't shake the thought that she might have been able to prevent whatever happened to Taryn.

"If she was hiding, we would have found her," said Nicola. She stared down at Sandrine. "You killed both of them, didn't you?"

Sandrine's eyes widened as she turned her face up to Nicola. Fear flashed across her face. "What? You think I killed Meg and Taryn? You think that I murdered two people? Why would I do such a thing?"

Josie tried to speak but her throat constricted. It still felt hard to breathe.

"You were conveniently alone when Taryn 'disappeared.' Just like you were with Meg. You woke us all up to tell us that Meg was gone. You could have easily killed her while we slept and then acted like she disappeared."

"Just a minute, Nicola. You were also alone when Taryn went missing," Alice pointed out. "You were in your cabin."

"No," said Nicola, gaze switching furiously back and forth between Alice and Sandrine. "I came back before that."

"How can we know that?" Alice shot back.

Sandrine stood up. "Stop! Stop this! None of us saw Meg leave her cabin. None of us saw Taryn leave this building. We can't start blaming one another. It's not going to do any good."

Nicola leveled a finger at Sandrine. "Don't try to distract us. Meg left this camp in the middle of the night. She tried to walk off this mountain in a blizzard. Why would she do something like that unless you drove her to it?"

Josie concentrated on getting oxygen to her lungs. But Taryn had asked Meg to come to her cabin that night. Meg had thought Taryn was stalking Sandrine. Perhaps she was fixated on Sandrine but not in the way that Meg suspected. Josie was sure that Taryn had been working with Brian and Nicola. For all Josie knew, Taryn had killed Meg to hide whatever they were trying to do.

Sandrine straightened her spine and scoffed. "You're really out to get me, aren't you? That is one of the most absurd things I have ever heard in my life."

Nicola took a step toward Sandrine, her eyes blazing with anger and hatred. "Is it? Is it so absurd to think that you would kill someone?"

Sandrine did not back away. She thrust her chin forward and gave Nicola a mirthless smile. "I suppose next you'll tell me that the blizzard is my fault as well."

In her way, she was trying to bring the temperature down in the room. Before anyone else could speak, a resounding crack came from the wood stove. It had the effect of a gunshot going off in the middle of the room. Everyone jumped. Alice bumped against her chair, sending it toppling.

Josie stood up and righted the chair. "I don't think it is in any of our best interests to start accusing one another of crimes right now. Yes, Meg was murdered. Perhaps I should have shared that with the group, but I didn't. Now all of you know. We don't know what happened to Taryn."

"Yes, we do!" Alice insisted, her tear-filled eyes turned toward Josie.

Josie gave her the best reassuring look she could muster. "No, Alice. We don't. All we know is that she walked up to her cabin and did not return. That's it. Jumping to conclusions, fighting—that's not going to help any of us. At first light, we can do another search for Taryn. Right now, we just need to focus on staying warm and fed until help arrives."

"You're kidding me, right?" said Nicola. "You just expect us all to sit here together and eat dinner like nothing is wrong?"

Alice shuddered. Then she walked toward the front door and took her coat from the rack beside it. "I can't stay here under these conditions. I know you're trying to keep us calm, Josie, but this is too much. Someone in this room killed Meg and Taryn. I can't just eat and sleep and chat with all of you knowing that. What's to stop the killer from coming after the rest of us? Especially now that he knows we know about him."

Brian jumped up out of his chair. "Him? Did you just say him? It has to be me, is that what you're saying? Because I'm the only guy here?"

Sandrine said, "Alice, where will you go? It's not safe out there alone and you need warmth and food."

Alice pulled her coat on. "Not as much as I need to stay alive."

Brian said, "Don't be ridiculous. If you are afraid of me then

I can leave. If that will make everyone feel better, I don't mind doing it, but I'm not leaving Nic alone with you three."

"Yeah," Nicola said, moving closer to Brian. "I don't want to be alone with you guys. What if—what if the cop did it?"

Josie felt a new pinch in her chest. All eyes went to her. Nicola pointed at her. "She's kept us away from Meg's body. She didn't tell us that Meg was murdered. She went to the rage room alone today. Why would she do that? What does she need to do there? The only thing down there is Meg's body, and she doesn't want any of us near it. She's hiding evidence! Plus, Taryn disappeared while she was there!"

Josie felt her face flush. It was tempting to confront both Nicola and Brian right now, in front of Alice and Sandrine, but without knowing more about why they were there and what they wanted, she wasn't comfortable doing it. For all she knew, they'd conspired together to kill Taryn. Maybe Taryn had decided not to go along with whatever plan they had in place so they eliminated her. All Josie wanted was to get off this mountain without anyone else being harmed. It was better to simply try to defuse the situation and bide her time. "I never even saw Taryn after I left here. I didn't do anything to her. I'm not 'hiding evidence.' I'm preserving it as best I can until rescue comes. I told you. I went to the rage room to try to contact my colleagues and see how soon they'll be here."

Alice's hand rested on the doorknob. "What did they say?"

"That they're working on it and to check back later."

"Later?" Alice said, tears in her eyes. "How are we supposed to do this? How are we all supposed to stay alive up here when one of us is a killer?"

"We split up," Brian said. "We already have—Nic and I are staying in the game room and you can all stay in the other room."

"No," said Sandrine. "The only way to do this is for all of us to stay together. No one does anything or goes anywhere alone.

We will all bring our mattresses back in here. We will all sleep together in the same room tonight just like last night."

"Are you crazy?" Nicola said. "What's to stop the killer from coming after any one of us in the middle of the night?"

"Numbers," Sandrine said. "Eyes. Two people stay awake while the others sleep. We can take shifts."

No one argued. Sandrine turned toward the breakout room. "I'll stay awake first," she said over her shoulder.

Josie said, "I can also take the first shift."

"This is a stupid plan," Nicola said.

Alice moved away from the door, turning to follow Sandrine into the breakout room. "Do you have a better plan?"

Brian said, "Sandrine is right. Staying together makes the most sense. But since we don't trust each other, I should take the first shift with one of you."

Without turning back, Sandrine waved a hand in the air. "Fine. Whatever. Brian and Josie can take the first shift. Hopefully we only have one more night to get through."

THIRTY-SEVEN

Abandoning dinner, they started dragging their mattresses back into the main hall. Josie, Sandrine and Alice clustered their mattresses on the opposite side of the room from Brian and Nicola. Sandrine put the pasta and salad in the fridge. Josie was afraid she would regret not eating later but she didn't think she could keep any food down at the moment. It was a surreal feeling knowing that someone there was a cold-blooded killer and that they were all forced to be civil to that person until rescue came. It hadn't felt quite so horrifying when she thought there might be a chance that an outsider or Cooper had killed Meg. She wanted badly to return to the rage room and check her phone to see if Gretchen had any more news, but they'd agreed to stay together. She also wanted to talk to Sandrine and Alice about what she had discovered but there was no opportunity for that either.

Josie took her blanket and curled up in one of the chairs near the stove while everyone settled into their beds. Brian joined her, sitting opposite her. He reached into the back pocket of his jeans and pulled out his vape pen. "Don't worry," he told her. "It still doesn't work."

"At this point," Josie said, "if it worked, I'd ask you to share it."

Brian laughed softly and turned the pen over in his hands.

They fell silent. Josie periodically glanced over at the mattresses. Sandrine, Alice, and Nicola were all under their covers. One of them snored lightly. Josie wasn't sure if anybody would be able to sleep under the circumstances, but everyone was exhausted, physically and emotionally. She was, as well, but her insomnia was stronger than ever. Only now, after a week under Sandrine's tutelage, she could identify the underlying anxiety and hypervigilance that went along with it. It felt like a low-level vibration coursing through her entire body, a buzz keeping her awake even at the height of her fatigue. Tension pulled the muscles of her neck taut. She had to concentrate on her breathing in order to slow her heart rate. If she didn't, she'd get lightheaded.

Her therapist would be so proud that she was able to do the body scan successfully.

She sat still as long as she could, noting all the sensations and the feelings attached to them, but the longer she did, the more uncomfortable she felt. A headache began pulsing in her temples. The more she focused on it, the worse it got. She had hours to go before she could rest in her own bed. Even if she didn't sleep, she had to distract herself.

She thought over Sandrine's lessons about moving her body, shaking things off, or even dancing. She couldn't shake or dance right at that moment, but she could get up and move around. She stood up and walked over to the stove. Sandrine had left a bucket beside it filled with random pieces of wood gathered from the rage room. Aware that Brian was watching her, she knelt and began loading more wood into the stove before returning to her chair.

Her headache was still there but the lightheadedness had gone. Her thoughts drifted to Brian, Nicola, and Taryn. She mentally reviewed the week, going over every interaction she'd seen them have together. They'd betrayed nothing. Even in an intimate setting where they were sharing deeply personal accounts of traumatic experiences, they hadn't slipped at all. Josie would never have guessed that Taryn knew Brian and Nicola. Even Brian and Nicola barely seemed to know one another, and they were married.

Perhaps the couple had not known Taryn well in real life. Maybe that part wasn't an act at all. But they had some connection that was compelling enough for them to team up, spend a great deal of money on the retreat, and lie about their true identities. What kind of connection could it be? She didn't even have enough information to form any theories.

Mettner's ghost voice whispered to her. *You're asking the wrong questions. Focusing on the wrong aspects.*

What are the right questions? she asked but she knew the answer already. She was, after all, constructing this entire conversation with Mettner in her own mind, based on what she believed he would say if he were here.

Stop wondering about what you don't know, Mett told her. *Zero in on what you do know.*

Staring across at Brian, Josie remembered that she had just spent a week with these people. What she knew was how they'd acted and how they'd conducted themselves. Nicola and Brian had appropriated Nicola's childhood tragedy in order to ensure that Nicola would be included on the retreat. It was clearly important enough that she attend the retreat for them to lie about it. The lie also explained why the two of them had seemed so shut down and mentally distanced from the tragedy. It wasn't really theirs. It belonged solely to Nicola, but she hadn't experienced it in the role of a mother. Yet, they'd both been engaged in all the group sessions. Things had been fine but as the week went on, Nicola grew more and more irritable. Josie assumed it was because they were digging so deep into their trauma, but now she wondered if it was because they were getting closer to the end of the retreat and their goal had not been accomplished.

Once the blizzard hit, Nicola began to openly accuse Sandrine of being a fraud. Josie had thought she was simply lashing out from the stress of Meg's death and being stuck on the mountain, but maybe she would have acted that way regardless since the retreat was coming to a close and they had limited time to achieve whatever they had come to do. Nicola had complained to Brian that she was the only one trying. But was that true?

While Nicola and Brian had played the grieving parents all week, Taryn had been firmly establishing herself as a sort of superfan of Sandrine's, always sitting beside her, mimicking the way she dressed, picking her brain about methods for processing trauma. She'd even kept notes in her binder. In fact, Sandrine had met her previously on several occasions in the last year. That meant that Taryn had been using a fake identity to get close to Sandrine for a very long time, maybe even longer than Brian and Nicola. Yet her approach this week, even as the retreat was ending, had been the opposite of what Brian and Nicola had done. She had even defended Sandrine to them on more than one occasion.

Had all of that been an act as well? Had they thought all of this out ahead of time to try to manipulate Sandrine into giving them whatever it was they wanted? Were they using a good cop, bad cop strategy? Make Nicola and Brian push Sandrine to her emotional breaking point so that Taryn could offer comfort as a way of manipulating her into telling them what they wanted to know?

Again, she wondered what that could possibly be.

"Hey. Josie." Brian said her name just loudly enough for her to hear but not so loud that he would disturb the others.

She startled. Blinking, she looked up from where his hands

cradled the vape pen, fingers tapping along its length, to his eyes. "Yes?"

"I can't take the staring anymore," he said. "Let's just get this out of the way since we have to sit here together for like four more hours. You think it's me, don't you? You think I'm a psycho killer."

Josie pulled her blanket up to her chin, prepared to lie. "I'm sorry I was staring. I didn't mean to make you uncomfortable. I wasn't thinking that at all."

He hunched forward, broad shoulders rounded, and put his elbows on his knees. "You don't have to lie."

Josie pointed at his hands. "I was looking at your wedding band."

He looked down at it as if it had just appeared. "My wedding band? Why?"

She slid her hand out of the blanket and wiggled her fingers. The light from the fire danced along her silver band. "My husband and I got matching rings. I wanted silver. He wanted titanium. I won. Now I'm wondering why it mattered at all. You two have different rings."

He let the vape pen rest on his thigh and rubbed a finger across the silicone band. "This was cheap. That's why I bought it."

"You didn't want an inscription?" Josie asked.

His brow furrowed. "What?"

Josie tapped her own ring for emphasis. "You had the inside of Nicola's band inscribed. You didn't want an inscription inside your own ring?"

"Did you and your husband both get inscriptions?"

He had answered her question with his own question. In Josie's experience, there was usually one of two reasons for this kind of deflection: to buy time so the person could think of an appropriate answer, or to deflect attention away from them in the hopes of avoiding the question altogether. It didn't surprise her since she already knew he was a liar but then again, she hadn't asked him a question he should need to buy time for or deflect from. The tiny ember of an idea slowly began to smolder in the back of her mind.

She answered him. "What we wanted to put inside them was too long, so on the outside of our bands it says, 'I'll always.'" She slid the ring off and handed it to him.

He had to get up and go over to the stove, holding it beside the glass to study it. "Oh yeah," he said. "It does. I'll always what?"

The words lodged in her throat momentarily as tears threatened. Just the thought of her husband and what they'd promised brought every complicated emotion she had racing to the surface. She swallowed and smiled. "Look inside."

He turned the ring and peered inside the band, reading the words slowly. "'Run to the danger. N.'"

"It should have been 'run toward the danger with you' but that was too long to fit," Josie said.

He handed it back to her. "That's what you guys have on your rings? I'll always run to the danger?"

She slid the band back onto her finger, feeling a modicum of comfort, as if it was Noah's touch. "No. His says, 'I'll always' on the outside and 'come home to you. J.' on the inside."

Brian returned to his chair, picking up the vape pen from the seat where he'd left it. He used the edge of it to scratch the side of his head. "I don't get it."

"Those were our vows," said Josie, the lump in her throat thicker than ever. "He promised to always run toward the danger with me and I promised to always come home to him. We had them inscribed onto our wedding bands a few months after the wedding."

"Huh," Brian said. "Weird."

Josie looked at the band sparkling on her finger. They hadn't gone through with the wedding they'd planned. Instead, they'd gotten married in the hospital next to her grandmother's bed. Lisette's dying wish had been to see them wed. They'd chosen to improvise on their vows, but they couldn't have been more perfect. Noah had kept his vow to her. He'd left Denton as soon as the snow started. He'd come to get her. But where was he now? She pushed the thought aside. The ember in the back of her mind glowed more brightly. "Yes," she agreed. "It's weird but it made sense for us. But yeah, it's not as traditional or as lovely as what you had inscribed inside Nicola's band. 'Forever & always. B.'"

Again, Brian used the edge of the vape pen to scratch at his temple. He gave her a strained smile. "Well, you know," he said. "That was what Nic wanted."

THIRTY-EIGHT

Josie pulled her blanket back up to her chin even though it was probably too dark for Brian to see her heartbeat fluttering wildly beneath the skin at the hollow of her throat. She was grateful when he settled back in his chair and turned to watch the flames licking the glass of the stove door. She quietly worked on her box breathing, trying to counteract the adrenaline that surged through her at this discovery.

Whoever they were, Brian and Nicola were not married. Josie had started to put most of the pieces together before she caught Brian in the lie about the inscription. The two of them had barely touched one another the entire week, and they seemed emotionally disconnected. Initially, she'd put it down to the strain on their marriage caused by the murder of their daughter. But they had no slain daughter. Then there were the smaller details like the fact that Brian hadn't known Nicola was lactose intolerant. Even more appalling was that Nicola had not known about Brian's peanut allergy—something that could possibly kill him. She'd claimed to have forgotten but her excuse had been brain fog from the death of her daughter. It was something no one would dare question—an excellent way to cover up the fact that she hadn't known about the allergy at all.

Maybe not all couples had the sort of intimacy that Josie and Noah shared but a potentially deadly food allergy and the inscription inside one's wedding band were definitely things a spouse would know, even if they hadn't been married for very long.

Across from her, Brian kept his attention on the wood stove, content not to talk. Josie did her best not to stare at him. A few hours passed in silence. Josie's mind was in a frenzy, trying to piece together what exactly was going on as well as wondering what had happened to Taryn and if it was her fault. When it felt like she was about to come out of her skin, she turned her focus to Sandrine and what she could possibly be hiding. Snippets of things she'd heard during the week came back to her, and she mentally replayed them, until another idea began to glow like a hot coal in the furnace of her mind. It was only a small thing, but she was sure it was important. To confirm it, however, she had to find a way to talk with Sandrine alone.

As the hours passed, the wind outside died down. With only the hum of the generator and the crackle of the wood stove, in the dark of night, Josie felt like they were the only people on the planet. Then from outside came a noise that she couldn't quite identify. It was loud. Some sort of dragging or sliding. It sounded almost mechanical. A machine? Before her mind could process it, she was on her feet.

"What the he—" Brian's words were swallowed up by some sort of crash outside.

Josie ran to the coatrack next to the door, searching for her coat and boots in the dim light. Behind her, she heard the voices of Sandrine, Alice, and Nicola, sleepy but alarmed.

"What was that?" asked Alice.

"Is someone here?" Sandrine said.

Nicola leapt up and raced toward the door. "Maybe it's Taryn!"

Brian, already at the door, yanked it open. Frozen air swept through the room. "Nic, just stay here. It might be the bear."

Josie put her winter stuff on and grabbed two of the lanterns. She handed one to Brian. He had sweatpants and sneakers on, but he didn't bother to put on his coat, instead rushing out onto the porch. Josie kept close behind. Their lanterns were almost dead, since they had used them earlier to search for Taryn, but Josie did her best to make out what she could with the little light they still gave off. They paused at the bottom of the steps, swinging their lights around, searching for the source of the clamor.

Now, the night was silent. The only thing Josie could hear outside was the whir of the generator.

Brian walked up the path, pausing between the main house and Sandrine's cabin, turning in a circle. "I don't see anything, but it sounded like it was close. I thought maybe it was someone here to rescue us."

Josie followed him, stepping off the path and into the snow. She started walking between the two buildings. "Josie," Brian said. "What are you doing? The bear might be back there."

Overhead, the clouds drifted, and the moon began to emerge, casting a silver glow over everything. Toward the back of the main house, where the roof wasn't as severely pitched as the A-frame portion of the building in the front, a massive slab of snow had fallen.

"It's not the bear," Josie called. She waved him over but he wouldn't move off the path. Holding her lantern out to the pile, she said, "Look! This slid off the roof. That's what we heard."

Brian took a tentative step and peered at what was now a mountain of snow along the side of the main house. "It made that much noise?"

Josie turned back toward him. "Well, yeah. It's almost three feet of snow sliding off a metal roof and falling onto this." She stomped her foot against an unbroken area of snow, making a cracking noise. "It froze overnight, but that, on the roof, probably got warm enough to slide off from the wood-burning stove."

"Holy shit," he said.

Back inside, Josie could see that the others were at once relieved that the source of the noise wasn't any sort of threat but disappointed that it wasn't a rescue. Brian and Nicola decided to switch places. Alice took Josie's place. While Nicola and Alice settled into chairs around the stove, Brian, Sandrine, and Josie went to their respective beds. Within minutes, Brian was snoring loudly enough to be heard across the room.

Josie stretched out on her mattress and looked over at Alice and Nicola, trying to gauge whether or not they'd be able to overhear if she spoke with Sandrine. Their mattresses were only a foot apart. Sandrine was already on her side, facing Josie, one hand tucked under her cheek. Confident that they wouldn't be overheard if they kept their voices down, Josie wriggled to the edge of her mattress and reached over, touching Sandrine's shoulder. She opened her eyes. "Is everything okay?" she asked.

Josie put her index finger to her lips to signal that they should be quiet. Sandrine shifted her body so that she, too, lay at the very edge of the mattress. With only a foot between them, it was easier to converse in whispers.

Sandrine said, "What is going on, Josie?"

"We need to talk. I'm sorry I didn't tell you about Meg. I felt it was necessary at the time."

Sandrine's eyes glowed with unshed tears in the flickering light from the stove. "Do you know what happened to Taryn?"

"No." Josie thought of what Nicola had said. *Her blood is on your hands.* Before her body went into overdrive, she pushed the accusation away. If they all got out of here alive, there would be time later to examine her role in all of this and whether she'd cost Taryn her life. For now, she was after information. "Today, when I was at the rage room, I learned from my colleague that Taryn, Nicola and Brian lied on their intake paperwork for the retreat."

A look of horror stretched across Sandrine's face. "What? What are you saying?"

"They're not who they're claiming to be." Josie explained what Gretchen had told her. "I don't even think that Brian and Nicola are actually married."

"What? No! That's ridiculous. It can't be."

Josie put her finger back to her lips so that Sandrine would lower her voice again. "I'm certain of it. I don't know how they know each other or Taryn but I believe all three of them knew each other before they arrived here, and they've come specifically for you."

With her free hand, Sandrine pulled her cover up to her shoulder. "For me? What does that mean?"

"I'm not exactly sure," said Josie. "But Sandrine, they want something from you."

"But what?"

"I don't know. Some sort of information, from what it looks like."

Sandrine frowned. "How can you know that?"

Josie told her about the cameras.

Sandrine leaned over the edge of the mattress, her face coming closer to Josie's. "Is there a camera in this room right now?"

"I couldn't find one in this room," Josie answered.

Sandrine lifted her head a couple of inches and looked over toward Alice and Nicola. Josie did the same. The two sat in the same chairs Brian and Josie had occupied, each one staring at the stove. Settling back into their pillows, Sandrine whispered, "But Taryn? She was so sweet. She was practically attached to my hip!"

"I know," Josie said. "I think that was the point. Taryn's job was to get close to you. I think she got so close to you that she had a change of heart about whatever they came here to do and maybe that's why she's gone."

"Listen to what you're saying, Josie. It sounds crazy. You're saying that these three people lied about their identities to come onto this retreat where they planted cameras because they hoped to get information from me? What do they think I am? A CIA agent?" She attempted a small laugh, but it died in her throat. Her lower lip trembled. "Do you think they're the ones who killed Meg?"

Josie glanced over at Alice and Nicola again but neither of them had moved. "It seems very likely. She must have found something out or seen something. I can't be sure if they're all in on it or not or if one of them has gone rogue and started killing. Regardless, I think Taryn refused to go along with the plan anymore and that Nicola and Brian may have killed her and hidden her body. I just don't know where."

"Oh God," Sandrine sniffled. "What do we do? We're stuck here. God knows how much longer we'll be here."

"Right," Josie said. "I don't want anyone else to die before we're rescued."

Sandrine's body quivered. "But Brian and Nicola know that we know Meg was murdered and that we suspect Taryn was as well—I mean, would they let us all go knowing that a police investigation will immediately begin? Every single one of us would be a suspect, right? Including them."

"Yes."

A tear slid from the corner of Sandrine's eye and over the bridge of her nose, onto the pillow. "How do we do this? How do we stay alive?"

"I think your plan of all of us staying together is safest."

"I don't want to be in the same room with them," Sandrine said. "Either of them."

"We have no choice," Josie said.

Sandrine buried her face in her pillow, sobbing. Her words were muffled but Josie made them out. "Oh God. I can't believe this. It's such a nightmare."

Josie touched her arm. "I know. Sandrine, we will get out of this, and I'll do everything I can to keep you and Alice safe."

A small voice at the back of her mind asked, *Like you kept Taryn safe?*

Josie did her best to ignore it. Another scan of the room told her that no one could hear them. She tapped Sandrine's shoulder again until she came up for air. "Sandrine, Nicola and Brian—whoever they are—have repeatedly insisted that you are a fraud and that you're not who you say you are. That makes me think they believe there is something about you that they can expose. I don't know why they think that or why it is so important to them, but they went to great lengths to get close to you."

Sandrine shook her head, hair swishing over her pillow. Then she went very still as a thought occurred to her. "Do you think they'll... come after me? Do they want to kill me?"

Josie rubbed her eyes. "If they wanted to kill you, they could have accomplished that with a lot less effort than following you to a retreat and spending the week participating in all of this."

"But what do they want? This is absolute madness. What could be so important to them that they were willing to kill Meg —and possibly Taryn?"

"I don't know," Josie answered. "But I want you to be honest with me. Our lives may depend on it."

"I have been honest with you," said Sandrine, her fingers gripping the edge of her blanket.

In her gentlest tone, Josie said, "We both know that you haven't."

Sandrine blinked. "What do you mean?"

"You can start by telling me your real name."

THIRTY-NINE

Sandrine propped herself up on one elbow, now looking down at Josie. In the faint firelight, Josie could see the shock on her face. Her skin was so pale that it was almost translucent. A vein in her forehead pulsed. "What are you talking about?"

"Shh," Josie cautioned, gesturing for her to lie back down so as not to draw the attention of Nicola or Alice. "I know that Sandrine Morrow is not your real name."

Sandrine laid her head back onto her pillow, one hand tucked under her cheek. "But how? How could you know that?"

This was the idea that had taken hold during the hours that she and Brian were sitting watch over the rest of the group. She'd been thinking about what Brian, Nicola, and Taryn could want so badly to find out from Sandrine. Whatever it was, they hadn't just wanted to hear it from her—they'd wanted it on video. Brian had outright told Josie that he and Nicola didn't think Sandrine was the person she claimed to be. They were accusing her of the same thing that they'd done to get onto the retreat. It made Josie wonder if Sandrine really was hiding something. Then she remembered the conversation she'd had with Sandrine in the rage room.

She had told Josie: *It took a long time and a lot of work to become who I am right now, standing before you. But I am just me. I'm Dr. Sandrine Morrow.*

She'd said she was Dr. Sandrine Morrow as if it were an identity she had assumed rather than her actual name.

"I didn't know it," Josie said. "I figured it out from things I heard in the last couple of days. You said your mother was an actress. Maybe she wasn't that famous but surely, with the success you've achieved in your career, you would have been linked to her at some point. I didn't do a major internet deep-dive on you before I came to this retreat, but I did some research. There's nothing about your mother—or any family—at all."

Sandrine took in a shuddering breath. "Fine. You're right. My real name is not Sandrine Morrow but, Josie, I can assure you that all of my credentials and my experience are very much real. Everything else about me is real. These people cannot possibly have come all this way and gone to all this trouble because I changed my name when I was twenty-one years old!"

Sandrine was right.

A creak from the other side of the room silenced them. Josie rolled over momentarily to see Alice loading more scraps of wood into the stove. She would love to discuss all of this with Alice. She was as close to a colleague as Josie had on this mountain. There just hadn't been an opportunity to get her alone in the last several hours. Then again, Alice was walking the emotional edge. She'd already revealed Meg's murder to the group after Josie had specifically asked her not to. Josie didn't fault her for doing so—after all, each one of them was on the mountain because they were dealing with the devastating effects of complex PTSD. Given the blizzard and Meg's death, they were all under a tremendous amount of stress. Add to that their physical fatigue and Taryn's strange disappearance, and it was enough to push any one of them to their breaking point.

Maybe it was best to keep all the new information between her and Sandrine for now.

Once Alice was seated again, wrapped in her blanket, Josie and Sandrine turned toward one another once more.

Josie said, "Think. Is there anything that might have happened—even if it is being misconstrued by them—that would drive them to seek you out like this, in these particular conditions? Maybe a patient with a bad outcome? Something like that?"

"What do you mean?" asked Sandrine. "You think they're related to a former patient?"

"Possibly. Have you had any issues with patients? Maybe a situation where the patient hurt themselves or someone else? Something that might make their family members think that you were a fraud?"

Sandrine scoffed. "I treat patients with complex PTSD, Josie. Of course I've had patients with tragic outcomes. I've been practicing for decades. Yes, I've had patients who died by suicide. I have treated patients with homicidal ideation though none have ever crossed that line. At least not that I am aware. What I have never experienced is a family member of one of those patients questioning my methods. The loved ones of my patients always understand just how badly their family member is affected by PTSD. They're usually relieved to know that they've come to me to work on it."

Josie could not discount the idea of a disgruntled patient or the family of such a person being the reason behind this week's machinations, but what if it was more personal than that?

"Why did you change your name?" Josie asked. "Was it because of your mom?"

"Yes, I didn't want my mother's name. I didn't want to be associated with her. You don't know how it was to have people find out she was my mother. They would get so excited and ask all these questions, thinking she must have been so amazing and it must have been so glamorous to grow up with her when, in reality, it was torture. She was a monster. Once I was free, I never wanted anything to do with her at all."

"She was—she's passed away?"

Sandrine nodded. "During my sophomore year of college."

"I'm sorry to hear that," Josie said automatically.

"Don't be," said Sandrine. "It set me free, finally."

"What was her name?" Josie asked.

"Why? Do you think this has something to do with my mother? How? It's been decades and these people aren't even old enough to remember her. I mean Taryn, Brian, and Nicola are all in their thirties and forties. They were just kids when she passed away. They've probably never heard of her."

Low chatter interrupted them. Josie lifted her head to see Nicola and Alice on their feet. Alice motioned to the bathroom. A discussion ensued and then she stomped off toward it alone. Nicola sat back down, arms folded, watching for Alice's return.

Josie waited until Alice was back in her seat before continuing their whispered conversation. "You said she was an actress. Was she wealthy? Maybe these people found out you were her daughter and they think you're hiding that? Their intention could have been to blackmail you with that information, for all we know."

Sandrine gave her head a small shake, her hair swishing against the pillow. "I suppose it would make a splash in the press if it came out that respected psychologist and trauma specialist, Dr. Sandrine Morrow was actually Lola Stowe, the daughter of Delilah Stowe. But I wouldn't pay someone to keep the secret."

"Delilah Stowe," Josie said. "That sounds familiar."

Sandrine rolled her eyes. "I forgot. Her name was back in the press a couple of years ago. When she was young, she starred in a bunch of films with this very famous actor, Dean Thurman. He was married to a bona fide Hollywood starlet but he cheated on her with my mother. It was very scandalous at the time. A black mark on Thurman's career. It was worse for my mother. In the press she was accused of seducing him. A home-wrecker, they called her. That's why her name always comes up when his does. Then, a few years ago, someone on his staff accused him of sexual assault. A housekeeper, I believe. He was quite old at the time but that never stops men like him. The housekeeper filed charges against him. Then a civil lawsuit. As soon as it hit the press, there were a dozen more women across decades accusing him of sexual misconduct, assault, rape."

"I remember that," Josie said. "The press coverage was endless. I remember Delilah Stowe being mentioned as well."

"Yes," said Sandrine. "The entire relationship between her and Thurman was re-examined through today's lens. People started to wonder if they'd gotten the narrative all wrong back then since my mother was so young, a co-star, and Dean was married. Journalists wrote about it. Maybe she wasn't some wanton vixen who had lured him away from his marriage bed. Maybe he was the one who had coerced her into an inappropriate relationship. I was too young and too worried about my own survival to notice. The point is that her name was on everyone's lips again."

"That's why I recognize it," Josie said.

"But Josie, my mother wasn't wealthy. She always did a good job of making it look like she was well-off but she wasn't. She squandered everything she ever made. She never earned much in residuals, even on her bigger films. Certainly not enough to live on. Near the end, she was destitute. She married a carpenter. Claimed that she actually loved him and that she was done being in the public eye. All they had was his salary and it wasn't much. It's not like she left me some grand estate. She left me with nothing but scars."

Josie nodded her head toward the others in the room. "But they wouldn't know that."

Sandrine groaned softly. "This is absurd. This can't be happening because of my mother."

"I didn't say it was," Josie replied. "It was just a theory."

"Here's a more likely theory," Sandrine said. "These people are lunatics. Josie, what kind of crazy people pretend to be someone else to come on a retreat to process trauma just to speak to me? Have you considered how insane that sounds? I've got an office. They could have just made appointments. They could have just looked up my home address and knocked on my door! Taryn came to three of my seminars! She had plenty of opportunity to speak with me after each one. Why go to all this trouble? It makes no sense!"

Josie shushed her again. "Keep your voice down. I agree, something is very off in this situation and if it was a single person, then yes, I'd say maybe they're dealing with a mental health issue but it was three of them, Sandrine! Three people. This was coordinated. They clearly believe you have something that they want."

"This is ridiculous!" Sandrine said. "I can't believe Meg and Taryn lost their lives over this foolishness. Oh God, I don't know how much more of this I can take. I'm sorry to say that to you, Josie. I'm supposed to be the calm one, the strong one, your therapist for the week. But now I just want to go home."

"I know," Josie replied. "Me, too. Sandrine, what if we just confronted them?"

"What?"

Her voice was loud enough to draw the attention of Nicola and Alice.

"You okay over there?" Alice called.

Sandrine waved a dismissive hand in the air. "Yes, yes. Just a nightmare."

They stared at one another as several minutes passed. Finally, Sandrine said, "I don't think we should confront them. If you're right about everything that has happened this week, that means we're dealing with at least one, if not two, cold-blooded killers. What if they feel threatened and try to hurt the rest of us? I know we outnumber them three to two but I'm not sure setting up a potential physical confrontation is wise." When Josie didn't answer, Sandrine reached across the distance between them and squeezed her arm. "I know you're thinking of Taryn. You think if you'd been honest about Meg's murder, Taryn would still be with us. I understand you're grappling with that but I'm telling you, confronting them will only put us all at greater risk. Not when we're so close to being rescued. Let's get off this mountain and let your colleagues in the police department take over from there."

Josie swallowed over a new lump in her throat. "Okay, but we should tell Alice."

Sandrine squeezed her arm again. "Maybe it's best we don't. She can't slip up if she doesn't know anything. She's already sufficiently scared that she'll be careful. Let's leave it at that."

FORTY

Noah's lower back spasmed for what felt like the hundredth time. The muscles of his shoulders felt like they were on fire. Sweat poured down his face, into his eyes, making them burn. He blinked, trying to stop the sting, but it did no good. He was sure the perspiration was blurring his vision but he couldn't know for certain. The darkness was never-ending. Yet he'd managed to squirm and roll and wiggle his way to the bottom of the wooden stairs. He'd positioned his bound wrists along the edge of the post that ran up from the bottom step, anchoring the railing. He'd been rubbing the duct tape against the edge of the post for what felt like hours, though it might only be minutes.

Time was meaningless here.

He started to mark it by how many times the furnace kicked on and off before he realized that that didn't really tell him anything about how much time was passing. The furnace kicked on when the temperature in the house went below a certain number and then turned back off when it got back up to that number.

His bladder was full and every muscle in his body screamed for relief. Several times he'd been close to defeat. The only thing that kept him going, kept his wrists sawing against the post, was the thought of Josie. He'd lost his mother a few years back, in the worst way possible. His father had been an asshole of the highest degree. Noah didn't believe his father had ever loved his mother. He'd left her pretty much the day that Noah, their youngest, turned eighteen. He'd immediately started a new family with another woman, leaving Noah and his brother and sister behind as if they had never existed. His mother had taken all of this with the stoicism of a statue. Noah had always wondered if she cried in her most private moments. Then he decided he didn't want to know. His own pain was enough. With his brother and sister out of the house, he and Colette had gotten through the storm of his father's betrayal together. She refused to let grief beat her. She had been his rock, the guiding light in his life for so long.

Until he met Josie.

He wasn't sure he would have survived Colette's death if it wasn't for her. On the outside, he'd handled it with the same stoicism his mother exuded in life but on the inside, he'd been a mess. Josie was his lighthouse, his beacon. When grief dragged him into its murky depths, he found his way to the surface by following her light.

He could not lose her.

He could not die.

The bindings came loose. Pain arced across Noah's shoulders as he flexed them, rolling them forward. A flick of his wrists outward and he heard the tape tear a fraction. Moments later, his arms were free. Adrenaline surged through his body, numbing the pain in his extremities from hours of being bound. He forgot all about his full bladder. He went to work on his feet, hoping he could get them loose before Cooper returned to make use of him.

FORTY-ONE

Josie didn't think she'd be able to sleep but after the conversation with Sandrine, she closed her eyes and soon, she was dreaming of Noah. He was trying to get to her but he was trapped. Mettner was there on the mountain with her but this time, she was the one dying and he couldn't save her. She woke in a cold sweat, just before dawn. Sitting up on her mattress, she noticed that Sandrine and Brian's beds were empty. Alice and Nicola were on their feet, walking around testing lamps and light switches. Nothing worked. Josie rubbed the sleep from her eyes. "What's going on?"

Alice threw open the door to the game room and reached inside, flipping the light switch up and down. Nothing happened. "We're pretty sure the generator ran out of fuel. Brian went out back to check. Don't worry, Sandrine is watching him from the back door."

This drew a glare from Nicola, who flopped into one of the chairs with a huff. "That means we're officially out of power. All we've got is heat now. Until the wood runs out."

"How long will that last?" Josie asked. She had lost track of how much they were using to load the wood-burning stove.

Nicola shrugged. "Not sure. Brian thinks a day? Two, if we're lucky?"

Alice walked over to the remaining pile of wood they'd gathered from the rage room and kicked it. "Son of a bitch!"

Josie stood up and walked over to her. "Hey, it's going to be okay. We're going to get out of here soon."

Alice's eyes filled with tears. "What about the food?"

Sandrine walked in from the kitchen, followed by Brian. Their faces were red and pinched with cold. "The food?" she said. "We have enough for today and probably tomorrow, as well. We can make it last longer now that..."

The silence stretched on a beat too long. Everyone stared at Sandrine. She wiped a tear from her cheek.

Nicola scowled at Sandrine. "Just say it. Now that Taryn's gone. We have one less mouth to feed thanks to someone in this room."

Brian went around Sandrine and plopped into the chair next to Nicola. He pushed a hand through his shaggy brown hair. "Let's not start that again."

The faint smell of wood burning infiltrated the room, growing stronger. Josie looked at the stove, but it wasn't emitting smoke. No, this smell was much stronger than what normally came from the stove, and it seemed to come from somewhere else.

Sandrine looked around the room. "Does anyone smell that?"

Brian pointed at the stove. "Something burning? Yeah. We're literally burning wood."

"No," said Alice, walking toward the center of the room. She lifted her chin, nostrils flaring as she sniffed the air. "That's not the stove."

From behind Sandrine, a tendril of smoke curled like a floating snake from the kitchen, slithering along the wall and up toward the ceiling.

Josie's heart stuttered. "Fire! It's coming from the kitchen."

"No!" Brian cried, springing to his feet.

Josie had only a second to glance over at him and see his eyes wide with terror. He grabbed Nicola by her upper arm and dragged her up out of the chair, pushing her toward the front door. "Everyone get outside. Get your coats and boots—everything you can grab to keep warm out there—and go!"

Josie raced toward the kitchen, pulling the collar of her shirt up over her mouth and nose. Flames raged along the back wall, from the back door to the countertop that held the kitchen sink. One of the shelves with the coffee mugs burned so quickly, it bowed in the middle, sending all the mugs crashing to the floor. More flames licked across the tile, overtaking the refrigerator and kitchen cabinets on the other side of the room. Josie went as far into the room as she could, searching for the fire extinguisher Cooper kept there, but it was already engulfed. She knew there was another one in the main hall near the stove. She ran back in there. The front door hung open. Everyone had fled except for Alice who stood in the doorway, holding Josie's coat in one hand and her phone in the other.

Josie yanked the fire extinguisher off the wall and yelled at Alice. "Go! Get out! Stay with Sandrine."

With a nod, Alice disappeared.

Back in the kitchen, the flames neared Cooper's closet room. The smoke was black and thick. Josie's eyes watered. Soot coated the roof of her mouth and the back of her throat. She pulled the pin and aimed the nozzle toward the base of the wall of flames closest to her. Squeezing the lever, she swept the nozzle back and forth. The chemical agent shot out, a white cloud, battling the flames, but the fire was already too big, eating up the entire kitchen now and roaring through Cooper's closet bedroom. Josie tossed the empty canister aside and pulled her collar back over her face. The main hall was now thick with smoke. A figure swallowed up the doorway. Brian.

Josie waved him outside. "Get out! Get out!"

The fresh air hit her like a slap. As her lungs labored to take in clean air, she almost fell. A coughing fit seized Brian's body as he stumbled down the steps behind her. Alice, Sandrine, and Nicola waited along the shoveled path. Josie coughed for what felt like hours but was probably only a few minutes. Pain sliced across her back. Her eyes watered again and she nearly vomited, the spasms in her throat and chest were so powerful. She bent, hands on knees, willing her body to calm down. When the coughing stopped, she felt Alice wrap her coat around her shoulders.

Next to her, Brian was doing somewhat better. Once they both stopped coughing, Josie slid her arms into her coat. Clustered together, the five of them looked up at the main house. Behind it, thick black smoke billowed into the air, marring the cloudless sky, now going from a midnight blue to a periwinkle as the sun rose.

"What do we do?" Nicola said.

Josie took a moment to get her bearings. Lucky for them, the wind had died down overnight although a slight breeze sent the smoke listing toward the top of the mountain. "We go downwind. To the rage room," Josie said. "We just have to hope that it doesn't burn down along with the main house."

FORTY-TWO

In the rage room, Alice and Sandrine went to work, clearing a space for all of them to sit. Brian stood at the doorway, watching the fire destroy the main house. Nicola found a broom and swept up as much broken glass as she could, pushing it all into a pile in the center of the room.

Josie was still trying to catch her breath. She couldn't get the thick sooty feel out of her throat. She wished she had water but all of their supplies had gone up with the main house. Although the cabins still had running water, the rage room did not. She didn't have the energy, or the wind, to walk past the main house and up to one of the cabins for water. Not yet. She leaned against a wall and zipped up her coat. Plunging her hands into the pockets, she was relieved to find her gloves and her phone. She'd had her phone on the charger in the house, but it was already at eighty-nine percent. Her heart sank at the realization that this time, when the battery ran out, she had no way to charge it.

Once enough area had been cleared, Sandrine, Alice, and Nicola sat down, backs against the wall. Brian stayed in the doorway.

Nicola pulled her knees to her chest, hugging her legs. "What the hell just happened?"

Over his shoulder, Brian said, "I think it's pretty obvious."

Josie moved around the room, pretending to pace, until she felt her phone buzz inside her hand, text notifications arriving. She froze in place, waiting until they stopped.

"No shit," Nicola said irritably. "I mean how did this happen? How did the fire start?"

"How would we know?" Alice said. "You were there! Do you know how it started?"

Nicola shot her a dirty look. "You know what I mean! What could have caused it?"

"It came from the kitchen," Sandrine said. She zipped up her utility jacket and hunched down inside it. It didn't feel too cold at the moment, but Josie knew as the hours passed, they would slowly freeze.

Alice scuttled closer to Sandrine. "You and Brian were in there. Did you see anything?"

Over his shoulder, Brian answered, "I didn't."

Sandrine narrowed her eyes at his back. "You were messing with the generator. Did you do something?"

Nicola said, "You were supposed to be watching him! Wouldn't you have seen it if he 'did something'? What are you saying, exactly, Sandrine? You think Brian—whose childhood trauma was a fire that destroyed his group home—set this fire?"

Josie found a space along one of the walls away from everyone else.

"I didn't say that," Sandrine said quickly.

A cloud of smoke pushed through the doors. Alice, Nicola, and Sandrine began coughing.

"Cl-close the doors, please," Alice stammered.

Brian took one last look at the inferno and then pulled them closed. He walked over and sat beside Nicola. "I didn't 'do' anything to the generator," he mumbled. "I was trying to see if we could get anything more out of it, but it was completely out of fuel."

Alice rubbed her face with both hands. "Does it matter what happened or how? The only question we should be asking ourselves is what do we do now?"

Josie pulled out her phone and checked the text messages. No one noticed, or if they did, they didn't mention it. Nothing from Noah but several messages from Gretchen.

> *Got new info for you. Heather checked out Cooper Riggs. He's retired army, 10th Mountain Division. No criminal record. No one's heard from him since the storm began. Sheriff's office said they'll look into it. No word from Noah so also looking into that.*

Josie tried to quell the worry that bloomed in her stomach at the sight of Noah's name. Why wasn't he in touch with the team? Where was he? Where was Cooper? What was going on down there? She pushed her worries aside, trying to focus on the rest of the messages from Gretchen. There were many.

> *Haven't forgotten you. Deputy from Sullivan County said they're trying to figure out the best way to get up there and then get all of you off the mountain. They're coordinating with the state police. Hopefully not much longer. Also, we think we found two of your people. Tara Pietro, age 39. Originally from Florida. No priors. No warrants. Here's the article. Pasting it since you probably can't follow the link.*

Josie scrolled down. Tara Pietro had to be Taryn Pederson. She'd chosen a name similar to hers. The article was from the *St. Augustine Record*, dated twenty-two months ago.

St. Augustine Man Dead After Whale Collides
with Boat

Josie skimmed through it, noting that the details were exactly as Taryn had given during the week. She and her husband had been out on a small fishing boat off the coast of Florida when a whale crashed into the boat, causing it to tip. Taryn's husband had fallen into the water and drowned. She'd been able to get his body back onto the boat and perform CPR, but he couldn't be saved. Alone at sea, shaken and not as skilled at handling the vessel as her husband, she had made a distress call. Local authorities had come to her aid.

Gretchen had followed up the story with a message that said:

Tara Pietro moved to South Jersey after the accident. We talked with a neighbor who is bringing in her mail. Tara doesn't work. Got a payout from her husband's accident. Travels a lot. Neighbor said she's away on vacation for two weeks right now but didn't know where so I'm pretty sure this is who you're looking for.

Alice's voice brought Josie back to the situation at hand. "What do we do if the fire spreads?"

Smoke slid beneath the door, lingering inside the space.

"Oh God," Brian groaned. His face was in his hands.

Sandrine said, "The wind is pretty calm right now. I don't think it will. Maybe this will be good. Emergency services might respond more quickly. They won't want a forest fire on their hands."

"But should we stay here?" asked Nicola.

Josie scrolled down to the next message.

Next one is Bradley Davison. Currently residing in Los Angeles. Copying and pasting again.

"What choice do we have?" Alice said. "We need shelter."

Josie looked up from her phone. "We could go to one of the cabins. They, at least, have water. It might be easier to stay warm if all of us are in a more confined space."

"But all of our food is gone," Nicola said. "Our source of heat is gone. Sure, the cabins have stoves, but we don't have anything left to burn, and we can't chop anything down because the axe was in the main house!"

Alice said, "Our source of heat is right outside those doors. That place is going to be burning for a long time."

Josie scrolled down and quickly read the next article, which was fourteen years old.

Survivors of North Star Boys' Home Fire Still Struggle with Loss Fifteen Years Later

Bradley Davison remembers the day his group home went up in flames like it happened yesterday. "That kind of thing gets permanently imprinted on your memory, you know? I still think about it almost every day. I have lots of triggers. Nightmares. It's tough."

The other two survivors, who Davison thinks of as brothers, agree with him. They were only a year younger than Davison when a fire tore through the home for foster children on the outskirts of Los Angeles. Thirteen children and four counselors died that day. It was one of the most tragic days in the city's history.

"I don't think I've recovered, really," says Chance Fields. "I still hear their screams in my sleep. The kids who got trapped up on the top floors and couldn't get out in time."

Micah Hewlitt says, "Yeah. That was one of the worst things. I think I've got survivor's guilt or something. I've had trouble with drugs and alcohol ever since. Can't hold down a job. It affects everything."

The three boys went to individual foster homes after the fire. Although they kept in touch, they never spent much time together after the tragedy.

"It was too hard," says Bradley. "We remind each other of what happened."

The subsequent investigation revealed that the cause of the fire was undetermined. Foul play could not be ruled out. Fifteen years later, the site of one of the city's most tragic chapters is now North Star Park. Although a plaque commemorates the fire, most families who come to enjoy the playground and picnic area don't remember the building that used to stand there and later burned to the ground.

All three survivors toured the new park recently on the anniversary of the fire. The mood was somber. "I guess this is nice," Bradley said. "Making something good for the community from this place, but it doesn't take away the pain. Nothing will ever take away the pain."

"We're going to starve up here," Nicola said. "How long can we go without food?"

"You don't need food to survive a couple of days," said Alice. "We can get by on water."

More smoke seeped around the edges of the doors. Nicola coughed again.

Brian watched the smoke undulate along the floor, like vipers slithering straight at him. He leapt up. "I can't stay here."

"We have to stay here," Sandrine said. "It's okay, Brian. Please. Sit back down."

Alice said, "I've been thinking about it. We'll never make it if we try to walk to the bottom of the mountain. The snow is too deep. It's a few miles. We'll be soaked and frozen and even once we get down there, the nearest house or town or anything is miles away. We're stuck here."

Josie scrolled to the final messages from Gretchen.

By the way, this guy, Bradley Davison, is not married. Doesn't even have a girlfriend but I do think we've got the right person based on the information you gave us. He has no priors although he did have a restraining order against him a few years back. It was that actor who had the big sexual assault scandal, Dean Thurman.

FORTY-THREE

Josie's heart kicked into overdrive. Blood roared in her ears. There was the connection she had been looking for between any of the imposters and Sandrine. Thurman had starred in a movie with Sandrine's mother and then had an affair with her. The last of Gretchen's messages glowed on the screen.

Still working on Nicola Davies.

Gretchen and Detective Loughlin hadn't bothered to check out the connection between Thurman and Brian. Thurman was dead. Whatever issues there had been between him and Brian, it would seem irrelevant to Josie's colleagues from where they sat. They didn't know what Josie knew.

Brian walked toward the door again.

Josie typed back a quick message.

Thanks. Things here are deteriorating rapidly. Tara Pietro is missing. Possibly murdered. The main house is burning. No food. No heat. Supplies gone. Phone will run out soon. No way to charge. Please help.

She hit send but a small clock beneath the message twirled, indicating that it would not go through. "Shit," she muttered under her breath.

Brian opened the door. More smoke wafted inside. "I can't stay here. I just can't. You don't understand. The smell. I can't stay."

Sandrine leapt to her feet and strode over to him, taking both his hands in hers. "Brian, look at me. It's okay. You're safe. Remember your flashback-halting protocol. Breathe. I'll help you with it."

Sandrine counted off the seconds for the box breathing. Brian struggled to mirror her but eventually began to calm down a bit. Alice jumped up and shut the doors again, blocking out the smoke.

"Come on," Sandrine said, tugging Brian's hands toward the other end of the room where the rest of them waited. "For now, this is the best place for us to be."

Coughing, Nicola wiped at her watery eyes. "But the smoke."

Sandrine motioned for Brian to sit down on the floor again. "The wind is pushing most of it uphill. It will be worse if we try to get into one of the cabins than if we just stay here."

"And if we go outside, we'll freeze," Alice pointed out. "It's at least dry here and we have some barrier against the smoke."

Sandrine sat down on the floor, cross-legged, beside Brian. "I know this seems like the worst possible time to do this," she said. "But let's circle up and try some grounding exercises."

"That is the stupidest thing I've ever heard," Nicola said. She looked to Brian but his eyes had gone unfocused and vacant. He was lost in some pocket of memory.

Alice scooted over and sat on the other side of Sandrine. "Do you have a better idea? Because right now all we can do is sit here and freak out. Didn't we come here to learn how to not freak out so much?"

Josie slipped her phone into her pocket and sat down beside Alice. Nicola glared at each one of them before scuttling over and sitting next to Brian to complete the circle. Sandrine said, "I know these aren't the best circumstances, but let's try to take some deep breaths."

Josie looked over at the door, but no more smoke filtered around it. The wind must have shifted again. Still, she could smell the fire raging outside. She wondered if the flames had spread to any of the cabins or nearby trees. What would happen to them if it began to spread? They'd have to do their best to get down the trail, wading through nearly three feet of snow with very little clothing to warm them. They'd never be able to outrace the fire if it spread. The vise took hold of her chest again and she knew immediately it was from fear and anxiety and not the remnants of smoke in the air.

But Alice was right. This was not the time to freak out. Josie couldn't control anything that was happening outside, but she could try to control her thoughts and her breathing. She tuned back in to Sandrine's words, following her instructions as she guided them through a breathing exercise. She had fallen right back into her role as a therapist and guide. The remarkable calm she'd exuded all week returned, in spite of everything that Josie had revealed to her the night before.

Josie noticed that Sandrine wasn't using any of the grounding techniques she had taught them during the week, probably because they all involved being in touch with your surroundings in sensory ways and they were already over-whelmed by their present circumstances. Instead, she had them focus more on their bodies. "Rub your hands together," she instructed softly. "Feel the friction, the warmth that your palms create."

Josie immediately thought of Mettner. Again, she felt his hand in hers as the life bled away from him. She was glad when Sandrine moved on. "Put one hand on your heart. Feel it beating. Feel how it pumps your blood so effortlessly, bringing oxygen to the rest of your body. This heart has sustained you through all the days of your life. It has seen you through the best and worst times of your life. Feel it now and know it will see you through more."

Josie knew her heartbeat should be slowing but it was still on overdrive as her mind returned to a safer topic than the inferno raging outside: the connection between the imposters and Sandrine. Brian, Dean Thurman, Delilah Stowe, Sandrine. What reason would Brian have for harassing Dean Thurman to such a degree that a restraining order was necessary?

"Now put one of your hands on the back of your neck," Sandrine instructed. "Feel how solid and comforting it feels, like when you were an infant being cradled by a parent."

A parent.

Josie looked across the circle where Sandrine and Brian sat side by side, heads bent, their left hands on the back of their necks. Josie hadn't seen any physical similarities between them before but she hadn't been looking for them. Why would she? But now, she stared at them, searching for a resemblance and flipping through her mental snapshots from the week. It was their eyes, Josie thought. They both had blue eyes and their eyebrows arced over them in the same configuration. When they smiled, their cheeks bunched in the same way, making the same lines in their faces. It was incredibly subtle but once you saw it, you couldn't unsee it.

But Sandrine could not have children. Even if she could have had them, she was not old enough to be Brian's mother. Yet he had grown up in foster care, parentless. From what Josie had gathered, he had been in the system since birth, never adopted. No one had asked him that week if he had ever made any attempts to find his biological parents but that didn't mean he hadn't.

A puff of cold air, tinged with smoke, came from under the

door. Alice coughed but quickly regained her focus, dipping her chin to her chest and continuing to follow the breathing instructions Sandrine was giving like a mantra.

Josie remembered what Sandrine had said about her mother. *She left me with 'friends' for months at a time. I was never sure if she'd come back or not but she always did. I never knew where she went or why.* Had Delilah disappeared for months at a time to give birth to another child? A child she'd had with a married co-star? Was Dean Thurman Brian's father? That would make Sandrine and Brian siblings.

All along, Brian had said that he didn't think Sandrine was the person she claimed to be. *I'm not sure she is who she says she is.* Somehow, he had found out that Delilah Stowe was his mother. Even though Sandrine had long ago changed her name, he had tracked her down. But if that was the case, why hadn't he just called her on the phone or gone to her office and told her that they were long-lost siblings? Why was he here, at this retreat, with two other imposters?

More smoke reached them. This time, as Josie inhaled, it tickled her throat. She coughed, using the hand over her heart to cover her mouth. The rest of them followed suit. Alice's face was red, tears streaming down her cheeks. "We should try to block the bottom of the door with something."

Nicola looked around. "Like what?"

"No," said Brian. "I can't stay in here."

Sandrine reached over and took his hand. "It's okay, Brian. I think Alice has a good idea. It will keep some of the smell out."

"No," he said. Then he yanked his hand from hers and jumped up, sprinting toward the door. He threw it open and plunged out into the snow.

FORTY-FOUR

Noah paced the dark cellar, hands extended in front of him so that he didn't bump into walls or anything else that might be down there. He had to get the feeling back into all of his limbs. He had to be ready. He'd found a corner to relieve himself. He'd been around the room enough times now to make a mental map. There were several shelves along one of the walls. He'd identified as many of the objects lining them as he could by feel. Paint cans, paintbrushes, tape, a few tarps, multiple cans and bottles of chemicals, what felt like holiday decorations, light bulbs, a host of other miscellaneous things that he didn't bother trying to puzzle out because they weren't of any use to him. The only thing on those shelves he cared about was the hammer. He'd tucked it into the back of his waistband so it would be easily accessible when Cooper returned.

Except that he had not heard Cooper's footsteps overhead for a very long time. No light had come from around the door at the top of the steps.

He had a choice to make. He could try smashing the door-knob off and opening the door, or he could wait. If Cooper heard him trying to get out, there was a chance he would just shoot through the door and kill Noah. If Cooper wasn't there and Noah couldn't get out, when he did eventually come back, he'd see whatever damage Noah made trying to escape and then maybe kill Noah.

Perhaps it was best to wait for him. Noah had the advantage down here in the dark. Cooper didn't know he had freed himself of his bindings. He didn't know he had the hammer. Noah could wait until he got to the bottom of the steps and attack. Except that if Cooper opened the door or turned on any light, Noah would be blinded, and he'd not only lose his advantage but once again be at Cooper's mercy. He needed a plan for when Cooper returned, with a contingency that wouldn't leave him helpless in the event that the lights came on.

He paced the cellar again, mind working to come up with something. The furnace kicked on and off. Up above, the house was silent. There wasn't even wind to make it groan. There was no sound at all.

Noah stopped in the middle of the room. "Fuck this," he muttered. "Plans are stupid."

He pulled the hammer from his waistband and jogged up the steps. Before he had time to think about it, he lifted the hammer over his head and brought it down where he thought the doorknob was located. A satisfying clang reverberated through his arms.

He kept going. When the knob fell off, he used the claw end of the hammer along the edge of the door to pry it open. Then he was standing in the dated kitchen. The light was dim. Noah blinked several times to get his eyes acclimated. He found the clock on the wall. It was the afternoon but of what day?

"Just what the hell do you think you're doing?"

Cooper stood in the doorway that led to the living room. Noah's mind took in his appearance. Oversized jeans, coat, hat pulled over his bald head, gloves on his hands. Snow wet on his boots. No pistol.

Noah rushed at him.

FORTY-FIVE

Josie got to her feet and ran after Brian. Outside, the smoke from the main house continued to rise upward into the sky. An occasional burst of wind sent plumes of it toward the rage room but for the most part, the air was still breathable. Still, she reached down into her coat and pulled the collar of her shirt up over her nose. Looking around, she saw no fresh footprints leading away from the building. There was only the shoveled path which was filled with all their tracks. The heat from the fire had turned those to slush. She looked down the slope but didn't see him. Had he gone up toward the cabins? She turned to follow the path that way, but Alice's voice stopped her.

"Josie! Where are you going?"

Josie lowered her collar. "I have to find Brian and bring him back. He's not well. He could die out here."

Alice stepped forward and grabbed Josie's arm. "He could kill you! He could be the killer, Josie! Have you thought of that?"

"Yes," Josie said. "But I still have to go after him."

"Why? Is this because of what Nicola said? That Taryn's blood is on your hands? She's wrong, Josie. I hope you know that. If something bad happened to her, you couldn't have predicted that. You did the right thing."

Josie looked into her hazel eyes, now gold and amber in the sun. She didn't believe Alice but there was no point in arguing.

"Thank you, Alice."

Alice pulled at her arm, urging her back into the rage room. "Come back inside."

Gently, Josie peeled her fingers away and squeezed her hand. "I'll come back when I find Brian. But listen—" She broke off. She had told Sandrine she would not tell Alice about what she'd discovered regarding Taryn, Brian, and Nicola. Even if she had wanted to tell her, there hadn't been an opportunity but now, Josie worried about leaving Alice behind with Nicola and Sandrine, in a situation in which she didn't have all the information. She'd been too exhausted and overwhelmed the night before to question Sandrine's motives for keeping Alice out of the loop. At this point, did it matter if Alice slipped up or lost her composure again? If something happened to Alice before they got off this mountain because Josie didn't tell her everything, could she live with herself? The answer was no. She wasn't even sure she could live with the fact that whatever fate Taryn had met was likely her fault.

"What is it?" Alice said, still clutching Josie's hand.

"I need to tell you some things. We don't have much time so I'm going to tell you everything I know as quickly as I can and then I'm going to go find Brian and bring him back to the group. I need you to stay calm."

Alice's posture straightened. The fear in her eyes receded, replaced by something Josie had seen among many of her colleagues when they had to stow their personal emotions in order to get the job done. It was the ER nurse, comfortable in crisis and chaos, taking over. She was prepared for anything. Relief coursed through Josie's body, loosening the tense muscles in her shoulder blades.

A blast of smoke from the main house hit them. Josie pulled her shirt up over her face again and led Alice down toward the shed. Then she told her everything she'd learned so far, leaving out her theory that Brian might be Sandrine's sibling. Alice listened, her hand gripping Josie's more tightly with each word until Josie's knuckles ached. Sensing Josie's urgency and knowing they could be interrupted at any moment, she didn't ask any questions. Instead, when Josie finished, she said, "I can't let you go after Brian alone."

"I'll be fine," Josie said.

"You don't know that."

"I've taken on people a lot more frightening than Brian."

Alice gave a weak smile. "That doesn't make me feel better. What about the rest of us?"

"You'll be fine here as long as you stay together," Josie told her. "There's no sense in all of us freezing outside. Go back inside. Stay close to Sandrine and wait for me. I promise you I'm not going to provoke Brian. I just want to bring him back to the rage room. I can't risk any more of us disappearing or getting injured or killed."

Reluctantly, Alice left her and ran back inside the rage room. Josie waited until the door closed and then she followed the melted path up past the main house, keeping her nose and mouth covered and going as quickly as she could. As she passed in front of it, a blistering wave of heat hit her so hard, she felt like she might fall over. She veered off into the snow to get away from it. As she passed Sandrine's cabin, she saw that the siding had begun to melt. Josie willed her feet to move faster but the snow was still high and difficult to push through. Her chest was tight. It felt impossible to take a deep breath. She was regretting her decision to go after Brian when she saw him sitting on the front steps of his and Nicola's cabin. He was hunched over, elbows on knees, head turned toward the fire. It was still smoky here but no more so than in the rage room.

Standing in front of him, she spoke through the fabric of her shirt. "Brian, please come back to the camp."

He didn't move, didn't look at her. His voice was flat when he spoke. "I don't want to go back. I'd rather be out here, in the open air."

Josie lowered her shirt. The back of her throat still felt thick and coated with soot. "You can sit out in front of the rage room, then. Just come back. No one goes anywhere alone, remember? It's not safe."

"The smell brings it back," he said, eyes still fixed on the fire. The middle of the building had started to collapse onto itself. The glass of the large windows in front had already cracked and shattered in some places. Flames licked through the openings. "You know, the others, they heard the screams. That was the thing that always stayed with them, but for me it's the smell. It takes me right back to that time in my life."

Josie's eyes watered. "I know the smell is a trigger for you but you're not safe out here. Please, just come back. It's important that we all stay together for when we're rescued, which should be soon, I hope."

His eyes were glassy and unfocused again. He was back in some place she couldn't touch. Los Angeles, probably. During the fire that had killed over a dozen people in his group foster home.

Josie climbed up onto the first step, holding the railing to keep her balance. The lack of clean air was making her dizzy. She said, "You don't have much more time to get what you want from Sandrine."

He blinked, alertness returning to his face. Slowly, his head swiveled toward her. His Adam's apple bobbed up and down in his throat as he swallowed twice. When he next spoke, his voice was scratchy. "Wait. How did you... you couldn't... does Sandrine know that..."

Josie was in dangerous territory now. She had to be careful

what she said so he didn't realize that she was bluffing her way through getting information from him. "Sandrine doesn't know anything. Neither does Alice."

"Then how? How do you know why I'm here?"

"It's my job, Brian. Or should I call you Bradley?"

FORTY-SIX

"How long?" he croaked. "How long have you known?"

Sweat beaded along Josie's hairline. "Not that long."

He reached into one of his coat pockets. Josie's body tensed immediately. Her hand itched to reach for a service weapon she wasn't carrying. Luckily for her, Brian was only fishing around for his broken vape pen. He held the pen in one of his gloved hands and stared down at it. "You didn't tell Sandrine?"

"I thought, as her brother, you should have that honor."

She could see the shock hit him like a punch. He flinched a little and curled his fingers around the vape pen. Josie looked back down the path they'd shoveled which was wider now that much of the snow out front of the main house was melting. No one had emerged from the rage room from what she could tell. They had some time, if she could stand being this close to the fire a bit longer. She said, "When did you find out that you had siblings?"

She deliberately used the plural, again bluffing her way to getting information from him. As they'd sat in the circle in the freezing rage room during Sandrine's grounding exercise, some part of her mind had been trying to put more of the pieces together. She hadn't had time to lay out all of those puzzle pieces and examine their edges to see just how they fit together, but she had a vague notion of the bigger picture they formed.

Brian watched her carefully now. Without taking his eyes off her, he turned the vape pen over in his hands. She saw the hesitation in his eyes, him trying to decide just how much to tell her. Finally, he said, "A few years ago. But I don't understand, how could you possibly...?"

"You weren't the only person not raised by his biological parents," Josie pointed out.

He sighed. "Fucking Taryn."

Josie reminded herself not to show any delight in having guessed correctly.

"She told you?" Brian asked.

"She told me that her mother had adopted her as an infant," Josie said.

Like Brian, Taryn was also too old to be Sandrine's biological child. Josie remembered Taryn and Sandrine clearing plates from the dining table in the main hall, how they had looked almost like twins. In fact, Taryn physically resembled Sandrine more than Brian. If they'd teamed up together for some common goal, it made sense that Taryn was also one of Sandrine's siblings although Josie still couldn't guess what they were after. She also still didn't know where Nicola fit into things. Gretchen hadn't been able to track down her true identity.

Brian switched the vape pen from one hand to another, muttering, "I can't believe this."

Nicola had never said she was adopted—though Taryn hadn't either until the private conversation with Josie. Nicola didn't bear much of a resemblance to the others. Josie thought she could see some resemblance between her and Sandrine— they had similar chins and more or less the same nose—but now Josie couldn't be certain if the likeness was really there or if her mind was tricking her into seeing it because of her theories.

Was she following the evidence or trying to force the evidence to fit her theory?

Only one way to find out, said Mett's ghost voice. *You've come this far.*

Why else would Nicola be on the retreat? Why go to the trouble of lying about her past trauma to ensure that she made it onto the retreat? Although it was possible she and Brian were a couple and just pretending to be married, Josie still would have expected to see more intimacy and closeness between them.

Josie pictured Sandrine, Brian, and Nicola seated in the rage room, their hands behind their necks. Their left hands. They were all left-handed, just like Taryn. In fact, now that Josie thought about it, she, Alice, and Meg were the only right-handed people at the retreat. It had been an issue while sitting for meals with the left-handers always bumping the right-handed eaters. Plus, most people Josie knew were right-handed. Mett's voice floated through her mind again, a memory this time. *Only about eight to ten percent of the world's population is left-handed.* They'd been working a stabbing case with two potential suspects. Forensics told them the perpetrator had been left-handed. Mettner had argued that they should question the left-handed suspect first and put the case to bed in no time at all. He'd been right. They'd gotten a confession within an hour.

What were the odds that of seven people on this retreat, four of them were left-handed?

Mettner had also told her left-handedness was hereditary.

She was sure that four half-siblings all being left-handed was extremely rare, but it was enough for Josie to take a chance on questioning Brian in that moment to see if her working theory was correct.

"When did the three of you find each other?"

Brian hung his head. "About five years ago. DNA testing and all that. One of those websites where you mail in your saliva, and they tell you your heritage, but you also have the option of making your profile public to see who you're related to."

Glass shattered in the distance. A large part of the A-frame in the front of the main house collapsed onto the porch. Embers flew over their heads.

"It must have been a shock to know you had two half-sisters," Josie said. "In different parts of the country. Did you meet up right away?"

He glanced to the side, eyes following the smoke that rose into the sky. "I was the last one to do the DNA test. Nic and Tara had already met. Once my DNA went live on the site, they both contacted me. We met up a month later."

"How did you know you were all Delilah Stowe's children?"

A grim smile stretched across his face as he turned back to her. "Wow. You really dug deep. Damn. It took us years to figure this shit out and you did it in a week. We should have just hired you from the beginning."

She was a police officer, not a private investigator, but she didn't remind him of that, hoping to get more information out of him before again trying to get him to return to the rage room.

He went on, "The website tells you which side you're related on—the father or the mother. We knew right away we all had the same mother. We didn't know about Delilah but according to the site we used to process our DNA, I was related to someone who was like the fifth cousin twice removed of this fairly famous actor. He died a few years ago."

"Dean Thurman," Josie said.

"Holy shit. How did you—" He shook his head. "You know what, never mind. Yeah. Dean Thurman. Taryn told me I should follow that, like a lead, and I did. I was able to confirm that I was Dean Thurman's illegitimate son. Unfortunately, that wasn't very good news for me."

"Because of the sexual assault scandals?" Josie asked.

"Yeah, and the fact that by the time I got a meeting with him, he was about to be sentenced to house arrest for the rest of his natural life! I was so disappointed. I spent a lifetime dreaming about meeting my birth father, and he was just this old perverted asshole who didn't care about other people at all."

"What did he tell you when you met with him?"

Brian laughed bitterly. "That he didn't have any money left, if that's what I was after. It wasn't. I mean, I'm not going to lie, it would have been nice, but at that point, I just wanted information. He was the one who told me my mother was Delilah Stowe. Then he said some really disgusting things about her that, honestly, I wish I could unhear."

His face turned beet-red at the memory.

"You didn't take it very well," Josie said. "That's why he took out a restraining order against you?"

He didn't answer. His eyes started to take on that faraway look again. Josie tried to keep him in the present. "Then you knew," she said. "About Delilah."

He blinked, focusing on her once more. "Yeah. We started researching her. We found out she had another daughter, one she kept."

"Lola Stowe," Josie filled in.

"You're actually very impressive," Brian said. "Yeah. She was our last link to our mother. We'd been so happy to find one another. It was really something. I felt like I had family for the first time in my life. But what we couldn't understand, what we could not get over, was why our mother had kept Lola but given all of us up. We wanted answers."

Sweat dripped down Josie's face and she wiped it away with her coat sleeve. "How did you find Sandrine then?"

"Nic had a lead on her father's side, too. There were still

some people alive in New York who remembered him. Someone she got in touch with confirmed Delilah was her mother and remembered that Delilah had had another daughter, one who was older by the time Nic was born. He'd seen her on TV once. He said she was a 'woo-woo head shrinker that burned incense and sang to crystals.'" Here he rolled his eyes. "So it took us a while to track down who he meant. It was Sandrine."

The siding on the front of Sandrine's cabin now looked like syrup, melting from the white heat of the main house next to it. Even where they were, it felt intensely hot. Josie wanted to claw all of her clothes off and roll around in the snow. She tried to maintain her composure. There were a lot of things she still wanted to know but she jumped right to the most pressing one. "Brian—Bradley—if you wanted answers, why didn't you just call Sandrine or go to her office? Why are the three of you here on this retreat? Why lie?"

He pocketed the vape pen. "Why lie?"

Josie knew he was buying time to come up with another lie. She didn't fill the silence. His hand wrapped over his wrist, where his burn scar lay beneath the sleeve of his coat. "We were afraid that she would reject us," he said. "She has the perfect life. What if knowing she had siblings ruined it? As far as the retreat? It's perfect if you think about it. We're isolated, alone with her. She's a captive audience. She's forced to get to know us."

Josie wiped more sweat from her face. It was getting more and more difficult to breathe. "You'll have to do better than that," she told him. "I know that's not your only reason for being here."

FORTY-SEVEN

Josie used the railing to pull herself up another step so that she was eye to eye with Brian. Down at the main house, the other side of the A-frame crashed down, destroying the porch. Flaming pieces of wood rolled onto the path and shot out across the snow. Soon, it was going to be even more difficult to get back to the rage room. Brian watched, his expression oddly blank.

"You all lied about your identities and flew from all over the country just to get to know Sandrine on this retreat? You expect me to believe that was all the three of you intended to do?"

"What else do you think we were planning?" he asked, eyes still on the debris flaming at the foot of the main house.

"I don't know but Meg is dead and Taryn is gone."

"I don't know anything about that," he said, squeezing his wrist.

"You don't? The three of you came here to 'get to know' Sandrine, your older sister, and by the end of the week, someone's been murdered and one of you is missing. I'm trying to do that math, Brian, but it's not adding up."

His forefinger worked under the edge of his glove and then

beneath the sleeve of his coat. "You think I know what happened to Meg and Taryn?"

"I think you know something."

His forefinger found the scar and rubbed across it.

He met her eyes. "I don't know anything about what happened to them. I didn't kill Meg and I don't know what happened to Taryn. You think I'm not worried about her? She's my big sister! She's my family. My real family!"

Josie pulled herself up another step, crowding him now. "Taryn seemed far more attached to Sandrine than to you or Nicola."

"So what?" he said irritably. "It wasn't a contest! I'm not the one who got pissed off about how close she got to Sandrine."

"Nicola didn't like it," Josie said. Nicola had been downright nasty to Taryn as the week progressed although Josie thought that was part of an act they were all putting on to cover their true motives.

With the tip of his gloved finger, Brian picked at the scab on his scar until a small bead of blood appeared. "If you really want to know what the plan was for this week, you need to talk to Nicola. She had different reasons for being here than us."

Before Josie could respond, shouting came from below them. Josie couldn't make it out at first but she knew it was coming from the other side of the main house. Grabbing Brian's arm, she dragged him to his feet and pushed him down the steps. "Let's go."

They took a wide berth around the front of the main house as they fought their way back to the rage-room building. The voice calling out became clearer. Alice. She was yelling Josie's name, and by the high-pitched waver in her voice, something bad had happened.

Josie nudged Brian along, trying to hurry the pace. From the door of the rage room, Alice lurched toward them, one arm wrapped around Sandrine's waist, holding her up. Blood was splattered down both their coats.

Brian stopped in his tracks, staring at them. "What the hell happened?" He looked behind them. "Where's Nicola?"

Alice glared at him. "She attacked Sandrine."

"What?" Brian said. In spite of what he'd just implied to Josie about Nicola, he seemed surprised.

"She stabbed Sandrine with a piece of broken glass," Alice said.

Sandrine dropped to her knees. Alice could no longer hold her up. Keeping her eye on Brian, Josie knelt as well and looked Sandrine over. "Where are you hurt?"

"It's superficial," Alice said.

Sandrine held up her hands, showing a large, bloody slash across one of her palms. Below that, there were more slices in her coat. Luckily, the weapon hadn't penetrated the thick fabric.

"She's in shock," said Alice.

She was right. Sandrine's breathing was labored. Her lips were almost blue. When Josie touched her cheek, it was cold and clammy. She pressed her fingers to Sandrine's throat and could barely feel her pulse.

"It's Nicola," Alice said, her eyes on Brian. "She's the killer. She's crazy. Out of control."

Josie leaned in and spoke softly into Sandrine's ear. "Is that what happened? Nicola attacked you?"

Sandrine nodded.

Brian said, "Where is she now?"

"Where do you think?" Alice snapped.

Pushing past them, he rushed through the doors of the rage room.

Alice slid an arm under one of Sandrine's armpits. "We need to get her out of the snow."

Josie looked around. The closest option was the shed, but Meg's body was inside, and she didn't want it disturbed. So much had already been lost in the past forty-eight hours. "Where?"

"We have to use one of the cabins. We have no choice."

Josie got on the other side of Sandrine, hooking a hand under her other armpit. "It's going to be a tough climb."

Together, they started hauling Sandrine toward the main house. "I don't care," Alice said. "We can't stay here. Josie, I'm telling you, Nicola is batshit crazy. She just completely lost it."

Josie guided them toward the tracks she and Brian had made on their way back from his cabin. "Walk and talk," she told Alice.

As the three of them hobbled back up the trail, Alice recounted what had happened; Josie kept panning the woods on either side of them, searching for any additional threats. Every nerve in her body was stretched taut.

"We were just sitting there, against the wall, waiting for you to come back. Nicola got up and went to the door. I don't know if she was watching the fire or waiting to see if Brian was coming back but I asked if she could close the door. More smoke was getting inside. She told me to shut my mouth. So I said she should shut her own mouth—that I wouldn't have to say anything if she would just stop letting all the damn smoke inside, and that I didn't understand why she let you go after Brian while she stayed behind. Then I said... I said... that if he came back but you didn't, I would make both of them pay."

"Alice," Josie said. They passed Sandrine's cabin. Now the side of it closest to the main house sagged, as if it was an ice cream cake that had begun to melt.

"I know, I know, but I was so frustrated and afraid and I'm tired of being afraid, Josie. I'm sick and tired of it. I don't even know why I said that! What am I going to do? Fight them both? I was sorry as soon as the words came out of my mouth. Then Nicola picked up a piece of glass and threatened me. Sandrine stood up and said we should both calm down."

Josie felt Sandrine's body shivering between them but she said nothing.

Alice went on. "Then Nicola told Sandrine to stay out of it or she would kill her. Then she said, 'You deserve it, you heartless bitch,' and she just started stabbing her. I pulled her away and I grabbed Sandrine and we got out of there."

A gust of wind blew a plume of smoke directly at them. They buried their mouths and noses in the crooks of their elbows. The smoke was thick but luckily, it passed over them quickly. Every muscle in Josie's body ached with the effort of helping Sandrine up the hill through the smoke. She didn't know that much about fires or their ability to jump or whether the snow would offer any insulation against the fire spreading but she prayed that it would stay contained to the main house and not spread to the other buildings, or worse, cause a forest fire.

"Which cabin?" Alice asked, once they were past it.

Josie pointed to the top of the slope. "Yours. It's the last one, furthest from the fire and we can see the entire camp from there."

What she meant was that they'd be able to see if Nicola or Brian tried to come after them.

FORTY-EIGHT

Time slowed down. It seemed to take hours to cross the tiny kitchen. As he got closer, Noah noticed Cooper's eyes widen. His hands started to lift. His mouth opened. Before he could do anything more than that, Noah tackled him, driving his shoulder square into Cooper's chest. He heard a puff of air expel from Cooper's mouth. Then they were flying together, feet completely off the ground for a short moment before they landed on the coffee table in the living room. It splintered under their combined weight. As Noah straddled Cooper, he felt some satisfaction realizing that he'd knocked the wind out of him. He watched him struggle for oxygen for a second before he looked around the room for his gun—or any gun—or something to restrain him with.

There were only curtains.

Before Cooper could get his breath back, Noah tore the curtains from their rods. He flipped Cooper onto his stomach and started to tie his hands behind his back. The fabric was slippery. Noah wasn't fast enough. Cooper flailed and bucked. His hands slipped out of the flimsy binding, and he wriggled off the remnants of the coffee table onto the floor. Noah followed but tripped over the discarded curtain and fell, landing next to Cooper.

Before he could get his bearings, Cooper hooked a leg across Noah's body, straddling him. His hands squeezed Noah's throat. "I told you I would kill you," he snarled. "You can't keep me away from her. No one will keep me away from her."

Noah swung a wild fist at Cooper's head, glancing a blow off his jaw. It was enough to stun him. Folding his arms across Cooper's wrists, Noah broke his grip. He lifted his hips and rolled Cooper onto his back. He had no idea where the hammer went. He had nothing but his hands.

He took great pleasure in smashing his fist into Cooper's nose.

Bone crunched. Blood poured from Cooper's nostrils. "You son of a bitch," he cried. "I'm gonna fucking kill you!"

Noah shifted his weight, getting onto one foot so he could roll Cooper onto his stomach. Wrenching his hands behind his back again, Noah said, "Not today, asshole."

Into the carpet, Cooper mumbled a long stream of expletives.

Noah leaned down and into his ear, asked, "Who are you? Who are you really and what are you doing here?"

A blast of cold air smacked against his back. He looked over his shoulder to see the front door wide open. A man filled its frame, tall and broad. He had thick, curly gray hair, and penetrating blue eyes. A dark purple bruise shadowed one side of his face. A deep cut scored his bottom lip. His clothes were wet. When he took a step inside, his right leg dragged behind him. Blood streaked his pantleg.

In his hands was a rifle, the barrel pointed at Noah. "Who the hell are you two and what are you doing in my damn house?"

FORTY-NINE

It was only marginally warmer inside Alice's cabin. At first, it felt cloying. Josie stripped off her coat and helped Alice get Sandrine's utility jacket off in order to assess her injuries. Then Josie locked the door and pushed the metal bed frame in front of it. It was precious little weight to keep someone from breaking inside, but it was something. Soon, the sweat on her face and running down her back dried and the cold set in. She quickly put her coat back on. "How bad is it?" she asked Alice.

"It's just this one cut on the palm." Alice held Sandrine's left hand out. "It's pretty bad. You'll definitely need stitches," she told Sandrine. "But it will have to wait till we get off this mountain. If we ever do. I need something to wrap this."

But there was nothing. Like Josie, Alice had removed all her belongings after Meg died and the blizzard had kept them to the main house. "Sandrine is wearing a dress under her jacket. She started tying it up near her waist so she could move around in the snow more easily but if you can loosen the knot, we can use the bottom of her dress," Josie said. "See if you can tear some of it off. Then put her glove over it. It won't be very sanitary but it's the best we can do."

Tearing fabric was not as easy as it looked in the movies. After struggling to untangle the knot that Sandrine had tied into her dress, it took both Josie and Alice several attempts before they tore a strip of it long enough to wrap her hand. Sandrine continued to shiver silently under their ministrations. Josie helped Alice to put her coat back on and then her gloves and hat. They leaned her against the wall and she slumped over onto her side, mumbling a thank you and closing her eyes.

Josie went to the window at the front of the cabin, but she didn't see anyone approaching. Alice walked over to the wood-burning stove and picked up the long-necked lighter on top of it. "We should light the stove. There must be something we can burn. The shower liner."

"It's toxic," Josie said. "And it won't burn long enough to give off any heat. Besides, I don't want to telegraph our position."

Alice laughed. "Our position? For all we know, that crazy bitch watched us walk all the way up here. There are a finite number of places we could have gone. If her and Brian want to get to us, they'll probably be able to do it."

Josie turned away from the window. She gestured toward Sandrine. "Then we'll need some rest. Let's sit."

They took their places on each side of Sandrine, huddling close together to share body heat. Now that they were away from the heat of the fire, the cold was relentless. Josie wondered if she should try to find some sticks outside, maybe break some small, low-hanging branches from trees and try to burn them. Alice was right that if Brian and Nicola really wanted to find them, it would take no time at all. Trying to hide was largely an exercise in futility. But Josie was desperately hoping that every hour that passed was an hour closer to being rescued. They should try to stretch the time they were hidden and secure in this cabin for as long as they could.

"Josie," Alice said. "What happened with Brian? Why were

you gone so long?"

Josie stood and quickly checked the window again. No sign of anyone. She resumed her place beside Sandrine and filled Alice in on what she'd figured out and confirmed by talking with Brian. Josie thought that Sandrine had slept through all of it but when she was finished speaking, she felt Sandrine's body quivering against hers. Josie looked over at her. Tears rolled down her bloodstained cheeks and she mumbled "sorry" over and over again.

Alice slid an arm across Sandrine's shoulders and pulled her close. "Wait just a minute," she said to Josie. "You're telling me that Sandrine's mother, an actress who pimped Sandrine out as a child in order to get parts, gave birth to three other children and gave them up for adoption and that they found one another as adults and decided they'd use fake names to get onto this retreat, and that Brian claims the reason was so they could get closer to Sandrine?"

"Yeah," said Josie. "But obviously that wasn't the real reason they came. They wouldn't have planted cameras or been pushing Sandrine so hard for information if all they wanted to do was 'get to know her.'"

"Then why? Why did they really come? Why kill Meg? And what the hell did they do to Taryn?"

"I don't know," Josie said. "I suspect that Meg saw something or found something and was killed so she wouldn't talk. I also think that whatever their plan was originally, after what Sandrine told us about her mother, Taryn didn't want to go through with it anymore."

Tremors shook Sandrine's body. Alice gathered her closer. "So they killed her, too? Hid her body somewhere?"

Josie scooted closer to Sandrine, again trying to share her body warmth although she knew that Sandrine's shivers were more due to shock than cold. "I don't know if they did it. Brian made it sound like it was Nicola. Whether he knew about it or was in on it, I can't say. The only thing I know for sure is that we can't trust either of them."

Alice tapped Sandrine's shoulder. "You knew about this? These siblings?"

Sandrine blinked more tears from her eyes. "No, of course not. I don't remember my mother ever being pregnant. Yes, she left me alone with virtual strangers for months at a time, but it never occurred to me she was going off to have a baby! I told you, I was only trying to survive. I didn't have the bandwidth for much else."

"But what do they want?" Alice said, her voice rising almost to a shout.

Sandrine shuddered and pulled away from Alice. Josie took one of her hands. "It's okay. Alice is just frustrated. We're not going to hurt you."

"I'm sorry," Alice mumbled.

They fell into silence. There was only the sound of Sandrine weeping quietly as she leaned into Josie's shoulder. This time, Alice checked the window. "No one," she said before returning to her seat. Josie's feet had grown numb with the cold. Inside her boots, she flexed her toes, hoping to bring feeling back. Her mind returned to the imposters. The siblings. In Josie's experience, most crimes came down to only a handful of motives. Drugs, money, heartbreak, to name a few. There was also revenge.

What had Nicola said to Sandrine before the revelations about Delilah Stowe?

You lived a golden life. I mean, look at you! The picture of success.

Brian had bemoaned the fact that Delilah had kept Sandrine, who she'd had while still a teenager, but given up her other three children. He and Taryn had had horrible upbringings. Josie still didn't know Nicola's story but if it was true that she'd been adopted by a family who had another daughter and that daughter had been abducted and killed, her childhood had not been very good either. Josie tried to imagine what it must have been like for them when they finally found Lola Stowe and saw that she was actually the super-successful psychologist, Dr. Sandrine Morrow. Not only had Delilah chosen to keep her while rejecting all of them, but she'd turned out extremely well. By all appearances, she had had a golden life.

They'd had no idea of the truth.

Josie said, "I think they came here for revenge."

Alice pulled her knees to her chest and hugged her legs. "What?"

"I'm not sure how they hoped to achieve it," Josie said. "But I think they wanted revenge on Sandrine for being their mother's chosen one."

"They were better off without her!" Sandrine cried. "They were! No matter what happened to them, it was better than being raised by her!"

"But they didn't know that," Josie said.

Sandrine wiped at the snot pouring from her nose. "None of them will ever understand. They probably don't even believe me. What she did to me—no human being deserves that. They were lucky. They were lucky. They were lucky."

She slouched even lower, eyes going unfocused much the way that Brian's tended to do when he was disassociating.

"They were lucky. They were lucky," Sandrine repeated, the words now a mantra.

Josie squeezed her hand. "Okay, Sandrine. Okay. That's enough. I think right now the best thing we can do is try to get some rest. I'll stay awake. You two close your eyes for a bit."

She expected Alice to object, but she didn't. Instead, she turned her back to Sandrine and curled onto her side. Josie waited until they both settled into a regular pattern of breathing before she took out her phone. It was down to twenty-three percent. She sent up a silent prayer for that she'd gotten service in the last couple of hours and then checked to see if her message had gone through to Gretchen. She took in a deep breath of relief when she saw that it had. One hour and thirteen minutes ago. There wasn't a response to it but that only meant that whatever Gretchen wrote back had simply not yet reached her.

Josie stood up and went to the window, checking again to see if the others were nearby. All she could see was the black smoke from the main house floating up into the sky. The path they had all shoveled was empty. She sat back down beside Sandrine who stirred briefly, eyes popping open, blind with terror. Josie put a gentle hand on her back. "It's okay. You're safe for now. Go back to sleep."

Sandrine blinked until her eyes focused on Josie. She smiled and patted Josie's hand with her good one. Then she closed her eyes once more. She shifted a few times before finding a comfortable enough position to go back to sleep. Josie stayed upright, concentrating on the sensations in her body. The low vibration she'd come to know as her hypervigilance, her body on guard for any and all threats. The dull pounding in her temples. The aches in her feet and calves. The tension in her shoulder blades. The punishing cold enveloping her entire body.

Nothing good was coming of this body scan.

Instead, she turned to thoughts of Noah, trying to drown out her worry, and focus on him. She pictured his face, his thick dark hair, the puckered scar near his right shoulder where she'd shot him.

How had there ever been any question as to his devotion to her? She'd shot him and he'd still married her!

In her mind, she was snug in bed with him, his arms wrapped around her. Their dog, Trout, warmed her feet. She could feel his breath in her hair. She was so deep into the memory that she never even heard the crunch of feet over snow outside.

FIFTY

A pounding on the cabin door startled Josie back to reality. She jumped up and ran to the window. On the tiny stoop outside the cabin's front door stood Nicola. Her coat was in shreds. Gone was the knit hat she'd been wearing the last time Josie saw her. Blood stained her strawberry-blonde hair and smudged her cheeks. When she lifted her arm to pound on the door again, blood flew from her fist. Josie couldn't see where it landed from the angle of the window, but she imagined quite an impressive blood spatter on the front door. Beyond her, Brian lurched up the shoveled path, holding his head. Blood poured from between his fingers. He swayed and stumbled, fell to one knee and stayed there. He opened his mouth, calling out, but Josie couldn't hear what he said.

Coming up behind her, Alice said, "We can't let them in."

Josie said, "They're injured."

Sandrine sat upright. "Nicola tried to kill me."

"I know," Josie said. "But they're both bleeding."

Alice craned her neck around Josie to peek out the window. "Maybe they tried to kill one another. Either way, it is not our problem."

Nicola turned toward Brian and called back to him. Josie could see blood streaking down the side of her scalp, her neck, and inside the collar of her coat. She turned and rushed down the steps toward Brian. As she ran, her gaze remained locked on the path below them, as if she was expecting someone or something to follow.

The bear? Josie wondered. "They're bleeding a lot."

"That's not our problem," Alice said. "They can take shelter in another cabin until help arrives."

Brian fell again, this time taking Nicola with him. Now crumpled onto the ground, Josie could see a trail of blood behind them.

"If they're that badly hurt," Josie said. "They're not going to attack us. Alice, they need help."

Once again, Nicola stood and got Brian to his feet. She slipped her shoulders under his arm and kept him upright. They had a small conversation. Nicola looked behind them—no one on the path—and they started toward the cabin again.

"No," Sandrine said. "No. We can't let them in here. Brian, maybe, but not Nicola. She attacked me!"

Alice said, "Josie, even if we did let them in, I've got nothing to work with. No first aid kit. No bandages, nothing to clean wounds with. Nothing! Sandrine is right, though. I was there! Nicola meant to kill her."

Nicola and Brian reached the bottom of the steps. Brian waved her away, holding onto the railing with one hand while he touched the side of his head with the other. Nicola kept glancing from him to the lower path. He swayed a bit more but was able to remain standing.

Josie said, "They're in bad shape."

"I don't care!" Alice said. "We cannot let them in."

Nicola climbed the steps and started pounding on the door again. "I know you're all in there!" she shouted. "Please! Let us in."

Sandrine stood and shuffled over to the window, looking out at them. Nicola spotted them and jumped at the window, pounding her fist against it. Bloody splotches appeared in irregular patterns. Sandrine jumped back, crying out.

"Stop!" Josie shouted, banging back at her.

Nicola froze and pulled back, holding her bloodied fist to her chest. Brian had climbed up behind her. He, too, came to the window. Lines creased his pale face, as if he were in pain. He glanced back down the path. Still, no one emerged.

"Please," Brian shouted. "Please let us in. The bear attacked us! I scared him off, but he might still be out there."

"He almost killed us!" Nicola said, opening her fist and pulling up her sleeve. She had a defensive wound along her forearm at least four inches long. "He might come back! Please let us in."

Alice pressed her face to the window. "Just go to the next cabin! We're not letting you inside."

"But we need help!" Nicola cried. "Alice, please! You're a nurse. We need your help!"

From behind them, Sandrine said, "Nicola tried to kill me. You cannot let them in here. You cannot!"

"Come on!" Brian shouted. "We won't hurt you. We promise."

"I made a mistake earlier," Nicola called. "I'm sorry. I won't hurt Sandrine. I promise. Please, just let us in. You can tie me up if you want but please, let us in!"

Brian pounded against the glass again until it bowed. Nicola went back to the door and started throwing her body against it.

"You can't just stand there and watch us get slaughtered!" Brian said, eyes pleading.

The door shook in its frame. Josie moved over to it and put her back against it. Nicola kept throwing her weight against it. She was stronger than Josie would have thought.

"Just go to one of the other cabins!" Alice repeated. "You'll be fine."

Brian left the window and joined Nicola. The impact of his weight barreling into the flimsy door jarred Josie's bones. Wood splintered. One of the hinges popped off.

"No!" Sandrine said, shrinking back against the wall. "No! You can't let them in."

Alice rushed over to help Josie, trying to hold the door back with her hands. It was pointless. With two more hits, the door flew open, knocking both Josie and Alice back. They stumbled over the bed frame and fell. Josie's hands shot out to break her fall. Alice landed on her back. Looking over her shoulder, Josie watched Brian force his way inside. The bed frame screeched across the wood floor. Sandrine shrieked as Josie jumped to her feet again, ready to fight Brian off, but he simply staggered over the bed frame and to the nearest wall. He held one hand over his bleeding scalp and sank to the floor. Nicola stumbled in behind him. She tripped over the bed frame and toppled, landing at Sandrine's feet. With a yelp, Sandrine jumped up and edged around her, moving closer to Josie.

Alice got to her feet, dusting off her bottom, and looked at them. Fury and fear warred for domination of her expression. Nicola was still flat on her back, staring up at all of them. Blood trickled from her hand, leaving large droplets on the wood floor.

"How dare you?" Alice snarled.

The door hung by a single hinge. Cold air sailed through it. Keeping an eye on Brian, Josie walked over and started to close it.

"Stop!" Alice said. "No. I'm not staying in here with these maniacs. We'll just leave them here and go down to the next cabin."

Sandrine shuffled over to the door, stepping over the bed frame and giving Nicola a wide berth. "Yes, let's go."

"Fine," Brian said. "But can you at least look at our injuries to see if we need stitches?"

"I feel dizzy," Nicola added, lifting her blood-soaked arm in the air.

"What good will that do?" Alice demanded. "Even if you need stitches, there's nothing I can do for you. We've got no first aid. Nothing."

Nicola rolled over onto her hands and knees. Her body swayed side to side. Josie thought she might fall but instead, she crawled over to Brian and collapsed next to him. "Forget it then. Just leave us here. But watch out for the bear."

Sandrine stepped behind Alice and Josie, almost through the doorway. "Let's go," she said.

Josie looked over at Alice who was now staring at Nicola and Brian. The nurse in her couldn't turn away. With a sigh, she said, "Fine. One look but then we're leaving."

"Alice!" Sandrine complained.

"It's fine. It won't take me long. Close the door."

Reluctantly, Sandrine helped Josie wedge the door back into its frame. It kept the cold air out but one strong gust of wind would probably knock it out of place. Sandrine hovered near Josie's elbow, watching Nicola and Brian warily. Alice stepped over the bed frame and knelt in front of them. "Take off your coats."

"It's freezing," Nicola complained.

"You literally broke the door down to get in here," Alice snapped. "You don't get to complain. Coats off. I need to see how bad it is, and then we're leaving."

Brian started to take his off and hissed in pain. "I don't think I can," he said. "He got me here." He pointed to his ribs. "It hurts really bad."

"Fine," said Alice. "Let me see your head."

While Alice used her own sleeve to wipe away some of the blood from the slice in his head, Josie said, "What happened?"

"What happened is that we were standing outside the rage room and the bear came out of the woods," said Nicola. "It attacked me. Brian grabbed a piece of pipe from inside and started hitting it. The bear swiped at him, too. It all happened so fast but then Brian dragged me back inside and we made a bunch of noise, and it ran off."

Brian pointed to his forehead. "But he got us pretty good. I felt lightheaded. We got scared so Nic said we should find you guys."

FIFTY-ONE

Josie could feel the anxiety rolling off Sandrine's body. Alice eventually gave up trying to stop the bleeding from Brian's head, instead lifting his arm up and pressing the sleeve of his coat against it. "Hold this here," she told him and moved toward Nicola, who had already taken off what was left of her coat.

Sandrine said, "It serves you right. Now you know how it feels!"

"Not helping," Alice said over her shoulder.

Nicola eyed Sandrine with disdain. "Does it?" she said. "Does it serve me right, sister?"

She said the word "sister" with such venom that Sandrine shrank behind Josie and went silent.

Alice held Nicola's arm out. "I have nothing I can wrap this with. I'm sorry. I don't think it needs stitches though. Just put your coat back on." She looked back at Josie. "What's wrong?"

Josie stared at the long slice along Nicola's arm. Something wasn't right. Her mind worked to figure out what.

"Josie?" said Alice.

Brian raised his head. "Is the bear out there?"

This time, Sandrine went to the window. "I don't see anything."

"Josie," Alice said, voice louder this time. "Are you okay?"

Her eyes moved from the clean slice along Brian's hairline to the clean slice along Nicola's arm. "Nicola's head," she said. "Check her head."

"Oh no," Nicola said, putting a hand to the top of her head. "It's fine. That one's not bad."

Alice scoffed and started pushing her fingers through Nicola's locks, searching for the source of the blood. "How do you know? You can't see it."

Brian watched Josie, eyes suddenly wary. "Put pressure on that," she told him, pointing to his forehead. He obeyed, lifting his forearm to cover his head once more. Josie frantically looked around the room for anything she could use as a weapon, but there was nothing. The only thing in this entire cabin that could possibly be used as an effective weapon was the lid from the back of the toilet and that was too far for Josie to reach in time. Now that it was broken, the door wouldn't be that easy to open in a rush. Josie could still try to get it open and push Sandrine out but there was a chance Brian and Nicola would grab Alice before she made it out with them.

Alice finished checking Nicola's head. "I don't see anything. Where did all this blood come from?"

Nicola squirmed away from her. "I told you it wasn't bad."

Alice arched a brow. "You don't lose that much blood from nowhere, Nicola. Let me check again."

Josie stepped forward. "We need something to clean her up." She looked over at Sandrine, whose dress was already torn from their earlier efforts. "I need a piece of your dress."

Sandrine tried to step back, away from Josie, but the room was too small. She banged into the wall. "No," she said.

Josie reached down and gripped the edge of her dress where she and Alice had torn it earlier. "I'm sorry," she said.

This time, it ripped more easily. Josie clutched the fabric in her hand victoriously and walked into the bathroom. She tossed the scrap onto the floor and went right to the toilet, lifting the lid from the back of it. Holding it in both hands, she returned to the main room. It was warmer now with all their bodies pressed inside. Or maybe it was Josie's nerves making her sweat again.

Brian noticed the lid first. "What is that?"

Alice's brow furrowed. "Where is my wet cloth?"

Josie raised the lid in front of her. "Alice, step away from Nicola."

Slowly, Alice stood and backed away, joining Sandrine on the other side of the room from Nicola and Brian. They were much closer to the door than the others. Josie was in the center of the room with her back to the bathroom.

Nicola scowled at Josie. "Just what the hell are you doing?"

Josie's heart began to gallop. "You two did not get mauled by a bear."

Brian laughed. Nicola held her arm out. It had stopped bleeding. "Then what the hell is this?"

Josie's knuckles were white from gripping the lid so hard. "Those wounds are not consistent with a bear attack. They're too clean to have come from a bear. I've seen that bear's claws and his teeth up close. If you'd been attacked by a bear—even just a swipe—you'd have larger, messier, more jagged gashes."

Alice said, "Then how did they get hurt? Wait, did you do this to yourselves? To each other? To trick us? Why would you do that?"

Josie took a step closer to them, brandishing the lid. "We're going to leave. Do not follow us."

"Why should we leave?" Sandrine said. "They're the ones who broke in. They should leave us in peace. They could have any other cabin. They don't need to be here."

Brian didn't stand up but he raised both hands, palms

outward in a gesture of surrender. "Just calm down. We're not going to hurt you."

Sandrine surged forward and pointed to the door. She screamed. Josie winced at the pitch of her voice. It was unnatural coming from her after how calm and seemingly filled with inner peace she had been all week. "Get out! Get out this instant! You're not welcome here! I don't want you here!"

"Oh shut up!" Nicola hollered back. "You selfish bitch! After what you did to me, do you think I care about what you want?"

"Oh God," said Alice. "Please don't start. Sandrine is right. You shouldn't be here, and we shouldn't have to leave. Just go. Take one of the other cabins and wait for rescue. Please."

"Selfish?" Sandrine said, a hint of indignation in her voice. "What I 'did to' you? I have no idea what you're talking about. I didn't even know I had siblings! How could I have done something to you?"

"You are such a liar," Nicola said, staggering to her feet. "You have always known about me!"

Sandrine shook her head. "No, no. I didn't know that my mother was having all these children and giving them up."

Josie held the toilet lid in front of her and moved closer to the door, positioning herself so that she was between Nicola and Sandrine. Brian remained seated. Had she overestimated the threat? No, she was certain that their wounds were self-inflicted. They'd wanted to get into this cabin for some reason.

"Maybe you didn't know about Bradley or Tara," Nicola said. "But you knew about me. You knew about me!"

Why would they want to go to such lengths to get into this cabin?

Sandrine, said Mett's ghost voice. *This one is pretty obvious.*

They were still trying to get something from her. Some sort of information.

"I didn't know about any of you!" Sandrine insisted.

"Stop lying!" Nicola shrieked. "You knew! You knew about me!"

Josie started making calculations based on the information that Gretchen had sent her. The age difference between Nicola and Sandrine was the biggest but Sandrine would still have been eighteen or nineteen when Nicola was born.

Brian had said that Nicola had found someone on her father's side who remembered him. That person also remembered Delilah and that she had had an older daughter. What had Sandrine told Josie about Delilah?

Near the end, she was destitute. She married a carpenter. Claimed that she actually loved him and that she was done being in the public eye.

Josie lowered the lid. "Sandrine, did you ever meet the carpenter?"

Nicola's body went still. She glanced back at Brian, who was watching the entire exchange with interest. Alice moved a few inches away from Sandrine but kept staring at her.

"What carpenter?" Sandrine said.

Answering a question with a question. Deflecting. Buying time.

"The carpenter your mother married," Josie said. "Near the end of her life. The man she said she was in love with—did you meet him?"

"Of course I met him," Sandrine said. "She made me be her maid of honor at their stupid, cheap little wedding. It was humiliating. She acted like we were so close, like she was such a good mother. I felt sorry for him at first because he had no idea who he was really marrying."

"Did you live with them?" Josie asked.

Sandrine stiffened. "Why are you asking me this?"

"Because Brian told me that Nicola tracked you down by speaking to someone on her father's side. If Delilah had given Nicola up in secret after she was born, like she did with Brian and Taryn, then how would someone who knew Nicola's father remember both Delilah and you? Unless, at some point, the four of you were a family?"

Alice gasped. "Is that true, Sandrine? You were there when Nicola was born?"

Sandrine's voice shook with rage. "We were not a family."

Before Josie could stop her, Nicola crossed the tiny room, pushing past her to get to Sandrine. She pointed an accusing finger at Sandrine's face. "That carpenter was my father! He was in love with our mother, and she loved him back. We were a family and you destroyed it! You ruined my life—twice!"

FIFTY-TWO

Sandrine's head reared back. She swatted at Nicola's finger until she retracted it. "No, no. I didn't."

"Twice?" Alice shuffled closer to the door, keeping her wide eyes on Sandrine. "What does that mean?"

Near the end, Sandrine had said. Near the end of Delilah's life she had met the carpenter which meant that she must have died when Nicola was fairly young. Since Nicola hadn't ended up with her father, he must have died around the same time. In the last forty-eight hours, Nicola had outright accused Sandrine of killing Meg and doing something to Taryn. Brian had said that Nicola had other reasons for being on the retreat than him and Taryn. Nicola had lied to ensure her place on the retreat.

Josie had been right. The siblings were there for revenge but not because Delilah had chosen to keep Sandrine while discarding all of them. Nausea roiled in her empty stomach as she realized why they'd felt the cameras were necessary.

The lid was heavy in Josie's hands, but she wasn't ready to put it down. "Sandrine, what happened to Delilah and her carpenter? How did they die?"

Sandrine's face paled beneath the dried blood from the cut that Nicola had given her. "What? What are you—"

Nicola cut her off. "Tell her! Just tell her!"

From her periphery, Josie noticed Brian take the vape pen out of his pocket. He held it in one of his fists.

Sandrine sagged, shoulders slumping. "It was an accident. They were hiking to the top of a mountain they frequently climbed in upstate New York. Mother fell. She was trying to take a picture and she slipped. Nicola, your father tried pulling her back up and he went over, too. It was a horrible, tragic accident."

Nicola advanced on her again. Sandrine's head banged against the wall behind her as she tried to keep away. Josie said, "Nicola."

She stopped moving toward Sandrine but narrowed her eyes. "That's what I read in old newspapers, too, after I did the DNA test and tracked down my lineage. Embattled actress finally finds true love and settles down only to fall off a cliff a few years later."

"Delilah wasn't capable of love, Nicola," Sandrine said quietly. "You were too young to remember her or know her true nature."

"We're not talking about her nature," Nicola said. "We're talking about yours. You were on that hike with them. They had asked you to come home from college because there was something they wanted to tell you. I still don't know why you came. Was it because you had to stay in their good graces to keep your college tuition coming?"

Josie watched Sandrine's face. One of her eyelids twitched but she said nothing.

Nicola continued, "I found my father's family, you know. He had a distant cousin only a couple of years older than him. They were close. He remembered everything. He told me you were with them. I confirmed it with the local police. One of the officers said that all of them suspected you'd pushed my parents off the cliff, but they couldn't prove it."

"You have no proof," Sandrine said, voice shaking.

No proof. In Josie's experience, those were not the words of an innocent person. Sandrine hadn't said, "I would never" or "I did no such thing." She'd said there was "no proof."

Josie glanced first at Brian, still seated along the wall, and then at Alice, inching closer to the door. Both watched the exchange with rapt attention. It seemed as though no one in the room had taken a breath in ages. Forgotten was the alleged bear attack. Josie's fingers ached from gripping the lid.

"But he had proof!" Nicola held up her left hand and waggled her ring finger, showing off her old, pitted wedding band. "My mother's wedding band. The police found it in your jacket pocket when they got to the scene. You left your backpack and jacket when they took you in for questioning. This was inside one of the outer pockets. How did it get there?"

"That is not proof!" Sandrine cried.

"Not by the standard of a court of law, maybe," Nicola answered. "They couldn't make a case out of it but the officers who were there that day never forgot it. Since they could never make a case, he gave it to me. He thought it came off during some sort of struggle between you and Delilah and that after you pushed her and my father, Ben, off the cliff, you hid it. You told them that Delilah slipped and fell, and he tried to save her and they both went over. But if that was the case, how did you get her ring?"

"No one can prove any of this," Sandrine said. "No one knows what happened that day except me! I was there!"

"If you didn't kill them, then why didn't you take custody of me after they died?" Nicola shot back. "Child services wanted you to take me in. You were my next of kin. You had enough money from the estate that you could have managed but you rejected me. A two-year-old child. My dad's cousin wanted to take me, but he was single and back then, the court didn't want to award custody of a little girl to a single man who traveled a lot for work. So I went to strangers."

"And you were lucky!" Sandrine screeched suddenly, making everyone in the room startle. Spittle flew from her mouth. "You were lucky! I did you a favor! All of you! Do you think Delilah Stowe had changed so much by the time you came around that she wasn't capable of evil? Nicola, do you think that she would have stayed with your father and raised you? She was an evil, heartless psychopath with more than one personality disorder. I saved you!"

"No, you didn't!" Nicola shot back. "I went to a childless couple who had their own baby after they had already adopted me. She was their little miracle and then when I was seven and she was five, we were out front of our house playing and the ice cream man came and he took her. He took her instead of me and they blamed me after that. Until the day I left their home, I lived with their blame and their hatred. My mother—my adopted mother—actually said, 'why didn't they take you instead of our little miracle?'"

The words were a punch to Josie's gut as she imagined innocent little Nicola growing up in such a sad and cruel environment. Even Alice recoiled.

Sandrine threw her hands into the air. "You were still lucky. You have no idea how evil Delilah was—I'm telling you, I did you a favor!"

Brian lurched to his feet. The vape pen was still in his hand. He looked past Josie to Nicola. "I told you we were never going to get a confession out of this bitch."

"Sandrine," Alice whispered. "You killed your mother and stepfather?"

Sandrine ignored the question, shrinking down inside her jacket, trying to make herself smaller.

Alice's eyes flicked from Brian to Nicola and back. "That's

why the three of you planted the cameras that Josie found. To get her confession on tape?"

Nicola said, "We wanted the world to know what she had done."

"Your recordings would not have been admissible," Josie said. "Because of the laws here."

"So?" said Brian. His fingers were still wrapped around the vape pen. With his thumbnail, he dug under the edge of it where the cartridge normally slid in and out. "We could still blast it over the internet and ruin her life."

"You'd be guilty of a felony here," Josie said.

Brian laughed. "So we didn't check the laws in Pennsylvania. So what? It doesn't even matter now because she's never going to confess."

An expression of horror stretched across Alice's face. "You did all of this for a confession you can't even use? You killed Meg and Taryn for this? Two murders to get another killer to confess?"

Nicola frowned. "What? We didn't kill anyone! The only killer on this mountain is Sandrine!"

Sandrine stomped her foot. "I didn't kill anyone! I didn't!"

Nicola shook her head. "Then who did? I know the cop and the nurse didn't do it. I know Brian didn't do it. I didn't do it. You murdered two people in cold blood. You had the opportunity. Meg and Taryn trusted you. It would have been easy for you to get close to them and murder them. I don't know why you killed poor Meg, but I'm assuming that Taryn told you who we were and so you killed her to shut her up. Where is her body, Sandrine?"

Sandrine's hands shook at her sides, but she didn't respond. Josie glanced at Alice. Tears slid down her cheeks. She hugged herself. Brian's thumbnail still worked the edge of the vape pen. The small white cap suddenly flipped off and sailed across the room. It landed at Nicola's feet.

She shot him a look of disdain. "Will you stop playing with that stupid thing?"

Brian took a couple of steps, stopping in front of Josie, and leaned over to pick up the cap. A bunch of small black squares spilled out of the hollow of the vape pen.

"What the hell is that?" Alice asked as he knelt to quickly scoop up the squares.

No, not squares. Micro SD cards. Josie took a closer look at the pen, now gripped loosely in Brian's hand. It wasn't broken. It was fake. He'd been using it to store the recordings they'd taken that week. As he loaded the minuscule cards back into the hollow, his thumb pressed against the metal rim of the pen. Josie was close enough to see the imprint it left in the pad of his thumb.

A small, thin line only half an inch long with a curve at the end. Just like the cut Josie had found on Meg's cheek.

Nicola turned back to Sandrine. "What did you do with Taryn? We deserve to know that, at least."

Sandrine put her trembling hands to her heart. "I did not kill Taryn—or Meg."

Josie couldn't take her eyes off the vape pen. Brian picked up the cap and pressed it back on. It was still in his hand when he noticed Josie staring at him. Their eyes met. He looked down at his thumb where the mark was now fading. Josie raised the lid, resting it on her left shoulder, ready to swing.

"It wasn't Sandrine," Josie said. "She didn't kill Meg or Taryn. Brian did."

Nicola's head swiveled toward Josie. She laughed. "Don't be absurd and don't take Sandrine's side. We're not murderers."

Brian didn't take his eyes off Josie but when he spoke, it was to Nicola. "Speak for yourself."

Then his fist shot out, connecting with Nicola's temple. She dropped where she stood.

FIFTY-THREE

Sandrine and Alice screamed at the same time. Alice turned and tried to pull the door open, but Brian was too quick. He grabbed her by the collar, whipping her entire body down, over the bed frame, and onto the floor. He put a boot across her throat. Her hands shook violently as she tried to pry it away. Sandrine slid along the wall, as far from him as she could get. Josie bent her knees, lid at the ready. She tried to stay out of his swinging range though. His left hook was nasty. Under his foot, Alice squirmed.

Staring at Josie, he shook his head. "So fucking nosy. You can't help yourself, can you? You're worse than Meg."

"She saw you with that pen," Josie said. "With the SD cards."

"Yes, she came out of her cabin that first night it snowed. I don't know where she was going but she saw me coming from the main house. Except I didn't realize it because it was really dark and neither one of us had our lanterns with us. Both sneaking around. I don't know if she was spying on me or what."

Josie knew she'd been headed to see Taryn but to Meg,

almost everyone was suspicious. She'd happened on Brian at the wrong time and approached him.

"I had this thing in my hand. I'd been changing out the cards. I was trying to get the stupid cap on and dropped it. I had my phone with me. I was using the flashlight app to find all the cards. She saw. Didn't give me a chance to explain. Just called me a pervert and said she was going to get off the mountain and call the police. So I hit her with this and then I dragged her down the path and strangled her with her own scarf. I took some of her clothes off to make it look like she got hypothermia. What else do you want to know before I crush your friend's windpipe?"

Alice squirmed harder, squeaking like an animal caught in a trap.

Josie tried to keep Brian talking so he wouldn't hurt Alice anymore while another part of her brain worked to figure a way out. Sandrine, now cowering in the corner, couldn't be counted on to help. Nicola was a heap on the floor. Josie wasn't even sure if she was still alive.

Alice wrapped her hands around Brian's ankle and tried to twist it, but he pressed down harder, leaving her gasping for breath.

Josie took in the room. Her options. She could drop the lid and launch herself at him. Drive her shoulder into his hip. Fold him in half and send them both flying backward over the bed frame and into the door. But then she'd have no weapon and he'd still have a lot of advantage over her. It would come down to hand-to-hand battle. Close quarters. He was a lot bigger than her. Even at close range, he could do some damage. Then again, she'd taken on bigger, angrier men than him before.

"Why did you kill Taryn?" Josie asked.

"She was going to blow up the entire plan," he replied. "She said she loved Sandrine and only wanted to have a relationship with her. She didn't care what Sandrine had done in the past.

She was going to expose all of us and excuse this piece of garbage, even though she is a murderer. I couldn't let her do it."

"Where is her body?" asked Josie.

"You're the one who knows everything," Brian said. "You tell me."

Josie thought about the night Taryn had disappeared, now knowing that Brian had been behind it. Alice had said Taryn was going to her cabin but hadn't actually seen her leave. No one had seen her on the path. Brian had been in the main house the entire time. When Josie arrived, he'd been by the fire. He said he'd been there the whole time except when he went to check the generator.

When Taryn came out of the breakout room to go to her cabin, she would have seen him. They would have been alone in the great room.

"You killed her in the main house," Josie said. "She never went to the cabin."

An evil smile slithered across Brian's face, but he let up on Alice's throat slightly. Josie watched her suck in several breaths.

"You're too smart for your own good," Brian told Josie. "Makes me kind of sad that I have to kill you."

Brian had admitted to going out back to the generator when asked about what he'd been doing when Taryn went missing. Why bother with that detail?

"You took her out back," Josie said. "Through the kitchen. That's why there were no tracks anywhere. You hid her body near the generator."

His smile widened.

But they'd checked the back of the main house and not found Taryn. There had only been snow and more snow. It had been falling from the roof of the house in huge chunks.

"Oh my God," Josie said. "You didn't hide her."

His grin made him look like a completely different person than the man they'd spent the week with. "Didn't have to," he said. "I got her out back, put her next to the house, and while I was trying to figure out how the hell to hide her, a big avalanche came down off the roof and buried her in three feet of snow. No muss, no fuss. It was meant to be."

Sandrine's voice was small. "You monster."

Brian scoffed. "Oh, I'm the monster? Do you have any idea how many lives you ruined when you killed our mother and her new husband?"

Josie shifted the lid against her shoulder and studied Brian's position. He was off-balance with one foot on Alice's neck. If she swung the lid hard enough, she might knock him over. Then she would have an advantage. Before he even got up, she could be on him, swinging again and again. But Alice. She was in the middle of everything. Josie couldn't risk getting her injured or even killed.

"You never even knew them!" Sandrine said. "You were lucky that you didn't! You have no idea what you're talking about."

"I guess you killed them before they had a chance to tell you, then," Brian said.

Then again, Alice was going to run out of breath if Josie didn't do something soon.

Sandrine stood up straighter but stayed in the corner. "What's that? Their big news? That they were having another child? That wasn't good news for anyone."

"They weren't *having* another child," Brian said.

While Brian's focus was on Sandrine, Josie inched her way closer, making a small arc so that she was more to his right side than in front of him. She would have to swing at his head and make sure that she got the angle right so that when he fell, his body would go backward, relieving the weight on Alice's throat instead of adding more pressure.

"They were *getting* another child," Brian continued. "Me."

Josie bent her knees, running through the scenario in her

head. She'd probably have to jump if she wanted to get a good swing at his head. Good enough to knock him off-balance.

"Oh please," Sandrine responded. "You're just as crazy as she was!"

"No, I'm not!" Brian said, voice rising now. "They came for me! Delilah and Ben came to the group home to get me. She had told Ben about me. She knew I was still young enough to be in the system somewhere. They tracked me down and saw I had never been adopted. They found me. They came to the home and met with me. She told me she was my real mother and that she was sorry that she had to leave me behind, but she was in a better place now. She introduced me to Ben. They wanted us all to be a family. They told me I had three sisters although they hadn't yet found Tara, but they promised they were going to locate her and bring all of us together."

"No," Sandrine breathed. "No. No. That didn't happen. She wouldn't do that. She wasn't like that!"

"It did happen, and she was like that. She told me the only thing was that because we were in two different states, it would be harder. They had to get a lawyer. She would have to fight to get me back, but she was going to do it. They were going to do it."

Alice squeaked again, the sound going right through Josie like a jolt of pain.

"No," Sandrine said.

"Yes!" Brian said. "Except then they went home, and they never came back because they died. My counselor told me. I never even knew their last name. I was so stunned when they came to see me. I was young. If they told me their last name, I didn't remember it. I didn't care. All that mattered was that my mother had come back for me. When my counselor told me she was dead, I asked him to tell me her full name at least and he said there was no point. So I burned that entire fucking place to the ground."

"Oh God." Sandrine put a hand against the wall to steady herself. "You started the fire at the main house, too, didn't you?"

He laughed. "What do you think?"

All his talk about being triggered by the smell of the fire had been an act, Josie realized. A convincing one, at that.

"You're just like her," Sandrine said. "A monster."

While his venomous stare was locked onto Sandrine, Josie took her chance. She sprang forward, leaping into the air. She timed the swing of the lid just right, making solid contact with the side of his skull. He flew backward, banging into the door, and setting it askew. Josie landed beside him. She was on her knees before he had a chance to recover, bringing the lid back over her shoulder. As he tried to get up, Josie swung at his head again, knocking him flat. She got to her feet and pulled at the door until there was enough room for someone to pass through it.

"Run!" she shouted. "Alice! Sandrine! Run. Get out!"

Alice staggered to her feet. Sandrine stared warily at the floor where Nicola lay in a heap.

Brian started to get to his feet again, one hand reaching toward Josie, nearly catching the edge of her coat. She jumped back, waving the lid between them.

"Stop!" she commanded.

From one knee, Brian sprang up and rushed at her, knocking her back. Her body crashed into the wall. She tried to sidestep him but instead, tripped over the bed frame and fell on her back. He was immediately on top of her. He was so much taller, and in the small space it felt like he was everywhere at once, limbs like an octopus. Josie held the lid up near her face, trying to block the blows he rained down on her head.

"You're dead," he growled.

Josie was vaguely aware of Alice and Sandrine shrieking as their hands wrapped around his arms and shoulders, pulling him back, away from her. With a single swat, he knocked

Sandrine clear across the room. Alice kept trying, staying behind him to keep him from getting enough power behind his backhand to hurt her. She moved with him, keeping out of reach while controlling his left arm. While his attention was on Alice, Josie got to one knee and raised the lid high over her head. She brought it down on the side of Brian's left knee. She was rewarded with the sickening sound of bones crunching. As he started to go down, she sprang up and advanced on him, delivering a kick to his groin. The cabin shook as he landed on his back. He immediately curled his body onto its side, howling in agony.

Alice was beside Josie then, patting her shoulder. Together, they stood over Brian. Josie kept her weapon at the ready. Alice rubbed her throat. "Nicely done, Detective. Nicely done."

FIFTY-FOUR

It was still hours before help arrived. Josie started to worry when the sun sank lower and lower in the sky. She and Alice stood watch over Brian, who had the good sense not to try anything with the two of them looming over him and his injured knee—one with a makeshift knife and the other with a length of pipe that Sandrine had retrieved from the rage room. They had also torn the shower curtain down and managed to rip it into enough pieces to bind his hands and feet. Sandrine kept her distance across the room, sitting next to Nicola. She had not regained consciousness but still had a weak pulse. Alice had assessed her but concluded there was little they could do for her. After some time, Sandrine had braved the snow behind the cabins to find enough low-hanging branches she could break off to feed the wood-burning stove. It gave them a little heat. It didn't last long but it felt glorious.

Josie was trying to figure out how they could manage to watch over Brian in the dark when they heard the squeal of some sort of engine. At first, Josie thought she was hallucinating. With everything that had happened in such a short amount of time, rescue had felt impossible.

Alice motioned toward the door with the pipe. "Go," she said. "Look. I've got him."

Josie took the toilet lid with her. If Brian tried anything with Alice, she didn't want to leave a weapon lying around for him, though the last time she'd glanced at him, he was asleep, his mouth hanging open, drool pooling on the floor under his face.

Outside, Josie bounded down the steps of the cabin and stood on the path, trying to find the source of the noise. The fire at the main house was only a smolder now, the smoke down to wisps of black. With the building now only a pile of rubble, the red outbuilding that housed the rage room was visible.

The noise got louder, seeming to multiply.

Then something appeared at the mouth of the trail, passing the rage room, and making its way higher.

"Oh my God!" Sandrine had come onto the cabin porch. She dropped to her knees and put her face into her hands. "Thank God!"

Josie blinked, her brain trying to process what she was seeing. She didn't want to be wrong. She hoped she wasn't hallucinating. Noah glided toward her, over the snow, alongside the shoveled path, on top of a snowmobile. Behind him, two other crafts appeared. He skittered to a stop when he saw her, the snowmobile bucking. She was running toward him before he had one leg on the ground.

"Noah!"

He got his footing, sinking into the snow, and started to come toward her, doing his best to rush, pushing through the deep drifts.

Josie crashed into him so hard, he fell onto his back. She went with him, feeling the solid wall of him beneath her. Her face was in his neck. He smelled like day-old sweat, WD-40, and home. His hands were on her face, then her shoulders and hands, feeling every inch of her. "You're okay?" he said. "You're okay?"

"Yes," she said, breathless. "I'm fine. I'm just glad you're here. What took you so long?"

Into her hair, he said, "I had some trouble. You ever hear of a guy named Austin Cawley?"

The name sent a shiver through her body. She held more tightly to him. "He was stalking one of the women here."

"I went to Cooper Riggs's house to see if he could get me up the mountain and ran into Cawley."

The skin of his neck was warm against her cheek. "Where's Cooper? Is he okay?"

Noah's hands kept roaming her body, his touch sending a powerful surge of relief through her. It was like a sedative. "He's fine now. He got into a car accident right after he left the camp the other night. The truck got stuck on the bank of the creek. The SAT phone was destroyed in the crash. He couldn't make it up to the road at first so he stayed in his truck. Today he was able to get up the incline. When he finally did, he came to his house since it was the closest place. Lucky for me, he brought the rifle he always keeps in his truck. We got Cawley into custody. Cooper went to the hospital to get checked out and the sheriff and state police let me come up here with them. Everything's okay now, Josie."

She couldn't stop herself from crying as she lifted her upper body to look into his hazel eyes. His thumbs found her cheeks and brushed away the tears. He looked at her with a half-smile, half-grimace. "I'm sorry it took me so long to get to you," he said.

Then he kissed her.

FIFTY-FIVE

DENTON

One Week Later

Josie used her hip to push open the door to the great room at Denton police headquarters. In her hands was a flimsy cupholder from Kommorah's Koffee, all four of its compartments filled and a fifth cup nestled precariously among them in the center. She held it with two hands as she made her way over to the desks. Noah grinned when he saw her and jumped up to help, pulling two cups out of the carrier. He handed one to Gretchen, who was typing away at her computer, and put the other on his own desk.

"Quinn!" the Chief hollered, emerging from his office. "What the hell are you doing here?"

Josie set the cupholder on her desk and took out the cup marked Red Eye. "This is for you," she said.

One of the Chief's brows kinked as he looked down his nose at her. She braced herself for one of his signature tirades but all he said was, "You're not supposed to be here." Then he took the drink from her.

She looked over at what used to be Mettner's desk, noticing with some dismay how different it looked. Files were tossed haphazardly across it. The pen holder was gone. A tiny desk-sized basketball net was affixed to its side. Noah had warned her, but it still felt like a bucket of cold water over her head. No matter how many times she was reminded of the reality, she would never be inured to it.

Mettner was gone.

She stared at the desk and let the ache bloom in her chest. The hurt, like a toothache and the jab of a pin at the same time. Like her heart was stepping on one of Harris's Legos. There was no help for it, and that was simply that. It would feel that way probably her whole life, and there wasn't a damn thing she could do about it. There was no comfort. No salve. Only this pain where love used to be. So she let it exist. Let it ache and prick and jab and swell until she thought her eyes might water and then she turned away from it. Until next time.

This is what sitting with her feelings was truly like. Sandrine had taught her that. It wasn't throwing up walls or barricades when the pain threatened to roll in. It wasn't searching desperately for an oxygen tank when the hurt took her breath away. It was letting it come. It was standing in the path of the tornado without flinching. It was taking grief's throat punch without trying to dodge it.

Because as big and overwhelming and impossible to withstand as the pain seemed, it wouldn't kill her. It was a chronic pain she had to learn to manage.

"Quinn!" the Chief said. "Are you listening to me?"

"Sorry," Josie said, tearing her eyes from Mettner's old desk. "I didn't know what the new guy drinks so I just got him a plain coffee."

Gretchen said, "He's late again."

Noah had also told her that both he and Gretchen were not

very pleased with the new guy. Neither was Josie, considering he'd hung up on her after answering Noah's desk phone. But she was determined to give him the benefit of the doubt now that she was no longer roughing it on the top of a mountain under threat of death.

"I'm not staying," she said. "I just came to pick up my husband."

Noah shut his computer down and started to put his coat on. The stairwell door whooshed open. Josie turned just as the Chief gestured in the direction of the door. "Quinn, this is our new investigator, Detective Kyle Turner."

Turner towered over her, long limbs, broad shoulders. His hair was thick and curly, brown shot through with gray. Mid-forties, Josie thought. Around Gretchen's age. His beard and moustache were still all brown. Deep-set blue eyes stared down at her. When he smiled, only one corner of his mouth lifted. In his hand was a small plastic bottle containing an energy drink called Turbo Powr. Apparently, the creators had been so energized, they'd blown right past the E at the end of the word "power."

"Well, well, well," Turner said, studying Josie from head to toe. "The great Josie Quinn. Thought you'd be taller, honestly." He leaned in, craning his neck to see behind her. "And have a cape. I don't mind saying I'm disappointed."

"Turner," growled the Chief. "Play nice."

Josie took a slow scan, starting at the top of his head, moving down to his shiny loafers, and back up to the crow's feet gathering at the corners of his eyes. "That makes two of us," she deadpanned.

Behind her, she heard Gretchen choke on her pecan latte.

Turner gave her a quizzical look, evidently decided not to respond and walked around her. "Parker," he said. "What've we got?"

"It's Palmer, you jackass," Gretchen replied.

"Palmer," said the Chief. "Don't say jackass."

"You can't stop me from saying jackass to this jackass," Gretchen said.

Josie felt Noah's hand at her elbow. His breath was warm against her neck. "Let's get out of here," he said.

FIFTY-SIX

The sun warmed Josie's back as she knelt to leave flowers on Mettner's grave. The ground beneath her was hard and cold even though the temperature was in the forties. Practically tropical compared to the blizzard at the retreat. She cleared away some of the old bouquets other family and friends had left, gathering them in her arms and standing up. She dumped them in the nearest trash can and looked around for Noah. When she didn't see him, she walked over to the part of the cemetery where his mother was buried. She found him standing in front of Colette Fraley's headstone, chin almost on his chest, staring down at it.

Josie put a hand on his back. He lifted his arm and she ducked under it, slipping both arms around his waist.

"I don't think she's here," he said.

"What do you mean?"

"My mom. Sometimes, it's like I can feel her all around me. I like coming here, paying tribute, keeping her stone clean and flowers fresh, but it doesn't feel like she's here."

Josie thought about her own losses. Ray. Lisette. Mettner. She'd had experiences in the past when it felt as though Ray or

Lisette were there, guiding her, as sure as if they were physically standing beside her. She squeezed Noah hard. "I think you're right."

She lifted her face to his and he smiled at her. "Have you heard from Cooper?" she asked.

"Yeah, he had only minor injuries from the car accident. He wasn't upset about me destroying his basement door. Turns out that he was worried about Cawley turning up at the retreat almost all week. Meg Cleary talked to him several times privately about it."

That explained why Alice had seen Meg and Cooper together behind Meg's cabin on more than one occasion. "She thought Cawley would find her?"

"She was convinced, and she didn't want to endanger anyone. She kept asking Cooper if he had seen anything unusual. He tried to reassure her that there was no way Cawley would find the place, but she wouldn't let it go. Finally, he started patrolling the mountain once a day from the summit to the parking lot to make sure no one else was lurking."

"Oh," Josie breathed. "That's why he was up there on the top of the mountain." It was also why he had avoided her question about his purpose for being there.

Noah pushed a strand of hair out of Josie's face. "You hear anything about Sandrine?" he asked.

"The prosecutor in New York has declined to bring charges against her. She never did explicitly confess in front of any of us. Apparently, her saying, 'I did you a favor' in front of all of us wasn't enough for a conviction. Plus she still insists it was an accident. She says she got into a fight with Delilah and that was what caused her to go over the cliff—then Ben tried to help her and also went over—but she says she didn't do it on purpose. She, however, is pressing charges against Nicola for coming after her. Once Nicola gets out of the hospital."

Surprisingly, Brian's blow had not killed Nicola, but it had given her a subdural hematoma. She remained in the hospital with a slew of charges waiting to be levied against her. Austin Cawley was already in custody and the Pennsylvania judge wasn't letting him out on bail. Brian was also in custody and had already been arraigned on two murder charges as well as a bevy of lesser charges, including violating Pennsylvania's two-party consent law. All of his secret recordings had been taken into evidence by the state police. Josie wasn't thrilled about her confidential sessions with Sandrine being out there, but if it helped put Brian in prison longer, she could live with it. Alice had returned home, relatively unscathed physically, but emotionally scarred. They'd all eventually have to testify at the trials of Brian and Nicola—and Noah at Cawley's trial—should none of them make plea deals, but for now, they were scattered.

Josie was back to her normal life. "Are we going to talk about it?" she asked Noah.

He laughed. "I was waiting for you to bring it up. When you were ready."

She sighed, burying her face momentarily in his chest. Against his coat, she said, "I don't think I'll ever be ready to have this conversation but we should."

He tightened his grip on her. "I'll go first. I'm sorry for the way I reacted."

She shook her head. "There's nothing to be sorry for, Noah. I'm the one who overreacted. I feel like a failure because I can't give you a baby. Give us a baby. When you were disappointed, I took it personally. I thought—I thought you had lied to me all those times you said that I was enough."

He kissed the top of her head. "I would never lie to you, and I won't lie to you now. I was disappointed. Once we talked about having a baby, about trying for one, of course I imagined what it would be like. I thought about how it would feel to hold a baby that would be half yours and half mine. I wanted it. So yeah, I'm disappointed, but Josie, it doesn't change how I feel about you. How I've always felt. The only thing I have ever wanted was you and you are enough, baby or no baby. I can live without having kids, but I can't live without you."

Josie blinked back tears. The only thing that kept her from ugly crying was staring at Colette Fraley's name on the headstone in front of them. Noah's mother had never liked her. She could only imagine what she'd have to say now.

Good. You shouldn't be having babies with the woman who shot you.

Josie said, "I'm sorry I didn't... trust you, and that I shut you down when you wanted to talk it over."

They held each other in silence for a few minutes. A light breeze tickled the petals of the flowers Noah had arranged on Colette's grave. Somewhere in the cemetery, birds called to one another. Josie felt warm and safe in her husband's arms. Loved.

"Noah, you said you imagined a baby half mine and half yours. Was that why you wanted to have kids? To make a person together?"

He laughed. "Make a person together?"

She slapped his chest lightly. "You know what I mean."

He stroked her back, pulling her more tightly to his body. "No, not really."

"Then why? Why did you agree to try to have kids? Was it just because I wanted to do it?"

He shook his head. "No. I hadn't really thought about why, to be honest. I guess I just thought..."

He went silent. She waited for him to finish the sentence, but he didn't.

"Thought what?" she prompted.

"We see so many horrific things on the job. So much violence and chaos and just... pure evil."

Josie nodded into his chest. "Yeah, we do."

"I guess I just thought that you and I, we can do more than just bring shitty people to justice. We could actually bring some happiness into the world." He paused. Josie felt his chest rising and falling evenly against her cheek. "But we don't need to make a baby to accomplish that. We can do other things."

"Like what?" Josie asked.

"I don't know. Haven't thought about it yet. I was too busy trying to get you to talk to me and then trying to get you off that mountain alive."

He shifted, staring down at her. Bringing his hands to her cheeks, he leaned down and kissed her deeply. Her entire body melted into him. When their lips parted, he kept his forehead pressed to hers. "Want to go home?"

"Yeah, I do," she replied.

Home. With or without a baby. Happiness.

He took her hand. They started walking toward the car.

"Noah. There's more than one way to become parents. If you don't care whether a child is biologically ours, then shouldn't we talk about other avenues?"

He smiled at her. "Yeah, I think we probably should."

She grinned back at him, swinging their joined hands. "But first, take me home to bed."

A LETTER FROM LISA

Thank you so much for choosing to read *Face Her Fear*. If you enjoyed the book and want to keep up to date with all my latest releases, just sign up at the following link. Your email address will never be shared, and you can unsubscribe at any time.

www.bookouture.com/lisa-regan

This book presented some unique challenges. I'm used to Josie being in charge of a case and being able to use her police resources to solve the crime. This remote retreat outside of her jurisdiction was a big change for Josie. I consulted with law enforcement officers to try to keep the police procedure piece of the story as authentic as possible. I did my best to make sure that Josie behaved as any law enforcement officer would in such a scenario. Even though she was not acting as a police officer at the retreat, nor was she in her own jurisdiction, my thinking was that she would still behave as a law enforcement officer and rely on her training. That said, any mistakes or inaccuracies are entirely my own! Also, I know it's hard to believe that there are still places in the world where cell service is spotty or non-existent, but I'm writing from experience. I've had the exact experience Josie has with cell service in this book. Very frustrating. In addition, the real-life locations that I mention in this book are all places I've been. Some I've spent significant time in. But the retreat property is entirely made up based on an amalgamation of properties I've seen and visited across Central Pennsylvania over many, many years. Also, although Sullivan County is a real place, the sheriff and deputies in this book have been fictionalized by me.

I am so thankful for each and every single one of my readers and I am thrilled that even this deep into the series, it's still gaining new readers. I love hearing from all of you. You can get in touch with me through my website or any of the social media outlets below, as well as my Goodreads page. Also, I'd really appreciate it if you'd leave a review and perhaps recommend *Face Her Fear*, or perhaps other books in the series, to other readers. Reviews and word-of-mouth recommendations continue to be a huge factor in helping readers discover my books for the first time. Thank you so much for your dedication and enthusiasm for this series. Josie and I are so grateful, and we hope to see you next time!

Thanks,

Lisa Regan

www.lisaregan.com

facebook.com/LisaReganCrimeAuthor

x.com/Lisa1Regan

ACKNOWLEDGMENTS

Fabulous readers: I can't believe we're on Book 19 together! Thank you so much for your continued dedication to this series. I am humbled and amazed by your ongoing passion for Josie and all things Denton! I love hearing your thoughts. I love hearing from you via social media and email. You pick me up on my lowest writing days and you always make me want to be a better writer. You make every word worth writing. I am so grateful for each and every one of you. Thank you so much for being on this incredible journey with me. Thank you to everyone in my Reader Lounge. You have created a fun online space that is filled with kindness and thoughtful consideration. That is no easy feat these days, and I think it's pretty awesome. It's also really cool to have an online space where fans of Josie can congregate and share their thoughts. You make me smile every day!

Thank you, as always, to my husband, Fred, for taking care of everything while I worked on this book for way, way, way longer than expected and for being a steady and unending source of calm and support. Thank you for answering all my questions about the outdoors in winter in Central PA and for letting me borrow your extensive bear knowledge! Thank you to my daughter, Morgan, for your constant encouragement, hugs, and willingness to brainstorm. Also, thanks to both of you for just generally being awesome!

Thank you to my absolutely incredible assistant, friend and

first reader, Maureen Downey for talking me off multiple emotional ledges. You are a saint and I love you. Thank you to my first readers and friends: Katie Mettner, Dana Mason, Nancy S. Thompson, and Torese Hummel. Thank you to Matty Dalrymple and Jane Kelly for always being available should I have any plotting emergencies or should I need a good brainstorming session. You are both brilliant and I adore you!

Thank you to my grandmothers: Helen Conlen and Marilyn House; my parents: Donna House, Joyce Regan, the late Billy Regan, Rusty House, and Julie House; my brothers and sisters-in-law: Sean and Cassie House, Kevin and Christine Brock and Andy Brock; as well as my lovely sisters: Ava McKittrick and Melissia McKittrick. Thank you as well to all of the usual suspects for spreading the word—Debbie Tralies, Jean and Dennis Regan, Tracy Dauphin, Claire Pacell, Jeanne Cassidy, Susan Sole, the Regans, the Conlens, the Houses, the McDowells, the Kays, the Funks, the Bowmans, and the Bottingers! I am eternally grateful to all the wonderful bloggers and reviewers who faithfully join Josie and her team on every adventure. I'm also extremely grateful to those bloggers and reviewers who have picked up this book as their first Josie Quinn tale. Thank you for giving her a chance!

Thank you, as always, to Lt. Jason Jay for all your help and for answering each one of my questions, no matter how specific or bizarre. Thank you to Stephanie Kelley, my fantastic law enforcement consultant, for helping make this book work as much as possible. I know it was quite the challenge, but I sincerely appreciate your answering my endless stream of questions so patiently.

Thank you to Jenny Geras for always being so kind, patient, and reassuring each time I panicked, which was a lot. Thank you for always being available for a chat, even on a moment's notice, which was also a lot. Thank you for believing in me and in this book. No matter how shaky my confidence, you always brought me back to the page feeling like I could do this book justice! You're truly wonderful. Finally, thank you to Noelle Holten, Kim Nash, my new copy editor, Liz Hatherell, and proofreader, Jenny Page, as well as the entire team at Bookouture.

PUBLISHING TEAM

Turning a manuscript into a book requires the efforts of many people. The publishing team at Bookouture would like to acknowledge everyone who contributed to this publication.

Audio
Alba Proko
Sinead O'Connor
Melissa Tran

Commercial
Lauren Morrissette
Jil Thielen
Imogen Allport

Cover design
The Brewster Project

Data and analysis
Mark Alder
Mohamed Bussuri

Editorial
Jenny Geras
Lizzie Brien

Copyeditor
Liz Hatherell

Proofreader
Jenny Page

Marketing
Alex Crow
Melanie Price
Occy Carr
Cíara Rosney

Operations and distribution
Marina Valles
Stephanie Straub

Production
Hannah Snetsinger
Mandy Kullar
Jen Shannon

Publicity
Kim Nash
Noelle Holten
Myrto Kalavrezou
Jess Readett
Sarah Hardy

Rights and contracts
Peta Nightingale
Richard King
Saidah Graham